PRAISE FOR

THE BOY AT THE DOOR

"Dahl savagely delineates the price of living in a society that insists women must try to be perfect wives and mothers and have successful careers, too, or they'll be inevitably made to feel they're never good enough." —*Publishers Weekly* (starred review)

"A tangled web, masterfully constructed and certain to satisfy fans of the genre." —Booklist

"Scandi Noir at its best. . . . Atmospheric and beautifully written. . . . Combines complex and believable characters with a heartbreaking and head-spinning plot."
—Mary Torjussen, author of *Gone Without a Trace* and *The Girl I Used to Be*

"A stunning debut! Alex Dahl has crafted an extraordinary plot; intricate and twisted, with dark secrets emerging at every turn."
—Alexandra Burt, international bestselling author of *Remember Mia* and *The Good Daughter*

"Suspenseful, vivid, and ice-cold, *The Boy at the Door* deftly shows that things are always messier than they appear."
—Kristen Lepionka, author of the Roxane Weary mysteries

"A genuine page-turner, a fascinating psychological study and a must-read for people who can't resist twisty thrillers with unreliable narrators." —Saturday Reader

THE
HEART
KEEPER

ALEX DAHL

BERKLEY
New York

BERKLEY
An imprint of Penguin Random House LLC
1745 Broadway, New York, NY 10019

Library of Congress Cataloging-in-Publication Data

Names: Dahl, Alex, author.
Title: The heart keeper / Alex Dahl.
Description: New York: Berkley, 2019.
Identifiers: LCCN 2019008860 | ISBN 9780451491817 (paperback) |
ISBN 9780451491824 (ebook)
Subjects: | BISAC: FICTION / Suspense. | GSAFD: Suspense fiction.
Classification: LCC PR9170.N83 D354 2019 | DDC 813/.6—dc23
LC record available at https://lccn.loc.gov/2019008860

First Edition: July 2019

Printed in the United States of America
1 3 5 7 9 10 8 6 4 2

Cover art: *Cracked ice* by Patrick Chondon / EyeEm /
Getty Images; *Locket* by Carolyn Jenkins / Alamy Stock Photo
Cover design by RedLine Graphics
Book design by Tiffany Estreicher

This book is dedicated to organ donors everywhere.

ACKNOWLEDGMENTS

A novel is a hugely collaborative undertaking—if it takes a village to raise a child, it takes a medium-sized city to produce a book. I have a lot of thanking to do. Firstly, thank you to the wonderful team at MBA Literary Agents, and above all my agent, Laura Longrigg, for the enthusiasm, encouragement, support, and the incredible way you look after me. Thank you also to Jill Marsal and Louisa Pritchard, how very fortunate I am to work with you both.

Thank you to the whole team at Head of Zeus—I enjoy working with all of you so much. A big thank-you is due to Madeleine O'Shea, my editor at Head of Zeus—it is a real pleasure to work with you. Your instinct and insights are pitch-perfect and have hugely benefitted *The Heart Keeper*.

Thank you to the whole team at Berkley/Penguin Random House, above all Michelle Vega, my U.S. editor, whose wise insight and enthusiasm has helped me enormously in crafting *The Heart Keeper*.

Thank you to my writing community—to Tricia Wastvedt for so many years of support, both creative and personal, and for wisdom and friendship. And thank you to Barbara Jaques—writers need writer friends and your support is very much appreciated. And to everyone in my writing group—Christine, Mina, Mary, Di, Jane, and Fiona.

The Heart Keeper was also a heartbreaker to write, and I was fortunate to have an incredible support system around me. Rhonda Guttulsrod—thank you for the walks and the laughter and the teary phone calls and the endless unicorn jokes and octopus emojis; your friendship means so much and has been nothing short but a lifeline. Thank you to Sinéad McClafferty L'Orange for the regular bubbles and the philosophical discussions that were also lifelines. A very big thank-you to Krisha Leer for the medical input, the walks and the coffees, and for making me feel sane and understood. Thank you to Trine Bretteville and Elisabeth Hersoug, whose friendship has withstood decades and is very important to me. Thank you to Lisa L— for listening, and for teaching me to listen. (And for caring.)

Thank you to Laura, for being my person, my forever; my heart keeper. Thank you to my mother, Marianne, for everything, as always. Thank you also to Judy and Chris Hadfield, for your enthusiasm, support, and endless dog-sitting. Thank you to my children, Oscar and Anastasia, for being the measures for what is important, for what is not important, and most of all—for love itself.

This book had a pretty fabulous soundtrack, but still, it was written largely to a single song—*House on Fire* by Sia, so thank you, Sia, for the song that will always be *the* Heart Keeper song for me.

A very big thank-you is also due the staff at the neonatal intensive care unit at Ulleval University Hospital, who saved my firstborn's life against all the odds in December 2006/January 2007, in particular Stefan Kutzsche. Many of the experiences of the characters in this book were drawn from that very traumatic time. I will never forget how hard you fought to save my son—there are no thank-yous big enough.

Tears come from the heart and not from the brain.

—LEONARDO DA VINCI

PART I

1

ALISON

I wake all the time; that is, if I sleep at all. The alarm clock projects the time onto the wall on Sindre's side of the bed and I lie staring at the pulsating dots separating the numbers. It's just after two o'clock in the morning and Sindre isn't here. He was here when I fell asleep. At least I think he was. I pull my hand out from underneath the warm duvet and stroke the cool, empty space where my husband should be.

A few nights ago, the same thing happened. I woke, suddenly, bursting from a dream I couldn't remember into this black, silent room. I blinked repeatedly, trying to make out the bulky shape of Sindre in the dark—I didn't want to reach for him in case he'd think I wanted something; I wouldn't have been able to bear his warm, careful hands on my skin. It took me several moments to realize he wasn't there. I got out of bed and sat on the windowsill, looking out at the forest and beyond, to the lights of the city rising up the hillsides to meet the stars. It was a very cold night for early October, and an orange moon hung low over Tryvann. I felt glad Sindre wasn't there—it was good to not have to pretend to sleep, even if only for a while.

I was about to return to bed when I spotted something moving in between the trees directly opposite the house, off the gravel path. I moved slightly back from the window as Sindre came out of the forest, dressed in a light blue shirt, half tucked into his trousers, and his expensive leather loafers. His shirt was smeared with a streak of dirt across his chest and he stood awhile in the narrow stretch in between the house and the car, as though he couldn't decide whether to come back inside or drive away. He turned toward where I stood on the first floor, and only then could I clearly see his face, which was twisted into an uncensored, almost unrecognizable grimace. If the man standing outside our house hadn't been wearing my husband's clothes, I'm not sure I'd have recognized him.

Has he gone back out there tonight? I get up and stand awhile by the window. Tonight is stormy, with gray, dripping clouds and a brisk breeze hustling leaves in the garden. The forest stands solid at the far end of our lawn, mist seeping from it and joining the wind in translucent coils. It might feel good to walk into that forest, listening to the whip of the wind cracking branches, to let the cold night inside me, to breathe its moist air all the way into my stomach. It might lessen the burning, even if only for a moment. I sharpen my eyes and focus on the spot from where Sindre emerged the other night, but without the light of the moon, I can't separate the shape of a man from that of a tree, even if he were standing right there. He could be standing directly in front of me, looking at me, and I wouldn't see him.

I walk over to the door and stand listening before opening it a crack. This house is rarely silent—it's as though a faint hum reverberates from within its walls, the bass to every other sound our family layers on top of it—but it's quiet tonight. I stand on the landing, my eyes smarting in the bright light from the overhead spotlights, listening for that comforting murmur, or for the reassuring signs of some of its occupants, but I hear nothing. I glance over at the door to Amalie's room and am struck by a wild terror at the thought of what lies behind it. The burning flares up in my gut, as though live flames were shooting around the myriad, dark corridors inside me. I clutch my stomach and force my eyes away from Amalie's room. I try to think of something to count, anything, and can only think of the steps. Seventeen. Seventeen steps, I can do it. I can go downstairs and get some water and then I can go back upstairs, past Oliver's room, past Amalie's room, just like that; I can do it, I've done it before, it's just a bad night, that's all, and when I get back upstairs I can take a pill from the bedside table, and even if it won't give me real sleep, it will give me dense, dreamless rest.

In the kitchen, I stand by the sink in the dark. I hear it now, that humming sound. My hands are still holding my abdomen, as though only they stop my insides from spilling out. The burning sensation is fading, and now it feels more like corrosion—as if I'd chewed through a battery.

Severe anxiety, says the doctor.

Hey, baby bear, I whisper. *I bet you can see me right now even if I can't see you. If you can hear me, can you give me a sign, any sign, the smallest of signs? A plate flung to the floor, a light suddenly coming on, an animal screeching outside? I'd see you in those shards, in that bright pool of light, I'd hear you in that sound . . . A sign, baby, my darling angel—please, please speak to me . . .*

A light comes on somewhere—a square splash of it spills in

through the window and spreads out on the floor behind me. I hold on to the sink with both of my hands; my heart is pounding so hard I can hardly breathe. I want to open my mouth to speak her name again, but no sound will come. I lean toward the window and then I realize that the light is coming from the garage across the narrow pathway.

Sindre is standing at the counter which runs alongside an entire wall of the garage. It's where he usually stands in winter, patiently prepping our family's cross-country skis with wax before the weekends—Oliver's slim racing skis first, then his own, then my beginner ones, and finally Amalie's short, broad ones with sparkly snow crystals and Queen Elsa's face stretching toward the tips. I am standing in the space between the house and the garage, bracing myself against the wind, which is much fiercer than I'd thought, and I can just make out those little skis on a hook high up on the wall. Sindre stands with his back to me, but I can make out most of what is on the worktop in front of him. He moves strangely, at times fast and jerkily, at times slowly and smoothly, and it takes me a while to realize that he is polishing weapons. He detaches the telescope from a long, matte hunting rifle, holds it up to the light, then runs a red cloth over the lens. He's going away in a couple of weeks, moose hunting. I'd forgotten. He goes every year at this time—of course he needs to prepare for that.

A volley of rain surges around the corner of the house and shoots down the pathway, pricking my face and hands painfully, and I draw my cardigan around me tighter, but I'm so cold, and perhaps a little cry escapes me, because Sindre suddenly turns around and walks over to the narrow window to peer out. Though I'm not sure why, I press myself against the wall next to the window so he can't see me. I could just knock lightly on the door and slip into the garage and hug my husband from behind. I could offer him a coffee—I can't imagine either of us will return to bed tonight. But I don't. I remain in the passageway, watching him carefully dismantle and reassemble the two rifles, running the cloth in and out of their nooks and crannies. When he has finished he reaches up and lifts a cardboard box down from a shelf above him. It looks like a nondescript brown shoe box. He opens it and removes some newspaper, a kitchen towel, and then, an object.

At first, I can't tell what it is; it isn't big, and because Sindre's back is turned toward me, he is partially blocking my view. Then he puts whatever it is down and takes a couple of steps away to his right, presumably to get something else. I can see it clearly now—it is a steel-gray handgun I've never seen before. He opens another box, this one much smaller than the one that held the gun, and shakes several bullets out into his hand. He holds one up to the light, turning it over and around before slotting it, and the others, into the gun's chambers.

I sometimes think about Sindre's other life, the life he lived before me. Before our family. I imagine him as he would have been then: in his army helmet and fatigues, trekking in the mountains of the Hindu Kush and Badakhshan, circling in on some of the most wanted war criminals and terrorists in the world. He'd take shelter in caves and sheepherders' huts, drink from impossibly clear mountain streams, inching his way toward a target until he was close enough to take them out clean. I see him squinting into the sight block—a man's skull framed, the absolute certainty of his finger on the trigger, the precise, muffled shot. I've never asked Sindre how many men he's killed. *Neutralized*, he calls it. I don't know if he knows. Would he count something like that? I know I would.

The life Sindre lived before me and our family seems an almost impossible contrast to the life I lived: growing up in the San Francisco Bay Area, then traveling the world—first for fun, and later for work, writing features for glossy magazines and newspaper supplements. I've interviewed female heads of state from New Zealand to Iceland, I've explored the drug cultures of South American women's prisons and looked into the increasing wine consumption of the American middle class. When Sindre traveled, it would be to Iraq, Afghanistan, Pakistan—places he'd go to kill.

He picks up the handgun again, weighs it in his hands, turns it over, and smiles slightly down at it. It occurs to me that he may be about to use it, that he could bring it quickly to his temple and just fire. Still I don't go in; still I stand watching. What would my husband need a pistol for? I can understand that he needs to keep the hunting rifles, but I can't imagine what use he could have for a handgun. Maybe he's always had it, but just hasn't mentioned it to me? There are many things I don't know about Sindre, and that air of mystery that seems innate rather than deliberate is precisely one of the things that drew me to him in the first place.

Sindre places the gun back in the box, and the box back up on the shelf. He stands still for a while at the worktop, head bent. I look at his hands—how soft and innocent they look in the meager light. Perhaps he is thinking the same thing because he raises them up toward the light and watches them, turning them over a couple of times. Then he cups them, holding them a few inches apart: his exact pose the first time he held our baby, slick from the womb—one hand underneath her bottom, one cradling her skull. I turn away from him, letting my eyes rest on the scrambling leaves at my feet. When I look back up again, Sindre is studying the palms of his hands, as though searching for clues as to what they're capable of. I walk back into the house.

* * *

I've been in bed for less than five minutes when the door softly opens. If my husband touches my face or my hands, he'll feel the cold clinging to my skin and know that I was outside. But he doesn't. He lies down on the bed, breathing heavily, as though he is already asleep. He emits a strange smell, like metal and wet earth, and I assume it is the scent of the oil he used to polish the weapons. Suddenly I do want him to touch me—I want to feel his wonderfully soft hands slowly caress my hairline, moving down and around my neck, then across my chest, back to my neck, down my spine . . . I turn slowly toward him and place my hand in the space between us. It's wide and daunting. My hand reaches his lower back, and he twitches at my touch. I slip my hand inside his T-shirt and lightly circle his skin, but he doesn't acknowledge my touch or move toward me. In the end, I retract my hand and hold it close to my chest, as though touching him had hurt it.

Mommy, do you ever feel sad for the things that haven't happened yet, like when I'm big?

Yes. Yes, I do.

Why?

Because then you won't need me anymore and you'll be independent and sassy and too cool to hang out with your old mom.

That will never happen, Mommy!

Come here and give your mommy a hug, little bear.

Both sides!

Okay, both sides.

Mommy, what would you do if you didn't have me?

My heart would break.

Hearts can't break!

Yes, they can.

How do you live with a breaked heart?
I don't know.

I wake, torn from the dream and delivered, panting, to our cool, familiar bedroom. It's morning and Sindre's gone. He's left a window wide open, though the temperature drops below freezing at night. I sit up in bed, my mind churning, closing my eyes and trying to let go of the dream.

How do you live with a breaked heart?

I get up and put my dressing gown over my pajamas. I can't remember when I last washed them. The storm has left a glowing, blue sky behind and I stand awhile on the landing, admiring it. I bring my eyes to Amalie's room, her door firmly shut. I could open it. I could push the door open just a crack and shout, *Time to get up, Mills.* Usually, she'd be up already, playing with her Sylvanians on the floor or drawing at her desk. I turn away and go downstairs.

"Hi," says a voice, and I jump, dropping the tea bag I was holding. It's Oliver, sitting at the kitchen table, cradling his iPad in his hands, his face serious, his brown eyes surrounded by purple circles, so dark it looks as though he's been punched in the face.

"Oh. Oh, hi, Oliver," I say, my voice emerging in a scratchy whisper. I flick the switch on the kettle, avoiding my stepson's gaze. I didn't realize he was here, though, come to think of it, I can't seem to keep track of when he was last here and when he is supposed to go to his mother's.

"I was supposed to go to Mom's last night," he says, as if to explain.

"Oh."

"I decided to stay. With you guys."

"Okay, sweetie," I say. "That's . . . that's great." I move clumsily around the kitchen, looking for my sweeteners, my favorite mug, the milk, as though I don't know where they all belong. He's worried, poor boy; he doesn't think that Sindre and I should be here alone, together. My thoughts dart to last night, to Sindre in the garage at 2:00 A.M., surrounded by weapons. Perhaps Oliver is right, perhaps we shouldn't be here alone together. The burning is carving out a bigger and bigger space for itself inside me, and I want to fling the steaming mug to the floor and just scream. If Oliver wasn't here, I'd take a tranquilizer. Perhaps I'd put a shot of vodka into the tea. Or two. I don't want him to be here, watching me, trying to comfort me in his awkward way, I want him to go to his mother's and stay there so I can scream out loud and throw plates to the floor and pass out on the sofa in the middle of the day, lulled and held by alcohol, if only for a while.

"Ali?"

"Yes. What is it?" I say, my voice stronger now, too strong, sharp. I sense him shrinking back and force a slight smile onto my face before turning back around.

"I . . . I was wondering if you could help me with my homework before I go. Uh. Geography."

"Sure," I say, and sit down next to him.

He pulls out a crumpled piece of paper from his backpack. "'Use evidence to support or negate the following statement: the weather in Scandinavia is becoming more extreme,'" he reads.

"Right," I say, but just then, a fat tear drops from Oliver's eye onto the paper, blurring the word *more*. Another falls, then another and another.

"Hey," I say, and turn toward him, but his face is suddenly so like Amalie's that I drop my eyes back to the table. She's there in his fuzzy, low eyebrows, in the soulful brown eyes beneath them, in the freckled, thin nose and the dark blond messy curls. It happens often, that she haunts me for a fleeting moment in the expression or gestures of Sindre or Oliver. "Hey," I say again, but I'm not only speaking to him now, I'm speaking to her. "Come here," I whisper, and pull him close because I can't bear to keep looking at him. It's as though he finally gives himself permission to cry, and he shudders in my arms for a long time before his sobs subdue and he relaxes in my embrace like a small, exhausted child.

"Do you want to come with me to the lake today? Or to see Misty?" I ask. Misty is Amalie's pony and several times a week I go and just stand beside her, placing my hands gently on her warm, soft body.

"I . . . I have to go to school . . ."

"No, you don't, sweetheart," I say.

We walk around the lake on the gravel path, stopping occasionally, shielding our eyes from the sun and gazing out at the water. Oliver's eyes are red and a splotchy rash surrounds them. His lips are firmly clamped shut and they're red, too, as though he's bitten down hard on them. Oliver has inherited Sindre's ability to be comfortable in sustained silence. I focus on my breath, on controlling the burning in my stomach, but still, I have to count. Leaves, trees, steps, days since Amalie was here—no, not that. No. Try again. The stones Oliver hurls into the water, the number of ripples they carve on the water's surface, the last few scraggly birds heading south. We sit for a while on the pebbled beach.

"My mom says it's worse for you than for Pappa," says Oliver. I tighten my hand around a smooth, small rock. "But . . . But I think maybe it's even worse for him," he says, carefully, looking straight at me with his almond-shaped eyes, his Amalie-eyes, his wavy fringe dropping into his eyelashes. "Because he has me, he can't just, like, die. Or run away. But you could. If you wanted to. You could just disappear and never come back to the house, where it's like she's everywhere. I . . . I hope you don't." I stare at my stepson: at his knobby, white fingers and his chewed nails, at the spots creeping from the collar of his shirt up his throat to his jaw, at his wan face still clinging to childhood, though he's thirteen. I nod, and Oliver and I both look out at the steely water, as calm today as though it were covered in ice, and I don't have any words, so I begin to count again; I count the pebbles my hands touch upon, trying not to think about my flaming gut, and keep my eyes on the cool sweep of the lake, but I want to run into the water, leaving the boy on the shore.

2

ISELIN

Three months earlier

It's the hottest day of the year so far. *In many years*, they said on the news earlier. Kaia hasn't spent it outside with her skipping rope, or bouncing on a trampoline, or running through a sprinkler. She's been on the sofa all day, dozing, holding tattered old Bobby Cat, *Dora the Explorer* flickering on the screen. I watch her through the open door from where I'm sitting out on the deck by the entrance, drinking a glass of cheap, sweet rosé. Dark clouds are coming in, and I won't be surprised if it starts to rain within the hour. Kaia has been even more tired than usual, and I haven't been able to get her to eat anything other than a couple of lemon ice lollies. The heat makes the apartment unbearably hot, even though it's in the basement of the other family's home and the walls are made of concrete. In the winter, Kaia and I often wear down jackets inside.

I can hear the boys who live upstairs playing in their garden on the other side of the house. They're three boisterous little boys, and Kaia sometimes watches them from the high window overlooking their garden; they're always moving, playing, running, fighting, jumping—activities Kaia knows little of. At home, she mostly sits and draws, or watches cartoons from the sofa. On a good day she might sit and play with the Sylvanians tree house I managed to get her for her seventh birthday. I take a sip of the wine, my one luxury of the day, and watch an ambulance helicopter fly fast overhead, so close I cover my ears for a moment. Kaia doesn't stir. It's the second one I've seen this afternoon; earlier, I heard the continuous whir of rotor blades hovering in the distance. Perhaps something has happened in the city—I wouldn't have known about it.

Another sound emerges from the silence the helicopter leaves behind. At first, I think it's part of the cartoon—it's that tinny kind of merry sound, music for children, but then I realize it's the phone. When I finally reach it, it has stopped ringing. Four missed calls from the hospital. I glance at Kaia, whose ashen little face is pressed against a cushion. My heart beats wildly. I pull the cushion away and Kaia slumps gently against the seat of the sofa, still without stirring. She's wearing a white cotton vest, stained lightly yellow from the ice lollies. Her thick, dark hair is braided tight against her scalp the way she likes it, a couple of stray curls escaping at the temples. *I can't live without you*, I whisper. I press the dial button and pick up Kaia's limp hand, squeezing it hard.

"How soon can you be here?" asks the voice on the other end.

In the taxi, I watch as the helicopter, or another helicopter, rises rapidly from somewhere near the side of the big ski jump and flies fast beneath swollen, black clouds in the direction we are heading.

Could it have to do with . . . ? Kaia lies slumped in my lap, sucking her thumb and lightly twirling Bobby Cat's worn-out ear. Tears flow from my eyes, so fast I have no chance of stopping them, and they drip onto Kaia, disappearing in her hair. I watch the rise and fall of her back and put my hand over where I think her heart is. I can feel it, tapping steadily against my fingertips. A little cry escapes from my clenched lips and I catch the eye of the taxi driver in the rear-view mirror. He smiles uncertainly but I look away. Kaia slowly and laboriously turns around so that she's looking up at me. Her lips are almost as pale as her skin, with a bluish undertone, and the veins on her forehead stand out against her pasty skin like black swirls in marble.

"Don't worry, Mamma," she whispers. I nod and lean in to kiss the top of her head, drawing in the scent of her, more tears dropping from my eyes, as the taxi pulls up on the curb at Rikshospitalet's children's clinic.

3

ALISON

I'm landing at nine, reads the text message, and I have to scroll up through the messages for a clue as to where he'd gone in the first place. **Landed at Charles de Gaulle**, one reads, from yesterday morning. Paris, a conference. I remember now. I remember last night, too; how I woke in the middle of the night on the floor beside Amalie's bed and spent several minutes staring at the ceiling, not daring to turn my head even an inch toward the bed. In those minutes, she was still there, in her Queen Elsa fleece onesie, curled around Dinky Bear, facing the wall, frail bird-like shoulders rising and falling in the safe, soft darkness. Eventually I placed a hand on the empty, cool sheet. Then I went downstairs to the kitchen, where I sat drinking vodka and scrolling through Instagram for hours. I woke up there, at the kitchen table, my hair slick with spilled vodka, still holding my phone, daggers of autumn sun stabbing at my eyes.

It's almost midday, and my husband is landing at nine. We will be here alone together until Monday, when Oliver comes back. I look around the room for clues as to what to do next. I'll need to leave soon, to go see Karen Fritz. I consider not going; she would sit there calmly waiting, fingers fiddling with the yarn, her eyes on the clock above the door. Would she worry about me, or just breathe a sigh of relief at not having to spend an hour sitting across from the crumbling, sorry mess I have become? I check my phone, glancing through the many unopened messages. A new one from Halvor Bringi, my old boss at *Speilet*: **We are thinking about you so much. Call me when you feel ready. Hugs, Halvor.** I press delete. Another message from Erica, my only other American friend in Norway, though she now feels so distant to me I can't clearly recall her face. **Please call me, honey.** Delete.

I open the French doors to the front garden and sit down on the stone steps, though it has clouded over and the hairs on my arms stand up in the chilly breeze. I imagine my husband at the conference, his tired, blank face turned toward a figure speaking at the front of a huge auditorium, not listening, drifting on the muddled currents in his mind. Later, the evening spent at the deserted hotel bar, drinking one scotch after another, watching the flickering lights of Paris in the distance. A sparse hotel room with pink and lime-green cushions, medicated sleep. We are like each other now, and yet further apart than we have ever been.

A couple of weeks ago, I went to see Dr. Bauer again about my frequent spells of confusion and disorientation. I've known him for many years, and he was the one who first recommended Karen Fritz. He listened seriously as I tried to explain the terror of suddenly not knowing where you are, or what you are doing. *Early-onset demen-*

tia, perhaps, I said, my voice trembling at the idea of losing my mind, patch by patch. *Or Creutzfeldt-Jacob, even. It happens to some people, after all.* Or a brain tumor—perhaps the dull headaches and the tingling sensation I feel in my fingers, together with the forgetfulness and bewilderment, are symptoms of something sinister growing deep in my brain? *I go upstairs*, I said, *and can't remember why, over and over. The other day I put my MacBook in the dishwasher, as if it were a plate. I hear my husband's voice and I can't decipher his words.*

The doctor waited until I finished speaking. *Does your heart race? Do you suffer flashbacks? Do you sleep?*

All the time. Yes. Not much. He handed me a folded blue pamphlet that read "Overcoming Bereavement." He wrote more prescriptions.

A sound, tinny and insistent. By the time I realize it is the phone, it has stopped ringing. Two messages tick in.

Do you want anything from Paris, baby?

Then: **On my way to the airport.**

There was a time I would have wanted many things from Paris. A soft leather handbag, vintage champagne, hand-poured ecological essential oil candles from Merci, pencil sketches of Pont Alexandre III, bought straight from the artist. I laugh softly to myself, that such things even exist. That I cared. Expensive quick fixes that once worked but will never work again. I turn my face toward the sun, which has briefly appeared between two large, somber patches of swirling clouds. **No, honey, thank you. Hurry home,** I reply eventually, but I don't mean it; I don't want my husband to hurry home, I don't want us to move around each other like polite strangers in this house.

* * *

When I arrive, late, Karen is holding the door open to me and I slip past her into the sparse, small room. I sit down in a deep, white armchair and wait for her to ask how I am, but she doesn't. She begins to knit and waits for me to speak.

"I dream of her," I say, my eyes on Karen Fritz's fast hands, winding the thread up and around itself, over and over.

"How does that make you feel?"

"I dreamed that she asked me what I would do if I didn't have her anymore. She really did that once."

"That sounds very distressing, Alison." I don't answer, and Karen doesn't push me to continue. She just knits and waits. We could sit out the whole session like this, in complete silence, and we have, on a couple of occasions.

"I went back to the lake." Needles paused, no comment. "Aren't you going to ask me why, or tell me not to, or something?"

"Is that what you want me to do?"

"No . . . I don't know what I want. Or that I want anything at all."

"Do you think that's bad?" There was a time when I found therapy as useful and necessary as breathing air or drinking water, like most American professionals I knew back then. I'd spend countless hours on various sofas, unloading my tangled thoughts onto strangers, then walk away feeling as though I had gained some clarity. I found it useful in processing all the stories I heard, because it just isn't possible to spend any length of time traveling the world as a features journalist without gathering material for future therapy. But now the irony of it is inescapable, a Band-Aid for a gunshot wound. I look at Karen Fritz, and try to count the rows of fuzzy, ocher wool spilling from underneath her ever-moving hands. Twenty, twenty-one.

"My husband has a gun," I say, enjoying the alarmed look on her face.

By eight, it's long dark, and I go to bed. I haven't taken anything, or had anything to drink. I consider getting up and taking temazepam; my limbs would go mercifully leaden, I could get some real sleep, but I don't like taking it when I am here alone—the thought of Sindre arriving home and observing me in heavily medicated sleep unsettles me, as though he might scrutinize my uncensored face and be repulsed.

I think about Sindre on the plane, his broad feet planted on the carpeted floor, his big knees pressing against the seat in front of him, cradling a drink in his hand. He'll be leaning against the window, watching the tiny lights below, like golden beads sewn into black cloth, as the plane heads north. After a while, when the lights become interspersed, his mind will clear—and the everyday noise of bills, transportation, relationships, cooking, parenting, and long-established routines will feel far away. The plane will settle into a smooth, quiet purr at cruising altitude, cabin lights dimmed, and Sindre will press his face to the plastic window, the stars almost as clear and close as high up in the mountains. I imagine that flying soothes him, that it helps him to let his mind run blank, life stripped back to the bare bones. But the truth is, I don't know what soothes him, or what my husband thinks or feels about anything anymore.

Hours pass before I hear his key in the lock downstairs. Hours spent counting and whispering to Amalie. I counted time as it passed, two hundred and nine minutes, and the number of sleeping pills I have taken so far this week—nine—and the unexplained sounds from outside that traveled through the open window into the bedroom: eleven. I counted the number of times I've been to see Amalie's beloved little pony, Misty, in the last month: twice. I counted the number of birthday cakes I have baked for my daughter—five—and summoned each of them to mind. I counted the number of times my phone bleeped—two—and then how many times I flew on a plane with Amalie: at least thirty-two. She loved it and would purse her mouth into a tight little O as the plane rose above the clouds.

I begin to count the seconds between the key in the lock and Sindre's footsteps on the stairs, but reach four hundred and still he has not come. What is he doing down there? I wait in the dark, wide-awake, though I will pretend to sleep when he lies down beside me. He doesn't come. I get out of bed and walk quietly across the room, listening at the door. I hear a muffled voice from downstairs; my husband must be on the sofa, watching TV, or dozing in front of its flickering light. There will be an empty bottle of wine at his feet, maybe two. I cross the landing and stand at the top of the stairs, looking directly across at the wall where the huge canvas photograph of Amalie used to hang. It has left a slightly darker, dusty rectangle on the wall, a ghost-frame. I glance at the door to Oliver's room, wide open but empty, and at Amalie's, tightly shut, also empty. I listen, and realize it's Sindre's voice I hear, not TV voices.

I take the stairs slowly, careful not to step in the middle of the fourth from the bottom as it creaks. I stand still in the hallway downstairs, and the voice is indeed Sindre's, coming from his office. He's shut the door, but a soft sliver of light spreads from underneath it onto the tiles. His voice is low, and though I can't make out the words, I can make out occasional laughter. My hand hurts and I realize I have dug my nails into my flesh, so hard I've left deep half-moon grooves in the pale skin. I turn around and go back upstairs. In the bathroom I swallow a temazepam dry. I avoid my gaze in the mirror and go back to bed, flexing and unflexing my throbbing hand in the dark until my limbs lose their painful tension and my eyelids grow so heavy I can't peel them apart and—

Pappa sat by my feet in the muddy sand, clutching his ears against the shouting and my sobbing and the deafening roar of the helicopter descending rapidly toward us, whipping the lake water up into brown ridges. It wasn't until we were in the helicopter that our eyes met. Come on, come on, come on—I said to the jagged line, the lifeline, the line that decided if you would stay or go. I couldn't look at you, though I held your hand. Did you feel it? Did you know that I was there? I could only look at the line. Come on, come on, come on, baby bear, I said. Then the line began to settle from spiky lurches to gentle rolls and I thought this must be good—surely everybody wants the lifeline to become calm and predictable, but it kept dropping from the gentle rolls to a flattened line with the smallest of spikes and I was screaming at it come on come on come on but it kept evening out until it was nothing but the cruelest unbroken line, a constant, bone-chilling tone cutting through the chop of the rotor blades.

4

ISELIN

Three months earlier

"Please," I whisper, again and again. *Please, please.* It isn't the first time I've been here, on this chair, in this same room. It isn't the first time I've prayed for her. I prayed for her life long before I knew I'd have to. I stare at the polished floor, then at some plastic lilies on the table, then at my hands, fingernails all chewed except for the thumbs.

Strangely calm.

I've steeled myself for her death so many times that by now I can look it in the eye. I've known it is likely to come before my own, so I've had to.

Still, I pray.

My sister, Noa, often tells me to visualize what I can't control, so I do; Kaia on the operating table in this exact moment, eyes closed, face ashen but peaceful, a couple of wisps of dark hair emerging from a tight green cap, palms upturned and vulnerable, receiving. What I would give to have Noa here in this moment, just holding my hand.

Somewhere in this building, someone else will have stopped praying. They will be suddenly swallowed up by the same death that has been tearing at Kaia's shadow since the day she was born. Before she was born, even. This death is the brightest light, so bright it will sear whoever comes near it, like an evil star. It is shining that cold, fierce light onto my baby in this very moment, but she doesn't move toward its glow; she is flying faster than the speed of light back to me. She is going to open her eyes and look into mine; she has to. Her heart, the new heart, her last chance, her only chance, will resume its beat in her chest; it *has* to.

It's the middle of the night and I've alternated between sitting, standing, and pacing for hours and hours.

"Look," says Dr. Harari. She takes me down the corridor and into a big room filled with the sounds of machines whooshing and bleeping. "Over there." I nod and stare at my child on the bed, half-buried underneath tubes and equipment. I can only make out a patch of her dark hair against the pillow and the tip of her nose beneath an oxygen mask. Dr. Harari points to a screen where neon-green spikes lurch and fall rhythmically. "It's beating steadily," she says.

5

ALISON

It is not yet six o'clock but already it's as dark as the darkest night. I wish I was in the forest, where the only light would be that of the moon and the stars and the soft glow of the snow, which began to fall this morning. Instead, I'm in the shoe department of Steen & Strøm, staring at the shelves, trying to choose a pair. Any pair. Sindre said we don't have to go to the dinner, but I said we should try. At some point we have to try. Don't we? And yet, the thought of making polite conversation with Sindre's work colleagues and their wives makes me want to cry.

I grab some plain black stilettos from the shelf and pull my feet out of my sheepskin boots. I push my socked feet into the heels, but they don't fit. I push harder and they hurt my toes, and this is what brings tears to my eyes—at least that is what I pretend. A woman is looking at me. I blink at the tears, but I'm suddenly tired and feel like I can't get up from the little stool I'm sitting on. I count to ninety-four. I stand up and present the shoes to a girl at the till wearing a Halloween witch hat with a spider-web veil. Sindre was right. Pretending to live, making plans for a dinner party, leaving the house, trying on shoes—it's all wrong. I walk away from the cash register though the girl has just rung up the sale and she says something, but I run up the escalators and then I'm outside on Nedre Slottsgate in the freezing air, letting tears fall freely, blurring the glare from the fairy-light installation strung overhead. Just then, a taxi pulls up at a red light right next to me, and I get in, and only when I'm collapsed on the backseat do I realize I've left my UGGs in the shoe department. My socks are soaked through and my feet are stinging with the cold.

"Go," I whisper. "Please, just go." I begin to count—streetlights and red lights and stark trees and people and the beat of the song playing on the radio, but I can't stop my mind from slipping into darkness.

Ninety-four days without you, Mills. Ninety-four nights awake. 2,256 hours since I closed my eyes for one moment and lost you forever. I have not asked your forgiveness, but I know that I should. Everything that has been lost, everything that you were, everything you would have become, is lost because of me. I am going to do it. I will bring Dinky Bear with me, and we will sit underneath the tree in the quiet, shaded corner we chose for you, next to your grandparents. Or I will go to the lake; you feel close, there. Or I will just spend the rest of my life, like this, saying those words over and over and over in my heart:

I'm sorry.
I'm sorry.
I'm sorry.

I walk up the snowy driveway in my bare feet, feeling the disbelieving eyes of the taxi driver on me as he reverses back out onto the road.

The house is lit up, but when I open the door, it's completely quiet. Our house is never quiet. I used to think that it was the house itself making an underlying sound, but it occurred to me when Sindre was in Paris that the sounds must be coming from Sindre in a consistent effort to stave off silence. Even at night. He runs the washing machine overnight with his running shoes inside, so I lie in the solid darkness listening to the thud of them tumbling in the drum. Or he pretends to forget to turn off the radio in his study, so the distant murmur of voices occasionally reaches me in that strange place that is not quite wakefulness, and not quite rest. Some evenings, when everything that needs doing is done, and there's just him and me in the house, he puts the TV on in the den, music on in the kitchen, and the radio on in his study, as if I then won't notice what isn't here.

And yet, now—quiet. I feel a sharp tug in my stomach, a dreadful fear. What if Sindre couldn't stand it any longer, what if he's just shrugged off this whole broken life and left me to it? He could be hanging upstairs, still warm to the touch. Or what if he's blown his brains out? I take the stairs slowly, leaving a trail of mud and melting snow. I listen for sounds, unsettled by the absence of the constant background noise I've gotten used to, but still I don't shout his name. I couldn't bear it if I'm met with silence. I pick out a faint rustling coming from our bedroom at the end of the corridor.

Sindre is in front of the floor-to-ceiling mirror in our en suite bathroom, trying to tie the knot on his tie, just like he has done so many times in his life, but his hands are shaking too hard, and when he sees me, he pulls it from his neck in one swift tug and tosses it toward the bathtub. He sinks down to the floor and I sit down next to him and that is where we stay; me picking at the grouting between two of the floor tiles, him leaning his head against the wall, closing his eyes, a faint hum rising from his throat, his hand trembling in mine.

* * *

It's me who leaves the TV on downstairs this time. Long into the night we lie holding each other in bed, for the first time in a long while.

"I feel like I've lost you, too," Sindre whispers.

"You have," I whisper back, and we both cry, then. "I'm not me anymore."

"Neither am I."

"No."

"This is so crazy, but . . . Sometimes I blame *her*, you know? I know how insane that sounds. But I do." I want to say that I feel the same; *I* blame her, too, sometimes. I once slammed her bedroom door shut incredibly hard because I was so angry with her for leaving me. I've screamed at her, my lost child, in a wild rage. I took the large photograph of Amalie that hung above the landing, taken on her last day at nursery, and flung it down the stairs. But how can I say out loud, that I, too, sometimes blame a small child for her own death when it happened on my watch? Everybody knows it was my fault.

I'm sorry.

I'm sorry.

I'm sorry.

The silence is so long and so heavy, I assume that Sindre has finally fallen asleep. I listen to the prerecorded laughter from some old comedy reruns coming from downstairs and lightly stroke Sindre's back. Suddenly he jerks and takes my hand in his own, turning around to face me.

"I have to tell you something," he says. "Once, I shot a kid . . . I . . . I always told myself it was a mistake, collateral damage, of course it was, but . . ." He trails off for a moment, tries to control his breath.

"Shhh," I whisper, and place my index finger to his lips. He kisses my finger softly, but tears stream down his face. I draw him so close that every part of Sindre is pressed against me.

"I've done bad things, Ali. More than I had to."

"No," I whisper. My hands travel gently across his eyebrows, then across his scalp to his neck, where I knead his tense muscles with my thumbs.

"I have."

"No," I whisper again, because I don't want to know.

"What if what happened to us is punishment? You know, karma. Karma," he repeats, as though he has never heard the word before. "I can't bear it. I can't. I can't stop thinking that I brought this on to us."

"Shhh," I say, more forcefully now. I press my finger against his lips again and then I turn slowly away from him. I feel a strange movement from his side of the bed and at first I think he's getting up, but then I realize he is sobbing and pushing against the headboard with his fists. I turn back around and hold my husband close. I place my hand on his chest and feel his heart rush inside him, as though he were happy and not desperate. I don't know how to be me, and I don't know how to be anything at all for Sindre.

In the earliest days, we vowed that we would stay together, that we would learn to live this life instead of the other one, that we would do the right thing and donate her organs so we could save someone else from such loss. We felt very deeply that she wouldn't have wanted us to come undone, that if we lay down to die, her life would have been for nothing. We meant it, and right at the beginning, when people constantly rallied around, when the world expected nothing from us, when prescription-drug apathy was still a novelty, I almost believed that it could be true—that it was possible to get through it. I couldn't have grasped, then, that it would grow bigger and sharper every day, that it would rot my heart, that it would devour everything that was once good, like a tumor in my head, pressing every normal function to the tight, dark corners of my skull.

I turn away from Sindre and clamp my eyes shut.

There you are, baby bear. Your hair is loose, and when I pick you up, its ends tickle the tip of my nose. I hold you close, the way a koala carries her baby. When I call you my little koala bear, you laugh straight into my ear, your voice pouring into my entire being. I place you gently down onto the beach and your stubby pink toes sink into the wet sand. You stand awhile looking out at the sun-speckled water before wading in, sunlight spilling down your back. You turn around to make sure I'm watching you, and I am; I'd never take my eyes off you. You splash around for a long while, shrieking and laughing, and I laugh, too, at the faces you pull, at your flailing arms, your legs pummeling at the water. After a while, I tell you to come back, but you don't listen.

You half swim, half wade farther out into the lake, where the water goes from golden and translucent to glittery and inky, like the night sky. Come back, I say, then I scream it, my voice thundering across the water, but you don't come back—you are a mere speck in the middle of the lake now. In this state, held beneath consciousness but aware of it, I can't move, not even an inch. I can only stand here, screaming. Come back, baby bear. Please, please come back. When you do come back, after a very long time, after I have screamed my voice bone-dry, I pull you from the water and your face is stricken and frightened by my urgency. I pick you up and you wrap your legs around my waist and my heart gallops against your cheek and I whisper into your hair: You scared me so much, baby bear.

6

ISELIN

Two months earlier

"Are you ready?" I ask. Kaia nods and I pick her up as gently as I would a newly hatched nestling. Her hands are cold against my neck and I place her down into the wheelchair on the curb and spread her thick purple blanket around her shoulders. Kaia looks at the house as though she's never seen it before, although it has only been five weeks. I've come back weekly, for clean clothes and quickly prepared meals, before heading back to Kaia at the hospital.

"Guess what?" I say as I unlock the door and push her inside. She looks up at me with her big, questioning eyes, but they seem far away, as though she can't entirely understand what I said. "I got you a surprise. Two, actually."

I pick Kaia back up from the wheelchair and half carry, half walk her into the main room. I've tidied everything up—we left in a hurry, leaving toys scattered about—but the apartment still looks small. I place her down on the sofa and she leans back, drawing her feet up, looking around the room slowly. Her eyes find the huge, crudely wrapped object by the curtain that separates her bedroom alcove from the rest of the room.

"What's that?" she asks.

"It's for you."

"What is it?"

"It's a welcome-home present, sweetie."

"Can I open it?"

"Yes."

"Can you please open it for me, Mamma?"

"Why don't I help you down to the floor and we can open it together?"

"Can you just open it for me?" My daughter looks tiny and exhausted where she sits on the sofa. Though she looks frail, there is a glint of strength in her eyes, and I tell myself it isn't strange that she's both exhausted and overwhelmed after what she's been through. But she made it.

I slowly and theatrically unpeel the yellow-and-pink wrapping paper, revealing an enormous, uneven cardboard box beneath. Kaia giggles, then her eyes grow wide as she realizes what it is.

"The Sylvanian Grand Regency Hotel!"

"Yeah," I say, pushing the box over to Kaia so she can run her fingers across it. "With all the Sylvanians you could possibly want, too." I hand her a second package, which had been concealed behind the first. This one she unwraps herself, serious and concentrated, and she keeps looking up at me with an expression of pure joy in her eyes. Many, many boxes of Sylvanians have been wrapped together: bears, bunnies, dogs and cats, tiny happy families.

"Thank you," she whispers. "Wow."

"It's from the Heart Foundation," I say, and Kaia nods.

"I'm so lucky."

You have no idea how lucky you are, baby, I think to myself. *No idea.*

That night, Kaia sleeps next to me, spreading out on the bed like a little starfish, but I don't want to move her for fear of hurting her. She stirs occasionally, mewling like an injured cat, her face twisting into grimaces, and I watch her in the soft glow of the streetlamps outside. I might have come back here alone. I might have been faced with a future without Kaia. I swallow hard and lie awhile listening to the soft gurgle of water flowing in the drains upstairs somewhere.

When I wake again, Kaia is crying softly.

"It hurts," she says. "I can't breathe."

I sit up, alarmed. "Where does it hurt? You're breathing just fine." Kaia doesn't answer, and I'm fumbling with the light switch when I realize that she is asleep, that these are words from a dream.

"Please," she whispers after a while, and then, "Mamma!"

"Shhh," I say into the soft, limp hair covering her ears. "Mamma's here." And that's how we stay, wrapped in each other, me listening to my daughter breathing until the late-summer sun appears in the sky.

7

ALISON

"I can't breathe," I say after a prolonged silence. Karen Fritz knits, carefully looping the needles in and around a delicate spool of violet yarn. She doesn't look particularly disturbed by what I just said, trained as she is in professional sympathy. Behind her hangs a drawing of a flock of birds flying above a seaside town of huddled, deep red houses. Lofoten or Greenland, maybe? I count the birds: twenty-two. I close my eyes and imagine myself among them; the pull of the salty wind on my face, the only sound the rhythmic, soft flap of wide wings, the navy sweep of the ocean rolling out ahead.

"Alison."

"Yes," I say, my voice as weak as though I'd just been punched in the stomach. I try to take a deep breath, but the air meets a wall of obstruction at the top of my lungs. "I can't breathe," I repeat.

"You're breathing, though."

"Yes, but it feels strained, like I just can't get enough air." I stare at the birds streaking through the sky, at the shimmery steel-blue sea. I see myself far beneath its surface, clawing at dark water, drinking great gulps of salt water, opening my eyes and blinking at a hazy, staticky medley of gray-blues, my limbs growing slow and cold, then still.

"It doesn't seem strange to me that you would experience that sensation."

"I can't . . ." I begin, but I can't finish the sentence because I don't know what I was going to say. I contemplate getting up and walking out; I've done that more than once before. But there isn't anywhere to run. The birds again, free, soaring above the ocean, beady eyes locked on the horizon, no thoughts besides flight, rest, food. I don't understand where the awful, keening sound is coming from until Karen Fritz gently places her knitting down on her table, gets up, crosses the space between our armchairs, and kneels next to me.

"It's okay," she says, nudging a soft tissue into my closed fist. "Close your eyes, Alison. That's it, keep them closed, just focus on your breath."

But I can't breathe.

"I need to go home," I whisper.

In the kitchen I pour vodka into a water glass and drink it quickly. I listen out for Sindre, but hear nothing. The door to his office is shut and a sliver of light illuminates the floor in the hallway. Has he fallen asleep in his chair again? I put my sheepskin boots on and slip outside. I decide to walk, though it's quite far.

The lake appears different now, in the autumn, than it did in July. The water is black, lightening to gold-flecked brown in the shallows, and the smoke from the surrounding farms' bonfires drifts across to where I stand on the soggy beach. I breathe in the smoke, trying to control my breathing. It's still very early in the morning, not yet eight, and the vodka I drank before I came here stings in my stomach. Fall used to be my favorite time; I loved the trampled orange leaves, the sharp morning air, the scent of smoke and spice and upturned, emptied earth.

Far out on the lake the water is rippling, as though someone is turning it from deep within. I pick up a small rock and throw it toward the curling water, and then another and another. I throw thirty-one rocks, and then I force myself to stop counting. I close my eyes and just stand here, focusing on the feel of my feet pressing into the muddy beach that is scattered with sharp stones.

Karen says direct speech can be a powerful tool in managing grief, so I try, but all the words I speak to her out loud dissolve into dark air. It's like praying, though I've never prayed in all my life— I never felt the need for a God. Why speak to someone who most likely does not exist? I understand it now; I imagine every lost child becomes its mother's God.

Amalie never answers and the silence seeps through my skin and chills me from inside. Still I can't stop because maybe one day it will take me closer to where she is now.

I open my eyes and glance around. She's here—my baby is here with me now; I can feel her. I feel her in the earthy, cool breath of the forest, in the dark glint of the lake, *her* lake. She's in the quiet air trapped in the shadows of our home. She's in her pappa's eyes when he thinks about her. She's in her brother's blank expression, in his shaking hands—his poor, chewed hands. She's in every thought that passes through my muddled mind, in every drop of blood that rushes through my broken heart. I watch the thin contrails of a jet reflected on the black water, like parallel lines of chalk drawn on a blackboard, then I close my eyes.

I wonder if it is a sign of actual madness, to have come out here, and for a moment I open my eyes, expecting the moment to be gone, to stop feeling her, but it isn't like that; I am still here, my feet firmly fixed to the ground, and so is she: in the trees, in the smoky, cool air. In the water.

You're here, I whisper.

I stay awhile longer, completely still, as though anchored to this spot, just focusing on breathing and feeling. When I speak again, my voice is hollow and flat, like a badly remembered song.

I can't breathe without you.

Peas on Oliver's plate: sixteen. Raindrops from earlier showers still studding the window: forty-six. Times I reach for my water glass before realizing I left it by the sink: three. Books left on the lounge table: seven. Number of Xanax I took when I got home from the lake: one. And a half.

"Alison?" I hear Sindre's voice, and glancing around from him to Oliver, I realize they're waiting for me to answer a question. "You looked far away there," he says kindly.

"Sorry," I say.

"Is the fish okay?" Sindre indicates the mess of flaky salmon pieces I've pushed around on my plate.

"Yes. Thank you. It's . . . it's really nice. Thank you for . . . doing this." It is the first time we've sat down together for a meal in a very long time, and the first time the three of us are here, together at the table, since July. I pointedly put a piece of salmon in my mouth and count as I chew. Eighteen, nineteen.

"Alison?"

I look up.

THE HEART KEEPER · 39

"Today at school we learned about transplants in biology." Oliver's face is pale and red along the hairline, and his too-big teeth glint as he speaks.

"Oliver!" Sindre says, voice sharp.

"No," I say, softly. "Let him speak."

"We learned that one person's organs can save up to eight lives."

"Oh," I say. *One, two, three, four, five, six, seven, eight.*

"I . . . I think that's amazing," he says, looking from Sindre to me. "Like, she would have wanted that, you know? She—"

"Oliver," interrupts Sindre. "Please. Please, let's just eat."

"I want to hear what he has to say, honey," I say as kindly as I can manage.

"I don't." Sindre drops his knife so it clatters loudly to the floor. I place a hand on Oliver's hand, and it twitches but he doesn't move it away.

"What else did you learn, sweet boy?"

"We read about a woman who was a strict vegetarian her whole life and then she received a heart from someone who had, like, really loved burgers and stuff, and after that she began to eat meat all the time." I nod, then realize I should smile at this. I smile.

"Wow."

"Yeah. It's called cell memory." He pauses a long while, stabs at a couple of peas on his plate, and then he speaks again. "Do we know which parts of Amalie were given to other people?"

The burning, again, those snapping flames in my gut, that searing heat behind my closed eyes. The consultant's sterile, clasped hands, the downcast, unmistakable tilt of his head, his impossible words, *I'm so sorry.* The sticky silence of a windowless room, the kind, unflinching presence of two nurses, one old and one young, how good it was of them to cry for Amalie in those moments, when we couldn't yet. Me counting the minutes that had passed since my hands ran through her wet, dense hair, the drum of my heart interfering with the counting I couldn't stop myself from doing, so I started doing it out loud, spitting those ugly minutes out, until the younger nurse got up and sat by my feet and made me look into her wet, red eyes. And later, the papers we had to sign, me counting the words on the page, rather than reading them, words I'd never really considered before those moments, though I must have on some level, because I knew without a doubt that it was the right thing to do.

"Sorry," Oliver says, when I don't, *can't*, respond.

"For fuck's sake," says Sindre, his gloomy, tense face turned toward the window.

"Sorry," says Oliver, again. Which parts of Amalie did we give away? Which parts of Amalie are now embedded in other bodies, parts of other living beings? Cell memory, he said. Cell memory—I roll the words over and over and over in my mind. My hands are hot, suddenly weak. I force my mind to Karen Fritz's birds and make them fly over me in my mind while I count them, twenty-two. Rubbery, gnarled feet held close to feathered bellies, hard eyes locked on the obsidian line of the horizon, air torn to shreds. I try to come back to my own body, back to Oliver and Sindre staring at me, but my mind is flying free with the impossibility of the words Oliver spoke. I bring him into focus, taking in his drawn, battered expression, his Amalie-eyes, his bloody, chewed fingertips.

"Her heart," I whisper. "We gave away her heart."

8

ISELIN

One month earlier

My daughter's heartbeat taps gently against my fingertips. I rub the ointment down the length of her scar and Kaia sits patiently, waiting.

"Dr. Harari is going to be pleased to see you."

"Yeah."

"She'll be really impressed with the progress you've been making," I say, smiling down at her and wiping my hand clean of the sticky ointment on a kitchen towel.

"Yeah. Last time she saw me, I was sick. I'm not sick now."

"No," I say.

"She's seen the inside of my body," says Kaia.

"Yes. Yes, she has."

"Lots of people have."

"I guess that's true, Kaia."

"Dr. Harari said that my old heart was a bit gray and too small. It didn't take the blood around fast enough."

"No, it didn't." I feel struck by sadness at the too-small, gray heart. What did they do with it? Did they just throw it away, the useless, crumbling heart that once formed in my womb? I remember hearing its rapid scatter during my first ultrasound scan in pregnancy, how I cried at first with despair, but also wonder. I kiss the top of Kaia's head and help her into the loose cardigan that doesn't rub against her scar.

I sit at the kitchen table, looking at myself in the mirror on the opposite wall. I'm wearing a red hooded sweater and gray yoga pants. My hair is scraped up into a high bun, but a few lank strands have come loose. My hair is bleached, but dark brown at the roots, the way I like it. Grungy—Kurt Cobain meets Cara Delevingne. I smile to myself. On my left wrist, three fine tattoos weave in and out of each other like doodles. I don't think it would be that easy to tell how old I am; though I am in my midtwenties, I'm a little overweight in the way teenagers sometimes are, but my face has the kind of weary expression of someone who has lived longer than that. I'm not beautiful, though I have been called that. I'm tired. If I wasn't tired, if I committed to eating food that didn't come out of plastic microwave trays, if I made use of the running track at the end of the road, then perhaps I could be beautiful.

But I'm so tired. In this moment, my eyes are red, and I squint even in the dimmed light from above the kitchen sink. I flick the radio on and smile as the Supremes start to sing. I turn my left wrist over, absentmindedly running a finger across one of the tattoos, the one that Noa and I both have. I stare at the soft, white flesh of my palm and then I pick up one of the pens in front of me. I draw a bird's wing so that it appears to flap when I open and close my hand.

I wonder what Noa's doing. I haven't heard from her in several days, but it's not like my sister has to check in with me. She's probably playing sets tonight—being a super-successful DJ is nothing if not busy.

In the next room, my daughter is asleep. Every night, she wakes numerous times, sometimes every hour. She wakes whimpering, or sometimes screaming. This is new. It's eaten away at my nerves so badly I can barely sleep at all. I should be in bed right now, but I find the hours ticking by with my thoughts racing so disturbing I prefer to sit here until I can't keep my eyes open.

Kate Bush is playing now, and I turn the page in my drawing pad, smoothing the blank new page with my hand. I am about to start drawing with a blunt charcoal pencil, sketching myself the way I just observed myself in the mirror, or perhaps just the palm of my hand holding the delicate bird's wing, when I hear a sound from the other room. I say room, but really it's just a windowless alcove, sectioned off from the living room. I get up and stand watching my daughter's slight frame. She's moving about, her head turning from side to side, her feet jerking. Her face is twisted in an anxious expression and her brow is moist with sweat. I know what will happen next. She will flail around more and more until her nightmares force her eyes to open and her voice will ring out into the cramped space of our apartment.

I sit down next to her to try to calm her down before it escalates even further. I place one hand on her shoulder and another on her forehead but her entire body is trembling now, and I'm not sure what to do. Nobody has ever told me what to do if this happens. Maybe it's medical and I'm supposed to make it stop but I don't know how, so I just sit there, tears flowing from my eyes at the sight of her. After several minutes, Kaia releases a guttural kind of roar and sits up in the bed, heaving for breath.

"No!" she screams, over and over, and doesn't react when I pull her close, smoothing her long, limp hair down.

"I'm here, honey," I say. "Mamma's here."

"No! No!" wheezes Kaia, scrambling in my arms like a bird caught in a bush, and we stay like that for a long while, me holding her tight until the strength seeps from her and she collapses back onto the mattress. I lie down next to her and imagine myself seen from above. Immobile, as if I'd been dropped onto my back from a thousand feet, exhausted, my expression matching Kaia's; a mix of anguished and blank.

9

ALISON

After dinner Oliver went upstairs to his room. Sindre didn't return from his run. Long into the evening I sat in the living room with the lights off. Sindre only came back after several hours, and I imagine he knew I was in there, but he headed straight upstairs without turning on the lights. I waited until I was sure he'd be asleep, and then I went up. Now it's two forty-eight in the morning and I've been sitting in the armchair by the window for thirty-seven minutes. My husband's face is serious and concentrated in sleep, as though he were solving puzzles in his dreams. Outside, a brisk wind sweeps up from the valley, launching itself hard against these houses at the very top of the hill.

Eight lives, Oliver said. I try to imagine eight people, strangers, powered by my daughter's organs. Other children alive because she is not. If what Oliver talked about has any truth to it, my daughter's cells could be altering the bodies of the recipients, growing into them. What does this mean? What *could* it mean? My daughter was a part of me long before she was born. She was made from every cell in my body, nourished by every drop of blood. She was my heart incarnated, a carrier of all that I am and all I ever could be. She's part of me still, held in every cell, forever, but she's dead and that means that, inside, so am I.

I envision her heart beating in this moment, sutured in place in a little stranger's chest. I see fresh, clean blood pumped out and around a young body, carrying minuscule particles of my own child. I stand up and press my face to the window. Out there, somewhere, her heart is beating.

10

ISELIN

"I don't want to go," says Kaia. I knew this would happen. I squat down next to her and take both of her gloved hands in my own.

"Hey," I say. "It's totally normal to be nervous. But you're going to have a great time, I know it."

"No."

"You will. Remember how nice your teacher is? She is so excited you're coming. And the other kids? It's a small class, honey, and they all looked really lovely."

"What if they laugh at me?"

"Why would they laugh at you?"

"Because I don't know the things they know."

"Oh, sweetie. You've learned so much, Kaia. We've already finished the third grade's reading book, remember? You might know more than most of them, even."

"But they've been in school for more than a year already."

"Yes, but we've done a lot of schoolwork at home. You're right on track."

"My heart hurts."

"Hurts?"

"It's going too fast. Like chug-a-chug-a-chug."

I pull my girl onto my lap and hold her close for a long moment. "Kaia, that's just nerves. Come on. We have to go now."

At the school gates, it's as though Kaia toughens up at the sight of the other children. Some are milling around the playground, some are jumping in huge leaf-covered puddles, some are standing quietly beside their mothers. A little girl who I vaguely remember from our visitation day comes running over, smiling widely.

"Kaia," she says, and Kaia smiles back at her. "Come!"

Kaia lets go of my hand and takes the girl's hand. "Bye, Mamma," she says, face excited and flushed a healthy red in the sharp autumn air. As I give her a quick hug, she pulls back and says, "Both sides, Mamma. We have to hug on the other side, too." She presses her left cheek to mine, and then she walks off as fast as she's able, still holding the hand of her new friend.

"Bye," I whisper.

11

ALISON

"Bye," I say, tenderly because I can see he's upset. It seems he doesn't want to go on the hunting trip to Norefjell by the way he holds me, his arms locking behind my back, his stubbled cheek nestled in the crook of my neck.

"Are you sure it's okay?" he says, his eyes searching mine, and I look away, because they are *her* eyes, too. I slide the gearshift from park back into drive, move my hand from my husband's to the hand brake, and glance at the door and the train station beyond it.

"Just go, babe," I say, forcing a smile.

"I'm worried that . . ."

"Don't be," I say, keeping my voice steady and reassuring. "Sindre. Look. We have to . . . keep moving. You know?"

"Could Erica come and stay with you or something? Or you

could come with us? I told you, the guys wouldn't mind at all if you came. Seriously."

"Go, honey," I say, and he does go now, slowly dragging himself from the car. I watch him in the rearview mirror, standing on the curb, his back to Skøyen Station's old, yellow building, his big backpack slouching off one shoulder, his rifle bag held in his hand, letting the onslaught of torrential rain run off his scalp.

At home, I am finally alone. Oliver has gone to his mother's, Sindre is away until Sunday, and I am expected nowhere and by no one. I stand awhile in the hallway. Heavy rain shimmies down the tall windows in the stairwell, and the sound of it drumming on the roof echoes around the house. I go into the kitchen and find my MacBook in a drawer. It won't start up—its charging cable has been put away somewhere. Sometimes, in the last few months, I have missed the mindless surfing on the Internet I used to devote a lot of time to. I'd let myself drift from a restaurant review to a travel article to a book review and on and on, but these days, I steer clear of the Internet. I can't face any of my social media channels—the instant-chat windows popping up if I log on to Facebook, the deluge of sympathy alongside banal reminders of other people's lives moving on. I've also feared where an unplanned browsing session might take me. Until now. I know what I'm looking for now, and feel a deep trepidation in my gut, not unlike the burning. I consider Oliver's desktop computer upstairs, but can't recall the password. I push the door to Sindre's office open, and am immediately struck by how long it's been since I came in here. It looks different, though I can't quite put my finger on how.

There was a time when the door to Sindre's office was always open, and after putting Amalie to bed around seven, I'd signal the beginning of the evening by bringing him a glass of red wine. I'd perch on the edge of his desk, we'd clink our glasses softly together and talk about the day. I might show him an article I'd been working on, and I loved how he'd always take his time reading it, face serious and concentrated. I'd watch him, his strong profile and full lips pressed together, the way his T-shirt would strain at his biceps, and I'd think I was lucky. Or I might tell him something funny Amalie had said on her way home from nursery that day. I'd laugh at the memory of her giggling hysterically at her own jokes in the backseat of the car, and Sindre would chuckle, too, at this strange little creature we'd made.

Sometimes, he'd reach for me, a big hand inching up my thigh, and I'd straddle him in his chair, kissing him hard, laughing, the evening stretching out in front of us.

I sit down in his chair and glance around, trying to decide what's different. The first thing I notice is that Sindre has removed all the photographs on his desk, as well as the kids' drawings he'd hung on the wall to the left of the window. Then I see that he has neatly filed all his paperwork and placed it in gray IKEA boxes on the bookshelf, like I've been asking him to for years.

I touch a random key on his iMac and it leaps to life, the screen saver a picture of me I can't remember seeing before, though I remember when it was taken. I am wearing a wide-brimmed straw hat and a white lace dress, standing barefoot on a beach, smiling at the man holding the camera—the man I love. My hair is honey blond and my skin is deep brown and glowing. It was taken in Maui on our honeymoon, eight years ago. I was thirty-six, but look much younger, or maybe I just think that compared with how I look now. I type in the password but it fails, so I try again. Sindre has had the same password for as long as I can remember, but maybe I'm remembering it wrong—my mind keeps pulling these tricks on me. I try again—*JuulOliSin40*—but again, it fails. I feel a strange sensation, not quite anger, and not quite fear, but a mixture of both. I don't know what to do. I leave Sindre's office and go upstairs to our bedroom. I open all the closets and cupboards and throw anything that isn't properly hung onto the floor. Finally, at the bottom of the chest of drawers, in a drawer crammed full of electrical converters and old invoices and detachable bra straps and foreign coins, I find my laptop charging cable.

In the kitchen, I pour myself half a glass of orange juice and then fill it to the brim with vodka while I wait for the computer to start up. I swallow hard as I take in the background picture—me and Amalie sitting close together at a restaurant in the old town of Rhodes, a whitewashed wall with climbing pink roses behind us. I make myself look at it for several seconds before going to Google and typing in *cellular memory* with my badly shaking hands.

12

ISELIN

We leave the house half an hour before the bell sounds at eight thirty even though it's less than fifteen minutes on foot. Walking is good for Kaia, though she needs to stop frequently. We walk down Lijordveien toward Nadderudveien when an orange forest cat, big as a fox, shoots out from a garden onto the pavement in front of us. It watches us for a moment and then it approaches Kaia, rubbing the side of its body against her trouser leg. Before I have time to react, she drops to her knees and starts stroking the animal. I pull her back up and march her away, but she wails and tries to wrench her arm loose.

"Ow!" she screams. "Let me go!"

"Why can't you think a little?" I ask. "A cat bite could kill you, Kaia!"

"No!"

"Yes, it could. You need to know this!"

"It was a nice kitty!"

"You don't know that."

"Yes, I do."

I feel my face flush hot with anger and begin to walk faster, so fast Kaia almost has to run to keep up. By the time I look at her again, we are approaching the school and her expression is both dejected and fearful. Poor Kaia—it isn't easy to explain to a seven-year-old all the ways she's different from other children.

"I love you," I say, pushing my face into the soft, warm hollow of her neck as I pull her close in a hug.

"Both sides," says Kaia, hugging me on the left side, too, in that funny new way of hers. Then she runs off into the throng of children lining up to go inside, braids flying, arms flapping like wings.

I walk home slowly, the day stretching out in front of me. I wish I knew someone in the neighborhood, someone I might meet for a coffee or a walk. Not that I can spend money on coffee, and I can't imagine I'd have much in common with the stylish, polished mothers at Kaia's school. They step from their Range Rovers, swishy hair tossed over a shoulder, clutching the hands of children dressed in Ralph Lauren. Then they drive off, probably to their fancy offices, leaving the kids to be collected by the au pair. How am I supposed to find common ground with people like that?

The only reason we can afford to live in this area is because we receive government benefits to be within ten kilometers of the hospital, and because we rent the tiny basement of another family's house. The Vikdal family who own the house live upstairs, and our apartment is really just their basement storage units converted into a little home.

It's hard being poor in Norway, where pretty much everyone has so much money. It's not even an age thing—I see young mothers only a little older than myself, pushing ten-thousand-kroner strollers, sipping fifty-kroner lattes without a care in the world, Gucci bags casually hanging off their arm, and it's hard to not become consumed by resentfulness and bitterness because I could have been like them, had I made different choices.

I walk down the paved path to the apartment entrance, and just then, Hanne Vikdal, our landlady, appears at her front door, as though she'd been waiting behind it for me to appear.

"Hi," I say, fumbling with the key in my pocket.

"Oh, hi there," she says, looking me up and down. "Cold today."

"Yeah."

"You know, I'm not sure it's a great idea for you and Kaia to walk to school in this cold. If she really is sick, I mean—"

"The doctor says it's good for her to walk."

"But in this weather?"

I nod and smile a tight smile at her, slipping the key into the lock. When I push the door open, Hanne angles her head, trying to get a glimpse inside. I stare at her for a moment, then close the door a little harder than I need to. I stand a moment in front of the shut door, unpeeling the gloves from my hands and listening to the unfamiliar silence.

Sometimes, I'm kind of glad the apartment is as tiny as it is. It still feels strange and almost frightening to be alone at home during the day after having Kaia for constant company for so many years. I walk into the main room and look around: corridor, toilet, shower room, living room where I sleep on the pull-out sofa bed, kitchen with a tiny table, Kaia's bedroom alcove just off the kitchen. That's it. I lie down on Kaia's bed and breathe in the familiar scent of her: the lime-and-honey shower cream we both like, something sweet like cookie dough, and underneath it, something medicinal. I close my eyes, and again I feel bad for how this morning started. I feel weak with regret just replaying it in my mind now. Poor Kaia. It's only her first month at school, ever. It's not like she's had it easy with all of her challenges, and then she got me as a mother on top of it.

Why can't you think a little? I'd said. Why can't I learn to control myself? I'm so tired. I am so, so tired, and for a minute, I consider just closing my eyes and napping for a couple of hours, because what exactly am I supposed to do with myself all day now that Kaia has started school? For seven years I have been her full-time carer. I haven't had more than a handful of days with any kind of time to myself, and now everything has changed.

I get up because I can't fall asleep in case the school rings, which I think they probably will—Kaia isn't used to being away from me, or to being around other children. I sit at the kitchen table; I could draw. Or I could see if my computer will start—NAV has said I have to register as a job seeker or they'll cut our benefits. I tried to say that I don't have any qualifications and that it might be almost impossible to fit a job around caring for Kaia, but the lady across the table just stared at me and said, "If you get a job, there are additional benefits for childcare you can apply for."

I make a cup of tea and sit on the sofa. A strange noise is coming from upstairs, but then I remember it's Wednesday and it's just the Vikdals' cleaner dragging the Hoover across their polished wooden floorboards. I try the computer, but it won't start. Sometimes I have to leave it for days, and then suddenly it decides to work again.

I decide to have a shower, and undress in Kaia's alcove—I'd be visible from the road if I got undressed in the living room, and the bathroom is so small my clothes would get splashed with water if I did it in there. I avoid looking at myself in the mirror opposite because I don't particularly like what I see. I like my face and my hair, but my legs are too fat and my stomach is crisscrossed with ugly, purple stretch marks. My breasts are heavy and look like they belong to someone much older.

I stand a long while under the hot water. When I'm dried off, I lie down on Kaia's bed again, just listening to the occasional sound from upstairs. I decide to bake buns—I think I have all the ingredients. She'll be so pleased when she arrives home from school to the smell of freshly baked buns dusted with cardamom and brushed with egg yolk. I feel energized again, and smile to myself at the thought of my daughter's little face lighting up.

It's early evening when there is a knock on the door. Kaia looks up from where she's sitting on the floor in front of the TV, an empty plate in front of her. The buns worked. She lit up and licked her lips theatrically when we came home, the apartment's air sweet and fragrant with the freshly made buns.

"Who is it?" says Kaia, her eyes back on the screen.

"I don't know," I say. I open the door and our landlady is standing there. She's never come knocking before, though I often feel as though she's watching me and Kaia as we come and go. She annoyed me this morning, and I feel a flush of irritation at the sight of her.

"Hi," I say, but don't invite her in. She glances past me into the apartment, and I silently curse the heap of helter-skelter shoes in the corridor.

"Hi, Iselin," she says, then pauses, most likely waiting for me to ask her inside. It's a drizzly, cool evening, but my basement entrance is sheltered by the upstairs terrace and she won't get wet standing there, so I don't feel that bad. "You were so quick to go inside this morning, but I've been meaning to check in with you, to see how everything is going here."

"Fine."

"Look . . . we've been hearing a lot of noise of late. At night. Screaming."

"Kaia's been having nightmares."

"Right. Just . . . It's a little worrying. Sound carries in this house."

"I'm sorry you've been hearing it. I'm afraid there isn't anything much I can do about it. I'm hoping it will gradually stop. She's been through a lot. It could have to do with some of the medication she is taking."

"Right."

"I mean, I hear you guys, too." At this, Hanne Vikdal raises an eyebrow. She might think I'm brazen saying that, but her three boys have disturbed us on so many occasions, and now she has the nerve to knock on my door to complain about the nightmares of a little girl with a life-threatening medical condition? "Anyway, I will try to keep the noise down so her nightmares don't disturb you," I say.

"I . . . Well, what I am getting at, is more whether I have cause for concern when a child screams like that night after night."

"Good night," I say, closing the door softly and leaving her standing there. I can practically see the stunned expression on her face. I lean against the door and take several deep breaths before going back inside to where Kaia has started building a Lego tower in front of the television. I imagine that bitch upstairs, in her big house with her gleaming Audi outside, reporting back to her husband that the tenant shut the door in her face, and my skin prickles with a sudden chill. Maybe we should move, but where and how? Not like I have any money, and Hanne Vikdal is hardly going to give me a glowing reference. I decide to speak to my caseworker at NAV about it; maybe we could get rehoused for medical reasons—it can't be good for Kaia to breathe the humid, stale air in this flat.

I tidy up in the kitchen, scrubbing the baking tray covered in lumpy, hardened bits of dough from the buns, then sit down at the fold-out table. Kaia is concentrating, carefully pressing each Lego piece down onto the one beneath. Her cheeks are pink and her movements are quick and easy. She looks like a healthy child. I close my eyes and fiddle with the crochet tablecloth, my mind racing.

13

ALISON

Every cell in the human body holds a person's complete genetic material. Neuropeptides, the transmitters used by the brain to communicate with the body, exist in all bodily tissue, making cellular memory a possibility, says Google. I type in *cellular memory heart transplants* and Google returns 707,000 hits. *Could transplant organs hold the donor's memories?* asks one article. This is already too much. Way too much. I get up and stand a moment by the kitchen window. Outside, everything is still the same. Rainwater streams off the branches of the spruce trees, the sky is dark and close, the city in the valley is entirely hidden by fog. My breath catches, I have to bend forward to fully fill my lungs. I stay there, and tears drop off the tip of my nose; I just want to be switched off, to stop, to have one moment away from my restless mind and my cracked heart.

I think of Sindre, out in the forest, clutching his rifle, expert eyes trained on an unsuspecting moose. Hooves moving this way and that in the shrubbery, jaw churning, a froth of berry juice and spittle strung from its mouth, soft eyes blinking in the incandescent morning light, sunlight shredded by the dense trees, only seconds left to live. I turn back toward the computer and bring my thoughts back to the notion of cellular memory. What if memories, and the essence of a person, are held not only in the brain, or in the soul, but in every single cell of a body? Would those cells then somehow influence or change their recipient in the event of organ donations? I press my face to the window, the cool pane soothing my flushed cheek, and stare out at the bulbous whiteness concealing Oslo beneath it—somewhere out there is a person who received my daughter's organs. Could it be that they received more than just a life-giving body part?

Once, my thoughts felt straightforward and were easily discernible from one another. Now I visualize them as hungry worms squirming in a can: ugly, and jumbled together. It's almost 2:00 A.M. and outside the rain has let up, leaving a spent and starless sky. I've been here for hours, fixed to the screen, the seconds of the night slowly bleeding away, drinking wine mixed with vodka and cranberry juice in big gulps.

I've read about the woman in New England who began having vivid dreams about a man named Tim L. after her heart transplant. She also experienced intense food cravings for things she'd never liked before, like beer and chicken nuggets, and when she tracked down the donor's family, they confirmed he was indeed a beer and chicken nugget lover named Tim L. I've read about the man who married the widow of his donor and then killed himself in the same way as the donor two years later. I read about the guy who turned into an art prodigy after a heart transplant, apparently thanks to his artist donor. I've read about the French actress who reported vivid memories of the car crash in which her heart donor apparently died. Then there was the little girl whose unexplained memories of a brutal murder were so strong and so detailed they led to the arrest of the man who killed her heart donor. All of these people received someone else's heart. I consider myself a rational person; I don't know how I could believe in these things, but then, how could I not? I read and read and read, trying to derive some meaning from all the words, and they swim around in my head, bleeding into each other. This concept is so full of possibilities, I can feel myself coming alive again.

The phone is vibrating in my hand, twitching and bleeping, its insistent electronic tune ringing in my ears. I sit up, disoriented, but as I do, the room spins and nausea washes over me, bitter splashes of bile shooting into my mouth. I swallow hard, squint at the bright screen, Sindre's name flashing. It's 5:52 A.M., and as I slide the button to take the call, I just know it isn't Sindre's voice I will hear, but someone else's, calling from his phone to tell me something has happened to him.

I'm right.

"Alison?" whispers a man.

"Yes?" *Please, please, not Sindre, too.* I see him, in the middle of the night, in the forest, not running now, just hanging still, strung by his neck from a black rope looped around a thick, mossy branch, watched by blinking stars and silent, roaming animals. "Tell me, goddammit!" The man is breathing hard into the phone, and his voice breaks as he speaks.

"Sindre . . . Sindre has completely lost it."

14

ISELIN

She eats properly now, merrily chewing her fish cakes and peas and mashed potatoes, her fork stabbing at the next morsel as soon as she's swallowed the one before. This, too, is new. She used to eat half a piece of bread with Nutella here, a quarter of an apple there. I watch her and smile and she smiles back, little face lit up and animated as she chats on and on about her school day. I listen intently and nod, asking all the right follow-up questions. *So, Solveig is nicer than Oda? Why did they fight, did you say? Oh, yeah, Ludvig sounds like a right joker.* Kaia accidentally drops her fork on the ground and the loud clattering noise almost makes me jump out of my skin. She must sense me tense up because when I look at her again her face is serious.

"Mamma," she says, spoon carrying a cluster of peas close to her mouth, "can I go to Solveig's house for a sleepover? She asked me."

"Oh, honey," I say. "Maybe at some point. But not just now."

"Why not?"

"Because you are still in the early phase after surgery. I can't expect someone else's parents to look after you in the right way."

"I know what to do if I feel bad! I know which medicines I need and when I need them."

"Kaia, you're seven. Planning lots of different medicines at different times is not your responsibility, though I know you know when and how much." She ponders this for a moment, chewing on the last spoonful of food.

"Solveig can come here for a sleepover, then," she says.

"Honey . . ."

"Why can't she? She doesn't have to take any pills at all! She said." I don't want to tell Kaia that the main reason is that I'd be embarrassed to have someone else's child here, in this tiny, crowded apartment we call home. Before, I had the convenient excuse that we couldn't have kids visiting due to infection risk, and while that is still true to a certain extent, Kaia is pretty much cured now, and I do want her to be like other children her age—she has missed out on so much.

"We'll see," I say, though I imagine most kids realize that means no.

She hasn't even woken up tonight. It's me who has jerked awake, maybe just preempting when Kaia starts screaming. I walk into her bedroom and watch the rise and fall of her chest shadowed on the wall in the faint light from the streetlights outside. I wish I wasn't so alone, that I had a partner who could put his arms around me and draw me gently back to bed, whispering, *It's okay, babe.*

15

ALISON

Espen and I sit close together on orange plastic chairs. My husband is heavily sedated in a room farther down the corridor. The doctors are going to take him off the meds this evening, and hopefully he can come home tomorrow.

"I'm just glad we're not at the morgue," says Espen, staring into his paper cup. Leftover drops of weak coffee stud its waxy inside. I nod. His right arm is in a sling, and his left hand, holding the empty coffee cup, is shaking badly. Espen has been my husband's closest friend for almost three decades, since they met in the military at age eighteen. His eyes are red and his bald, smooth head shines in the brilliant sunlight coming in from the window behind us.

"I think he must have thought he was back there," says Espen, his eyes clouding over, and I know that he is back *there* now, too.

"You know, in combat. It really was as though he was unreachable, that he had lost grasp of reality."

"Will you tell me everything, from the beginning?"

Espen nods, then begins to speak. "We got to the clearing at around five thirty. It was earlier than we'd hoped, so we just waited. It was still completely dark."

"Was there anything strange about Sindre on the way there? Or the night before?"

"Well. He's not himself, of course. Understandably. But he didn't seem much different from when I saw him last week."

"Did he talk to you about Amalie?" Her name catches in my throat like a badly swallowed painkiller.

Espen shakes his head slowly. "No. He's never been chatty, and now he's just more withdrawn than usual."

"So. You waited. For how long?"

"Maybe an hour. No, it must have been longer. It started to get light. It was cold, but we were well dressed."

"Did you speak in that time?"

"No, we just lay there, waiting. Listening. Sindre in the middle, Victor to his left, and me to his right. It was all agreed ahead of time, of course. It always is. We were there for a huge female; we'd stalked her the entire day before. She had a calf with her, probably around four months old. Sindre would shoot the calf first, that was the plan."

"Why would you shoot a calf?"

"Because . . ." Espen hesitates a long while, looking up at the ceiling as though to find words, but then I realize that he is blinking back tears. "Because the mother always comes back."

The mother always comes back. I see them: a big, gentle moose mamma and her baby, moving unselfconsciously through the dewy, cool grass of the morning forest. At the clearing, the mother would look around, blinking, trying to detect humans and danger.

"I see," I whisper.

Espen stares miserably at the cup in his hands. I see the loaded rifle in his hand, the alert concentration of framing the shot. "I was supposed to shoot the mother when she came back for her baby; we'd have her at a perfect distance. But. It didn't happen like that. We could just make them out, emerging from the forest and coming slowly toward us. I nodded at Sindre to get ready, and he looked calm and focused. But then . . . he didn't do what he was supposed to. He shot at the mother, and the calf immediately bolted. Victor managed to shoot it, but Sindre had stood up by then and moved toward where the mother was in the middle of the clearing, trying to get back up. He walked almost all the way up to her and then he started firing again. Again and again. She was . . . He shot her to pieces."

"What did you do?"

"Well, I made toward him when he stood up, but Victor held me back. It was pretty obvious he was totally out of control. I made my way along the back of the clearing toward him, in between the trees. Sindre noticed me, then, standing just a few feet away from him, holding my palms up toward him. 'Back the fuck off,' he screamed. 'Back off,' he screamed, over and over." Espen won't look at me. I won't look at him, either. I open my hand and look at the faint lifeline in my palm.

"We . . . We didn't know what to do. When I tried to approach him, he waved the rifle at me and then he turned it toward himself."

"Jesus Christ. He could have shot you."

"He didn't, though."

"What happened next?"

"I threw myself at him and wrenched the rifle from his hand. He was covered in blood spray, screaming."

"Jesus," I say again. Espen nods. His face is stricken, disbelieving, as though he's watching the scene unfolding itself in this moment. We fall silent but images of my husband going amok with a rifle in the deep forests of Buskerud repeatedly flash through my mind.

"Here," I say, into the quiet, dim room, and sit down on the edge of the bed next to Sindre, placing the steaming coffee on the low table by his head. He's awake—I can see the glint of an open eye. He has only been home for three days and already he wants to go back to work. The doctor says it's out of the question until after New Year, at least, after what happened.

"Thank you," says Sindre, and turns toward me with a tired smile. "How are you doing?"

I nod. Sindre sits up and sips from the mug, closing his eyes. I glance at the time—another hour until he has to take his meds.

"I was thinking that . . . that maybe we should go away for Christmas. With Oliver," he says, staring seriously into the mug. My mind darts to suitcases stacked on a trolley, to long, blue flights, to the brazen sun beating down on a remote beach, to Dinky Bear left on the pillow, to the browning mounds of rotting leaves in the garden, to the empty, black lake covered by a lid of ice . . .

"Yes," I whisper. "Yes, let's." Our eyes meet, pleading with each other, turning this possibility over and over.

"Where?"

"Um, maybe . . . maybe Mexico?"

"Mexico," repeats Sindre, as though he's never heard of such a place.

"Yeah, or . . ." I'm trying to think of other places, places where we'll be known to no one, where we will look complete: a man, a woman, a lanky, sweet teenage boy. "Uh, Tenerife. Sarasota? Maybe . . ."

"Mexico," says Sindre again, staring at me through the drifts of steam rising from his coffee. I nod and am about to get up, but happen to glance at his pink, full fingers clutching the mug, and an uncomfortable vision of those same hands firing the rifle uncontrollably appears in my mind. I see Sindre's blank, focused face as he kept shooting, over and over. I see him turning the gun from the moose to Espen, to himself. My husband might have been a murderer, but then I remembered that he already is, though they don't call it that. Neutralizer. *He was unreachable*, said Espen, later. *Wild.* What if . . . What if it happens again? What if I wake in the dead of the night and he's pointing that gun in my face?

"What is it?" says Sindre, dark brows scrunched close together.

"Nothing," I say. "Nothing, babe. Just . . . It's almost time for your meds. I'll be back up in an hour."

"Okay."

I lie down on Amalie's bed.

Daddy is getting better. He came home. He had to go away for a while so he could get better. He's not back at work yet; he's napping in our room, so I'm here, just resting and listening for your presence. It's eleven o'clock in the morning but gloomy outside. It makes me smile to remember how you never noticed the weather much, and if I ever complained about a particularly dreary day, you'd laugh and look around as though it hadn't registered with you that icy-cold rain was crashing down all around us. You were such a happy person.

I'm trying to get better, I'm trying so hard. Sometimes, like now, lying on your bed, I feel so close to you that it's almost okay you can't come all the way here to be with me. I know now that something of you remains.

I come to her room almost every day now. At first, I couldn't bear it; I would literally be itching and clawing at my own skin at the impossible truth of her absence from her own room. It was easier with the door shut—I could almost make myself believe she was in there. But Karen said that I'd be more likely to feel close to Amalie in the space she'd lived her whole life than in the space she left us from, and she was right. But could there be a way to feel even closer?

I shut the door softly and step back outside into that other world. She's sitting at her desk, I tell myself. She's making those beautiful swirly patterns she's so good at with her glitter gel markers, and she's smiling to herself, humming the songs she always makes up.

But she isn't.

I let go of the door handle and stumble toward the stairs. Seventeen steps done in five, through the double doors in the hallway, outside, fast across the soggy lawn, rain stabbing at me, into the hushed clutch of the trees, onto my knees, hands digging into squelchy earth, breath short, hiccupy, gasping. I'm trying to get better, I've been trying so hard, and I'm trying even harder now because Sindre and I can't both fall to pieces at the same time. I'm on my fucking knees, I want to shout out loud, but not a sound will come, and in the end there's nothing to do but get back up and stand staring at our house through the gaps in the trees.

Downstairs in the kitchen, I scrub my nails clean with a wire brush until my skin breaks and bleeds. Will I be like those other wives, the wives of men who fire at a group of innocents, who turn guns on strangers, whose faces are all over the newspapers in my country—angry, armed, with nothing to lose? Will it be me next, weeping, saying, "I didn't see it coming, how could he do something like this?"

The mother always comes back, said Espen. *Always.*

* * *

It's late, and Sindre is passed out on the sofa, an almost empty bottle of scotch on the floor beside him. I stand there watching him, thinking about what has become of us. I almost say it out loud: *Goodbye.*

Goodbye.

In the garage, I find what I'm looking for easily enough. The gun is even heavier in my hand than I'd imagined it would be, and I hold it for a moment, then place it back in the box. I remove a few other things, things I know could be dangerous. A blue coil of rope. A glinting hunting knife. A bottle of sulfuric acid. I place the rope and the knife in the box with the gun, then I remain in the dark, musty room for a while—what a strange and difficult situation I find myself in. But I know, with every fiber of my being, that I *have* to do this; there is no other way. I carry the box carefully around the side of the house down the narrow passageway, as though danger were a live thing. I return for the acid. In the car, I place the box and the bottle on the floor of the passenger seat, and then I sit in the driver's seat, clutching the ice-cold wheel, breathing frosty clouds into the still air. It's past midnight, and time to go.

I drive into the forest along a narrow dirt track and choose a quiet spot on the north side of the lake. I'm doing this to save us. I know that I can't trust myself around the dangerous objects any more than I could trust my husband, and walking into the forest, I finger the frayed coil of a blue rope with numb fingers, imagining looping it over a bare branch and then around my neck. By the water, I tie the rope to a chunky rock and fling it out into the darkness. I pour the acid out at my feet and it makes a hissing hole in the ice. Next, the long, curved knife Sindre has had since his teens—it gives me the chills every time I look at its glinting blade. Then, the gun and the cartridges. It takes me an age to fling all the objects into the lake, one after the other, listening to the sharp cracks as they smash the surface layer of ice and disappear into the blackness beneath.

Now, afterward, I regret throwing those unpleasant objects into the lake—it's *her* lake, and it will forever hold something of her within its waters. I drop to my knees on the brown, frozen beach, clutching at a stabbing pain in my stomach, my sobs leaping out across the surface of the lake like skipping stones, before being sucked into a shrill wind tearing at the trees. The fragile hope I have felt in the last few weeks melted away at the sight of the lake and the inescapable reality of what it has taken from me. I need a sign to get up, to keep moving, to take even one more breath.

A sign, baby bear. Can you give me another sign?

I sit holding myself tight against the cold, trying to regain control of my breath. And then, unmistakably, unbelievably, a sound separates itself from the whoosh of the wind—it is the rapid beat of a heart, and I stand up, turning my head away from the wind to hear more clearly. I'm not imagining it. It's getting louder and louder, slicing through all the other sounds of the night, this delicious, rhythmic thump, and even when I spot the T-bane train's lights at the far end of the lake, slithering through a gap in the bare trees, it's still a sign.

16

ISELIN

"What are you doing?" I ask, taking in the sight of her, caught red-handed, pen held against the baseboard in the kitchen. I grab the pen out of her hand and squat down next to her, spraying her with my wet hair from the shower, bringing my face close to the wall. She's drawn a long line of little bears along the baseboard. In permanent black marker pen. "Kaia . . ." Kaia won't look at me, and stares at her hand instead, still held in a half grip as though she were holding the pen. "Hey, look at me! Why would you draw this . . . this stuff on the walls in this house?"

"Don't be angry," she says.

"Kaia, how could I not be angry when you go and do stuff like this?"

"Stop it! Stop shouting! You always shout at me! Other moms

don't shout." *The other moms don't have to put up with being an un-employed single mother to a kid who has never had a healthy day in her life, who requires constant attention, who doesn't sleep at night, who answers back, and who thinks it's okay to draw eleven fucking bears on the walls of our rented home*, I want to say, but I manage to keep my mouth shut and instead I just walk away from her and slam the door to the corridor shut behind me.

I lean back against the door and imagine having the kind of life lived by the moms in this neighborhood. They go home to nice, successful husbands, they go to delis or fancy supermarkets like Meny to buy food without having to add up the cost of everything in the basket on the way to the checkout, they buy clothes without looking at the price tags, their kids get their hair cut at the parlor in CC West, not at home with a pair of old nail scissors, bending backward over the washbasin. I bet those moms don't lie awake at night, stricken by worry and fear and regret. I want to be like them, not like me. I'm tired, poor, and alone. When I was younger, I was so driven, so hell-bent on escaping my drab childhood in that place I never bother to think about, and what kills me is that I came so damned close. I actually made it to where I wanted to be—Paris and art school. And then I went and got myself pregnant and ruined everything.

Still, I have something none of the other moms have: Kaia. I take a few deep breaths and manage to push the tears that sprang to my eyes back in their ducts. I go back into the kitchen, where Kaia is rubbing at a bear with a wet dishcloth.

"Hey," I say, taking the cloth from her and gently stroking her cheek. "I'm sorry. I didn't mean to raise my voice at you. I just don't understand why you would draw on the walls, Kaia. I worry we'll get into trouble."

"They're cute," she whispers, and she's right, they *are* cute and meticulously drawn—they could be from a professional cartoon.

"It's just . . . You have got to understand that we can't draw stuff on the walls in this house. It isn't ours, Kaia."

"Yes, it is. We live here."

"Yes, but that doesn't make it ours. Other people own it. When they find out that we draw on the walls, they'll get really angry."

"But they're cute," she whispers. I nod and pull her close, kissing the top of her head. I think of that woman upstairs, at how she watches me and judges. She'd be lucky to get some bears drawn on her walls. I take a pen from Kaia's box and begin to add to her mural. Two birds flying overhead, a bear in a boat, a duck dragging a cart full of tiny bear children. In the end we can't stop laughing, and then we collapse on the sofa watching *Dora* and eating strawberry ice cream straight from the tub.

17

ALISON

"Alison," says Karen.

"Yes," I say, dragging my eyes from the birds to Karen's mild face.

"I want to say that I'm sorry you felt like you couldn't stay last time. My job is to listen to what it is you're saying, and to make you feel held. I'm not sure I managed to do that."

"No . . . No, it wasn't your fault. At all. It was a bad day. An especially bad day," I add. Karen nods and looks at me for a while, perhaps waiting for me to start talking. I don't.

"Is your breathing better?"

"No. Maybe a little. It seems to come and go." Karen nods. When she doesn't speak, I continue. "I threw my husband's gun into the lake." A shadow of alarm moves across her professionally calm face.

"When did you do that?"

"Last night. And when I was there by the lake, it felt like she was close. So close. Like she was sending me a sign."

"A sign?"

"Yes, a sign." As I say the word *sign*, I realize how insane it sounds. I wanted to tell Karen about how I'd felt a flicker of hope when I stood by the lake and the sound of a heart beating appeared out of thin air, getting steadily louder and closer, but then I would have to tell her it was actually just the sound of the train hurtling along its track, though of course that was way too much of a coincidence *not* to be a sign, but from the way Karen is looking at me, I know she'd never understand. I straighten up in my chair, let my eyes rest on her birds for a moment. "What I mean is, she feels close, sometimes."

Karen nods, waits for me to continue, but I do not.

"You've been coming here for almost four months now," she says after a while. "I was thinking we might try to incorporate some regression techniques into these sessions." I shrug, return to the birds. Twenty-two of them, up high, slicing air, collectively organized into an arrow pointing south; how? Karen Fritz says something.

"What?"

"Will you tell me, just as you remember them, the events of July sixth?"

No, I think. *I can't.* How would I find the words? But I nod. I close my eyes. And then I'm back there.

I can practically taste the earthy, bitter lake water and feel the rush of muddy sand slithering through eager fingers. I'm sitting on the grass overlooking the lake, watching swarms of children. I grew up near the water, too, and feel moved watching my own child play in the shallows just the way I used to throughout my childhood in

California. I watch Amalie where she sits up to her waist in the sun-dappled murky water, clutching a yellow bucket and red spade, splashing and shrieking, droplets shooting from her loose, long hair. Only recently has she shrugged off the last remains of stocky toddlerhood and grown lean and tall for her age. She frequently looks over to where I'm sitting, scanning the throng of people for the familiar sight of me, an easy smile passing between us. I'm vaguely annoyed that Sindre isn't here with us. He carried the picnic blanket and cooler bag from the car, searching the grass lawn surrounding the beach for a tiny, free spot to sit, and then helped me spread the blanket out. Instead of sitting down next to me, he pulled a pair of running shoes from his sports bag and discarded his flip-flops. He smiled ruefully at me and gave me a quick kiss before darting off onto the forest path that encircles the lake.

I stand up and, shielding my eyes from the wonderfully warm summer sun, look across the calm, brown water to the far shore for signs of my husband running, thinking I might spot his bright yellow running vest between the birch trees, but I don't. Sometimes, I feel like I'm always alone. If Sindre isn't at work, he's cycling, or running, or skiing, or climbing, or hunting, or playing football with "the boys," who are no longer boys at all, but balding lawyers and businessmen in their late forties. What had started off as a much-encouraged bid to recover the fitness of his military days has exploded into a rather extreme pursuit of ultimate fitness, and every month he brings home increasingly expensive equipment, signing up for marathons, races, and various competitions across southern Norway. I've begun to miss the slightly tired-looking, normal Sindre I married.

I return my gaze to Amalie, but she's no longer sitting in the middle of a small circle of children of a similar age. There are so many kids running, splashing, and swimming that they have become a kind of collective body; one giant being made from shy, white skin, bright scraps of colored bathing suits, blow-up toys, armbands, and wet hair. Before I have time to feel really panicked, Amalie stands in front of me, shivering theatrically, pulling her armbands off and flinging them onto the picnic blanket.

"Can I have ice cream now, please?" I nod and take her cold, wet hand in my own. It takes us several minutes to get to the ice-cream kiosk a short distance away, inching forward on the tiny slivers of lawn not occupied by families sunbathing, eating, rubbing sun cream into tender, jutting shoulder blades. On the way back to our blanket, Amalie spots Sindre, sitting down and looking out at the sweet pandemonium in the water, wiping sweat from his forehead. *"Pappa,"* she shouts, and runs toward him, vanilla ice cream dripping off her thin wrist as she goes. He scoops her up and takes a little bite from her ice cream, making Amalie squeal. I smile and lie down next to them, resting my head on Sindre's knee.

"God, it's crazy here," he says. "I could hear the kids across the water all the way to the other side."

"Yeah, we shouldn't stay that much longer, actually. We need to pack this afternoon and get to bed early; the flight is at six thirty in the morning, remember?" Sindre grimaces and nods while simultaneously wiping at the sugary river running down the entire length of Amalie's arm, dripping onto her Queen Elsa bathing suit.

"Okay, let's leave in half an hour," says Sindre. "After we've packed, I, uh, might meet with Espen for a bike ride. Won't be long. Not like I'll get to exercise in Italy—I'm going to spend all my time snuggling by the pool with my gorgeous wife." He squeezes my shoulder and I roll my eyes but he doesn't notice through my dark sunglasses.

"Mm-hmm," I say.

"I want to swim more!" says Amalie.

"Finish your ice cream first, honey," I say. "You've still got half an hour."

"I'm going to run another fifteen minutes, okay?" Sindre moves my head from his lap and gently puts my handbag underneath it for support, then jumps to his feet with impressive speed, running off before I have a chance to say anything. I close my eyes and take a few deep breaths, lightly stroking Amalie's stringy, wet hair.

I must have fallen asleep for a moment. It can't have been more than a moment. Sindre is standing over me, saying something. I sit up fast, my head throbbing.

"What?"

"Can you get Amalie? I'll start getting our stuff together," he says, lifting his sunglasses, peering out at the water.

"But . . . weren't you going running?"

"I'm back. Where's Amalie?"

"She . . . she was just here," I say. "I'll get her."

"I can't see her."

I stand up and walk away from him, scanning the myriad children rushing back and forth, carrying full buckets of water, the toddlers with sandy bare bottoms, the older children farther out on the lake, sitting atop inflatable crocodiles and flamingos and giant ducks. I can't see Amalie anywhere, and begin to feel a dull ache in my stomach, a wild flutter of alarm. I didn't really fall asleep, I can't have, I must have just closed my eyes for a moment. And then there she is. She's standing with her back to us, thirty or so meters away, scooping water from a bucket into another little girl's bucket carefully. I watch her for a moment—the way her Elsa bathing suit is almost too small, even though we bought it less than a month ago, the way her skin seems to have taken on a slightly darker hue already, the sweet way she holds her arms out from her body, encumbered by the matching Queen Elsa armbands, how all her movements seem joyful.

"Look—there she is," I say, turning back toward Sindre, pointing her out.

"Where?"

"Over there. With that girl."

"Where?"

I take his arm and point it in the direction of the little girls. "There."

"Ali, that's not her." His words are blurry, like they've been spoken underwater. I lift my sunglasses—it *is* her, it *has* to be her, of course it's her. I begin to walk toward them, shouting "Amalie," but the girl doesn't turn around, and Sindre follows behind me, then grabs my arm, his eyes anxious, and in his hand, he's holding one of Amalie's discarded armbands.

"Look," he shouts, though he's right in front of me, "she isn't wearing her armbands. That girl is!" I run up to them, stepping into the water so I can get in front of them to see their faces. He's right, it isn't her. Snub nose, broad forehead, blue eyes, not brown. A strange sound, it must be coming from me. The little girls stare, alarmed. I begin to run. Fast, through ankle-deep water, shouting her name. People come running. Everyone looking for her. Voices, many voices, calling her sweet name. *Amalie*, they shout; *Amalie, Amalie, Amalie.*

But she's gone.

18

ISELIN

"Mamma," screams Kaia.

"I'm here, baby," I whisper, and she looks at me, lucid and serious.

"I almost drowned," she says, crying softly.

"What? No, baby. No . . . You had a bad dream, my sweet girl. Everything's going to be okay."

"No, I almost drowned."

"Shhh," I whisper. "It was just a dream. A bad, bad dream. You're going to be okay, my darling." I bury my face in her neck, wisps of hair tickling my cheek, and cry with relief. She's awake, she's alive, and in spite of everything, I am still the luckiest girl in the world.

Kaia has been up three times already, and it's not yet 1:00 A.M. Each time, I sit with her, smoothing her hair down, singing "Clementine" into her ear, tucking the blankets tighter around her until sleep catches her again. I've gotten used to these sleepless nights now and almost can't remember the way it was before, how she'd sleep the coma-like sleep of the heavily medicated. I've taken to staying up until around two o'clock, and if I manage that, I stand a good chance of getting a few hours' sleep toward the morning. Besides, Kaia tends to wake more in the hour just before midnight and the hour after. Sometimes, I even think it's nice when she wakes up— the nights can be lonesome.

After the operation and the two weeks she spent asleep afterward, there's a part of me reluctant to let her sleep at all; my instinct is to constantly check that she's breathing, that she's fighting, and that her heart is steady and strong.

Tomorrow a journalist is coming to talk to us. I didn't want to do it at first, but when Noa was interviewed by *Se Her* magazine earlier this autumn, she mentioned her heroic little niece and then the magazine called me and convinced me to do a feature about Kaia to raise awareness for childhood heart disease. They're doing an "at-home" piece and I've tidied everything, so it's nice to sit here, on my fold-out sofa bed, looking at the familiar shapes of our few bits of furniture in the near darkness: the stretch of uncluttered, gleaming floor between the living room and the kitchen suddenly seeming vast. The sound of Kaia's soft breath travels from the next room and occasionally she lets out an odd little sound, like a kitten mewling. I bring my mind back to the summer day when everything changed, the day the journalist will want to hear all about. The day when the phone finally rang and we tumbled stunned into a taxi, Kaia's little body curled up in my lap, the way her favorite doctor, Dr. Harari, stood waiting on the curb when we arrived and carried her into the children's clinic, the cool, familiar air of the hospital building, the long hours alone in the waiting room, the prayers, watching rain slamming against the windows, washing away the hot summer air.

I've just fallen asleep when Kaia wakes again, or at least that's how it feels. I let her slip under the covers and glance at my phone screen—it's just after 2:00 A.M. and my eyes are heavy and sore.

"Shhh," I say, stroking her hair, gently rocking her tiny body back and forth.

"I'm afraid," says Kaia.

"What are you afraid of, Kaia?" I ask, yawning, still holding her tight.

"The things in the night."

"What things?"

"The stories when I sleep."

"Dreams."

Kaia's head bobs up and down in the snug space between my shoulder and my neck as she nods.

"Yeah."

"What kind of dreams are they?" She doesn't answer, just hangs in my arms like a rag doll. Kaia never used to remember her dreams before the last few months—the medicines she was on before were so strong any dream would be obliterated, and that is why she keeps waking in the nights now, again and again. The recurring nightmares have become less frequent in the last month, thankfully, and my guess is that it could be down to her feeling generally calmer and more settled in at school. "Dreams aren't dangerous, sweetie, even if they can be scary sometimes. They're your brain's way of processing different things." Still she doesn't answer and I realize she's fallen asleep again. I place her gently back on the bed, and she briefly opens her eyes before they roll back and slide shut. I get up and go into the kitchen.

I turn on the fluorescent tube light above the sink and pull out my notepad from the drawer where I keep our art supplies. I use a soft charcoal pencil to draw a web of crooked lines across the page. They will become the branches of a tree and on them I will place hundreds of birds, so many of them that their round little bodies will sit pressed closely together like an expectant audience at a pop concert. After penciling in just a couple of the birds, who turn out wobbly and ugly, I grow tired of the stupid drawing and crush it in my hand. I smooth another blank sheet down in front of me, but nothing comes to me. It never used to be like this. Before Kaia, I'd think almost entirely in images, and they'd always willingly be transcribed onto the page. I was often told my drawings were wonderful, and for a long while I thought drawing would become my career. But now it's as though the images in my mind have left me entirely. I guess that's hardly surprising. I try one more time, placing the pencil on the new sheet, very gently, and when it moves, it is as though by itself.

I don't know where I've picked up all the details from—perhaps from the endless images and diagrams and illustrations the doctors have presented me with over the years, but apparently, I know how to draw an anatomical heart. When I have finished I draw the outline of a girl around the heart, not much bigger than the organ that powers her.

When they first told me Kaia's heart was failing, I thought they would be able to fix it. That it could heal and grow strong. The thing that plays so painfully on my mind, the thing that keeps me up so often at night, is the fact that I never wanted her. That I couldn't love her until I almost lost her. When they placed her on my chest after almost thirty hours of hell, I turned away. I didn't want to know the little being who had taken over my body and my life, who had already cost me so much. It wasn't until I found her, limp and blue, in her cot on the ninth morning of her life, that I realized that everything would be nothing without her.

That the meningitis didn't kill her was nothing short of a miracle. A nurse stood all night by Kaia's incubator as she fought for her life, nudging her hard every few seconds as her heart rate dropped. There was a handicap toilet in the neonatal intensive care unit where I curled up on the floor, dug my nails into my palms, and prayed, probably for the first time in my life. Later, I looked up from where I was sitting by her cot and into the eyes of the hospital priest. *It's time to give her a name,* he said, *before she goes home to God.* I stood up very slowly and said, *Her name is Kaia. And she's not going anywhere.*

I get up from the kitchen table and sit on the edge of the sofa bed, watching Kaia sleep. She's not entirely like before. I always thought my daughter was calm and somewhat dreamy by nature, not just because she's spent most of her life poorly, but now I wonder if I was wrong. Since the end of July when she finally came home from the hospital after the operation, there's been something slightly restless about her. It's like she runs on a different gear from before. She's no longer content to spend a whole day indoors the way she used to. Now, instead of watching rain fall, she wants to splash about in it. It's what I always wanted for her, ever since the day when she got sick and I knew that my life would never be good unless she was in it, but still, I find this new jittery energy unsettling. Like I don't know her the way I used to.

The doctors prepared me for this. Children as young as Kaia who have been sick their whole lives sometimes show remarkable over-night improvement after receiving a new organ. The lucky ones, that is. The ones whose bodies don't reject the new organs, losing the second chance. I will spend the rest of my life grateful that Kaia got this chance, and I will also spend every day monitoring her for signs of rejection. Transplant patients, especially children, don't always live long lives, but I will make sure that Kaia lives a good life.

I run my finger very lightly down the bridge of her nose, and try to see something of myself in my child. Or something of *him*. I don't see either; she is so entirely her own person that I've sometimes thought I might as well have picked her up from a basket by the roadside. Noa says that Kaia is like a little animal—a strange and wonderful species that has never previously been observed. That always makes Kaia laugh. Noa is good at making her laugh; better than me. I'm good at making Kaia talk, and think; those were the things I could always develop in her, even during the years she spent in the hospital, or the months spent immobile in bed, so weak I had to carry her to the bathroom and bring the straw to her mouth so she could sip black currant juice, her favorite.

I wish Noa was here now. I miss her.

I lie down beside Kaia. I picture her heart beating inside her, easily sluicing the blood around its chambers, working like clockwork, the way a heart is supposed to. Then I begin to cry. I just can't stop myself, and there's no one here to comfort me.

I wake to the sound of my phone vibrating loudly on the floor: Noa.

"Kaia called me," she says casually, sounding exhausted. She was probably DJ-ing well into the morning hours. I feel a stab of jealousy picturing her in this moment; lounging on the bed she shares with her handsome boyfriend, Enzo, holding a cup of black coffee, looking out at rows of Parisian rooftops outside, a deep blue autumn sky above. I clutch the phone to my ear and glance over at Kaia watching a cartoon in her bedroom; I need to get her bathed and ready for the journalist. She's tried to braid her own hair the way Noa does it, but it doesn't look right, and I'll have to rebraid it before the journalist and her photographer get here. "She said she woke in the night because you were crying."

"That's not true," I say. I can practically see Noa raising her pierced left eyebrow and looking at me in that X-ray way. "I'm just tired," I say, but to my horror I begin to cry again.

"Hey," she says, suddenly alarmed, "hey, I'm sorry. That wasn't a criticism. Of course you're tired. What you've been through is almost impossible to compute."

"But it's over now," I say, my mind drifting to the incredible contrast between the ghost-child Kaia used to be, and the sprightly, quick-witted child in the next room, laughing raucously at her cartoon, her strong voice rising above Bugs Bunny's cackle.

"It isn't, though," says Noa, "it isn't over for *you*. You haven't processed what you've been through, Iselin. You've lived in crisis mode for seven years. You haven't stopped, even for a moment. You've been up all night, comforting, administering medicines, praying, loving her so hard, but not giving yourself even an inch of space or a smidgen of love. The rest of your life begins now, and you can start to think about how you want to live it."

Noa's words echo in my head as I speak with the journalist, Kaia playing on the floor by our feet with an expensive new doll the magazine brought as a gift. I speak of the new life, the strange wonderfulness of parenting a healthy child, of my eternal gratitude to the people who made the biggest sacrifice I can imagine so that my child could live, and these things are true, but still, Noa's words won't release their grip on my heart. *It's not over, though. It isn't over for you. The rest of your life begins now . . . What are you going to do with it?*

19

ALISON

When I finish speaking, Karen Fritz has tears in her eyes.

"She was gone," I say. "It was my fault."

"I feel so much empathy for you, Alison," says Karen, even though I've essentially just described to her how I killed my own child. I laugh a little at that, and I think she understands that it's the hollow laugh of disbelief. "I'd like us to work toward you being able to feel that same kind of empathy for yourself." I laugh again but now it's the softer kind that quickly becomes inseparable from the crying it tries to disguise.

"It was my fault."

"It was nobody's fault. It was an accident. A terrible, incomprehensible accident."

"It was my fault," I say, again. "Everybody knows that. If I hadn't fallen asleep . . ."

"But you did. That doesn't make it your fault. It makes it a very tragic accident."

"My husband blames me."

"Is that what he says?"

"No. But I can tell. He's different toward me now. Sometimes, when he looks at me, I can see pure, solid hate." Karen listens, inclines her head slightly, face serious.

"It must be difficult to be around someone you believe blames you."

"Of course he blames me. How could he not? If it were the other way around, I would have held him fully responsible."

"Or it could be that he empathizes with you in a way you are unable to accept?"

I shake my head curtly. It's always the same with these people—instead of just recognizing facts for facts, they have to read between the lines and draw conclusions that aren't correct. I don't want to talk to Karen anymore or pretend like this might help. I dig my nails into the sore skin of my palms and try to envision my mind as a calm, blank space.

"You know, every day I wonder if today is the day. The day I can't take it for another fucking second. Every day I wonder if today is that day."

"Alison. You know that I am morally and legally obliged to notify your GP if I believe you are at risk of taking your own life. Do I need to put you on suicide watch?" Karen Fritz speaks softly, her eyes searching mine. I wonder whether she ever thinks about me outside of these sessions, whether she finds it hard to let go of the images I speak of; the compulsive thoughts of death, the solid, terrifying darkness I live inside, the broken husband, the child underwater.

"No," I say, softly, though perhaps I should have said *yes*.

* * *

I walk slowly up Frognerveien toward Majorstuen Station; I'm the only one walking and the people in buses and trams stare at me as I push forward through onslaughts of rain. Or maybe they don't, maybe they don't see me at all, sensing that I'm only half here. My breath is short and painful, but my mouth is shut tight against the rainwater, and several times I have to stop in doorways to catch my breath before I can walk any farther.

I reach the station and sink down on a dry, warm seat on the 1-line toward home, resting my wet hair against the window glass, watching the blur of buildings slipping past. I contemplate whether what I said to Karen Fritz was true or not, whether I truly pose a risk to myself. I've always believed that the human instinct for survival is stronger than any other force. Even in my darkest hours, I have managed to refrain from playing out suicidal thoughts in my head. They would appear, constantly, but I somehow chased them away, directing my entire focus on breathing, drinking water, taking pills, screaming. I must have believed that if I could live through those first days and weeks, it would eventually get easier. But it doesn't.

I feel lulled by the rhythmic clunk of the train, reminded of the latest sign from Amalie. I get off at Vettakollen Station, though it isn't the stop closest to home. Up here, three hundred meters above sea level, the rain has thickened into slushy fat snowflakes. I start walking up the long hill toward the school we had chosen for Amalie; the school she never got to start at. I can already hear the children—it's almost two o'clock and they will be on their last recess before pickup time. I pause and glance down at my bare hands, raw from the cold, and try to find some of that empathy for myself Karen Fritz talked about. Are these the hands of a murderer? Are they the hands of a dead woman? I try to imagine Karen's face if she could see me now—standing silently in the falling snow, partially hidden by a red wooden fence, watching the busy bodies of other people's children rushing around a school yard.

I watch a little girl sitting alone on a bench, then a little boy lying on his back on a patch of snow, moving his arms and legs. I take in a chubby girl who looks a bit sickly. And another who looks vaguely like Amalie when I squint. Of course, I know that it isn't one of these children. He or she could be anyone, anywhere. But somewhere, my daughter's heart is guarded deep inside the body of a stranger. And I want to find it.

20

ALISON

The slushy snow has let up by the time I reach the top of the hill, and our house. I let myself in, push my feet into my slippers, and walk into the kitchen. Music is playing; the Beach Boys, I think, and Sindre stands at the kitchen counter, dicing onions and garlic. His movements are quick and precise, and he looks like any other guy, just going about his normal life. I'm surprised; he's barely been out of bed since the hunting trip.

"Hi," he says, smiling carefully, trying to gauge which version of Alison just walked through the door.

"Hi," I say.

"Your face is red. Have you been to see Misty? You okay?"

"No. No, I walked here from Vettakollen." He nods, and doesn't ask me why I would have chosen to do that. I make a mental note to go see Amalie's pony tomorrow. He stabs at a plastic packet of chicken strips with his knife and tosses its contents into the pan with the garlic and onion.

"I didn't realize you'd be cooking," I say. "I already bought dinner. But I guess we can have that tomorrow instead."

"It's my turn," he says, and I nod, as though it's completely normal he's suddenly started keeping tabs on whose turn it is. "Oliver will be here by six."

"I'm glad you're feeling better," I say, but my voice comes out harsh, like I'm accusing him of something, and perhaps I am. He notices and shoots me a sharp glance.

"We need to . . . to try. To keep moving. Right?"

"Of course," I say, softly now, and take the glass of wine my husband has poured me.

And now the three of us carefully and mechanically negotiate the ritual of Friday-night tacos. *Can you pass the cheese, is there any more cilantro, oh, yum, I do love tacos.* Sindre doesn't say a word, he just keeps his eyes on the food, chewing carefully, expression neutral, probably out of fear of saying or doing something that will bring that aching, black silence crashing down over us. Oliver looks from his father to me and back constantly, never succeeding in holding on to more than a quick glance from either of us. I feel a sudden stab of empathy for him.

"What's up, Oliver?" I say. "You look like there's something on your mind." Oliver shakes his head slowly, but when my eyes meet his, I can tell there's something he wants to say.

Sindre stares at him, and Oliver reverts his gaze to the plate. He's too hard on him. I don't think we should stop Oliver from asking questions, or talking about Amalie. I want to talk about her, and I want Oliver to feel that he can still mention her, but it's as though Sindre wants to pretend she never existed, as though she didn't change every single second of our lives for almost six years, and always will.

"Do you remember how Amalie's idea of the perfect taco was basically a tortilla with a couple of pieces of cucumber on it?" I say, smiling slightly at that memory, but the burning immediately flares up inside me and I have to focus on maintaining a little smile, on allowing myself one moment untouched by grief. Oliver lights up and nods.

"Yeah, and how she'd always say 'extra hot sauce, please,' meaning ketchup?"

"Yes," I continue, "and that time she insisted on putting strawberry jam on top of her chicken and cucumber and I made her eat the whole thing, and she pretended like it was the best thing she'd ever had? The stubbornest kid I've met in my entire life." We laugh a little. Sindre gets up, slowly.

"Running," he says.

When he's gone, and we've gathered the plates, my stepson and I sit listening to the drum of rain on the windowpanes. He used to call me Mamma Alison. I look at him and in this moment I don't know what he means to me—he could be anybody; a random teenager with a hoodie and unreadable eyes you might cross the road to avoid.

"I think I'll go for a walk," I say. I just have to get out of this house.

"But it's dark," says Oliver. "It might rain again."

"I don't mind," I say softly, smiling at him with affection I'm not sure I feel.

"Can I come?" says Oliver.

"No, sweetie. I . . . I just need to think a little."

* * *

The conference hotel farther down the road toward Voksenkollen is practically empty, and the receptionist looks at me with slight disdain as I walk in from the wet night, water pooling at my feet.

"Um, is the bar open?" I ask, and the receptionist, a young girl with hair dyed a silvery blond turns around, as if a colleague would suddenly materialize behind her.

"Yes . . ." she says. "We don't normally get walk-in guests, but . . . I'll see if someone can serve you."

I settle into a wide, cushy leather chair, and after a long while, a tall, boyish man with a thin goatee appears.

"What would you like to drink, madam?"

"A double vodka tonic," I say, smiling disarmingly to hopefully distract from the fact that I am a soaking-wet deranged woman who walked in from a forest in the middle of a rainstorm. When he returns with my drink, I notice how kind the young man's eyes are. I look away, and stare at the ice floating in my glass.

"Is everything okay, madam?" he asks. "We just had two hundred Danish doctors here all week, but they left this afternoon, so I'm all yours if you need an ear." I shake my head slowly, but smile at him. As he walks away I take my phone from my pocket and Google *heart transplant cellular memory* again. I want more stories, more hope. I finish my drink and order another and for a long while I just sit scrolling through articles and interviews, drinking in the words I long to hear. Stories of a mother meeting her daughter's donor recipient and recognizing traits of her lost child. Stories of close friendships forged between the families of donors and recipients, from Scotland to France to the States. It's real, and not just something I dreamed up. One woman even says she feels like she and her donor merged into one person after receiving a new heart.

I feel the bartender's eyes on me as the tears begin to fall from my eyes, onto the touch screen of my phone. I smile because these aren't sad tears; they are the happiest tears in the world, tears of hope. I feel the sudden need to be at home, to run my hands along the little plastic animals Amalie collected and lined up on the windowsill, to hold my stepson tight and show him that I do love him and want him around me. I want to tell him that it felt good to talk about Amalie with him at dinner, and that most of the time I can't feel anything other than the burning, but I did then. I place three hundred kroner on the table and walk back out into the night.

The house is quiet. Sindre's running shoes, caked in mud, are on the doormat. I hope he's gone to bed. Upstairs, I listen at Oliver's door before knocking softly. He opens the door immediately, as though he's been standing behind it, waiting for someone to come. I'm not sure what I'm doing here, but right now it feels as though Oliver is the only person I can speak to in this family. I was cold toward him earlier, and I want to make amends.

"I wondered about something," I say. "You know a while back, when we talked about the . . . the donations?" Oliver nods, his tired eyes blinking several times. "Well, I've been wondering about it. About whose lives were saved. And also, whether . . . God, it sounds so crazy . . . Just . . . I guess I wonder whether anything of her, even the tiniest thing, might have passed into whoever received her organs, you know?"

Oliver nods again, and he pulls me over to the little chair by the window. I sit, and he sits across from me on his messy unmade bed, our knees touching.

"I've been thinking about this stuff a lot." He looks both relieved and sheepish.

"I thought so."

"I've Googled a lot."

"Me too," I say.

"I want to believe it," says Oliver. "But also, I kind of . . . don't."

"I know what you mean. I also wanted to say that you can talk to me about it, and about Amalie, whenever you want, even if Pappa finds it very difficult."

"Yeah," he says finally, fiddling with the edge of the duvet cover. "Do you remember how much she loved strawberries? Like, strawberries everything—strawberry ice cream, strawberry prints, strawberry coulis, strawberries in a salad. Imagine if the kid who got her heart or whatever suddenly started liking them? Or something else she loved, like bears, or ponies, or the color green, or cheeseburgers with extra onion rings, or those funny little farm animals . . ."

"Sylvanians," I say, and we both smile. Amalie used to sleep with lots of Sylvanians in her bed, and when she rolled over at night, they'd leave imprints on her face, so she'd wake with vivid red bunny ears on her forehead, or a bear's tiny hand on her chin.

"What was that joke she was always telling?" asks Oliver.

"Oh God," I say, and start to laugh before I even fully remember it. "Oh, what was it? Oh! Why can't you give Queen Elsa a balloon?"

Oliver's face cracks into a wide smile, and he releases a muffled bark of a laugh. "Because she'll let it go!"

We both laugh so hard we're crying, but for once these tears are okay, the laughter doesn't turn into howling, and when we eventually settle down, it's wiping at running eyes but smiling. It's a long while before either of us breaks the silence.

"Can we find out who received her heart and stuff?" asks Oliver.

"I don't know . . . I don't think so. I'd imagine it would be anonymous."

"Maybe I wouldn't want to know," says Oliver. "It might make it even worse, that another kid is alive because Amalie isn't."

"But it isn't like that, honey. She wouldn't be here now even if we hadn't donated her organs. And the other child might be dead, too. At least this way, one child is still alive."

"I wish that child was Amalie," says Oliver. "I love having a sister."

His use of the present tense takes my breath away. I wonder if he sees her in his mind the way I do, chasing him around the house in her diaper as a toddler, laughing hysterically behind her pacifier, arms flailing, fat little legs pumping. Falling asleep in his lap at the cabin after a long day skiing, the way he'd just sit there, cradling her and smiling.

"Let's try to find her," he whispers.

I shake my head because we can't, we mustn't, of course we can't. I'm going to speak to Karen Fritz about this, and she'll tell me exactly how insane all of this surely is, but still, inside my heart is racing and insisting—*yes, yes, yes.*

21

ISELIN

It's Christmas in a week, and I have less than three thousand kroner in my account. Every month I have a meeting with the social workers at NAV, where I have to discuss my efforts to find a job or prove why I can't work. I'm hoping they will be understanding today—though Kaia is better now and I could technically start working, it's taking us a while to get settled in this new life. I push the door open and step into a crowded, overheated waiting room. Avoiding the eyes of the other people, I flick through a dog-eared copy of *Se Her* from September, and practice what I'm going to say in my head. Surely there must be some extra support for single parents of sick children in the run-up to Christmas?

"Iselin Berge?" It's the same lady I met with last month, a sour-faced woman in her fifties who reminds me of my mother. Her name badge reads *Else*. She shows me into a cramped office with a glass wall looking into another similar office, empty. I'm surprised to see a little star tattoo emerge from her sleeve as she shuffles my case papers around on the desk. For a terrible moment, I imagine ending up as her—an angry, faded woman in a boring job.

"So, Iselin," Else begins, saying my name as though it leaves a bad taste in her mouth. "How is the job search going?"

"Well, I've sent out quite a few applications in the last few weeks."

"Have you sent them through our website so we can track your progress?"

"Well, some of them, yeah."

"You know, job searching is a full-time job in itself. At least it should be treated as such."

"Okay."

"So, how many interviews have you been asked to?"

"None."

"None?"

"No."

"What kind of jobs have you been applying for, Iselin?" Her voice is condescending and a little smirk plays on her lips.

"Um. I applied for a job at the Munch Museum. As a part-time receptionist. And for a job at Henie Onstad Art Center—they were looking for a junior tour guide."

"And?"

"I haven't heard back from either of them."

"What else?"

"I've looked at other similar jobs. Jobs that could match my interests and would make it possible to work around my daughter."

Else raises an eyebrow. "You do realize you can't afford to be picky?"

"Yes," I answer. "I've applied for jobs in clothes shops, and in cafés, and in old people's homes—"

"Have you applied to the council?"

"No . . . What do you mean?"

"They have various jobs for unqualified people like yourself on a day-to-day basis. Litter picking, recovering and replacing broken road signs, that kind of thing."

"Oh," I say, because what am I supposed to say? That I went to Paris to become an artist, that I had dreams, that I have no skills besides looking after a sick child?

"New rules are coming into effect in the new year. If you do not register with the council as a job seeker, you will no longer be eligible for job-seeker benefits through NAV. And when you get called in for a job, you have to show up, or they will cut your benefits. Do you understand?"

"Yes." I'm furious and humiliated now, but determined not to show it. I'm not going to show this mean woman any reaction. "I went to art school. In Paris. For a while. It's on my CV."

Else glances briefly at the paper in front of her. "École Supérieure de Dessin Jean-Jacques Gareau, is that it?" She has clearly never read a word of French before and pronounces the words entirely as though she is speaking Norwegian.

"Yeah."

"Never heard of it. What kind of degree did you get out of it?"

"Well, I would have got a bachelor of arts, but I had to leave after just under a year, so . . ."

"So that doesn't count for anything, then, does it?" This woman reduces my proudest achievement besides Kaia to nothing with her cruel words. I practice my controlled breathing, the technique I taught myself as a child.

"I did learn a lot during the time I was there. I also speak French fairly well. That might be relevant to possible jobs?"

"I doubt there is much need for a French-speaking illustrator at the council, Miss Berge," says the mean-faced bitch, and I have a sudden jolt—a realization that no matter what, I have to get out of this myself. I will find a way to support us without having to come here month after month, begging for the bare minimum to survive.

"Goodbye," I say, and stand up.

"Miss Berge, these meetings are mandatory and I will let you know when we are finished here. Now—"

"I said goodbye. I'm not coming back."

"You know very well that you are legally obliged to meet with NAV monthly to monitor your progress as a job seeker. I will have no choice but to recommend your benefits be terminated if you do not uphold your commitment." I slam the door to Else's office and walk fast into the darkening afternoon outside.

It felt good, in that moment, to walk away. But now, as Kaia sleeps fitfully in her alcove and I sit doodling at the kitchen table, my bravado has faded. How will I feed us? And how will I explain to Hanne Vikdal that I won't be able to pay rent? I have a terrifying vision of having to return to my parents' farm in Svartberget, with a grandchild whom they have never even met. Our basement flat in Østerås is no fancy home, but compared to where I came from, it's heaven. What would Kaia make of such a place? And what would my parents do, if we just turned up one day?

I try to imagine Noa's reaction if I told her I'm taking Kaia with me and moving back to Nordland, but find I can't. I consider asking her to lend me some money, just until after Christmas, but again, I just can't. She's my younger sister, and while I love her dearly, it hurts that she's living her dream and making lots of money in Paris while my own life is what it is. It isn't envy, exactly, it's just sadness.

* * *

It's gone one in the morning, but I'm not tired tonight. I feel sharp, and wired. It probably comes from the pressure of somehow working this situation out. I look around the apartment, and feel a rush of gratitude for this home. I am never going back to Svartberget. Never. I am also never going back to NAV. That means I need to make some money fast. My eyes land on the pile of new drawings over by the window. Thirty, by now. I go and sit down on the floor next to them, going through them one by one. They are different from anything I've ever seen, and certainly different from anything else I've ever drawn before. And they're good. Could I sell them? Math was never my strongest subject, but if I could find a part-time job, say three days a week, and sold five drawings per month, I'd make more money than I've had in handouts from NAV. And I'd be free.

Something shifted in me this morning at Else's plain little office, watching her stutter her way through my CV, the CV that I was once so proud of. I just can't sit around waiting for a fairy god-mother any longer. I need to become the mistress of my own destiny and achieve my dreams on my own terms. I spend a long while taking good shots of the drawings on my Samsung, then I upload the twenty-seven best ones to my Instagram account, and change its name from @iselinberge to @IsbergArt.

22

ALISON

Karen is clutching a short swath of red wool, and is holding the needles still in place, ready, when I sit down in the chair. I stare at the bird picture on the wall behind her.

"How are things at home now?" she asks.

"Good," I say. "Well. You know. Not good. Up and down, I guess." Karen nods slightly and looks down at the yarn pooling in her lap. Her eyebrows are drawn together, like she's trying to figure something out. "We're going to Mexico the day after tomorrow."

"Mexico?"

"Yes."

"I haven't heard you mention that before," says Karen, frowning, as though I might be making it up.

"Yes, well, I haven't thought about it much if I'm honest."

"How do you feel about that?"

"I said I haven't thought about it. I'm sure the sun will be nice."

"Are you sleeping better?"

I nod. I do sleep, just not much.

"Eating?"

I nod again. I do eat. Just not much.

"You seem . . . You seem less present in these sessions. Are you still taking the Zoloft and the Klonopin?"

"Yes," I say. I'm not. I can't bear the flatness, the struggle to grasp the simplest of thoughts. I wanted to be clearheaded again, I *need* to be. I have decided to broach the subject of cell memory gently with Karen; I need to know if I am clinically insane, or if I'm actually onto something.

"I . . . I have so many strange thoughts," I say.

"Strange thoughts?"

"Yes. I see her everywhere."

"You've described that previously. It doesn't seem so strange that you would see her, Alison. The mind can conjure up incredible things—"

"No. No, this is different," I say. "I see her as she is now. You know?"

"What do you mean, exactly?" I realize that Karen thinks I mean that I see Amalie dead.

"I mean I see her in other people. The people who received her organs. Her heart especially. I always thought of it as her giving new life to someone else, but now I realize that someone else is giving new life to her."

"I'm . . . I'm not sure I follow?"

"I've been thinking about this so much. It seems to me that it would make sense that something of Amalie lingers in the people, or person, who received her organs."

"That might be a really constructive way of thinking about it, Alison, but . . ."

"And if something remains of her," I continue, "even the littlest thing—a transferred mannerism, a fraction of a memory, whatever it is, it means she's still here. I could find her."

After a prolonged pause Karen speaks; her face is calm, but etched with concern. "What do you mean when you say you could find her?"

"You know, find whoever received her organs." Karen is watching me carefully, waiting for me to continue, but I don't. I wonder if she has kids, but feel certain she doesn't—she's too serene. I imagine she has a cat, and that she lives alone in a small, cozy apartment where she sits knitting in front of Netflix. How could this woman ever understand?

"I'd imagine that would be impossible. It could even be illegal to strike up contact. Alison, I'm not sure I entirely understand, but if what you're asking is, do I think it is okay to seek out whichever impulses make Amalie feel close to you, then I think you need to decide for yourself whether it is something that contributes to a continued improvement in managing your grief. From what you are describing, it sounds as though it is. But talking about trying to somehow find Amalie through her donor, I feel that that is a very dangerous way to think." I focus on keeping my expression neutral and untouched by her words, because this woman knows nothing. Nothing at all. She hasn't seen what I've seen, or felt what I feel. She hasn't lost what I have lost.

"Never mind," I say, fixing my gaze to my hands held tightly together in my lap.

"Do you remember what we've talked about in terms of focus and directing energy when grieving?" I look at the clock above the door, seventeen minutes left of the session, but I can't stay, not today; I can't spend another second trying to explain to Karen the thoughts that consume me—as soon as I opened my mouth, I saw how crazy I sounded to her. The tears flowing from my eyes blur the clock face and I stand up, mouth "sorry," and dash awkwardly for the door like a teenager fleeing math class. Once I'm outside in the corridor I begin to run. I run out of the building, past my car parked outside Peppes Pizza, down Cort Adelersgate past throngs of shouting slick-haired teenage boys in pastel Ralph Lauren polo shirts emerging from the gates at Handelsgym, past the furniture shop where we bought Amalie's first bed, down toward the harbor at Aker Brygge. I need to see the water, to touch it, to know that lowering myself into it is a real option.

23

ISELIN

I'm woken by Kaia trailing a dry paintbrush down the length of my nose, hovering at my nostril, making me sneeze.

"Hey," I say groggily, holding her by her thin wrist. "You silly little monkey!" I pull her down onto the sofa bed and kiss her cool cheek.

"It's almost Christmas," she says. "Can we go buy the tree now?"

"Well, I was thinking we could wait until Aunt Noa gets here." I was, in fact, hoping Aunt Noa would offer to pay for it.

"No, I want it to be ready by the time she gets here. A surprise!"

"I don't know, honey." My account is practically empty and it's Christmas in two days. I have bought Kaia some secondhand toys, but I still need to buy some cheap decorations from the supermarket, and a little gift for Noa.

"Please," she says, theatrically fluttering her long black eyelashes.

"Can I at least make a coffee before you start up," I say, tickling her little drum-belly and hauling myself out of bed. In the kitchen I stir the instant coffee slowly in the mug, yawn a couple of times, and rub my eyes, which feel dry and sore. I was up until almost 3:00 A.M. working on my Instagram account. Hopefully some of the drawings will have had a few likes by now. I grab my phone and am just taking a sip of coffee as I open the app. I almost choke— sixty-one new followers and 879 new likes. Five direct messages. I scroll through them, and each of them is from someone who wants to buy one of my drawings. I sink onto the floor of the kitchen, my right hand holding the phone shaking hard. I burst into tears.

"Mamma?" says Kaia, appearing in the doorway, face pale and alarmed. "Don't cry, Mamma," she whispers, placing a careful hand on my shuddering shoulder.

"I'm not sad, honey bunny," I said. "These are happy tears. Now, what do you say we go and buy a beautiful tree? It was a great idea to get it ready as a surprise for Aunt Noa."

Noa's train pulls into the station at five to six. Kaia and I have been waiting awhile, jumping up and down on the platform to stay warm. A light drizzle of snow has started to fall; the forecasters have predicted a white Christmas, the first in several years. Noa steps from the carriage, hauling a huge suitcase. She looks tense and exhausted, and tumbles into my arms, Kaia snuggled in between us.

On the bus back out to Østerås, Kaia chats excitedly about the big surprise we have for Noa at home. I smile, listening to her, and at the thought of her carefully hanging the plastic supermarket baubles on the tree this afternoon, her concentrated face mirrored in each little silvery globe. At home, I'm about to place the key in the lock when a voice calls my name.

"Iselin!" It's Hanne from upstairs, clutching a package to her chest like a bird of prey holding a soft baby animal. "This came for you today when you were away. I offered to take it in."

"Thanks," I say, and give her a tight smile. She hovers, as though she expects me to open the envelope right here in front of her. Noa shoots her a quizzical look and Hanne takes her in disdainfully; she's probably never seen a girl with platinum-and-purple hair and an eyebrow stud at Østerås before.

"Merry Christmas," I say in a sarcastic, singsong voice, wrenching the door open. Kaia, Noa, and I rush inside, giggling.

"What a weirdo," says Noa before the door is even fully shut.

"Come, hurry," says Kaia, tugging at Noa's arm, pulling her down the corridor toward the living room, leaving lumps of hardened snow from her boots on the newly mopped floor.

"Oh, wow!" says Noa, clapping her hands and laughing at the sight of Kaia's huge tree, its tip bent against the ceiling, taking up most of the space in the room. "Amazing!" She and Kaia dance around the tree while I unwrap the parcel Hanne brought.

"Oh my God," I whisper, stopping Kaia and Noa. "Look at this!" It is a copy of *Se Her*'s big Christmas issue, on sale from tomorrow. Kaia is one of the cover stories, with the shout line *Hjertebarnet*— the heart-child. There's a note from the editor, as well as a five-thousand-kroner gift card from Meny, Norway's most exclusive supermarket, where I have, needless to say, never shopped. *Merry Christmas to an exceptional family*, reads the note, and my eyes blur with tears.

The three of us slump down into the sofa, close together, and read the article in awed silence.

Once Kaia is fast asleep, I pour a large glass of Shiraz for Noa and me. She smiles tiredly but takes the glass, and we sit across from each other at the tiny kitchen table.

"There's something I have to tell you," I say, pushing my phone across the table at her. "Look at my Instagram."

She opens the app and looks at me. "What's @IsbergArt?"

"I've done some new drawings. Take a look. I put them on Instagram, and sold five almost immediately."

"Shit, are you serious?" Noa scrolls through my feed, eyebrows lifting in surprise, her stud glinting in the sharp overhead light. "Issy, these are amazing. Wow. They are really something else."

"Thank you." I smile and take the phone back, scrolling quickly. Two more messages from potential buyers.

"This is the kind of stuff that could make a real name for you. You should have a studio space."

"Steady," I say, laughing. "I literally started selling, like, yesterday."

"Do you remember my friend Eline? Her mother's an artist and she's gone to Bali for the winter. She has a studio at her apartment in Majorstuen. She might consider subletting it to you."

Later, much later, I wake in one of those pockets of the night that is so dark and soundless it feels like being at the bottom of the ocean. Noa sleeps next to me, her breath so slow and even it takes me several moments to pick it out from the silence. When my eyes have adjusted to the dark, I can make out the faint outline of Kaia's huddled little shape next door and the tall, dense shape of the massive tree outside. I run through the incredible events of the last few days in my mind: the drawings, Kaia in *Se Her*, the five-thousand-kroner gift card, Noa arriving. My life, in this moment, is good. I smile to myself and whisper, "Merry Christmas, Iselin," before closing my eyes again.

24

ALISON

I step from the plane and blink hard at the fierce sun, like an animal caught in the sight block of a rifle. It feels strange that a place exists where the sun could shine like this in December. Sindre carries our hand luggage down the steps, into the humid air smelling faintly of sweet rot and salty sea, and onto a waiting bus. He looks fresh and cheerful, even after twenty hours in transit. He checks his phone and a little smile twitches at the corners of his mouth. Who is he talking to? I realize I don't care and turn my face to the window as the bus proceeds slowly toward the terminal building. Sunscorched palm trees sway halfheartedly by the highway that runs on the other side of the airport fencing.

"It's so hot," says Sindre.

"Mmm," I say, and feel a vicious dread spreading out in my gut at the thought of how we are going to pass the time in this place, alone together, for a whole week. We'll have to play the stilted pretense game. *Do you want another margarita, honey? Oh, yes, sure, how thoughtful of you, make it a double. Can you rub my back with sunscreen?*

Oliver didn't come in the end, choosing to spend the holidays with Monica and her family in Drøbak, even though he spent it there last year, too. I wonder if Monica didn't allow him to come. I wouldn't blame her—if he was my son, would I have allowed him to spend Christmas across the world with two adults who were falling to pieces?

Sindre and I have agreed not to talk about last Christmas, when we took Amalie to South Africa, but I think about it anyway. I think about how the new green and blue beads at the bottom of her braids swished as she skipped ahead of us on the beach.

It's still dark when I wake, but when I step onto the balcony, the sky is burning orange and pink in the east. I go back inside and change from my silk camisole and shorts into yoga pants and a thin hoodie. I take the elevator down to the empty reception and cross the marbled space barefoot. It's just a short walk on smooth, paved stones down to the sea, and I stand awhile at the top of the beach, listening to the murmur of the waves and watching the blossoming sky.

"Merry Christmas, baby bear," I whisper. At the far end of the hotel's beach, where it borders the public beach, some big rocks jut out into the water. I climb onto the one farthest out and pull the little soft toy from the pocket of my hoodie. Dinky Bear and I sit watching the Pacific waves surge and recede, each chasing the next, forever. I busy my mind counting the swells farther out, then the birds swooping down into them, emerging with wildly squirming fish. It isn't only Amalie who has left me behind. Every day, I'm making memories she will never share, however meaningless. I am becoming someone she will never know. I'm in a place she will never see, but the strange thing is that I feel close to her here. I count the hours: how many days are left of this year, and how many since I closed my eyes and Amalie walked away from me and into the water. I think about how there is an actual, numerical answer to these questions—to how many fish are in the sea, to how many times my heart has beat in my lifetime, how many tears I've cried, to how many times I've spoken her name.

"Amalie," I say. I hold Dinky Bear and count the beats of my own racing heart. And then—"I'm sorry." As I speak, a dolphin surges from the sea almost directly in front of me, its beautiful, slick back shimmering with the iridescent morning light. It drops slowly, then slices the surface and disappears. I stand up on the rock and watch the quivering water in its wake.

I hear the sound of Sindre's voice as I slip my key back into the lock. He's laughing. I twist the key with a soft click, and he doesn't hear me enter. I stand a moment in the space between the bathroom and the bedroom, next to the softly purring minibar.

"So, what are you doing today?" There is something flirtatious in my husband's voice. Just then, he glances up and sees me standing there, holding Dinky Bear to my chest. He presses a button on his phone and slips it into his pocket before whoever he was talking to has a chance to respond.

"That was Espen," he says. I stare at him, hard. "He called to wish us a Merry Christmas."

"Right."

"Come here," he says, reaching his arms out to me like a needy baby. I ignore him and cross the room. I stand on the balcony, watching the brilliant sun rise above the horizon and imagine the dolphin out there, the dolphin that was another sign from my daughter.

"Hey you," says Sindre, sidling up behind me and placing a heavy, warm hand on the small of my back, inside the hoodie. "What's got into you?"

"Can I see your phone?" I say. I'm not sure who's more surprised; Sindre or me. My husband holds my gaze without flinching, but there is something hard and mocking in his eyes.

"Are you serious?"

"I'm totally serious, Sindre," I say, keeping my voice level and calm.

"No," he says.

"No? Are *you* serious?" I hold my hand out, but Sindre doesn't even look at it—he's looking out at the ocean, carefully rearranging his features into his practiced, resigned sadness. I flush hot with fury, the skin at the back of my neck pricking uncomfortably, but I'm not going to back down now.

"Is this the kind of relationship you want, Ali? I thought what makes us strong is the trust between us."

"What *made* us strong," I say, and he has the decency to flinch at the past tense. "Nothing is strong anymore."

"What are you saying?"

"I'm saying I want you to show me your phone."

"No. Ali, you're acting crazy. Completely fucking paranoid. I don't know what's gotten into you—"

"You don't know what's gotten into me? It's Christmas morning, Sindre. I couldn't sleep, so I went down to the beach. I spoke to Amalie there, our daughter, and as I did, a huge dolphin came out of the water, so close it splashed me with seawater and there wasn't even the smallest doubt in my mind that somehow it was a sign, that she'd sent it, it was too beautiful to be just nothing, and then

I come back here to share that moment with you and you're on the fucking phone, laughing and fooling around, and now you won't let me see it and then you have the fucking nerve to say that I'm acting crazy?" I've raised my voice and it's so loud it hollers around the hotel atrium enclosing the pool. When I stop, Sindre and I stare at each other, his eyes narrowed into slits, mine streaming. Then my husband turns and walks away without a word.

25

ISELIN

"Faster," says Kaia, and when I turn around to look at her, she laughs
and claps her gloved hands together in glee. The new sled with steering wheel and chiming metal streamers shines in the bright, cold
sunlight. I tug on the string and drag Kaia up the last bit of the little
hill and then I position the sled before climbing onto the seat behind
her, reaching around her to grab the wheel. Noa takes a picture of
us on her phone, then returns to texting.

"Uh-oh!" screams Kaia, and then we set off, both of us whooping
and laughing as we shoot down the hill on the best, fastest sleigh
money can buy. Again and again we go, and as we horse around, I
feel a joy so easy and pure I can't remember ever having felt it before.
Ever since I came up with the plan, my moods have been much
better, and I've experienced a kind of optimism I'd forgotten existed.
As a kid, I used to have that kind of positive mind-set, the can-do

attitude; I had to, to get away from Svartberget, but I guess year after year of hospital life and poverty wore away at me.

I drag Kaia on the sled back up the hill and then Noa takes over. I jump from foot to foot against the cold and watch my sister and daughter hurtle down the long, icy hill. My phone vibrates in my pocket. Another sale. Since the article in *Se Her* ran at the beginning of the week, we've been inundated—both by well-wishers and buyers. I've sold another three drawings, bringing it to a total of nineteen, meaning I've earned more in a week than I did in a month on public assistance.

It's not even three o'clock when the light begins to fade to a pasty pink and we start to walk back to the apartment, Kaia skipping merrily ahead. I worry, sometimes, that she overexerts herself, but the doctors at Rikshospitalet have assured me that she can do as much as most other children, as long as she feels able to.

"I've been thinking," says Noa, keeping her voice low so Kaia won't hear. "Now that Kaia is improving and you're selling pictures, couldn't you think about coming back to Paris? You could reapply to your course, you'd get full state student funding from Lånekassen, it would be enough for a little apartment near us, we could—"

"Noa," I say. "Not now. Let's not get too carried away. Kaia will need medical attention for years to come."

"But—"

"Shhh."

"Iselin, you really are talented. It would be a shame not to pursue this."

"I said, shhh. I don't want to talk about this now." But inside, I make note to ask Dr. Harari about whether traveling with Kaia is even a possibility. We reach our road, which is gray and gloomy-looking in the weak December light, and I push away thoughts of me and Kaia wandering through the narrow streets of the Île Saint-Louis, stunned by all the beauty, laughing together.

The fireworks wake Kaia twice, and she takes a long while to settle down again.

"Is it the future now?" she asks groggily as I lower her back onto her pillow and kiss her hair.

"Yep. Welcome to 2019," I whisper, but she's already asleep.

Kaia and I wave Noa off as the airport train slides away from the platform in a blur of icy rain, all three of us in tears. It's hard to let her go, but I've entered this new year with a quiet optimism. Noa planted a seed in my mind when she tried to talk me into returning to Paris and continuing my studies. If the doctors said it was possible, and if I got a job to build some real savings, and if I kept selling drawings, I could do pretty much anything.

I place Kaia in front of an old rerun of *Full House* and am about to start the dreary task of tidying up the clutter and chaos of Christmas and New Year past, when Kaia turns to me and says, "Mamma, where's my granny who talks like them?" She nods at the Americans on television. *Sweetheart, please believe me, you did the right thing,* says a sexy young John Stamos in his drawn-out, smooth Californian drawl.

"What do you mean?" I say.

"My granny. The one who talks like that."

"Honey, your granny lives in Nordland and she definitely doesn't talk like that."

"Oh."

"There was a visiting doctor at the hospital. Just after you had your surgery. She was a little older and had an American accent. Maybe you're thinking of her?"

"Maybe," says Kaia, and lets her eyes slide back to the screen.

26

ALISON

It's evening and Sindre is in the bedroom, packing for our return to Norway tomorrow. I'm in the shower, letting the warm water rinse away the grains of sand and the dried sweat and whiff of chlorine on my skin. I picture Sindre walking outside onto the balcony, looking out at the darkening sky and the gently rippling purple ocean, shaking out beach towels, absentmindedly stroking the sunburned patch on his forehead, lost in thoughts.

It would be difficult to say that we've had a nice time in Mexico, but in spite of the bad start, we have at least been able to be together, putting on a show of reading by the pool in the mornings, eating lunch with several margaritas at one of the cute little restaurants in the town, before strolling on the beach in the afternoons. I dropped the issue with the phone and whoever he was communicating with;

I just don't have the energy to let my mind run wild with torturous thoughts of my husband with someone else. Besides, he is here, with me.

Let's just stay here, I have whispered night after night, resting my head on Sindre's chest—the closest we have come in many months. Every time I've said it, he's grown slightly rigid, exhaling slowly. *And do what? Abandon my son and open a smoothie shack?* I've dropped it, then, but inside, a part of me thinks—*yes*.

Sindre looks disheveled and exhausted; puffy bags and dark shadows have gathered underneath his eyes, and the gray-specked stubble I once found sexy now just adds to his unkempt appearance. He drives slowly from the airport; the roads are icy, and I angle my body slightly away from him, staring out the window, drawing my woolen cardigan tight against the cold.

We sit silently for a while in the car in our driveway, watching our home in the brilliant January sunshine. On the plane we talked about what it would be like to come home, how it might feel good, but I didn't believe it even then. I feel consumed by the need to keep moving, to travel and take myself out of the constrictions of my life here in Oslo with Sindre and Oliver—the endless monotony of it, my lack of friends, my suddenly lost and hollow marriage, the hole in my heart . . .

"We can just leave," I whisper to him again. "Turn back around and see where the road takes us. You and me, babe. We don't have to do this . . ." Sindre stares at me, then laughs a little, but in his eyes are tears.

"You and me, babe," he repeats, but there is something hollow in his voice—like he no longer believes it.

Sindre is out the door in his running gear less than five minutes after we arrive home, and I stand at the kitchen window watching him dash into the forest like a startled deer. I drink tequila we brought home with a splash of orange juice, but it doesn't take the edge off my nerves, it just makes me feel sick, so I take a Valium. For a while, I sit at the breakfast bar, riding out waves of nausea, closing my eyes, trying to summon to mind the soft, ocher sand in Sayulita, the soothing crash of the waves, how I felt a profound sense of peace there. When I get up from the stool, bile rises in my throat and I don't even make it to the bathroom, throwing up a vile splash of tequila and stomach acid on the kitchen floor.

I spend the afternoon drifting aimlessly from room to room under the pretense of unpacking and tidying, but after several hours my suitcase is only half-empty. Just before four o'clock, Oliver comes home, shutting the front door softly behind him, waiting in the hallway to see if anyone is home.

"Hey you," I say, wrapping my arms around him. "I've missed you."

"I've missed you, too. You're so brown!" He looks taller than just two weeks ago, and I realize that what I said is true: I have missed him. A thin line of fuzzy, blond hair has appeared on his upper lip, and I wonder whether he's trying to grow it into a mustache. I remember him as the little boy he was the first time I met him, when Sindre and I had been together for a year and I came back to Norway with him at the end of his final tour. He was only four, and I was immediately taken with him. I had never particularly wanted to become a mother, probably because I hadn't met anyone I wanted to have children with. I was well into my thirties when I met Sindre, and thought I'd left it too late. My focus had been firmly on my career and my freedom to travel the world. It wasn't until I saw Sindre with his son that I realized I did want to have children— with him—so I unpacked the little suitcase I'd dragged behind me around the world for a decade and stayed in Norway. I long for it now, that battered case that had held most of my possessions for so many years. It's in the attic somewhere, and I could easily bring it downstairs, fill it with a few things, and walk out the door. What would I take?

I'm not attached to many things, but I would pack Dinky Bear and Amalie's pillowcase. I'd bring my favorite picture of the four of us together: Sindre, me, Oliver, and Amalie. It was taken last Easter in the Old Town of Rhodes when I still had everything. We're standing close together, squinting at the sun, Amalie perched on Sindre's arm. We're all wearing white and look like one giant, strange, smiling being.

"Where's Pappa?" Oliver looks at me oddly and I realize my face is scrunched up in a grimace. I smile at him but he doesn't return it.

"He's gone to Meny to pick up some stuff for dinner."

"Oh. I'm, uh, going to head back out again in a bit."

"Will you be home for dinner?"

"I'm not sure. I'm . . . I'm meeting my . . . girlfriend."

"Girlfriend? Oh, wow, Oliver. You haven't told me about this! How exciting!"

He smiles ruefully. "Yeah."

"How long have you been seeing her? What's her name? Is she nice?"

"Of course she's nice," he says, and we both laugh. "Her name is Celine and she's a year above me in school. We've been together since August."

"August?"

He nods, uncomfortably.

"But why haven't you told me?"

"Uh . . ."

"Of course I understand, sweetie. Don't worry about it. I'm so happy for you." He nods again and begins to fill his backpack with stuff from various jacket pockets and shelves in the hallway: gum, headphones, a fifty-kroner bill, bus card, gloves. I stroke his arm awkwardly and he turns around in the doorway and gives me another quick hug. I wave him off, watching him walk across the courtyard space we share with the neighbors, down the gravel path that leads to the road to Frognerseteren, then disappearing from view.

In the kitchen I pour another tequila, despite what happened earlier. I can hardly bear to sip from it, but I force it down. I sit at the window, looking out over the city, the last twilight-blue sky fading into black across the fjord, Oslo's myriad lights twinkling. Oliver is out there somewhere, just being a kid, meeting his girl, laughing and flirting. All the months since Amalie left us, he has been hiding this part of his life. It hurts to think of all the moments he would have had, away from the stunning blackness that has devoured our family; he would have kissed Celine, shared jokes with her, goofed around, searched for silly emojis to represent his teenage affection. I should be happy for him; I know that Oliver mourns his sister deeply, but I can't bear the thought that life moves on, that the world doesn't break apart without her.

Woozy, I lie down on the bed. The room is spinning and I am humming a melody I don't recognize. A strange noise penetrates my cushy, dream-like state. It's a phone vibrating somewhere in the room, but it's not my phone, because my phone is in my hand and I was going to scroll mindlessly through Instagram until I pass out. I stand up again but my stomach flutters, then rolls. I worry I'll be sick again, onto the bed. How disgusting would that be? Is that what I've become? I take a few deep breaths and swallow hard, trying to locate the sound. The phone is in the back pocket of Sindre's jeans, which he wore on our journey back and flung into a corner of the room before he went to Meny. If that's even where he's gone. I slide the bar on the touch screen to unlock it, but a code request pops up. This is new. Still, I can read the first line of the WhatsApp message, from someone named Mia.

Still laughing. Drive safe, talk later.

27

ALISON

I wake with a start and look around the bedroom feeling disoriented. Home. I'm home. I try to keep my mind blank, refusing even the thinnest thread of a thought. Still, I can't go back to sleep. Hardly surprising. After I read the message on Sindre's phone, I went downstairs to the kitchen and worked my way through the bottle of tequila. My mind was spinning with both exhaustion and fury but I refused to act hastily or in a way that didn't necessarily reflect my feelings.

He came home carrying several shopping bags, and found me slumped over the breakfast bar, a fresh splash of vomit on the floor. He half walked, half carried me through the living room and up the stairs, and I caught sight of us in the big gilded mirror at the top of the stairs. Sindre bore the grim expression of a man hauling an injured comrade to safety on the battlefield. I tried to tell him what happened, that I can't do this anymore, not for another second, that my mind runs wild with images and fantasies and impressions, that I just want to be away, away . . .

This morning, my mind is clear; the heavy muddled haze of the tequila has faded, leaving behind an uncomfortable transparency. I have lost my husband. I don't want him anyway. At the thought of Sindre fucking someone else, someone named Mia, I feel nothing at all. Nothing. Sindre sleeps heavily beside me—the pills he takes make him drowsy, so since the hunting trip he sleeps most nights. I turn to face him, though his back is turned to me. He has some nerve, coming back to our house and lying down beside me. We are mourning our only child, and he has used that time to pursue another woman. I bet he used our child as a sob story, a way of luring this woman into bed. *Poor Sindre—poor, poor man. I can fix him in a way his wife never could.*

I switch on the lamp on the bedside table and still he doesn't stir. I watch the mechanical rise and fall of his tanned, strong back and picture him as he would have been in previous incarnations: as a bald, chubby baby flung over his mother's shoulder, as a young man breathing hot, sandy air and training a weapon on other young men on the other side of the world, as a tired, middle-aged businessman taking his shoes off by the side of the bed, night after night, how that strong back suddenly seems fragile and vulnerable. I could kill him in this moment, plunging a knife into his neck, and he would be defenseless. After watching him a long while, I get up.

I hover a moment on the landing and pick out the usual soft whooshing sound of the house and some canned laughter from television, which Sindre must have left on, but there is no sign of Oliver. I open the door to Amalie's room and I lie for a while on her bed, my head nudging against Dinky Bear, calming my breath. Then I hear the door open a crack, casting a slice of light onto the floor.

It's Oliver in his flannel pajamas, holding something to his chest, his face twisted, streams of tears running down his face. I sit up, alarmed; I haven't seen him this distressed in all the time that has passed since July.

"I have to show you something," he whispers.

He sits down next to me, too close, hiccuping, and pressing the home button on the iPad he's holding, making the screen light up. *Look*, he says, finger scrolling fast through what looks like an article. There are several photographs of a little girl and a woman who is presumably her mother. In the main photo the girl sits on a blue-and-white stripy sofa, holding a tattered Eeyore toy, her mother standing behind her, both hands on the little girl's shoulders. *Miracle Girl* reads the headline.

"Oliver, what is this?" The burning flickers to life inside me.

"It's her," whispers Oliver. "The girl who got Amalie's heart." I stare at him, then at the little girl. A weak-looking child with very white skin, an awkward pointy nose, clear blue eyes, and chocolate-brown hair held in two long, uneven braids.

"How . . . Why would you think that it's her? There's no way to know that."

"Ali, they do two, or at most three heart transplants on children in Norway every year. What are the odds that there was another one at the beginning of July?"

I begin to read. *After seven years of life-threatening illness, Kaia Berge finally received a new heart at the beginning of July . . . Since then, she has gone from strength to strength, even starting school alongside other children, for the very first time. Se Her magazine met with brave little Kaia and her mother, Iselin, at their home on the outskirts of Oslo.* I wanted this so much, but now I close my eyes and wish I'd never seen her. I wanted this. What was it I'd hoped for? Perhaps I'd thought I'd wanted to know, but I know, now, that I didn't really.

I feel nothing for her. Nothing. She is a stranger, and looking at her face does not make me feel connected to my baby. How could I have thought finding this child would console me?

I hand the iPad back to Oliver, feeling his expectant gaze on my back as I leave the room.

I go downstairs and sit by the kitchen window, looking out over the city again. I'm calm now, calmer than I have been in a long time. I feel a sudden stark clarity, as clear as the pinprick stars in the sky. Everyone else's lives have moved on, but mine has ground to a halt. Everything has fallen apart; my life lies scattered on the ground like shreds of snow from a black sky. I think about Karen Fritz and know I will never go back there. I will never watch her hands spool the yarn again. I will never trust my husband again, nor can I hold him close knowing there's this secret between us. I will never again see my child, nor will I have another. I will never go to find that girl—why would I? There is nothing of her that is anything like Amalie. How could I have believed such a thing?

A heavy rain has started to fall, and the water running down the window distorts the twinkling lights of Oslo far below in the valley, making them flicker like they are about to go out. I get up.

Though it's unseasonably warm for January, it still can't be more than thirty-five degrees or so, and as I step outside, the heavy rain feels like blisters spreading across my face. I get out and sit on the hood of the car, listening to the crackling sound of the rain falling on the bare, wintry forest, and feeling the unpredictable thuds and lurches of my own heartbeat. I open the car door and switch on the fog lights, and in their misty beams I can make out the obsidian lake in between the trees. Where else but here?

I lift Sindre's heavy sailing lantern from the trunk and walk away from the car without locking it, my feet sinking into squelching moss as I move toward the lake. A sheet of thin ice has formed along the lake's shore, but farther out, the water ripples in the heavy downpour. I shine the beam of light far out onto the surface and watch the rushing rain, like flickering static on an old television.

I step onto a patch of ice. It crunches beneath my rain boots before the icy water surges over the tops, filling them. Can this really be the same lake that was filled with laughing children and their languidly happy parents, including me, sitting just over there, watching my little girl sifting muddy sand through her sieve? The difference between July and January by this lake is not just summer and winter, light and darkness, but life and death. I don't know what I'm doing here. I don't know where else I could go. I want to unsee that girl's face. I want to unknow everything I now know. Why did I think that finding her would help me?

I've tried so hard every day to look ahead, but the fact remains—everything is broken and nothing can be put back together. For a short while, I felt as though I had a sliver of hope, an imagined link to my lost girl, but I was wrong, I know that now.

I clear my throat and hug myself hard against the wet wind. *Hey, Mills,* I whisper, but immediately I feel stupid. Maybe I've forgotten how to speak to her. I bend down and touch the skin of ice on the lake's surface that holds black water still beneath.

This is her lake, but it could be mine, too. We could be together.

I shove both of my hands through a small crack in the ice, tearing it open wide, and it hurts more than I'd dared hope it would, shards slicing at my wrists. I let the icy water rush up into my sleeves, and farther still, until I'm forcing my hands down into the dense, hardened lake bed as though it could swallow me.

We could be together, my girl and me . . . It could be me and her again: the Juul girls. I could be where she is. I don't have to live like this, trying to find something, anything, to hold on to. I could be with Amalie, forever.

Give me a sign, baby bear, any sign. I need a sign to carry on.

There is nothing, nothing but the night and me.

My next movement follows naturally—I don't have to move more than an inch. As I fall, the lantern drops from my hand and strikes the rocky ground, and the sudden absence of its light is the last thing I see before I crash through the surface.

PART II

28

ALISON

Four days later

I could open my eyes if I wanted to, but I don't.

I'm back there, with them.

It's early morning and I'm reading with Oliver by the fire, his tiny face eerie and transfixed in the flickering orange glow. He helps me turn the pages. Amalie sleeps like a starfish on a sheepskin rug on the sofa. On her feet are faded yellow wool socks once knitted by Sindre's mother for Oliver. Her belly is like the rounded back of a whale and I want to press my lips to its soft, warm skin and blow raspberries.

It's the weekend, and after lunch we ski together in a long line; me at the front, a pioneer heading into the wilderness within the city borders of a capital. Behind me follows little Oliver, then Sindre, and all the way at the back—Amalie in her sleigh, silently watching towering firs rush past, tiny snowflakes churning on white air, a slit of milky sky high above.

The day becomes evening early, and Sindre and I have become used to watching movies in bed, stroking each other lightly and laughing in the same places.

It's daytime again and Amalie and I walk alongside the forest to Lake Øvreseter, where we park the stroller by the barbecue spot and totter down to the ice-covered lake, then across it, Amalie smiling with delight at the sudden slide of her stubby little legs.

But then, in a split second, she's gone. There, not there. I charge toward the dark gash in the ice but it's expanding fast across the lake until every patch of milky ice has disappeared. I scream her name out loud, my voice spreading out across the surface and rising up the hillsides.

I throw myself into the ice-cold water and dive down below the surface and open my eyes in the blackness. I am at the bottom of the lake and run my hands across some large, slick rocks, feeling around for my child, then sifting through empty water. I resurface for air, but in the moment my eyes rest on the glassy surface of the lake, the water ripples and rises into a silhouette and out comes a girl—*that* girl. The girl in the picture.

Kaia.

The heart keeper.

She looks at me and says *Mamma*.

Mamma. Again and again. *I need you, Mamma*.

I pull her out of the water and she clings to me like a castaway to a raft, like a baby koala bear to its mother, so close I feel the thud of her heart against my chest. I stare into her eyes. And it's all different now. The world, me, the child, the familiar glint in her eye. It's Amalie, looking at me through the eyes of a stranger. My child is inside this girl, held beneath her skin.

I open my eyes.

29

ISELIN

I guess life is rather samey for a lot of people: get up, sort the kids out, go to work, come home, make dinner, sit around watching something, go to bed. Sometimes I feel like I am just waiting for something to happen, that my life is the dragged-out opening to a movie, that boring bit before the action begins. My drawings are selling—not as many as just around Christmas, but that's probably to be expected. Kaia is thriving. Noa is coming back this week. It's all good. And yet, there's this itch to make something happen.

I check on Kaia, spreading out on the sofa octopus-style.

"Hey, sweetie, do you want to go somewhere?"

"No."

It's Saturday and a beautiful, clear day outside and I can't help but feel as though we ought to be out somewhere.

"We could go into town. We could go to the harbor front at Aker Brygge and get blue slush or something."

"No. I want to be home."

"We could head to the Henie Onstad Center? I think there's a children's art exhibit on at the moment."

"Mamma," says Kaia, looking sternly at me. "Can't we just be at home and do nothing?"

"Yes, but I just want you to be happy and have a fun day."

"I am happy. The happiest!" She gives me the biggest smile she can muster, tiny face cracked in halves, and I hop onto the sofa next to her, tickling her until she squeals.

It is evening when a message ticks in from Noa.

Remember I told you about that studio space in Majorstuen? My friend's mother says you can have it for free until June if you water her plants twice a week! N X

30

ALISON

I woke in the hospital. I was alone. Weak January light was seeping through the slat blinds. I felt thankful, then, for the crawl of the clock hand on the opposite wall, for more time, for being there, even if I was broken where I lay. Cracked open. But open to light, and to truth, as it came to me before I opened my eyes. I was thankful for my life, and for Kaia Berge's. And I was filled with a hope so pure and strong I'd never felt anything like it before.

And now, as of yesterday, I'm home again. Just like that. Everything was the same, but it was also entirely different. Last night, Sindre and I sat across from each other at the kitchen table for a while, talking. We discussed whether we should spend Easter at our cabin at Norefjell; reminiscing about past ones spent leisurely relaxing in the sun after a morning of skiing, peeling oranges and sharing a bar of chocolate between us. We talked about how the couple next door, Berit and Jan Olav, are most likely breaking the law by cutting down two large spruce trees at the end of their property, though we're glad they did, as we can now glimpse a teal slit of frozen fjord in the gap they left behind. We spoke about how, perhaps at the end of the year, we'll give in to Oliver's relentless pleas for a dog. *An older rescue*, I said, and in spite of everything, I gave in to an impulse to reach across to stroke the graying, fuzzy hair on Sindre's jaw.

It was nice, to sit there together like that. It was nice, because we both instinctively understood the new rules; we need to talk the way other husbands and wives do, about holidays and the little grievances caused by neighbors and the things we may or may not do with the kids. Perhaps that was the way we spoke before, I can't remember, but I know that is how we will need to speak in the future. There can't be any more conversations about lakes holding little girls or cells holding memories or what the hell is going to keep us alive. And still, my thoughts belong to me alone. My mind and heart are filled entirely by hope, making all of these little exchanges possible. I have something now; something bigger than me and my own life, or life itself, even. Bigger than death.

Sindre takes the task of looking after me very seriously, but we are both aware of how little time has passed since the tables were turned; since it was Sindre who was drugged and disoriented. Before I came back from the hospital, he sat Oliver down and explained to him that what happened to me at the lake was not a suicide attempt. Desperate and impulsive, but not born out of a real wish to be dead. I want to learn to live again and I wanted Sindre to tell Oliver that. I'm not sure Oliver believed it, and he followed me around the house all afternoon, constantly trying to keep me busy. I watched TV with him until I was so tired my eyes stung. I took the medication I am supposed to take, then I went to bed and blacked out.

Tonight, Oliver has gone to Monica's, and Sindre is next door in his home office on a call to Washington or somewhere. At least that's what he said. I can't find it in my heart to care. I have something more important to focus on now. So I'll pretend. I'll pretend like it's all better now. That I am going to take steps toward learning to live without my daughter. I need to pretend so I can focus on finding Kaia Berge to know whether something of my child really remains inside her.

I drink red wine and watch the last half of a show about people who meet for the first time at the altar. Occasionally I hear Sindre laugh through the wall and wonder what he could be laughing about—corporate security always seemed like a pretty dry profession to me. I want to be in bed pretending to sleep by the time he gets upstairs. But first: what I have been waiting for. I take the stairs two at a time but stop for a moment when I catch my reflection in the mirror at the top of the landing. It reminds me of that night, that darkest of nights, when the burning drove me into the frozen lake. The ice splintered easily into shards, and it felt good to push my hands through it, tearing my skin to shreds.

My hands still ache, and I hold them up to the mirror, examining them in the soft light; the swelling has gone down, the bruises have faded from red and purple to green-yellow, and the four shattered bones on the top of my left hand are taped into place by a strip of skin-colored tape. My hands don't look as shocking as they did when I came to at Rikshospitalet, but they still look like the hands of someone who has fought death off with her bare hands.

I rest my right hand against the cool, speckled surface of the mirror and hold my own gaze. I feel like a stranger to myself. Sometimes I felt the same when looking at Amalie. I'd watch her sleep, wondering where she'd come from and how I could uncover the essence of what made her *her*. I'd watch her play, running, jumping, dancing, fluttering, falling, and consider how utterly strange it was that she had come from me, out of me, and yet was so entirely separate. Sometimes I'd look into her eyes expecting to find the most intense connection but wouldn't feel it. And other times, that connection would suddenly spring forth in an unexpected moment, so powerful it could have floored me. I imagine looking into Kaia's eyes. Would she have the same effect on me in real life?

I slip into Oliver's room and sit down at his desk; as I press the space key, the screen saver on his iMac changes from a generic stock image of the Grand Canyon to a picture of him and Amalie in a pool in Spain two years ago. I study the picture carefully. Amalie is wearing a strawberry sun hat that partially obscures her face and she sits beaming on the side of the pool, next to her older brother. I can't remember taking the picture, though I must have; Sindre never remembers to take any photos of the kids. I try to isolate that moment in time from every other moment before and after it; the ocean beyond the pool must have shimmered in the sharp sun, all the children's laughter must have hung on the air, birds must have streaked past in the sky above, feathered smudges of black. I must have said *Smile*.

On Google, I type in the name of the girl's mother—Iselin Berge. Like her daughter, she has bland blue eyes, pale skin, and a rounded face, but the two of them don't actually bear much resemblance to one another. There aren't many hits for Iselin Berge, but I click on an old article. It's from *Nordlandsposten* from October 2006, and shows three young teenagers picking plastic waste from a bleak beach, their faces serious and pleading. *Save Nordland's*

Beaches from Plastic Waste, reads the headline, and below the picture are the names of the girls. Merethe Hansen, Nora and Iselin Berge. I stare at Iselin's face, trying to reconcile the fresh, sweet face with her adult face, which strikes me as sullen and somewhat younger than her years. She looks like the kind of girl who might have been a popular teenager: her eyebrows are skillfully plucked into even arches, her eyes are discreetly rimmed with eyeliner, she looks straight into the camera, confident in her conviction that she could save the world by picking straws and scraps of old plastic bags off the local beach. I return to Google and find the article Oliver showed me near the top of the search results. I scroll farther down to avoid it, but finding nothing of interest, I return to it and click on the link.

AT HOME WITH MIRACLE GIRL KAIA BERGE

"I still can't believe it," says Iselin Berge, gazing lovingly at her daughter, Kaia, who plays busily with dolls on the floor of their cozy flat . . . "I think I'd begun to let her go," she whispers. Life for this young single mother has been excessively hard. Some might say nearly impossible, but Iselin has fought relentlessly to give her daughter a chance for survival.

Se Her magazine has secured an exclusive at-home feature with Norway's possibly bravest child: seven-year-old Kaia Berge, who has suffered from life-threatening heart disease since she was a baby, and finally received a new heart in July after five years on the transplant list. Only a couple of heart transplants are performed on children in Norway every year, in spite of long waiting lists. Kaia was one of them, and after five years on the list with rapidly deteriorating health, Iselin was beginning to give up hope.

"It is an impossible situation to be in," she says. "Wishing so hard that your child will receive a new heart and a chance at life,

while also knowing what that wish entails—that someone has to die for it to happen."

We pay this charming mother-and-daughter duo a visit in late November. Their home is a compact basement apartment in a house a few hundred meters from the T-bane station in Østerås. On the day of our visit, a wet, drizzly fog hangs over the western fringes of Oslo, obscuring both Holmenkollen and Kolsåstoppen from view.

"I go to school now," says the frail-looking little girl as she opens the door to us, ushering us into a warm, brightly lit hallway. "I love school!" And then she's gone, twirling down the narrow hallway plastered with her accomplished drawings. Though she is pale and small for her age, Kaia's movements are quick and nimble. It's hard to believe that in the summer, she was at death's door after being struck down with pneumonia last winter and struggling to fully recover.

"These kids [on the transplant list] just can't withstand what other children can," says Iselin, handing us mugs of milky coffee. "More has to be done to draw attention to their plight, that is why we agreed to this feature."

I close the browser window and spin the chair slowly around, staring into the soft blue glow of Oliver's room. My heart is hammering hard in my chest. I'm a journalist; I've built my world around words, but I have no words for this; for what I'm feeling. I close my eyes, but Kaia's wan, white face is etched into my mind, and underneath her image is Amalie, like a ghostly hologram; shimmering, see-through, gone. I clench and unclench my hands so hard I leave dark purple grooves on my palms, then turn back around to the computer. I need to know more.

I go on Facebook for the first time in a long time. I used to check it numerous times a day, loving the ease of communicating with old friends scattered across the globe. Presumably she, too, will be here, and I will know even more. I type in *Iselin Berge* and she's easy to find—only one match.

Only her profile picture is available to me, but Iselin Berge appears even younger than in the magazine feature, no older than twenty-five, I'd imagine. She has a pretty face with a soft jawline thanks to a few extra pounds. Kaia is in the picture, too, standing behind her mother and resting her head on her shoulder. The child's skin tone is a strange gray, like the underbelly of a fish, all the more noticeable next to her mother's pink, healthy color, and I notice that it was posted last May, three months before she received the new heart.

Only eleven people have liked the photo, and I look at Iselin's friend list. Seventy-two friends, no mutual friends, unsurprisingly. She's most likely almost twenty years younger than me, and I don't know many people in Norway, even after eight years here. It doesn't seem like Iselin knows that many people, either, so perhaps we have that in common. I move on to her cover photo, a skillfully drawn anatomical heart in soft charcoal pencil, accentuated in slashes of neon yellow, and I wonder if she drew it herself. Somehow, I doubt it; she looks more like a receptionist or a shopgirl, but who am I to judge? I don't think anyone who could see me now, wearing my too-big old Levi's and Sindre's maroon cashmere sweater, my hair scraped back into my usual tight bun, would imagine that I once wrote for some of the world's biggest publications or traveled the world on my own. Above the heart is a quote in accomplished calligraphy: *Hearts are wild creatures, that's why our ribs are cages.* Underneath, someone called Anton Mehus has commented *Gorgeous, Iselin!* Someone else, a DJ Noa, has written *Bravo, my <3.*

I try to look for more pictures, but there is nothing—like me, she must have strict privacy settings. I'm about to shut Facebook down, but notice that her profile picture was uploaded from Instagram. I take my phone from my pocket and open the app. I've never posted on Instagram much, though I will scroll through from time to time. I realize that the last picture I posted, a selfie of Amalie and me two weeks before she died, has now had over five hundred likes and countless comments. But I'm not going there, not now.

I search for @IsbergArt, and as I hoped, her profile is open. She may be private on Facebook, but she's open to anyone on Instagram: she has posted over eight hundred times, and is followed by 1,311 people. I scroll down her feed, which is mostly her drawings, with occasional food pictures and pictures of Kaia. I open a recent one, taken two weeks ago, of Kaia standing in front of a brown, single-story building with a pyramid-shaped red climbing frame in front of it. She's grinning widely, forehead and ears obscured by a fluffy purple hat, arms spread out in a typical pose, her face almost as white as the winter sky and the snow on the trees. On the side of the building in the background, I can make out the words *Elvely Skole.*

My bubba loves school sooo much, reads the caption, followed by a long series of emojis, mostly hearts. Perhaps not so strange, considering Iselin looks very young. Elvely Skole. I know it—it's just down the road from the stables where we keep Amalie's pony. To think that I've driven past that building time and again, when all the while inside was the little girl with a very special heart. Maybe . . . Maybe I could make a little detour next time? All I need is to see her, just once, from afar.

"Hey, what are you doing?"

I jump in my chair, blinking at the sudden slash of light from the open doorway. Sindre is silhouetted in it; huge, his shoulders nearly touching the sides of the doorway.

"I . . . Uh, Oliver's computer was left on . . . I was just shutting it down." I quickly close the Facebook browser window and slip my phone back into my jeans pocket.

"Okay, I'm off to bed. You coming?" I nod in the soft darkness, but Sindre's already gone.

31

ALISON

At the bottom of the road is a junction and I hesitate there for a long moment, watching flurries of wet snow dropping fast before disintegrating on my windshield. There is no one behind me. I should turn around, head back home, take a hot bath, catch up on all the life admin neither Sindre nor I have been able to face. I think of the quiet house, the possibility of taking a couple of tranquilizers. I could finally return Karen Fritz's calls, ask if she would see me again.

I could find out if Oliver wanted to go for a walk this afternoon even though he's at Monica's this week; it might do us both good to breathe in the fresh forest air, to talk more. Or . . . Or I could take a right and just quickly drive past that school and see if I might spot her. Kaia.

It was I who insisted on the donations. I believed, and I still do, that any sane person should be a donor. The idea that healthy organs are routinely buried or cremated while people die on the transplant lists has never sat easily with me. But that was before; before I had to make that decision in a matter of minutes, holding my baby's cooling hand, deep in shock, just entering the world of ex-mothers. I close my eyes, gripping the steering wheel, consciously drawing breath slowly and deeply.

Your heart. Amalie, your heart is calling for me.

A loud noise breaks my thoughts; someone is honking. I sit up straighter and glance in the rearview mirror. It's a woman in a Chevy Suburban, and behind her are a couple of other cars, waiting, puffs of exhaust rising from them, streaking the white air. I wave in apology and flick my indicator to the right, heading toward the stables, and Kaia's school, in Østerås. The other cars all turn left, and I'm glad; I'm inching along the road, tears streaming down my face. I think of Misty in her box, waiting.

The school is brightly lit up, but quiet. I park across the road, on the sidewalk, discreetly concealed by a browning, gravel-studded snowbank made by the snowplows clearing the parking lot directly in front of the playground. I can see the main entrance from here, and most of the playground. It's a small school, and to the left of the building is a bumpy hill, its snow worn thin and icy in patches by little tobogganers. Their sledges and short plastic skis that strap onto winter boots, *stumpeskis*, are flung about at the bottom of the hill, ready for the next recess. I glance at the clock on the dashboard—it's 11:14, and I try to guess when the kids might come outside to play.

I hear a sustained muffled sound and turn toward it—the school bell. As if on cue, children appear in the glass corridor on the right side of the building; messy-haired, pale, tired-looking, smiling, jumping, carrying little boxes, all heading in one direction, and then suddenly, the building seems empty again. I stare at my hands on the steering wheel; veined, blue, dry. I imagine Kaia's little hands in this exact moment; perhaps unwrapping a sandwich. I wonder what's in it, what she likes. She might be sitting with a couple of friends; little girls like herself, buzzing with energy in the way only small children can, eyes roaming, smiles quick and wide, laughter loose. Or she might sit alone, chewing slowly and carefully, timidly scanning the room for a potential friend. From the pictures, she strikes me as the latter kind of child.

Is she consciously aware of the heart inside her, is she noticing its steady beat, the incredible work it does, sluicing her blood around her body, powering her every move? Does she ever think about where it came from? How, really, it belongs to somebody else?

I close my eyes against this onslaught of thoughts and try to bring my mind to a safe place. Once, it would have been Sindre. I go further back: childhood, home—I was happy then. Stinson Beach, its honey rocks, the wild, surging ocean, the fragrant California air; smoke, cloves, verbena, pine. I open them again and take it all in: the school full of strangers' children, the parking lot glistening with slushy, brown snow, the white sky merging with the gray-white fields behind the school. This is madness. I can end this right now. I need to go home and begin to put some of the pieces back together. I need to get the help I so clearly need; no one sane would come here, looking for someone else's little girl. My hand is on the key in the ignition when that muffled sound starts up again. Eleven thirty. The corridor becomes a swarming hive of little bodies stepping into snowsuits, pulling hats down over heads, shoving soft, pudgy hands into gloves.

I've started reversing slowly back off the sidewalk when the doors swing open and the kids burst into the playground like a spilled bag of beans. Kaia is one of the first ones to emerge. I recognize her immediately; her serious, pale face and blue eyes are etched on my mind. She is wearing a scruffy-looking purple ski jacket with mismatched turquoise ski pants, and a navy hat with something written across the forehead in gold letters. A couple of strands of hair peek out from underneath the hat and she pushes them away with her gloved hand. She is alone, indeed, and glances around before making her way toward the red pyramid jungle gym. Another little girl approaches and they chat a moment before pulling themselves up onto the lowest rung. They turn around and sit with their backs toward me, looking at the other kids milling around the playground. A boy runs past and chucks a little snowball toward Kaia and her friend.

Kaia jumps down, leaving her friend on the frame. At the bottom of the little hill, she picks up a red plastic sledge with handlebars on the sides, then joins the line of kids waiting their turn. She jumps up and down, looks around as if for another friend, kicks at the snow with the tip of her boot. When it is her turn she carefully places the tip of the sledge so it points straight ahead, like a plane getting into position on the runway before takeoff. Then she throws herself onto the sledge, propelling it forward, laughing and squinting in the sun, which has just come through the layers of white fog. I hold my breath, watching her. There is something about the way she smiles—I can't look away. Inside her chest, in this exact moment, Amalie's heart is beating.

I can't get out of the car; it would look pretty suspicious if a strange woman stood observing children at play; this is a small school, everybody would know that none of these children are mine. There are two adults sitting on a bench over by the main entrance, wearing reflective vests and occasionally rubbing hard at their arms against the cold, but they most likely can't see me from where they sit. I wish I could get closer, so close I could see the exact color of Kaia's eyes, the curve of her lip as she smiles, what is written on her hat—it isn't enough to just watch her from here, knowing what I know. Again and again she comes down the little hill on the red sledge, laughing carelessly, and I was right, after all; seeing her, knowing her face, even just for a few moments, was the right thing to do. But after this, I will have to let go.

She's nearing the top again, bouncing about as excitedly as if it were the first time. Sledge carefully positioned, she sits down on it and is about to nudge it into motion when a big, chunky boy steps forward and pushes her hard on the back, making the sledge lurch off, veering toward the right. A couple of tall trees fringe the hill and Kaia throws her weight to the left, trying to avoid them, but it's too late and the sledge hits the first one fast, head-on. Kaia soars through the air—a big, pastel bird—before crashing to the ground.

Two little girls run down the hill toward her, but for a long moment, she doesn't move. The girls pull her up, and they are facing toward me; Kaia's face is twisted in a grimace of pain, I can tell she's screaming, though I can't hear it, and blood is pouring from a gash above her left eyebrow. My breath is shallow and strained, as though I, too, am in acute pain. In this exact moment her heart, *Amalie's heart*, will be racing, pounding painfully in her chest, and I could run to her and pick her up and hold her close; I'd feel its panicked flutter like a tiny bird's wings caught in the sliver of space between us.

My hand rests completely still on the door handle, knuckles white with restraint. How can I not go to her, how could I not try to calm that frightened heart? One of the adults supervising has heard the commotion and runs across the playground to Kaia, scooping her up in his arms, her blood splattering onto his neon-yellow vest. As he carries her quickly back across the playground toward the school building, he happens to glance in my direction and his eyes meet mine. His eyes immediately narrow in suspicion—there must be something about the look on my face—and I push my foot hard down on the brake and put the car back into gear before driving off, my eyes streaming, my stomach hot and liquid, my heart booming in my chest.

At home, I make an excuse to Sindre, saying I caught a chill in the stables and need to lie down. In bed, I go through Iselin's entire Instagram account, poring over the pictures of Kaia, committing the curve of her jaw, the exact color of her eyes, her tight French braids to memory. Then an idea appears in my mind as clear and perilous as an iceberg on the horizon. I open my e-mail browser and begin to type.

32

ISELIN

I must have fallen asleep on the kitchen table, slumped over a new drawing. The pinging sound of an e-mail on the phone wakes me up. Kaia hasn't been up in the night as much in the last two weeks, but she's woken up twice so far tonight, leaving me with only scraps of sleep. Poor little one, she took a bad fall at school today and we had to go to A&E to get the deep cut above her eyebrow glued back together. All afternoon she was woozy and teary. I turn the phone over and squint at the screen; quite a few new likes on Instagram and an e-mail from an address I don't recognize.

FROM: **Alison Miller-Juul** <A.M.Juul@online.no>
TO: **Iselin Berge** <isberg@isberg.no>
DATE: Sat, Feb. 9, 2019, at 1:04 A.M.
SUBJECT: Inquiry

Hi,

I came across your illustrations on Instagram and thought they were very beautiful and special. Would it be possible to commission a couple for my home? I especially like your charcoal and calligraphy work featuring anatomical hearts. Could you e-mail me some prices and information on how to proceed?

Thank you,
Alison Miller-Juul

Another one! I almost want to wake Kaia and tell her that now, finally, we are getting somewhere. As Kaia has gone from strength to strength, I have found my mind clearing, as though it has been steeped in a thick fog for years and years. When I went to pick up the pencil, it would just hover there, above the page, not moving, because in my mind, I saw nothing. All the images and fantasies that had played out in my head from childhood, the need to draw that pulled me through my difficult teens, were just gone, replaced by an eerie, gray silence.

I consider texting Noa, but then I remember she's here, sleeping on the sofa bed. She's playing several sets in Oslo this week, so we get to see her twice in one month. I flick the switch on the reading lamp in front of me and then I can make her out from where I'm sitting; she's shrugged off the duvet, exposing the star tattoo on her ankle that matches mine. We got them together in Narvik when she turned sixteen and I was almost eighteen. She's covering her face with one hand, another tattoo creeping out of her pajama sleeve. I find a new piece of drawing paper, sharpen the pencil into a perfect point, and then I begin to draw her. I try to capture the fragile curve of her back, the milky, unblemished skin, the soft hollow of her stomach, and something of that uncompromising strength that defines Noa. I think of her when she was a little girl, when her name was still Nora Caroline Berge. She always possessed such a strong sense of self, even when we were children. She knew who she was, what she wanted, and where she was going, and sometimes, thinking back, it seems to me that she extended that determination to me, shaping me the way she wanted to, even though she is younger than me.

We're going to leave this shithole, me and you, she'd say, and I'd look around the quiet fjord-side village surrounded by barren mountains, listening to her voice, drawing pictures in my mind of all the places we would go. *We'll be artists*, she'd say. *We'll always be together. We'll live in Paris or London or New York, and we'll be famous and everyone from home will read about us in magazines and wish they'd been nicer to us.*

Yeah, I'd say, because that was what I usually said to Noa's grandiose plans. *Our parents will be sorry, so fucking sorry.* I'd always recoil a little bit, just thinking about them. *Yeah*, I said, *they'll be so fucking sorry.* I wonder if they ever were.

My pencil lingers on Noa's wrist tattoo and I exaggerate it, adding intricate designs that aren't really there. In the end, the Noa on paper is covered in tattoos, every last part of her face, even, and I smile at the thought that in this moment it is me defining her, not the other way around.

Noa stirs and makes an abrupt, growly noise—a cross between a yawn and a cough, and then she sits up, blinking hard in the shaft of light from the kitchen. When she sees me sitting at the table watching her, she stretches her arms out like a child would to its mother and I go to her. I don't know what I would do without her; she is my sister, the only person really close to me besides Kaia, but sometimes my love for her is contaminated by envy and becomes too complicated. I pat her knobby back, and draw in the familiar, sleepy scent of her. I'm glad I'm not here alone.

"Hey, guess what?" I say.

"What?"

"I got an e-mail from another lady who wants to buy some drawings from me. Two, I think."

"Awesome! You must be Østerås's most successful illustrator by now, big sis." Noa's dark blue eyes shimmer with pride and excitement.

"I know, right?"

"Issy, that's awesome! I swear, I always knew this would happen. You just needed some confidence. The new stuff is so cool. I've never seen anything like it before."

I wish it was always like this—Noa and me, here together, my daughter sleeping in the next room, an apartment filled with drawings, in an anonymous suburb of the capital. *We're going to leave this shithole, you and me. We'll be artists and we'll always be together* . . .

Sometimes it felt like I never had a choice, that my only option was to follow her on her journey from Nordland to Oslo, from Nora Berge to DJ Noa, from determined outcast schoolgirl to tattooed it-girl and celebrated songwriter-DJ, but somewhere along the way I lost my own way. I sense it again now, folding out in front of me.

"I drew you," I say, and show her the drawing.

"Your hand sees me more clearly than your eyes," she says, and laughs. I lie down beside her but can't sleep. When Noa's breath has dropped into the unmistakable steady rhythm of heavy sleep, I pull my phone out and reply to Alison Miller-Juul.

FROM: **Iselin Berge** <Isberg@Isberg.no>
TO: **Alison Miller-Juul** <A.M.Juul@online.no>
DATE: Sat, Feb. 9, 2019, at 01:49 A.M.
SUBJECT: Re Inquiry

Hi,

Thanks for getting in touch. I'm in my studio space in
Majorstuen two days a week (Monday and Wednesday). If
you're able to come by to discuss further, that would be great.
That way I can show you a selection of my work. The address is
Trudvangveien 30.

Best regards,
Iselin Berge

The reply comes almost immediately—*Monday is perfect*, it reads.
I move closer to Noa, snuggling against her shoulder like when we
were kids, and close my eyes.

33

ALISON

"I'm going to go and see Erica and the baby," I say, and Sindre looks up from where he's sitting at his computer in the home office, face blank. "I haven't seen her in a really long time. Since . . . well, since last summer."

"I didn't know they'd had a baby."

"Yeah. Quite recently. A boy called Alvin."

"Tell her I said hi."

I nod. My eyes linger on my husband for a drawn-out moment, as if a part of me wants him to question me, or stop me somehow. He seems to just automatically believe that I would suddenly feel the urge to go visit an old friend. So why would he question me?

This is a crazy thing to do. What would Sindre do if he knew where I was going? I imagine him holding me hard by the shoulders, like a naughty child, his gravelly voice booming in my ear: *Are you completely fucking insane?* But it isn't as if Sindre isn't crazy himself; shooting uncontrollably, concealing weapons, running for hours in the middle of the night, pursuing some woman. As if either of us could be anything but crazy. I shut the door softly behind me and, pulling my scarf tight around my neck, step outside. I've decided to walk to Iselin's studio, though it is far and very cold outside. It's all downhill into the city from our quiet neighborhood on the edge of the forest, and I think it might be good for me to physically tire myself before I arrive. My knees ache and I have a distant recollection of falling down, but I'm not sure I actually did.

I start walking down Ullveien, but my legs feel weak. I stop for a moment and think about turning back toward the house, but then I decide to keep walking; I'd rather be out in the frosty air than shut up inside. Besides, I don't have to go to Iselin's studio. I could just walk into town and get the T-bane back up—I haven't yet done anything that isn't entirely reversible.

I take a deep breath and feel soothed by the sight of the tall spruce trees fringing the road, branches laden with snow glinting in the sunlight. I haven't taken anything today, though perhaps I should have, but in this moment I feel able to just walk and breathe without the tranquilizers. Either way, they are in my pocket and I close my hand hard around the little rattling box as I walk.

Something happened in the time after I regained consciousness. The burning was gone. I had wanted it to be gone, of course, but I hadn't anticipated the vast, cold space it would leave behind. It felt so good, to be suspended in that semiconscious state, where memories and feelings and impressions layered over each other, where past and present could seamlessly coexist. Moving around in my mind, the years blurred and the kids were big and small and then big again. I wish the doctors had never woken me up. I stop for a moment and try to focus on the burning; to conjure up the way it felt like constant corrosion in my stomach—sometimes unbearable and searing hot, other times harder to discern, but nevertheless a constant presence—but it really is gone.

I pass Holmenkollen Station and stand awhile looking up at the ski jump, its nimble glass-and-metal body reflecting the sun. Some Asian tourists stand around in the slushy snow in their tennis shoes, chattering and halfheartedly photographing the famous structure before getting back on their tour bus. I'm about to walk on when I pick out a small black figure toward the top of the jump, inching toward the cabin. It's Monday morning, and they do train here throughout the winter. What might they be like, those moments spent hanging suspended above the drop, clutching the metallic railing on either side, before letting go and hurtling down the in-run? What makes people do such things? I wait for a bit, and sure enough, the figure slides down fast before arching smoothly through the sky, and for a moment it is as though I am him, as though it's me flying high above the city glittering through a haze of smog far below in the valley; fast, cold air tearing at my face. He lands, broad skis slamming down onto densely prepped snow, arms shooting from his sides to above his head, as if applauding his own perfect flight.

I start walking again, faster now, and it isn't until I reach Slemdal Station farther down the hillside that I realize my mistake. I've never walked this way before, and in the car I would have known to avoid it—Holmenkollen Montessori Klubb. Amalie's old nursery. How will I bear the chatter of other people's children, the sight of little busy bodies rushing around in the snow, encumbered by snowsuits? I listen out for voices, but the air is almost entirely silent, save for the distant whir from the highway. Rounding the corner, I'm relieved to see that all the children are inside, and I stand by the fence, looking at the myriad footprints in the empty playground, trying to calm my hammering heart. If Amalie hadn't left me, she wouldn't still be here—she'd have started at the school farther up the road. I turn around and can just about make out the large yellow school building in between the trees.

She's in there, I whisper to myself. She's in there, practicing letters with a carefully held pen, crossing *t*'s and dotting *i*'s. She's in there, the new green-and-purple Mummitroll backpack leaning against her desk. She's smiling to herself because she's finally at school, in the bright and airy classroom overlooking the tennis court, at the double desk next to Charlotte Bern, whose freckled, gentle face she's known her whole life, after so many months of thinking and talking about it nonstop. *She's in there.*

It's easier to keep walking when I tell myself this.

At Majorstuen, all the snow has melted, and I sit at Baker Hansen with a cappuccino, watching the half-empty number-twenty bus churn slowly through brown slush. I'm early, and despite the long walk, I feel restless and deeply anxious. This is a crazy thing to do. Crazy *and* dangerous. But since that night at the lake and in the blurred weeks since, I have become convinced that owning a couple of Iselin's drawings will bring me some comfort, giving me a connection to the recipient. Perhaps I could somehow find a way to ask her about her daughter, if she's noticed any changes that can't be ascribed to the surgery or the recovery. *No*, I tell myself, *stop now*. I'll buy the drawings, and then I will stop.

I check my phone and there's a text message from Sindre, reading **Be careful walking, it's icy out there, I love you.** My thoughts return to Amalie at her school desk, messy hair swept back from her face in a high ponytail, eyebrows scrunched in concentration, sharp new pencil held tight, little smile lurking, my heart—undone. I stand up, leaving the cappuccino untouched. I'm ready. I walk past Majorstuen Station as if in a daze, turn left after the library and down a quiet residential street. I repeat the quote from Iselin's Facebook cover photo over and over in my mind as I bring my finger to the doorbell at number thirty, which has a new white name sticker reading *Studio Isberg. Hearts are wild creatures, that's why our ribs are cages* . . . I press two fingers to my chest just above my breast, and the rapid throb of my heart is indeed like the scramble of a beast.

I'm buzzed in, and walk up two flights of stairs, where a woman is waiting in the open doorway. She's more beautiful than I anticipated from her photos, with translucent, pale skin and big, carefully made-up eyes, a flick of black eyeliner sweeping upward at the corners of her eyes. Her hair, which was brown in the pictures, is now dyed a punchy, icy blond and piled up high on her head. She smiles widely at me.

"Hi. You must be Alison," she says in English, and I don't bother offering to speak Norwegian, though my Norwegian is as good as her English, if not better. "I'm really happy you could stop by. I always think it's best to see these kinds of illustrations in person; they just don't photograph that well." I follow her through what looks like someone's apartment, which is filled with books and artwork.

"Is this your apartment?" I ask, my voice emerging as a hoarse croak. I try to imagine this young woman at the sick child's bedside, praying, praying, that her daughter would receive a new heart. Someone else's heart.

"No, this is my sister's friend's apartment. She's gone to Bali for the winter, and I'm just temporarily using the studio space here. I mostly work from home, but my daughter has just started school and I wanted to get out more. It's great to have a space where I can meet with potential buyers." Iselin shows me into a big, white space I'm guessing would have been the apartment's master bedroom. It looks out onto a wide, square backyard covered by thick snow, but I imagine it in the summer, bustling with people from all the apartments overlooking it, drinking beer and cooking together on big barbecues. I let my eyes travel around the room, taking in Alison's illustrations, which cover almost every surface. I feel her eyes on me expectantly, but just then, a thin voice from another room rings out.

"Mamma," it says. "Come, Mamma!" My heart drops in my chest, and the burning flares up again, a hot, searing sensation spreading out in my stomach. Iselin looks at me apologetically, eyes wide and startled when she sees the look on my face. I try to smile, but my face won't comply, so I look down at my feet.

"Sorry. Will you excuse me for a moment? My daughter's home from school today; she's had a bit of an accident."

"Of course," I say, using all my strength to keep my voice from shaking. She's here. "Poor thing." Iselin leaves the room, and I can hear her whispering in the next room, and the little girl's voice rising and falling. My eyes are stinging with hot tears. What am I doing here? What the hell was I thinking, finding this woman and her child online and striking up contact with them? It's beyond crazy. I eye the door and decide to quietly slip out—I can end this craziness, right now, and that is exactly what I need to do. But just then, Iselin returns, trailed by a little girl partially hiding behind her mother.

"Hi," I say, and Kaia peeks out from behind Iselin, a flash of cool blue eyes, before I look away.

"This is Kaia," says Iselin. "She wanted to say hi. She was really excited that someone was coming, you're actually the first, uh, customer to come here, so . . ."

"Oh," I say. "Hi, Kaia." I extend my hand but my face flushes hot and my mind is burning white, like if one looks at the sun for too long. The little girl steps forward to take it and I have to swallow hard several times before I'm able to lower my eyes and fully look at her. I needn't have worried; I feel nothing. She's unremarkable. Shorter than I'd have imagined a seven-year-old to be. She has a big cut above her right eyebrow, dressed with surgical tape, blueing at the edges.

"I know you," says Kaia, and my mouth drops open. I glance at Iselin, whose face looks a little bit flushed.

"No, Kaia, you've not met Alison before. Remember, I told you, she's come here to look at my drawings. She found them online."

"Yeah, but I know you," she says again, and looking into her eyes, I feel it, too; I *do* know her, and it is as though a powerful current passes between us. I fight the urge to reach for her, to pull the child close, feeling the beat of her heart against my chest.

"I . . . I was on TV," I say. "I wrote a book. Uh, maybe you saw me there." Kaia stares at me, then turns around and walks over to a little easel by the window, which I hadn't noticed. I'm struck by the unchildlike way she moves; she walks like an adult, with poise and control, unlike Amalie, who'd half dance and hop about.

"Look," she says, pointing to the drawing she's working on. "I draw, too." Kaia is clearly talented, and the drawing she points to could be the work of an adult. A little girl stands on the edge of a cliff, dark hair whipped up by the wind, and she's stretching out her hand to a big, black bird about to land on it. In its claws it holds a shiny red heart. I turn away from it, careful to avoid Iselin's eyes. I really need to leave, now; my head hurts and my heart is pounding.

"I fell down!" says Kaia, standing closely beside me.

"Oh, no," I say. Why doesn't Iselin call the child away, tell her not to disturb us?

"Kaia, I'm going to have a chat with Alison here for a little while now, okay?" Iselin smiles uncertainly at me; she must have sensed a strange atmosphere between me and her daughter. "I'll be with you again in a moment."

"I'm going to stay here and draw," says Kaia, turning away from us and pulling a little chair up to the easel. Iselin and I walk around the big room, and she points to the various drawings, most of them variations of the same themes: anatomical hearts, some birds, occasional calligraphy.

"They're beautiful," I say, trying to keep my voice steady and composed. In my head I'm counting the minutes back since I left the house: one hundred and fifty-two.

"Are you a teacher?" asks Kaia, suddenly.

"No," I say. "I'm a journalist." I expect her to ask me to explain what a journalist is, but she doesn't, she just nods, then returns to the drawing in front of her. Iselin and I talk for a while about the sudden thaw after the fierce cold of the past couple of weeks.

"I'm going to be a teacher when I grow up," says Kaia, eyes not leaving the drawing. I don't know if I want to bolt from the room and never return, or if I want to draw out these moments in Kaia's presence; my heart is beating fast, then very slow, then fast again, and my mind is both fuzzy and chaotic at once, thoughts darting about. Iselin hands me a steaming mug of hibiscus tea, which I don't recall being offered, and we stand in the middle of the floor, surrounded by her drawings, the child silent and focused in the corner. We talk about Kaia's school, which is just down the road from their home and apparently very nice. We stop talking for several long moments, Kaia's pen scratching at the silence.

"I've got a new heart," says Kaia suddenly, and as our eyes meet, that current passes between us again, so strong it strikes me mute. My mouth is open, but not a sound emerges.

"Kaia," says Iselin. "Not now, sweetie, okay?"

"It's true," she continues, her eyes still locked on mine, and I smile weakly at her, unable to say a single word. "Someone else had to die for me to get it. Or I would have died. I'd be dead by now, the doctor said it."

"Yes," I whisper, hibiscus steam rising up into my nostrils, those cool blue eyes fixing me to the spot. I could speak up now and stop this charade. I could tell Kaia that that someone was my little girl, that I don't have her anymore, that the only thing that remains of her, of everything that she was, is the strong, sweet heart inside Kaia's own chest.

Iselin says something to me, but I can't quite grasp the words, so I just listen to the murmur of her voice, my eyes still on Kaia. She has stopped drawing and is holding a chunky oat cookie her mother has just handed to her. Her fingers are thin and so pale they are almost translucent, the tips covered in sticky crumbs. She looks back up at me, unguardedly, and in the end, it's me who looks away, toward the window, where there is nothing to look at but the bare branches of a tree covered in a skin of ice. *Do you have any further questions?* I hear the girl's mother say, her words drifting past me like the thin snowflakes that have started falling outside.

I want to speak, now; I want to ask the little girl what she likes, what toys she plays with, who her friends are, whether strawberries might be her favorites, too, but I know my voice would emerge as a frightening croak. I look at Kaia again, but my eyes won't stay with her because everything about her is wrong—she's short and very thin, unlike Amalie, who looked older than her, aged five. There is something particularly unselfconscious about her; she chews with her mouth open, oats churning visibly around and around, slick with spit. Her feet are shuffling back and forth like she can't keep them still, and she fidgets with the buttons on her blouse with fast, restless fingers. Suddenly one pops open, exposing the top of a thick, fleshy scar reaching all the way up to her collarbone. I feel overcome with a sudden wild hatred for this girl, and the idea of Amalie's heart beating inside her seems deeply repulsive. It's not her heart. It's *Amalie's* heart. My heart.

The ugly stab of hatred suddenly fades into a kind of tenderness as I watch the girl try to open a box of charcoal pencils, her tiny fingers stumbling on the cardboard flap, and I find myself walking over to her to help her. And then something happens. Kaia turns to look at me again and in her eyes a kind of brilliant glow appears as our eyes meet. I feel drawn to her in the breathtaking way I was drawn to the first man I loved, immediately and eternally, a feeling only surpassed by the way my breath was sucked clean from my lungs the first time Amalie opened her eyes and looked into mine, my heart pummeled to pulp.

"I'd better get going," I say. "I'd love to buy two. Similar to that one, and that one. With the calligraphy quote on the one with the girl."

"Perfect," says Iselin. "I can have them with you in around a week if that works?"

"That would be fantastic," I say.

"Do you want to buy my drawing, too?" asks Kaia, a mischievous look in her eyes. I walk over to her and squat down next to her.

"I would love to buy your drawing, too. Why don't you finish it and when I come back for your mom's drawings I'll pay you with a big box of chocolates. Deal?" Kaia laughs, exposing round little teeth, her nose scrunching up sweetly. I commit her face to memory; I won't see her again. Coming here was a very bad lapse in judgment, and I got more than I'd bargained for, in actually meeting Kaia. Kaia Berge, the heart keeper. I suddenly feel distraught at the thought of never seeing her again; something unmistakable has passed between us. Kaia's proximity is irresistible; I want to grab her and hold her tight, smoothing her hair down, kissing her pale, dry cheeks, pressing my head to her chest. It's Kaia who reaches for my hand.

"Do you have a little girl?" she says, voice clear and neutral. I look at Iselin, who shakes her head almost imperceptibly, eyes soft, apologetic.

"Kaia . . . Remember we've talked about which questions we can and cannot ask people we don't know?"

"No," I whisper, the biggest betrayal of all my life.

Kaia seems to consider this, eyebrows scrunched tightly together. "Is your child a boy?"

"No, I . . . I don't have a child," I say. "Well, actually I have a stepson."

"Let Alison leave now, sweetie," says Iselin, her eyes imploring her daughter, and then the two of them walk me back through the apartment to the entrance, Kaia's wan little face serious and thoughtful.

"Bye," says Kaia, and steps forward to hug me. Iselin and I exchange another smile.

"Goodbye," I say, and step into the communal hallway. I remain awhile outside the closed door, just breathing and clenching and unclenching my hand.

34

ISELIN

I can't sleep, so I'm working. Kaia has already been up three times, unsettled and crying, voice hoarse, complaining about the cut on her forehead hurting. I'm feeling somewhat unsettled tonight, as though I'm no longer held in by skin and bone, like I could just melt away into anywhere, anytime. My thoughts keep returning to Alison Miller-Juul. I liked Alison; there was something so fragile and jittery about her that I almost asked her if she was okay, if she wanted to talk about it or whatever—sometimes it does help to talk to a stranger. I started working on her drawings almost as soon as she left; it felt like a challenge to land a commissioned job. I'm almost done with the first one, a copy of the one I did a while back of a little girl's outline with an oversized anatomical heart inside it. Alison wanted the "hearts are wild creatures" quote with it, and I'm about to start the calligraphy when Noa walks in. Her hair is plastered to her skull when she takes her woolly hat off, and her pale cheeks are rosy from the cold.

"Hey," she says, tossing her jacket onto the chair opposite mine but missing, so it slithers to the floor.

"Hey," I say, gently pressing my pen down in the first line of the letter *H*. "How was the gig?"

"It was crazy. Really buzzing." Noa pours herself a glass of red wine from the open carton, then leans over my shoulder to look at Alison Miller-Juul's drawing. "Wow."

"Like it?"

"It's amazing. Are you doing the 'hearts are wild creatures' quote?"

"Yep."

"It needs a bird," says a thin voice. Kaia is standing in the doorway, face serious, running her index finger absentmindedly around the outline of the cut on her forehead.

"A bird?" I draw my daughter close, kissing her cheek.

"Yeah. A little bird here." Kaia points to the upper left corner of the picture, just below where I've just outlined the *H*.

"Why don't you add the bird, baby, if you're sure?"

"Can I?"

"Sure," I say, and hand her a soft charcoal pencil. Kaia sits on my lap and meticulously draws a scraggly black bird with a hooked beak and tiny little dot eyes.

"See? It needed a bird."

"You were right, Kaia. Now, come on, you," I say when she's finished. "It's the middle of the night and you have school tomorrow."

"Can you tell me a story?"

"I already did, hours ago when you went to bed."

"Auntie Noa, can you tell me a story?"

"Go on, then, monkey," says Noa, and Kaia clambers from my

THE HEART KEEPER · 173

knee and into Noa's arms, who carries her like a damsel in distress to the alcove, then pretend-flings her in slow motion onto the bed.

"Tell me about when you and Mamma lived in Paris and then I arrived in Mamma's tummy!" Noa glances up at me, and I shake my head slowly. I don't want my thoughts to go there, back to that place that still feels like a gash in my heart, so many years later. Thinking about Paris, and the beginnings of Kaia, and how my life came to be as it is, is nothing but self-torture, like plucking at a scab to make it bleed again.

The next morning is beautiful and clear, and though I didn't get much sleep, I feel light and energetic. I've finished Alison's drawings sooner than I thought, and send her a message. I stand leaning against the kitchen sink, sipping my coffee and listening to the sounds of Kaia and Noa getting ready together in the bathroom. My phone pings in my pocket and it is Alison's response.

"Hey, Noa, I know it's your last night in Oslo, but would you be able to stay here with Kaia for a couple of hours tonight?" I ask as we leave the house, squinting in the bright morning sun. Before Noa has a chance to answer, we are interrupted by a shrill voice from upstairs.

"Miss Berge!" says Hanne Vikdal, standing on the terrace above my entranceway, looking down at us, her face pinched and stern.

"Yes," I say warily, taking a couple of steps away so I don't have to look straight up into her nostrils.

"I must say I'm a little concerned," she says. I glance at Noa, who is standing with her arms crossed, raising one eyebrow. I'm so glad she's here.

"What's the problem?"

"Well. As you know, it isn't just one thing. But I will say, last night has really given me reason to believe I am absolutely right to feel concerned."

"Last night?"

"Yes."

"Um. We were just here."

"My husband was out late, Miss Berge. He returned home at around one thirty in the morning. Your blinds were up and he happened to glance toward your flat as he came toward the house, and he was frankly shocked to see a small, sick child drawing at the kitchen table. Literally in the middle of the night. From what I understood, you two were drinking." The air is still and stunned between us after her tirade, but then a sound breaks it. It's the sound of Noa laughing loudly.

"Are you fucking kidding me?" she says, theatrically holding her hands to her stomach. "How dare you?" Hanne Vikdal's mouth drops open. Kaia's too. I take Kaia's hand and start to walk away.

"Hey," says Hanne Vikdal. "Hey! Kaia, which school do you go to?"

"Don't answer," I say, pulling Kaia away.

"How dare you?" Noa asks again, but Hanne Vikdal turns around and goes back inside, slamming the door shut behind her.

"Noa . . . I'm not sure that was a great idea," I say, my eyes on the brown slushy snow melting at my feet in the sharp sunlight. "She is our landlady."

"She's a bitch. Seriously, Issy, you need to get out of here." Noa takes Kaia's hand and stoops down to kiss her pale cheek, but Kaia turns away, little face startled and sad.

35

ALISON

This isn't quite sleep. I could open my eyes if I wanted to, but I don't.

I keep them closed; I can feel where my eyelids are fused together, and I think they must have been closed for a long while, but still, I can see. I see my mother standing by the lake we sometimes went to, wearing a wild, orange minidress, throwing chunks of bread to some large birds on the water, but when I manage to focus this strange gaze on them, I realize that they are vultures.

Amalie plays at the piano, her tiny fingers picking randomly at the keys, and had she been anybody else, I would have been annoyed by the scattered, jarring tones. But she's so beautiful. I don't have to open my eyes to see her, sitting there. I don't need to reach out to feel the feathery softness of her hair. I have tried to count how many different ways she took my breath away, still does, just by having existed, and this is the only uncountable thing I have managed to find in the whole world. She starts up again, stabbing hard and insistently on one key, and I am pulled out from this state of suspension.

I wake on the sofa, and that same sound is ringing out in the empty house. My hands are stiff and frozen, and the room is pitch-dark. For several long moments, I can't tell whether the sound is real or trapped inside my head. I can't immediately recall where everyone is. I look at the clock on the TV: it's only 6:40 P.M., but it feels like the middle of the night. The afternoon begins to come back to me: Sindre's lips pressed hard against mine, my hand stroking the stubble on his jaw, the way he made me look him in the eye before he got out of the car. *Be careful, Ali*, he said. Then he was walking away, disappearing into the revolving door to the terminal, merging with other travelers. He'll be in Geneva for five days, and though I find the empty house and the four blank days ahead unsettling, it's a relief to have some time away from my husband. There was a time when, if I had suspected Sindre of even the slightest indiscretion, I would have gone wild with jealousy and anger, but now, whatever he is doing in Geneva and who he's doing it with—I just don't care.

The sound starts up again, unmistakable this time—the doorbell. I move toward the hallway without switching on any lights; I want to see who it is without the person outside knowing someone is at home. Oliver is at Monica's, but if, for whatever reason, he's come here to pick something up, he has keys and won't be using the doorbell. One of my friends? I don't have many here in Norway, or anywhere at all, anymore. Fifteen years of traveling the world tends to displace the friends you had, especially when you make little effort at staying in touch.

Especially when you lose your daughter and no one knows what to say to you. My friends message me and say that they are praying for Amalie and for me, and when I don't respond, they seem to assume I want to be left alone. I don't. I wish they knew how to talk to me, that they knew that all I want is to talk about her; I want to rebuild her from my memories—I want to talk about how much I miss kissing her fingertips while she slept, how she used to swallow chewing gum and pretend she hadn't, how she used to mutter "Oh boy" under her breath, making Oliver laugh, how she'd arrange peas in a circle on a plate before eating them one by one; I want to tell people about the time she first roller-skated, in Venice Beach, or the way she used to smile into her hot chocolate at our cabin in Norefjell, the mountain sun painting streaks of gold on her hair. These are the things I want to talk about, because that is where Amalie is now; in each minute snippet of memory, in every episode brought back into the light.

My heart surges and I place a hand inside my sweatshirt to calm it, then I peer out from the narrow window on the far side of the dining room, which overlooks the raised porch. A woman, wrapped snugly in a huge navy down jacket, face turned away from my direction, holding a large cylindrical object. An ungloved hand emerging from her pocket, fingers pressing against the doorbell again, exposing a tattoo on the underside of her wrist. I remember that tattoo. Iselin. My heart lurches in my chest and I press my face harder against the window, trying to see if Kaia could be standing concealed behind her mother. I just can't stop thinking about her; it's as though her face is etched on my retinas. Iselin seems to be alone and turns slightly to look up at the windows upstairs. I could stay where I am and, surely, eventually she'd go away. What could she possibly want?

A thought occurs to me, or a vague memory, rather: Did I invite her here? I quickly pull out my phone and reread my messages, and there, clear as day, sent today at 9:30 A.M., just after I dropped Sindre off at Gardermoen, before I went home and started drinking.

> Hi Iselin, so excited the drawings are done! Do you want to pop
> round for a glass of wine tonight if you're free—it occurred to
> me that I have a couple of contacts who might be of interest re
> your illustrations. That way you could see where the drawings
> will hang, too. Let me know, Alison xo

I slip my phone back in my pocket and lean my head on the doorframe. Fuck. What the hell was I thinking? The stale taste of alcohol lingers in my mouth and I pop a piece of chewing gum from my jacket pocket in my mouth before switching the light in the hallway on and opening the door.

"Hi. Oh my God, come inside, it's so cold," I say, pulling Iselin into the hallway. "So glad you could make it! Where's Kaia?" Iselin looks around the hallway, smiling nervously.

"Kaia's at home. With my sister. Noa."

"You could have brought her if you'd wanted to," I say, focusing on maintaining my smile. I'm suddenly glad Iselin is here; maybe this was a good idea. If I were to befriend her, I'd be able to see Kaia again. I could stay close to Amalie, because in those intense moments that passed between Kaia and me, there was no doubt in my mind that there was something of Amalie there, in her eyes.

No, I say to myself. *No.*

"Well, come in," I say, holding my hand out for Iselin's jacket. She takes it off, stomps snow from her boots, then takes them off by the door, glancing self-consciously at the dirty puddles they've left on the floor tiles. I smile at her and beckon for her to follow me into the living room, switching on lights as we go. She follows, carrying the large cylinder presumably holding the drawings.

"Would you like red or white?" I say, following her eyes around the room.

"Um, either," she says, "I don't mind."

I suddenly realize that a photograph of the kids is on display on the glass table by the terrace doors, facing us directly. In it, Amalie is sitting on Oliver's lap. Behind them towers a Christmas tree laden with garlands and baubles, and there are stacks of presents surrounding the children. I turned the photo facedown, I know I did; Oliver must have turned it back around, and not for the first time. I keep talking, pointing out some of the artwork on the far side of the room to Iselin to distract her, while moving toward the terrace doors.

"See that one up there? To the left of the doorway. Yeah, that one with the mountains. I took that. I mean, I'm no photographer, but I used to take a lot of pictures back in my twenties." Iselin gazes at my shot of the Matterhorn beneath an inverted crescent moon, a wash of stars spreading out on the night sky like pulverized glass. I discreetly turn the photograph around, then lead her toward the kitchen.

Iselin takes a seat on a barstool in the kitchen and stares out of the window at the black night while I unscrew a bottle of Pinot Noir. I try to swallow away the rancid taste of alcohol in my mouth—I must have had more than a few glasses of wine on the sofa before I fell asleep; I often do. If I get the balance right, a bottle of wine mixed with my prescription meds leaves me mellow, unable to hold on to any thoughts, and I can sit and watch mindless television for hours, not hurting.

Iselin takes a long gulp of the wine and looks around the kitchen. It's a sleek, white space with little to look at; no children's drawings stuck to fridges, no school photographs beaming from the walls. In a metal mesh bowl some limes have been left to rot, and they are the only colorful objects in the room. Will I frame Iselin's drawings and hang them behind where she is sitting at the breakfast bar, clutching the glass with both hands as though it might warm them? Iselin has leaned the cylinder awkwardly against the breakfast bar but it clatters to the floor, and when she picks it up, I beckon to her to pass it to me. Her face lights up with a smile, but she's blushing, and when she hands me the cylinder her hand shakes slightly. As I take it from her an intense energy passes between us, not unlike the deep connection I felt with Kaia as she perched on the stool next to me, those thin, translucent hands clutching the pencil, staring at me with her unflinching, pale eyes. I smile at Iselin, a sensation of premonition and perhaps fear spreading out in my gut.

"I am so impressed you finished these in such a short time," I say. I take the cap off the cylinder's end and look inside at the rolled-up drawings. I glance at Iselin again and she looks very young and nervous.

"I hope . . . I hope that they will come to mean something to you." I unfold the first drawing; it's the one with the outline of a little girl with the big, intricate heart inside. In the top left corner is a black bird I don't remember seeing on any of Iselin's other versions of the drawing, but I love it. There is something so familiar and sweet in the way it's penciled—childlike and masterful in equal measures. I am reminded of Karen Fritz's birds, how it was easier to stay in that chair when I could imagine myself up there, among the migrating birds, high and free. It's been a while since I stopped seeing Karen now. I return to the drawing, lingering over every stroke of Iselin's pencil.

I imagine Sindre taking in the beautifully penciled heart, the medley of deep and bright reds nudged into its tiny chambers. I'll have to lie. I can't help the tears that flood my eyes, and one drops onto the edge of the drawing.

"I'm sorry . . ." I say. "I just felt so moved by your work from the moment I saw it."

"That means so much."

"Come, let's go through to the other room. I want to hear everything about what inspires you and how you came to draw like this."

"Uh, okay," she says, smoothing down her trousers, which are a little tight across her thighs, and then she sits down on the maroon velvet sofa, placing her wineglass on the low bronze table in front of her.

"The drawing is even more beautiful than I remembered. And thank you for coming up here with it. It's so nice to catch up with you again; I'm always intrigued to meet someone with such an enormous talent—there are always interesting stories there."

"I . . . Oh, well, thank you. Yeah, it's really nice to catch up again." She laughs a little, then looks around again, as though curious about whether we are here alone or if someone else might appear.

"My husband is away on business," I say. "In Geneva. Oliver is at his mother's this week."

"Oh." Iselin hesitates, pale eyes quickly scanning the room. "How old is he?"

"He just turned fourteen. It's so funny, he is suddenly really grown up. He even has a girlfriend."

"Oh, wow."

"Yeah."

"I like your house," says Iselin. "It must be nice to have the forest right outside like that. And the views. Wow."

"Yes," I say. "Yes, well . . . I . . ." It's almost as if I have forgotten how to converse with another person. "I grew up in California," I blurt out, and look beyond Iselin to the window behind her, to the lights of the city far below. I need somehow to bond with her, make her feel we can be friends. "It was really different from this." Iselin seems slightly relieved that I'm suddenly so socially awkward, and flashes me a quick, wide smile.

"I can only imagine," she says. "I've never been to the United States."

"No?"

"No . . . I always wanted to travel. I moved to Paris for a bit. To study. But then . . . I had Kaia, and, you know, it wasn't exactly like I could do much traveling after she was born."

"Do you have any help with her? Family, or . . . ?"

Iselin looks stricken. She peers into the wineglass for a long while and I silently curse myself for being so inconsiderate.

"I'm sorry," I say, but she smiles and waves her hand like it doesn't matter, but clearly it does, and I worry she may burst into tears. It would be disastrous if I've offended her; we're strangers, and I need her to feel like we have bonded, not like I've pried.

"No, no. It's fine," says Iselin, taking a sip of her wine and then looking straight at me, unflinchingly, with shining eyes. "But no, I don't have much family help with Kaia. Except for my sister, Noa— she does help me here and there when she can. She lives in Paris, and she tries to come every month or so; we're very close. The rest of my family lives, uh, far away, too. In Nordland." We remain silent a long while, and I wonder if Iselin is trying to come up with an excuse to leave. I wouldn't blame her—who would want to sit around drinking wine with a woman twice her age, whom she doesn't know and doesn't necessarily have anything in common with? But I don't want her to go.

"Tell me about Kaia," I say, softly, trying to give Iselin my most relaxed, uncomplicated smile. I wish she'd brought Kaia with her. Before, my every minute was consumed by thoughts of Amalie and the aching, black world I've lived in since she left us, but now I have found myself increasingly thinking about little Kaia.

Iselin brightens; perhaps she's more comfortable talking about Kaia than her own background. "Well, she's had a very, very hard start in life," she begins, and I nod sympathetically. "It's true, what she told you when you came to the studio. She had a heart transplant last summer after years of life-threatening illness. She tells everybody. She's really proud of it."

"My God, that must have been so stressful."

"Yes. I mean . . . It looked very bleak. I've had to say goodbye to her so many times. But somehow, she's pulled through."

"She must be very strong."

"Yeah, strangely strong for someone that little and fragile-looking."

"She struck me as a really interesting character. Grown-up, for, what, six, seven?"

"Seven. And yeah. Kaia is . . . funnily remarkable and unremarkable at the same time. You know? She likes the stuff most little girls like. She loves animals. She draws a lot. She likes cartoons, especially *Dora the Explorer*. She's eager to learn, and reads all the time. And yet . . . She's never sat on a pony, or even cuddled a dog. Too risky. She's never seen half of the things she likes to draw, like zoo animals, or the beach. She's never been on an airplane, or explored anything beyond our little apartment. And she was only able to go to school for the first time last year. She loves it, though."

"Wow," I say. "That must have been so tough. For both of you."

"Well, I've never been able to work much. I would have liked to. It's not . . . It's not how I imagined my life. Looking after a very sick little girl." Iselin stares into her wineglass. "Though, of course, I'm not complaining about that," she adds, nervously. "Not at all. It's just how it is. Or has been, until now. You can't . . . You can't imagine the changes in Kaia. It's just incredible . . ." She trails off, eyes shining.

"Changes?"

"Oh my gosh, it's almost like she's a different kid since before the transplant."

"Really? Tell me . . . Tell me more," I say, leaning across and patting Iselin's pale, plump hand lightly with my own. I pour her another full glass of Pinot Noir and she glances nervously at it, but doesn't say anything.

"Are you sure? Are you sure you want to talk about this? I mean, I don't want to bore you—"

"Iselin. It's lovely talking to you. My husband works away a lot and most of my friends are spread out across the world, so it's so nice for me to have some company. And I loved meeting Kaia. You have a wonderful daughter . . ." I say, intending to continue, but stop because a lump is growing in my throat, making my words trail off in a whisper. I take a big glug of wine, and clear my throat a couple of times, smiling reassuringly at Iselin. She nods.

"So," I continue. "You were going to tell me about the changes in Kaia since the transplant . . ."

"Yes." Iselin scrunches her eyebrows together in a frown, and it occurs to me again, just how young she is. When I was around twenty-five, I was drifting around Koh Samui, selling bric-a-brac at the market with my boyfriend at the time, Rex, building a portfolio as a budding freelance feature journalist on the side. I was completely free, and the most challenging decision I'd make in a day would be whether to go to Chica's or Lou's Beach Bar for a cheap dinner. I look at Iselin's sweet, unblemished hands, and imagine all the long nights she's sat there, by a sick child's bedside, clutching a clammy, limp hand, wiping a feverish brow.

"Yes, well, it's funny . . . She's changed a lot. In some ways, it's very obvious, and in others, it's more . . . subtle. And it's difficult to know whether all the changes are down to Kaia suddenly feeling healthy, for the first time in her life."

"What else do you think might have caused the changes?"

"Well, I mean, obviously she has more energy than before."

"Sure. I can imagine."

"Like, for example, she now loves to play outside, which she was never able to do before. She seems to really want to push the physical boundaries all the time, which I guess makes me a little worried, but the doctors tell me to trust her to decide when enough is enough."

"Right."

"She's more affectionate. Much more. She likes to hug me really tight, which she didn't before. But perhaps that kind of closeness would have felt uncomfortable when she was so sick."

I close my eyes for a moment. *I can feel your hugs, how tight they were, how strong your baby arms were.*

"Alison? Are you okay?" Iselin whispers, placing her warm hand on my cold, tense one. I nod, then gently retrieve my hand to pick up the wineglass. My heart trembles in my chest.

"Oh, yes. Sorry. I . . . I get these headaches sometimes. Like flashes. It helps to close my eyes. It's gone already." I smile at Iselin. "Tell me more. This is so . . . fascinating. How incredible modern medicine is."

"Yes. It really is incredible."

"You know . . ." I begin, watching Iselin's open face carefully as I speak, "I read this thing a while back, I think it might have been in *The New Yorker*, about how there is substantial scientific evidence that some fragments of preferences or memories may be passed to a recipient of a transplant organ from the donor."

Iselin draws her eyebrows together in a frown, and suddenly resembles her daughter exactly. She seems to form her words carefully in her mind before she speaks again. "That is interesting. I guess I don't spend much time thinking about that. You know, who the donor might have been. I am, of course, eternally grateful and I kind of wish they could know how much what they did for Kaia has meant."

"Yes. It *is* interesting, isn't it? Research seems to suggest that memory, and experiences, and the core essence of what makes us *us*, is stored in different parts of our anatomies, not just our brains, so I guess it could make some sense in that way. They're calling the gut the second brain now, aren't they?" I'm careful not to seem too interested in hearts.

Iselin nods, and takes another sip of her wine, and from the flush creeping across her throat, it would seem she's feeling the effect of the alcohol. "Yeah, I've read some stuff about, uh, the relationship between the mind and the body, too. And how psychological pain can, like, give you actual physical pain. So maybe it could be like that with memories or whatever."

"Yes. Do you think . . . Has Kaia, you know, done or said anything really odd since . . . since she received the new heart?"

Iselin raises an eyebrow briefly, like it suddenly occurs to her that it might be peculiar that I'm asking a virtual stranger such questions. "Well, Kaia says and does weird stuff all the time, being seven," she says, laughing a little, and I laugh, too.

"Yeah, I can imagine."

"But . . . yes. There have been a couple of things . . ." I have to use all of my mental energy to just sit here, a calm smile on my face, holding the wineglass in my hand still. "She's, uh, started doing this thing . . . this weird little thing. When she hugs me, she nestles her face in my neck on one side, then the other. And she goes, 'Both sides, Mamma. We have to do both sides.' It's little things like that, which she's suddenly started doing and consistently does, over and over."

I close my eyes. *Both sides, Mamma. We have to do both sides.*

Iselin is still talking, but I can't make out what she's saying. And then, a piercing, alarming feeling—a burst of pain, something wet, a scream, my own?

"Oh my God!" Iselin shouts, and I open my eyes and look into hers, which are wide open and frightened. "Oh God," she says again, standing up, and I follow her eyes to my hand, which has closed so hard around the wineglass it has shattered it, slicing open my palm. It's bleeding heavily, squirting blood and splashing red wine onto the table, onto Iselin, onto my jeans and the parquet floor. Iselin rushes into the kitchen and returns with a dish towel, which she ties quickly around my hand.

"I'm sorry," I whisper. "I'm so sorry." Iselin looks afraid, like I might suddenly hurt her the way I've hurt myself. I try to open my wounded hand but it is too painful and I can't stop the tears that begin to flow.

"There's glass stuck in my hand," I whisper, when I regain enough composure to bring the words out.

"I think we should call an ambulance," says Iselin.

"No!" I say, my voice sharper than I intended. "No, please," I whisper, imploring her with my eyes. "Listen. It's not as bad as it looks. These glasses are very fragile. Over there, in the kitchen, above the sink, the second cupboard to the left. There's iodine and bandages . . . Bring it here . . . Please . . ." Iselin does what I ask, her eyes not meeting mine.

Iselin sits gingerly on the edge of her seat and runs a cotton ball soaked in iodine across the inside of my palm. I instinctively pull my hand back; there really is a shard of glass stuck in the wound and it hurts badly.

"Tweezers?" asks Iselin, tilting my hand so that the embedded shard catches the overhead light.

"Upstairs bathroom. On the side of the sink, I think." Iselin gets up slowly, and walks uncertainly out toward the hall, then I hear her footsteps rushing on the stairs and I close my eyes again. I decide to try to pull the piece of glass out myself using my nails, and though it slips out easily, new, dark blood surges out of the jagged cut. This eases the pain, but I must have grazed an artery, judging by the amount of blood. I grab one of the bandages and start to wind it tight around my wrist, working my way up toward the gash in my palm. Is this cut deep enough to kill me? Could I just leave it unbandaged, go to bed, and never wake up?

"Let me help you," says Iselin, softly, and I open my eyes to see her standing there, holding the tweezers.

"I got it out," I say, and nod toward the bloodied splinter on the coffee table. "Could you just help me secure this?" Iselin moves toward me slowly, like I wasn't a middle-aged woman who'd cut herself on a wineglass, but a tiger in a trap. She purses her lips, concentrating on securing the end of the bandage with the metal hook. Already blood is seeping through the gauze and blossoming in the center of my palm. I watch her, and again I see the similarity between Iselin and her daughter, in the slightly pointy nose and the veins running visibly beneath the skin at the temples, like charcoal lines seen through an overlying sheet of paper.

"That . . . that thing you said," I whisper, "the thing about hugging on both sides . . . Did she not do that . . . before?"

"No."

"That's just so fascinating."

"There are other things, too . . ." Iselin looks at me intently, as if judging whether I can handle it if she continues. Her hand is resting gingerly on top of mine, though she has finished wrapping a second bandage around it. "Like, now she keeps wanting sparkling drinks. She hated them before. 'I love how it pops in my throat,' she says." Iselin pauses and it occurs to me that we hear what we want to hear—Amalie never cared for sparkling drinks, so I'm not interested in this piece of information. "Also," continues Iselin, "her drawings are different . . ."

"Different how?"

"When she was little she used to draw, I don't know, Disney stuff. Princesses and witches and that kind of thing. And then she got progressively really good at drawing, and used to copy a lot of the stuff I draw. Especially birds. Kaia loves birds. But lately she keeps drawing these bears . . . Funny little bears. They're very good, actually. I just find it a little odd, this sudden focus on them."

What was I playing at? Why did I ask her to come here? I can't think of a worse form of self-torture. I was wrong to think I could handle this—I cannot. I pull my hand out from underneath Iselin's, and mindful of every movement and the tone of my voice, I clear my throat and speak.

"Iselin, thank you so much for coming here, and for helping me. I'm sorry about the mess. I think I should lie down now. I'll call you a taxi." Iselin looks startled and mortified at my sudden change in tone, as though she has just said something extremely offensive.

"But . . . I can't just leave you here, like this." We both glance at the pool of red wine and blood, sprinkled with tiny shards of sparkling crystal on the floor, and at the sticky, darkening bloodstains on the coffee table.

"It's fine," I say, standing up, moving toward the kitchen to look for my phone so I can call her a taxi.

"Alison . . . Alison, is everything okay here? You know, at home? I . . . I know we don't know each other, I just . . . I just feel like maybe something is wrong."

"Iselin. It's fine," I say, steering her back toward the hallway, opening the Oslo Taxi app with my unbandaged left hand. She needs to go, right now. I feel faint and hot, and my right hand is throbbing hard.

"Sometimes it helps to talk to a stranger," she says, smiling sympathetically.

"Yes," I say. "But I just need to go to bed now. A taxi is on its way." I turn the screen to show her the taxi on the map, inching its way up toward us, at the very top of the city.

"A taxi will be hundreds of kroner . . . I live in Østerås . . . I can't . . ."

"It's prepaid," I say, smiling and handing her the bulky navy jacket, making a plume of feathers emerge from a rift on the underside of the sleeve. She looks embarrassed and upset, and I have to use all my control to stop myself from just shoving her out the door. The lights from the taxi finally sweep across the driveway outside and I open the door before Iselin has had a chance to put her shoes on. She looks on the verge of tears as she gets into the car, and I try my best to give her a reassuring smile, but like her little daughter, I have the uncomfortable feeling that she can see straight into me.

Inside, I walk fast back into the living room. It looks like a murder scene, and this actually makes me laugh out loud. It is a laugh that becomes coughing, then sobs, unleashing my horror and shock at Iselin's words. I go into the kitchen and a grunting, wild sound hollers around the room as I open the low cupboard where we kept Amalie's cups and special plates, the little pink plates with bear faces, because she loved them. Dinky Bear, Gruffalo, Goldilocks . . . I fling them to the floor, one after the other, until all that remains are shards.

I sit down on the floor in the kitchen among the pink shards, and stare into the living room through the wide archway, at the glass, the blood, the wine. I grab my phone and call Sindre. I want to tell him about the hugs on both sides. About the bears. It rings for a long time but then he picks up, voice groggy. I open my mouth to speak, but realize I can't, because how would I tell my husband that I sat around drinking wine with the mother of the girl with Amalie's heart, that I believe her to hold something of Amalie within her because she suddenly likes to hug her mother a certain way?

"Honey?" asks Sindre, no doubt hearing my short, heavy breathing.

I hang up. I put the phone on the floor and wait for him to call back, but he doesn't. I go into the kitchen and begin to clear up the mess, using only my left hand, exhaustion seeping into my limbs. When I finish, I wrap another gauze layer around my right hand—blood is still seeping through. Then I go upstairs and stand awhile at the door to Amalie's room before entering. In her desk drawer, I find what I'm looking for. A thick stack of drawings, page after page of bears. Bears riding bicycles, bears dining in restaurants—meticulously penciled food on the table in front of them, bears flying planes, bears playing volleyball on the beach.

36

ISELIN

I'm covered in blood. I only realized it in the taxi. My fingernails are encrusted with it, as though I'd fought Alison off; it's all over my shirt, and smudged on my face, even. I unlock the door as silently as I can and cross the corridor to the bathroom without switching the lights on, but even so, Noa has heard me and knocks on the door before I've finished washing the blood off. I don't open it until it's all gone, and the hand towel lies soaked and rust-colored beneath my scrunched-up shirt on the floor. I switch off the light as I pull the door open, trying my best to keep my expression neutral, but Noa stares suspiciously at me—she knows me too well.

"Ummm, what is going on?" she asks, taking in my upper body— bare except for my bra, my scrubbed, pink skin, goose bumps rising with her gaze.

"I, uh, walked home from the station and got really warm, so I decided to have a little rinse. That's all."

"Before even saying hi?"

"I thought you'd be asleep."

"Come on." Noa is a night owl and we both know that I know that. The problem with being around my sister is that there just isn't any room for pretense.

"How's Kaia?" I ask, walking into the living room, where Noa has already prepared the sofa bed for the night.

"Fine. Now, are you going to tell me what's going on?" I stare at her tired, pinched face. Her fingernails look painfully chewed down, and the skin on her neck is blotchy and red where her headphones have chafed against it. I burst into tears. I'm as surprised as Noa, but the tears come suddenly and feel unstoppable. Like I knew she would, she pulls me close. I stay there, closing my eyes and breathing in the scent of her—detergent, a simple, floral perfume, and something sweet like cookies or cake, perhaps she and Kaia baked. I try not to think of the strange and disturbing scenes at Alison's house, but I can't protect myself from the image of her sitting completely still on the floor, covered in blood and glass, just staring emptily out in front of her.

"Nothing," I say. "Just . . . I feel really tired. Overwhelmed, I guess."

"What did that lady think of the drawings?"

"I think she really liked them. Just . . . She's a little, I don't know . . ." Noa raises an eyebrow, and I want to continue, but I don't know what to say.

"A little what?"

"I can't really explain it. She just seems a little dazed. I mean, she clearly has this amazing life—you should have seen her house. Views across the city, all modern and sleek. I've never been to a house like it before."

"Why would you think she has an amazing life just because her house is all perfect?" This is typical Noa—always trying to second-guess what I'm saying, trying to catch me out as this shallow, twisted person. I exhale and sit down in the green chair, kicking my slippers off and undoing my hair.

"Never mind," I say. "I'm getting in the shower."

"I'm off to bed. My flight's at ten in the morning."

I scrub the skin on my arms and legs hard with the wiry side of a sponge, and let new tears run with the rushing water. It felt nice to talk to Alison about the changes in Kaia; sometimes it really does help to speak with a stranger. But there is something about her that unsettles me. She mentioned that she used to write features from all over the world; maybe she misses that kind of life. There is something fascinating about her, too; she's so intense, and clearly someone who would have a lot of stories to tell. I'd like to hear her stories, and could see us being friends, but can't imagine she'd find me very interesting, though she did seem interested in hearing about Kaia—maybe she was just being polite.

I think about Kaia sleeping in the next room, her new heart lumbering on, beneath all the scars. Again, I wonder what they did with the other heart, the one she was born with, the broken one. Most likely they incinerate the hearts and lungs and livers and kidneys that don't work anymore. It makes me sad to think of all biological trace of it being gone, but what would I have done with it? Buried it? Could it be that something of Kaia has gone with it? Could it really be that cells hold something that can be transferred to others? That memories and feelings are held not only in the brain, but also in the heart?

I switch off the shower and stand awhile in the steamy cubicle, a hand placed around my breast, over my heart. I imagine the thick veins and arteries anchoring it in my chest, the intricate chambers cleansing pool after pool of blood. I imagine it crumbling, cut open and torn apart, rotting and dried out. I'll be up tonight, alone with these thoughts, with my baby girl and Noa sleeping next door, with the images of Alison drenched in her own blood, with the new drawing I'm going to start on.

I sit at the kitchen table in the near dark. Two scented candles burn on the kitchen counter, sending flickering shadows up the walls. I begin to draw, and it comes easily to me tonight. Hearts again; I sketch the outline of two halves of an anatomical heart, in cross section, leaving a space open in the middle. I Google images of hearts for a while on my phone, making sure I get all the details right in the drawing; the soft curves of the semilunar valves, the pulmonary veins and arteries breaking off into thin air like snapped twigs, the thick bend of the aortic arch like the neck of a swan. When I've finished, I sit awhile looking at the sketch. I get up and look through the cupboards. I feel like another glass of wine, and am sure I've got a bottle left over from Christmas somewhere.

I pour the deep red Malbec slowly, my hand steadying the wine-glass as though it may suddenly shatter in my hand.

I must have fallen asleep. When I wake, Kaia is sitting across from me, watching me.

"Hey, honey," I say, sitting up, disoriented. I can't have been asleep long; the candles are still burning, the sky is pitch-black. "How long have you been sitting there?"

"A long time. Four minutes, maybe." I smile at her and take her hand across the table.

"Where were you last night?"

"I went to see a friend."

Kaia nods thoughtfully. "Can I draw with you?"

"Honey, it's two o'clock in the morning . . ." I can't even think which day tomorrow is, then remember it's Tuesday and Kaia will need to get up for school. "Let's go to bed, sweetie."

"Just one drawing." She gazes intently at me, and I have to look away—the flickering candlelight is making her look eerie and dangerously gaunt. I swallow hard, and again I think about the strange changes in Kaia since her surgery in July, and my conversation with Alison.

"Okay," I say, sliding a thick piece of sketching paper across the table to her. "Just one." We sit in silence a long while, the only sound in the room that of the crayons sweeping across the paper.

"Was it that lady who came to the studio?" asks Kaia, her voice startling me.

"Uh, yes, actually. It was."

"Alison," she says.

"Yes. Alison."

"I loved her."

"You loved her? You mean *liked*, probably."

"No, I mean *loved*. I loved her. You said if you like someone very, very much, then that's love." Kaia has stopped drawing and is looking at me with something unfamiliar—defiance, or annoyance.

"Well," I say, laughing dismissively, "she is a really nice lady. What . . . What did you like the most about her?"

"Her eyes," says Kaia. "She had old eyes."

"Old eyes?"

"Yeah."

"What does that mean?"

Kaia shrugs, then theatrically stretches her arms toward the ceiling. A thin crack runs from the top of the window to the center of the ceiling, where it disappears into the plastic fitting of the overhead lamp. I blink a couple of times; I am so tired I can barely keep my eyes open, but inside, I feel a growing disquiet. Kaia stands up slowly. "I want to go to bed."

I nod and pull her toward me.

She pulls back slightly and looks at me. "I missed you."

"When?"

"When you went to see Alison."

"But you were asleep."

"I still missed you."

"But I bet you had fun with Noa."

Kaia doesn't react to this, just keeps looking at me. "Can you take me with you next time you see her?"

"I don't know that there will be a next time, sweetie. We don't know each other well."

"Oh." She scrunches her eyebrows together, as though this is a surprise.

"What did you mean about Alison having old eyes, Kaia?"

Her expression remains intense and serious, and though she is looking at me, she seems far away. "Nothing, maybe."

This makes me smile—Kaia has been saying "nothing, maybe" since she was tiny. I pick her up—she is still as short and slight as a five-year-old—and carry her over to the sofa bed. She falls asleep immediately, mouth dropping open, eyes chasing dreams beneath her eyelids, clenched fists falling open. I go back into the kitchen to double-check that I blew out both candles. On my way back to bed I glance at the kitchen table, at my drawing, and then at Kaia's. She's drawn bears again, in school this time, five of them sitting on little desks in front of a big teacher bear in the front. I find the bears with their round black eyes unnerving, and without thinking I grab both Kaia's drawing and my own and crush them into a tight ball in my hand.

37

ALISON

I couldn't sleep. This is hardly a new thing, but even after I took temazepam I kept jerking into an alert, raw kind of consciousness, interspersed with periods of fitful rest. I finally fell asleep when the night sky was weakening into a pale gray. My first thought when I woke again just after ten this morning was how strangely I behaved toward Iselin. She's just a kid, and she came all the way here when I asked her to, even though it might have struck her as odd. I should have unwrapped both of the drawings, calmly admired them, and shown her where they would hang. I should have had a glass of wine with her and told her some of the old stories from when I was traipsing around Thailand instead of encouraging a dangerous conversation about cellular memory and heart transplants. It must have been a crazy turn, to strike up contact with Iselin and Kaia in the first place, and now I need to stay away. But I'm not sure I can. Because more than I need to stay away, I need to stay close to that which remains of my daughter, held inside Kaia.

My second thought is how badly my hand hurts—could I have severed something important? I hold my bandaged hand up to the shaft of light coming in through the gap in the curtains; it's soaked through with blood, and sitting up, I realize that the bed, too, is covered in long, brown streaks of dried blood.

I go downstairs, and in the daylight, it's obvious I missed more than a few places when cleaning up last night. There are splatters of blood or wine alongside the base of the sofa, and tiny shards of glass I've missed catch the sunlight, twinkling like stones in a river. I stand by the sink and unwind the red-brown gauze bandage. My uncovered right hand is swollen and blue all over, and the gash in the center of my palm produces fresh, black beads of blood when I gently flex my hand. I soak a cotton ball in iodine and place it over the wound, closing my eyes against the pain, then leave the cotton there before winding a new, long stream of gauze firmly around my hand. Then I get down on my hands and knees and run several moist pads over the floor.

I stand up and look out the window. An eerie mist is drifting out from the forest, lending the weak February sun a milky glow. I want to be out there, walking slowly into the forest without a plan, without going anywhere in particular. I open the door and take a couple of breaths of cold air. I feel sharp today, like I should do something other than sit at home. My phone vibrates in my back pocket: a text message from Sindre.

Hi honey, I tried to call you back last night but you didn't pick up. My dinner ran late. You okay? Looks like it would be really useful to stay another day—okay if I change my flight to tomorrow afternoon?

I take another couple of deep breaths, unsettled by how relieved I feel. I decide to go for a walk in the forest. But first, a phone call. It has just occurred to me how I might get Iselin to forgive me for my strange behavior.

"Hello?" Iselin picks up on the first ring. This isn't a thought-through conversation and at the sound of her voice I realize that I need to tread carefully here.

"Uh, hi," I say, softly. "Yeah. This is Alison. I wanted to apologize for last night."

"No need," says Iselin, though she sounds a little weary. "Are you okay?"

"Yes, absolutely. It wasn't half as bad as it looked. Just a cut. Anyway, listen. I was thinking about what you said, about wanting to work more. You're so talented—I just hung the drawings up this morning, and they really are just something else." I glance over at the cylinder still holding the drawings, and take a deep breath before continuing. "I used to work for *Dagbladet*, when I first came to Norway. And I've freelanced for pretty much everyone from *Aftenposten* to *VG* to *KK*. For the past three years, I've been features editor at *Speilet*. I'm . . . I'm taking some time out at the moment, to . . . to write a book. Maybe. Hopefully. But I . . . uh, I know a lot of people in the industry and good illustrators are always in demand. Would it be helpful if I, say, sent a couple of e-mails to some editors I know with a link to your work?"

Iselin draws sharply at the air, hesitates awhile before she speaks. "I . . . Well, that would be amazing . . . But . . ."

"Great!"

"But don't feel like you have to . . ."

"I don't, at all. I just figured I might be able to help. Seriously, if you need some pointers, I'd be happy to sit down over a coffee and talk about it some more. Sometime. If you want." I realize I'm holding my breath, like a teenager asking her crush out.

"Sure," says Iselin, after a slight pause. "I mean, thank you."

"Hey, I remember being young and starting out and there were so many things I wish someone had told me. And it doesn't hurt to come recommended. Besides, it was fun last night, until my little freak accident. I enjoyed speaking with you."

"I did, too," says Iselin.

"My stepson has a little horse and I check on it a couple of times a week. I have to go see to it tomorrow afternoon. It's in Sørkedalen, so not all that far from you guys. Would you want to meet for a walk or something after? I could bring a couple of my articles—I'll see if I can find some from back in the day that were illustrated by Sami Haley. I love her work—she reminds me a bit of you."

"Sami Haley . . . Oh, wow. Yeah, that sounds great." Iselin's voice is excited and gushing now. From Frognerseteren to Fresno, flattery never fails. "I have to pick Kaia up at three, but could meet before that, like maybe one thirty? A walk would be nice. I don't get nearly enough fresh air . . ."

I walk fast through the forest, drawing in icy air, holding my injured hand close to my chest. At the top of the long hill behind our house, I turn right where the track separates, toward Oslo Vinterpark. I stand awhile by the ski lift at the bottom of the run, watching the chairlifts pass, mostly empty. A little girl comes down the beginner's slope, held between her mother's legs, plowing hard, and there is something about her posture and height that reminds me of Amalie. I squint toward them and finally get a clear view of the girl's face as she lifts her ski goggles and lines up for the chairlift. It really is her. Honey-blond hair, almond eyes, pink, full lips. I blink hard and begin to walk toward them but they are nearing the front of the line, scanning their lift passes to get through the barriers, moving slowly toward the pickup spot.

"Hey," I scream, and a couple of other people waiting turn around. I come up behind where they are standing just as the lift arrives. A man holds it in place for a moment so they can get on, and Amalie expertly places her ski sticks between her legs.

"Hey," I scream again, and the girl turns toward me, but then, her face crumbles and blurs like a mirage and I realize she doesn't have brown, almond eyes at all, but blue, cold ones, rather, and an upturned nose. What I thought was honey-blond hair is the beige lining of her ski helmet, and emerging from it are strands of limp, dark brown hair. It's not Amalie, it's Kaia, and I scream *no, no, no* as the lift surges off the ground, and I run after it, scrambling over the barriers, but someone grabs me and says *hey, no, stop, lady what are you doing, hey.* The little stranger, who looks nothing like Amalie or Kaia, stares down at me from the lift with beady, blank, bird eyes and I hear a rising cacophony of voices around me, but I'm kneeling on the tightly prepped snow with my eyes closed, saying *I'm sorry, just a misunderstanding, sorry, sorry.*

At home, I drink tea with two tranquilizers. I unwind my bandage and pick at the still-fresh gash, making it bleed again, running my hand through my hair, and I just let myself cry and cry until the sky is dusky and velvet and long shadows spill across the floor. I pick up my phone and stare at my vague reflection in its screen, a haunted, twisted grimace etched across my face, and wonder who I could call. Sindre won't talk about her. My mother doesn't remember her, or anything at all now; she spends her days staring out the window of the old-age home at the empty, ocher desert sands, talking and laughing to herself. Oliver is just a kid and I can't expect him to carry me, it isn't fair. I open my mouth and just let my voice loose in the hushed air of the living room

I don't have anybody to talk to but you. You can't carry me, either, but you're going to have to. I need another sign. A sign, baby bear.

Karen Fritz said I should go to a grief support group, where I could sit around with others like myself: ex-mothers, angel parents, the bleeding-to-deaths. I could talk about her there, and people would listen; I could talk about the bears she draws, the way she never stops swinging her legs underneath the table, how she stares into Misty's eyes and the old horse falls as still as if Amalie had cast a spell on her. The ex-mothers would listen and cry and that's what I don't want, for her memory to always be steeped in sadness, for any mention of her to prompt tears. I want to speak about her and say that she is funny and silly and that even when she was little, she'd laugh gleefully at any unexpectedly comic occurrence. I never want to use the past tense about my baby, not ever. I want Sindre to see her the way I do, I want him to talk about her and laugh a little, I want to talk and talk and talk until my words restore everything she ever did, until I have rebuilt her, not leaving out even a single little freckle or scar or expression. But I don't have anyone to talk to.

38

ALISON

I'm on my way out when the phone rings. I let it go to voice mail and Karen Fritz's voice fills the room. It is the voice of a person trying to talk another off a bridge, and the familiar gentleness of it makes me linger for a moment, my hand on the door handle.

"Alison. Ali. It's me, Karen. If you can hear me, please pick up. Today was the seventh session you've missed. I am very concerned for you. Please call me back anytime. If it's too difficult for you to come to me, I will come to you. Alison. Are you there?"

I step outside and close the door. It's snowing heavily, and thick wet flakes cover my hair as I rush across the courtyard to the car.

I run a red light down by Røa, not on purpose, but because I was driving too fast and didn't realize it was red before I was already going through it. A car making a right turn has to brake hard, skidding on the snow and veering into the oncoming traffic lane. Thankfully it's empty, but I pull over as soon as I can, wheels sinking into pristine, new snow in someone's driveway. I pull the slide for the mirror cover back, the little light snaps on, and I stare at myself hard. Still here. Fleshy, dry skin has gathered at the corners of my eyes, dragging them down and giving me a look of permanent exhaustion. My face is very pale, and my cheeks have sunk beneath a protruding ridge of bone, making me look ill. My hair hasn't been colored since the end of May, and is pulled harshly back in a greasy ponytail, streaked through with gray. I am a little shocked at just how bad I look—I am forty-four years old but I have aged a decade in six months.

I try to recapture the memory of how I used to look, when I was a teenager in California. I remember that all my colors seemed to pick up warm, golden tones—my naturally highlighted hair from hours of surfing and running on the beach, my bronze skin, and the honey flecks in my eyes. I must have looked like the archetypal California girl. And now, this gray, crumbling shell of a woman. I open the door and step outside. I take a couple of steps forward, then place my feet about a foot apart in the snow before stepping back into my own footsteps so it looks like someone just dissolved into thin air.

"You are supposed to be here."

I look around to see who spoke, but there is nobody there, just the slow crawl of traffic toward Holmenkollen in one direction and Ullern in the other, the blur of heavy snow against a somber, fading sky. I heard the words, as clearly as I hear the wet crunch of metal-studded wheels gliding through thick snow, as clearly as the rumble of the T-bane speeding away in the distance. *You are supposed to be here.* Did it come from inside myself? My heart begins to race, and I get back in the car and switch on the ignition. I catch my own eye again, unguarded this time, and this moment feels pivotal in the intense empathy I feel for the woman looking back at me. *I am going to teach you how to live again*, I think, mouthing the words without a sound.

I am not going to give in to tears, not now. I am not going to be sucked down into the darkest corners of my mind and heart, not now. I am going to go to Misty, and then I am going to meet Iselin. I've decided to do whatever I can to help them—no matter that we are bound together by the strange circumstances of the heart transplant—I genuinely want Kaia to grow up in stable, comfortable surroundings with a mother who has some support. And I could be that support. Meeting Kaia has planted something inside me—an urge to see her again, to be close to her, to help her. I *need* to help her to help myself. I inch the car back onto the road, and before pushing the mirror holder back, I give myself one last, reassuring gaze.

Long gentle strokes with my uninjured hand, but still, Misty is restless. Her wide, wise eyes stare at the ground, ears sharp and alert. I brush her for a long while, then I cling to her mane, drawing her scent deep into my lungs. I change her water even though it was clean. I stand for a while, just watching her. She's different from before; it is as though a kind of lethargy has settled on the little horse, slowing her movements. Perhaps it's age—she'll be sixteen this summer. She was a feisty little thing when Amalie first rode her, her tiny body bobbing around in the saddle like a rag doll as Misty waddled about the track.

"Bye," I whisper, and turn around to leave, but Oliver is standing there. A girl is with him.

"Oh, hi, Oliver," I say. He looks nervous and not particularly happy to see me. I imagine he is afraid I might say or do something embarrassing in front of his girlfriend. "What are you doing here?"

"Well, I come here sometimes. You know, after school."

"You do?"

"Yeah."

"I didn't know that. You must be Celine," I say, turning to the girl. She's tall and dark-haired, with fine bone structure and brown doe-like eyes, not unlike Misty's. I smile and she nods.

"I'm Alison, Oliver's stepmother."

"Um, yes. We met before. A couple of weeks ago? At your house."

I smile coolly and try to think back—wouldn't I have remembered meeting Oliver's girlfriend? "Oh, yes. Of course, I'm sorry. Nice to see you again, Celine." Walking away from them, I feel Oliver's gaze on me. A vague memory comes back to me; waking up on the sofa to the sound of someone talking to me, my mind blank with alcohol, going unsteadily upstairs, Oliver behind me, catching his eye in the mirror at the top of the stairs, bumping briefly into someone on my way into our bedroom—Celine. In the car, I run my hands through my hair, and this reminds me of last night, the desperation of those hours, drinking and sobbing and talking to Amalie, my blood-soaked hand streaking my hair a grotesque red-brown. I look in the rearview mirror and feel the same strength I felt earlier. *You are meant to be here*, I whisper, and hold my own gaze for a long while before turning the key in the ignition.

We don't walk far; it's too cold, and the snow falling bites at any skin left exposed. Circling Iselin and Kaia's nondescript suburban neighborhood of detached family houses and low-rise apartment buildings, I tell Iselin about my early years as a journalist.

"So you just left home and moved to Istanbul?"

"Yeah, pretty much. I'd been traveling around for a few years, making a living as a freelance translator, and occasionally selling travel articles, at one point selling bracelets on the beach in Bali, then Thailand. I started to write quite a bit for Lonely Planet at the time. At first from Istanbul, and then Kyrgyzstan. Then I returned to Europe, and started writing more and more features."

"That must have been so fascinating."

"It was incredible. I loved learning some of the languages, and getting to know the cultures. Especially Central Asia. And Thailand. It is just so beautiful, and the people, the landscapes, the food, all absolutely amazing."

"It must have been a real shock to your system."

"Yes and no . . . I grew up in Walnut Creek, in the San Francisco Bay Area. I guess you'd say it's pretty fancy. But I think, even as a kid, I knew it wasn't real life, you know? And I was always so curious about other places and cultures."

"Yeah. I was like that, too." Iselin glances at me and I like the unmistakable look of admiration on her face.

"Yeah? Where did you grow up, Iselin?"

"In Nordland. In the most underwhelming place you can possibly imagine. I mean, it was beautiful, but there was always this sense that life was elsewhere, you know?"

"Oh, I know. Story of my life." We laugh a little, and I can tell I am winning Iselin over. We have come to a stop outside their apartment, having looped around the neighborhood, but it feels like she doesn't want our time together to end.

"I should go," I say. "I'm sure you need to pick up Kaia."

"You could come with me to get her if you wanted to and we can come back to ours for a coffee or something . . . If you have time, that is?"

"That sounds great," I say.

Iselin is twenty-six years old. I almost can't believe that she is the mother of a seven-year-old child and try to imagine myself in her shoes at that age. What if I'd had a kid with my high school boyfriend, Fred the Red, we used to call him, because of his thick, ginger hair. Would I have ended up there, in the scraggly hills of the Bay Area, living in a bungalow and raising red-haired kids who by now would be well into their twenties? I watch Iselin as we approach the school, how young and soft she is, and yet there is something hard there, beneath the surface. I wonder if she feels resentful. The thought of this makes me go cold—to think that any woman could resent being a mother. I want to grab her by the arm and make her look at me and shout *Cherish every second, because look at me. Look me in the eye.*

"Hey, Mamma," shouts Kaia, perched on the bottom rung of the red pyramid jungle gym in the playground. And then, "Hey, Alison!" I'm so surprised that she remembers my name that my mouth drops open. I keep my right hand close to my side and give her a little wave with my left. Kaia hops down easily and runs over to us, throwing herself into Iselin's arms and immediately retracting her legs, like an airplane pulling its landing gear up after takeoff, so Iselin is holding up her full weight. She looks cheekily over at me, and I notice that her bandage has been removed, leaving a fresh, puckered little scar.

"Hi there," I say. "What a cool playground you guys have here."

"Yeah." Kaia comes over to me and gives me a quick, surprising little hug.

"What is that *smell*?" asks Kaia, nestling her face at my waist.

"Kaia!" says Iselin. "Don't be rude!"

"It's . . . uh, from our horse," I say. "Misty."

"You have a horse?" Kaia's already big eyes swell.

"Yeah. Someone else takes care of it a lot of the time, but yeah."

"Why does somebody else take care of it?"

"Because, well, because I don't have time to go see it every day."

"Because you're a journalist!"

I smile at this. "I am, yes. But I'm not working that much right now. I'm . . . taking some time out." I pause, still focusing on maintaining a calm, controlled composure. "I am going to start working again soon, though. Writing and stuff."

Kaia tightens her brow into a frown, and it occurs to me that she of course has no idea what I'm talking about. "My mamma doesn't work."

"Kaia . . ." says Iselin.

"Your mom does work," I say. "She's a very talented artist."

"That's not a job."

"Of course it is," I say, giving Iselin a reassuring glance. Kaia runs ahead of us the last few meters to the apartment, then turns around at the door and beams at us. I notice how pale she looks, how short she is for her age. How must it have felt for a small child to know she was likely to die? Amalie had no concept of danger, or of death. Sindre and I created a dreamy bubble around her, trying to make ourselves believe that nothing bad could ever happen to her. I swallow hard and give Kaia a weak smile as she leads me into her home.

Kaia pulls me over to a slouchy, moss-green armchair with a tear partially covered by a fluffy cushion, and perches on the armrest, but Iselin gently leads her over to a blue-and-white stripy sofa across from me and puts an arm around her, as though she might otherwise rise up and away like a balloon. I glance around the apartment, overcome with the strange situation. The living room is small and quite cluttered, with shoe boxes overflowing with paper pushed underneath the sofa, dolls staring hard at us from a storage box by the window, bits of Lego studding the carpet. I wonder what Amalie would have made of this stuffy, messy space. I just can't picture her here, sitting by the toy box, pulling out random plastic pieces and starting to put them together.

"If I had a horse, I would go and see it every day," says Kaia.

"I bet you would," I say softly, letting the fragrant steam from the green tea Iselin has made rise into my face.

"What's his name again?"

"She's a girl. Her name is Misty."

"Misty! I like Misty!"

I smile and let my eyes discreetly travel around the room. Through the half-open door leading to what I presume is the only bedroom, I see a pile of clothes on the floor. I feel a profound pity for Kaia, and for Iselin, living in this cramped apartment, most likely originally built as basement storage for the house owners. It's freezing, too, frost gathering along the window frames, the floor shockingly chilled. For a moment, I wish I could take them home with me, and let them live with me and Sindre in Ullveien. I imagine Kaia, playing quietly at Amalie's desk, Iselin in the kitchen, unloading the dishwasher, chatting to Oliver. A dull ache spreads out in my stomach at this impossible fantasy and I stand up.

"Are you okay, Alison?" asks Iselin. I breathe in deeply, thinking of the peaceful moments in the stables with Misty's chunky little body standing close to me, and feel instantly more centered. *You are meant to be here.* Here, in the world, but not *here, in this house*, with this little girl and her mother.

"Yes," I whisper, and clear my throat. "Can I use your bathroom?"

I quickly grab my tranquilizers from my jacket pocket and then I sit on the closed toilet and swallow two dry. I focus on keeping my breathing deep and even. I try to separate the thoughts and emotions spinning through my head—just being around Kaia makes me feel like my insides are turning hot and liquid. If Sindre knew where I am in this moment, he would most likely have me sectioned. This must be what it's like to go crazy. To think one thing, knowing with every cell in your brain what is right and what isn't, and then doing the complete opposite. Because your heart tells you to. But hearts can't talk.

Yes, they can.

It is as if the words are spoken inside my head. I search for the image of my husband—thinking of Sindre always used to center me, but not anymore. I can't entirely bring his face into focus in my mind. I feel a strange sensation, but my mind is too fuzzy with this whole situation to properly analyze what it means. Geneva. He's in Geneva again. I don't know where he is staying, or who he has gone there with. He told me, he always does, but I didn't listen. There is no way for me to find out if he even told me the truth; maybe there is no conference, maybe he didn't go there with one of the guys from Maxicurity, but with Mia, whoever she is. The way he once told Monica he was going one place, and then went another with me. And does it even matter? I find it so hard to feel anything at all.

My mind, it's slipping. I can't separate one thought from another. I can't allow myself to lose hold of my thoughts, letting my mind charge off. *It isn't real, Ali. Your mind is running wild.* I try to summon Karen's face to mind, but it won't come. I vaguely recall that she called earlier today, leaving another voice message. Ali, are you there? she'd said, as though she really cared, as though she wasn't just paid to worry. If you can't come to me, I will come to you. But what would Karen do if she could see me in this moment, popping pills and muttering to myself, sitting on the closed lid of a tiny, cramped toilet in Østerås? She'd be afraid of me and what I might be capable of. I am, too. Because where can this go? What good could possibly come from this contact with Kaia? I should make an excuse to leave, then use my contact network to give Iselin a little boost, perhaps follow her from afar on Instagram. And yet, I feel so deeply that I *need* Kaia—it is as though she radiates solace, that she is a tiny island in this ferocious ocean of grief, that she is the only thing I can cling to.

I turn on the tap and scour my mind for a plan, some way to keep this fragile connection going. And then it comes to me. Risky, and perhaps immoral, but still, a plan. I need to stay close.

"Hey, Kaia," I say, sitting back down across from her, catching the child's eye and fixing her with my gaze. Right now, inside her, Amalie's heart dutifully powers this girl. My girl. "Have you ever skied?"

39

ALISON

It's nearly five o'clock and pitch-dark when I drive down to the bus station at the bottom of the hill. It has been snowing heavily all day, but now it's let up, leaving a crisp and silent early evening. I marvel at a long streak of white stars in the sky; so much brighter here, away from the lights of the city. The snowplows have not yet reached this part of Norefjell, and my 4x4 struggles to get through the loose, thick snow in places. I pass Ole's Kiosk, the boarded-up kebab shop, the Shell station, the children's ski lift where Amalie learned to ski. It's still running, slowly pulling little padded bodies up the hill on T-bars, huge floodlights casting their orange glow on the snow. I take my foot off the accelerator for a moment and watch them. It feels like the middle of the night and it's strange to watch the tiny figures meandering expertly through the blue and red gates.

At the end of the road is a lay-by and the bus is just driving away from it as I pull up. On the curb, I can make out the shapes of two people waiting. Kaia is holding a red backpack in front of her, a tatty cat toy peering out from it. She is staring down at the ground, making shapes in the fresh snow with her boot. She's wearing the same purple down jacket and hat she wore the first time I ever saw her, at her school. My mind goes to the awful moments after she was flung from the sledge, when all I wanted was to rush to her and calm her racing heart, but couldn't. I swallow hard and smile widely as Kaia looks up from the ground, my car's headlights sweeping across her face as I come to a stop. Iselin smiles nervously.

"Oh, hi," she says as I step out of the car, engine still running, spewing frosty bursts of exhaust into the air. "Thank you so much for coming to get us."

"Of course. No problem," I say, hugging her briefly, then Kaia, who offers herself to me to be hugged, but doesn't close her arms around me. "Were you guys okay getting here on the bus?"

"Yeah, it wasn't far at all, really."

"That's one of the reasons we chose Norefjell," I say, driving slowly back down the quiet main street. "It's so close to Oslo and we really didn't want to spend hours in the car every time we wanted to go to the cabin, you know?" Iselin nods, and I glance at Kaia in the rearview mirror, her blue eyes shining, taking in the exciting new place and the sight of the children rushing down the gentle slope.

"How long have you had your cabin?" Iselin asks. I like how she always attempts to fill a silence. I'm just not able to do it anymore, but I appreciate it in others.

"I guess it's five years now. The kids, uh, Oliver was about nine when we bought it." I don't think Iselin noticed my slip. Amalie was a baby the first time we came here. I spent two weeks over Christmas and New Year on the big blue sofa by the fire, just gazing at her soft baby face, learning her features, responding to her every need, holding her tiny hand as she slept. Iselin says something, but my mind feels thick and disoriented again.

"What?" I say, turning to her, smiling carefully.

"It's green," she says, softly, and it takes me a moment to realize that she means the traffic light at the intersection. I nod, flick the indicator, and turn left, the wheels spinning several rounds before gaining traction.

"So, your son is—what?—fourteen, did you say?"

"Stepson," I say, keeping my voice neutral. "Yeah. Oliver recently turned fourteen. He's a great kid. At that age now, when, you know . . ." I trail off, my attention diverted again by the myriad bright stars above the snow-laden spruce trees on the last stretch of track before our cabin. I need to get it together or Iselin will think I'm completely unhinged. "Yeah. So, he's at that age when it's all about his friends. He lives with me and my husband every other week, which is great, but he's generally either out with friends or shut up in his room playing video games."

"Yeah," says Iselin, smiling kindly at me, then turning to look outside as I pull up in front of our little cabin, Blåkroken—the "blue nook." We called it that because of its beautifully carved indigo shutters. The cabin is only vaguely visible from the track, but I've left the lights on and the soft glow from the windows can be seen through the tall trees by the parking spot. It's not unusual to get snowed in up here, and when I think back to our first couple of winters here, which were much colder than the last few, I remember often waking up in a dull gray light, snow covering most of the windows. Sindre and Oliver would dig us out, both of them giddy and red-faced with excitement while Amalie and I played on the rug in front of the fire, the room slowly brightening as the boys cleared the snow. In my mind's eye her sweet baby face shimmering in the flickering light of the fire is as clear as if she were sitting in front of me now, little busy hands moving toys around, mouth pursed in concentration, fine blond infant hair sticking up at the back of her head still, from the pillow.

"Wow," says a voice, loudly piercing my thoughts. "It's so cute!" Kaia is trudging toward the cabin through deep snow; she doesn't use the path through the trees I cleared with a shovel before coming to pick them up.

"Over there, Kaia," I say, but my voice comes out barely a whisper, and it's too late anyway; Kaia is wading through snow up to her thighs, giggling loudly, and looking at her, I have to laugh, too. As we step into the warm cottage, the three of us are chattering and laughing like old friends and I feel briefly, powerfully, alive again.

"Your room is the second on the left," I say, and Kaia dashes off down the narrow hallway to explore, clapping her hands. I take Iselin's jacket and hang it in the wardrobe and we smile at each other at the sound of Kaia's excited voice from the bedroom I've put her in.

Blåkroken has three bedrooms: one for the kids, one for guests, and one for Sindre and myself. Kaia is in the kids' room, though I debated whether I could bear it. It's a narrow room with triple bunk beds built into the wall. Oliver always sleeps at the top, directly underneath the ceiling; I imagine Kaia might, too. During the day, Amalie liked to play up there, drawing the bunk's blue-and-white-checked curtains shut, cocooned in the cozy space, a world all her own, chatting away to her dolls. I force my mind away.

"You're in here," I say to Iselin, showing her the guest room with its rounded timber walls and deep sleigh bed. At the foot of the bed is the skin of a brown bear, shot by Sindre's father in Trysil.

"It's lovely," she says, walking over to the window that overlooks the valley. It *is* a lovely room, the nicest of the cabin's bedrooms—Sindre and I wanted the guest room completed first, but then never really got around to putting the finishing touches to our own bedroom.

"I'll let you get settled in," I say.

In the kitchen, I open a bottle of Barolo I find on the wine rack. I think it's one of Sindre's expensive ones, and that suits me fine—I want Iselin to feel spoiled. And I want to impress her. I swirl it around in my glass, drawing in its peppery richness and intense black-cherry hue. When I look up I suddenly notice that Kaia is sitting on the long wooden bench that runs alongside the kitchen windows, a pen held suspended over a blank sheet of paper, staring at me.

"Oh, hi, Kaia," I say, my heart hammering. "You startled me." She says nothing, just keeps looking at me, and her cool blue gaze makes me irrationally nervous. "Hey, so, do you like board games?" Kaia stares at me blankly.

"Where's your girl?" she asks. I freeze, my hand tightening around the fragile wineglass. I remember what happened the last time—my hand still aches from it—and put the glass down on the counter before turning away from her. My heart is lurching in my chest, my nails digging into my palms. I pretend to look for something in the cupboard above the sink, taking several deep breaths before turning back around.

"I have a boy, Kaia. Oliver. My stepson." My voice is barely a whisper.

"You don't have a girl?"

"No," I say, my heart aching. My eyes drop to the bloodred wine in the glass. I pick it up again and take a long glug, closing my eyes against the tears I can feel rising.

"But . . . But whose is that?" I follow Kaia's pointed finger to the top shelf next to the fireplace in the adjoining living room. One of Amalie's Barbies sits in between two empty vases. I thought I'd

removed every trace of her before Iselin and Kaia's arrival: two boxes
of toys and clothes shoved into the attic space, her short wooden bed
that stood at the bottom of Sindre's and my bed—dismantled and
placed on top of the boxes. I lay on our bed, afterward, staring at the
swirls in the wood of the ceiling until the sky faded to a light purple.

"Oh, that," I say, forcing a shrill, merry laugh, dashing across
the room for it. I remember this particular one; it's the one whose
hair Amalie hacked off with nail scissors in the bathtub; I raised my
voice at her because of it. I remember her wet, sad face, the plastic
Barbie hair floating on the soapy water around her. *I'll never buy
you another toy if you're going to destroy them*, I'd said, angrily hauling her from the tub by a thin, slippery arm. I run my finger across
the doll's blunt bob now, regret so fierce it takes my breath away.

"Can I play with it?" asks Kaia. I turn toward her again, and
perhaps she notices something in my expression because her eyes
drop to the piece of paper on the table in front of her and she begins
to draw a long, shaky line. I open my mouth to say *No. No, Kaia,
you can't play with it, it isn't yours to play with. It's Amalie's. Just like
the heart beating inside you. It's Amalie's. It doesn't belong to you and
it never will.* No words emerge, and then Iselin walks into the
room, face open and unprepared for the tense atmosphere. I don't
want her to sense it. I *have* to keep her from finding out who I am,
or this all makes me look completely insane.

"Here," I say, and place the Barbie on the table in front of Kaia,
smiling at her. "A friend's daughter forgot this here. Perhaps you'd
like to play with it?" Kaia stares at the doll, at her tatty yellow
dress, her outstretched arms, her empty, plastic smile, the crudely
chopped hair.

"That's okay," she says, returning her gaze to her drawing, which
by now has taken on the shape of this cabin, surrounded by towering trees and a moon with a smiley face. "I don't like Barbie."

"Kaia," says Iselin, "don't be rude. Since when do you not like Barbie?" Iselin gives me a slight eye roll and the well-known exasperated-mother expression and I smile as warmly as I can manage.

"It's okay," I say, picking the doll back up from the table. I place it in a kitchen drawer and pour Iselin a large glass of wine, which she takes eagerly. "How about a game of Yatzy?"

It's almost nine o'clock by the time Kaia goes off to bed, after several rounds of Yatzy and homemade *knekkebrød* crackers with brown cheese. She enjoyed the board games, her little face lit up, tiny body animated and buzzing with excitement, my heart swelling with a growing affection for this little stranger, along with something else, too; something darker.

Iselin is in the room with her for quite a while, and I can hear their murmuring voices and occasional muffled laughter from where I'm sitting by the fire. I finally managed to get the fire going after trying for half an hour; it occurred to me how I've never come here without Sindre before. My mind is pleasantly foggy with the wine and I stare into the curling, snapping flames. My phone vibrates in my pocket, first once, then immediately again. I fish it out and glance at the neon screen, so out of place in this haven of roaring fires, ancient woods, and deep snow.

Landed, reads the first message from Sindre. And then: **I've missed you. Home in 45. Sx**

I try to think, but my mind feels slippery and murky. It's Thursday. He said in his last message that he needed to extend his stay in Geneva. Didn't he? I wonder what he will make of Iselin's drawings—I got them framed the day before I left and hung them in the living room. I'd thought I would get the chance to gently prepare him for the sight, but now he will get there before I do. Although, knowing my husband, he might not even realize they weren't there before. I decide to say nothing.

Hi honey, I write back. **Thought you were gone another couple of days—I've gone up to Blåkroken. Lots of snow, back on Saturday.**

A moment later, my phone buzzes again.

Alone?

Yes, I write.

Is everything okay?

Better than in a long while, I reply. **Don't worry. A x**

"God, she can be so hard to put to bed sometimes," Iselin says, slumping into the sofa next to me just as I press send, reaching for her newly refilled wineglass.

"Yeah?"

"Yeah. She used to be so easy with bedtime. Probably because she was on so much medication. Anyway. All good now."

"Is she asleep?"

"Not quite, but she'll be out cold in a minute. She just loves it here."

"Aw, good. It is a great place for kids. She'll love it in the morning; she can jump off the roof and into the snowdrifts."

"Oh, wow. Yeah, she'll love that. It's crazy . . . Just a year ago, she would never have been able to do stuff like that, you know? She was literally slumped on the couch in front of the TV, or napping, most of the time. I prayed so hard that she would make it, that somehow she would be one of the lucky ones, and of course I'm over the moon that everything has gone so well. But it's like I can't quite get my head around it sometimes. Someone will suggest something Kaia could or should do, and I open my mouth to say the words I've said so many times—'Unfortunately Kaia can't.' But now she can."

"It must have been so hard, waiting."

"It was. It was just . . . inhumane . . . It felt more like we were waiting for death than for life, most of the time. Life just didn't seem like a realistic option."

"Just waiting for someone to die," I say, focusing hard on an unwavering, neutral voice.

"Exactly." We fall silent for a while, Iselin looking out the window next to the fireplace, framing a waning moon high in the inky sky.

"I prayed that someone would die," Iselin says. "It sounds so awful. But it's true. I'd never wish for anyone else's child to be taken away, but that's how desperate you become in that situation."

"I can only imagine," I say, but I can't imagine, I won't imagine. I hate her now. Did this woman somehow manifest what happened to Amalie by wishing so hard for someone to die? *People's thoughts don't influence what unfolds in life*, Karen Fritz says, but, really, what does she know? What do any of us know? I pick up my wineglass and stare into it, my face reflecting on its surface . . . I could smash it into her face, tearing flesh from bone. Or I could . . . *Stop it*, Ali, *stop it*. I need to keep a firm grasp on reality. Iselin doesn't speak again, seemingly comfortable in our prolonged silence now. I look at her sideways, and again, I'm struck by how very young she is— her skin has that plump, almost moist tautness to it that becomes so coveted in your thirties and forties. I need to find empathy for her, and mutual ground. I can only stay close to my baby if I stay close to this woman. I wonder what Iselin wants from me. Does she believe we could really be friends? I need her to believe that. Or is she merely after some help with her career?

"You know, I'm so glad you two came up," I say. "You deserve some time away. If you want to head over to the hotel and use the spa tomorrow, I'm happy to watch Kaia at the children's ski area." Iselin's face lights up and she smiles at the prospect of a couple of hours on her own, but then the smile fades a little, leaving a slightly nervous expression behind. She's probably worried about the cost. "We're members," I continue. "You're welcome to use it; it's totally free."

"God, that would be so lovely," she says. I refill her glass again and she bursts out laughing. "This is all so nice! I'm a bit drunk, though . . ."

"Nice feeling, isn't it?" I say, touching my glass to hers, and we both laugh. "Look at the moon," I continue. "It's going to snow again."

"How do you know?"

"See the reddish ring around it?"

"Yeah?"

"That means snow."

I was right. I wake in the middle of the night to go to the bathroom, and stop for a moment at my bedroom window. Flurries of snow churn on brisk bursts of wind charging up the mountainsides. For a moment, I consider going out there, standing in front of the cabin, barefoot and in my nightdress, every snowflake landing on my skin like a tiny stabbing blade. Instead, I pad down the hallway toward the bathroom, but as I pass Kaia's room, I pick out some strange sounds from the hushed, heavy silence. I shudder and move closer to the door. I'm not imagining things; Kaia seems to be crying, perhaps in her sleep. I glance down the hallway toward the guest bedroom, and stand completely still, listening. Not a sound, except the child's muffled wailing. Iselin is probably fast asleep; she was so drunk she slurred her words when she went to bed.

224 · ALEX DAHL

I open the door to Kaia's bedroom a crack and the sound intensifies.

"Kaia?" I whisper, but there's no answer, just indiscernible words interspersed with soft crying. I step into the room and pad softly over to the bunk beds. I stand on the lower one and peer into the top bunk, the soft glow of the outdoor oil lamp streaming in through a gap in the curtains. Kaia is tossing and turning, her brow studded with sweat, her little pale face twisted in anguish. *No*, she says, several times. *No. No.* And then, *Help me.* I feel entirely overcome by a fierce maternal protectiveness for the distressed child. I place my hand lightly on her forehead and still she does not open her eyes.

"Help me," she says again.

"Shhh," I whisper. I place my other hand on her hands, which are clasped tightly together against her chest. "Shhh, little sweetheart." She tenses slightly, and suddenly I can feel the thud of her heart against my fingertips. It's beating wildly, and she lets out another cry, louder now.

"The water!" she says, clearly. "The water! Help me!" I shake her firmly by her bony shoulders; she needs to wake up now, *now*, and finally she opens her eyes, wide and terrorized.

"Mamma!" she whispers, and bursts into tears. "Where's my mamma?"

"Shhh, sweetheart," I say. "You were having a nightmare. It was just a dream."

"I dreamed I—"

"Shhh!" I interrupt her.

"There was water everywhere. Black. Cold water. I was drowning. I couldn't breathe. It hurt so much. I'm afraid." Kaia scoots down to the bottom of the bunk, clambers down the ladder, and runs down the hallway to Iselin's room, crying loudly, but I'm unable to move. I stand for a long while listening to her wailing and Iselin's soft soothing voice filling the hiccupy gaps between sobs.

It wasn't like that. I know it. The water wasn't black. It wasn't cold, either. She could breathe but she no longer needed to. It was like swimming inside the sweetest, softest cloud. It was like dancing in the sky.

She wasn't afraid. I need to know that she wasn't afraid.

I stand by the window, looking out at the falling snow, like little shavings of heaven.

A sign, baby bear, I whisper. My eyes are closed and my fists are clenched. The harder I clench, the more clearly I can feel the throb of my pulse, and I know now that my sign was the strength of Amalie's heart beating when I touched Kaia. She's still with me.

40

ALISON

When I wake, it's still dark outside. I pick my phone out from under my pillow and squint at its bright screen: 8:30 A.M. I sit up and look around—it isn't actually still dark outside, but we're snowed in. Though it's always quiet up here at Blåkroken, this is a different kind of silence, like being sealed inside a box and submerged in water. My mind returns to Kaia's nightmare last night, how distressed she was, the impossible words she spoke. After she ran into Iselin's room, I spent several hours awake, trying to think about something other than what she'd said. Black water, cold, fear.

I unhook the metal clasps on the window and try to push it outward, but it won't budge. As the cabin is built on a steep slope, the bedrooms at the back of the house are much closer to the ground than the living room and kitchen at the front. I listen for signs of Iselin and Kaia as I walk down the narrow hall, but the house is entirely quiet. As I thought, the front of the house is much better, with snow rising less than halfway up the windows. I'll be able to get out through the terrace door and can then use a shovel to dig the front door clear. I remember something I forgot last night after all the wine.

I get my phone and dial the number of Norefjell Høyfjellshotell, whose brochure we keep in a kitchen drawer. I give the lady on the other end of the line my credit-card details and tell her that I wish to treat a guest to whatever she wants at the spa and to give her access to all facilities for the day. When I told Iselin that we had a membership at the hotel, that wasn't strictly true, though we use it a lot when we're here. After all those years praying for someone's kid to die, I'm sure she deserves a day at the spa.

After I hang up, my phone begins to vibrate in my hand. It's Sindre, but I don't want to speak to him just now; I want to be here, in this moment, at Blåkroken, with Iselin and Kaia, far removed from my life in Oslo with my husband. And without my daughter. I crack four eggs into a bowl and whisk them together with cream and pepper as several messages tick in, making the phone twitch and bleep on the counter. Sindre has an annoying tendency to send five messages when he could have said everything he wants to say in one.

Morning Baby. I heard on the radio that there's heavy snow in Norefjell?

Oliver and I thought we'd pop up.

Are you okay for food or should we stop in Noresund? Also, what's up with the new pictures? A little weird?

Call me. S x

I am so startled by Sindre's messages that I forget the bowl on the countertop behind me and I lean straight back, knocking it over, spilling its slimy, yellow contents across the counter, down the front of the kitchen cabinets and onto the floor.

"Goddammit," I hiss. I stab at the phone, trying to find Sindre's number in the call history, but my heart is racing and my fingers are slick with the eggy mess. I have to call twice before he picks up, sounding flustered.

"Oh, hi, honey," he says, and the sound of his voice makes me suddenly yearn for him, for the safety and comfort of being held tight in his arms. What am I doing?

"Hi," I whisper.

"You okay, Ali?"

"Yeah."

"Did you see my message? I'm just grabbing a few bits and pieces, and then I thought we'd hop in the car and join you. Oliver hasn't been up since last year. Thought we'd catch a few hours on the powder in the afternoon."

"Listen, I . . . I really need to be alone."

Sindre hesitates and I can't tell if he's annoyed or worried. "Ali, I haven't seen you all week. I've missed you."

"I miss you, too. I'm coming back down tomorrow, okay? I'd really just like a little time to think." Sindre falls silent again, and I know he's worried now. "Listen, don't worry, babe, okay? I actually feel vaguely like myself again. It was a beautiful night last night. I looked at the stars and cooked a nice meal and gave Blåkroken a much-needed clean. I just need to be alone here for a couple of days. I think it will give me the headspace to really start to pick myself up again, you know? Maybe even go back to work. Okay?"

"Okay," says my husband.

I hang up and turn back to the spilled eggs, but Kaia is standing there, right behind me.

"Oh!" I say. "You have to stop sneaking up on me," I say, ruffling her hair and smiling at her, but her face is serious. "You okay?" She nods slowly, and nothing in her expression betrays whether she understood that I just lied to my husband on the phone.

"I'm just going to tidy this up," I say. "Then, if you want, you and I could go outside and dig the front door clear of all the snow, what do you think?"

Slight nod.

"Is your mom still asleep?"

Slight nod.

"Where's the man?"

"Which man?"

"Your man."

"Oh, you mean Sindre."

Slight nod.

"He's at home. In Oslo. He was working, so he couldn't come to the mountain."

"Oh."

"Is he much taller than you?"

"Um, yes, he's pretty big. Yeah, he's quite a bit taller than me," I say, rinsing the egg-stained cloth under scalding water, avoiding Kaia's serious and unnerving little face. "Why?"

"I just thought he looked like a giant in the drawing."

"Which drawing?"

"There's a drawing taped to the ceiling of the bunk I slept on."

"What? Show me!" I try to control my tone of voice, but it comes out shriller than I intended and Kaia looks at me warily.

"You can only see it when you lie down. I guess the big boy drew it." I walk her into the kids' bedroom and climb up to the top bunk, and there it is—a drawing in Amalie's hand I've never seen before. It is painstakingly sketched, but clearly the work of a very young child. She has drawn a sharp, pointy mountain and on the left side of it is me and Sindre—me a tiny little lady next to Sindre's gargantuan shape. On the right side of the mountain she's drawn Oliver and herself, smiling merrily, holding skis and sticks. I unpeel the drawing and climb back down without a word, leaving Kaia standing there.

"I'm cold," says Kaia, the moment she steps out of the car.

"You'll be fine," I say, sitting down inside the open boot, kicking my Uggs off, and then pushing my feet into my tight, clunky ski boots. Kaia has insisted that if she is going to try downhill skiing, I have to ski alongside her. "You won't feel the cold once we're up there." I smile encouragingly at her and we look up at the long, gentle slope and the mostly empty T-bars gliding up and around the turnstile, then down again. It's still early, but it's a beautiful day and half term, so soon the children's beginner run will inevitably be swarming with children much younger than Kaia.

In the ski rental shop, Kaia bounces excitedly up and down as we wait our turn. In Blåkroken's shed I have Amalie's brand-new skis and boots from last year, which she only got to use a couple of times, but I clearly couldn't have mentioned them, so here we are.

"How old are you, then, sweetheart?" asks the young woman behind the counter.

"Seven," says Kaia.

"Cool. What size shoes do you wear?"

"I don't know."

"Okay. What size shoes does your little nugget wear?" The young woman turns to me expectantly. Kaia and I exchange a brief glance and I open my mouth to say, *Actually, I'm not her mom*, but Kaia pulls her boot off and turns it upside down.

"It says number one!"

"Okay, great," says the girl, and walks over to the huge open shelves holding ski boots of every size. She picks out a purple metallic pair and Kaia's eyes light up.

"You like purple, huh?" I ask, awkwardly patting the top of her head.

"Yeah, it's my favorite color." The girl returns with the boots and a pair of short pink skis and a purple helmet. Kaia slips the helmet on, I help her with the boots, then we lock up our belongings and go back outside. I help Kaia slot the boots into the ski bindings and pull her by a ski stick toward the lift, slowly in my cumbersome gear. I turn back to look at her, and in that moment, I am overcome with a sense of profound déjà vu. How many times did I pull Amalie along, just like this, in this exact place? With the helmet and ski goggles on, Kaia could pass for my daughter. Even the wry little smile is similar. I stare at her and marvel at how, suddenly, it is as if some order has been restored, as if the universe has realigned itself—as if I have her back. I turn back around and keep sliding slowly toward the lift, a small, excited girl tugging at the stick, and underneath my ski goggles, my eyes are streaming.

Kaia loved it. After an hour or so, she was coming down the slope on her own, steering carefully around the padded penguins, snowmen, and monkeys placed on the run to practice turning. We came back to the cabin after a lunch of hot dogs from the slope-side barbecue, sitting side by side on the tightly prepped snow looking out over the valley down to Lake Krøderen far below. I almost didn't dare look at Kaia for fear of breaking the spell that had been cast. For the last run, we skied down together, holding hands as we set off, soon breaking apart, laughing, and it was the kind of laughter that isn't touched by despair. It was just happiness.

"When is my mamma coming back?" Kaia asks. She's sitting on the wooden bench by the window, drawing.

"Soon, I imagine. She's been up there for a good few hours now."

"Yeah. What is she doing?"

"Not sure exactly, sweetie. Probably relaxing in the sauna, getting a massage, stuff like that. It's good for your mom to have some time to herself to relax."

"Why?"

"Because it isn't easy to get much time to yourself when you're a mother." Kaia nods and seems to consider this. I take the milk, which has just begun to simmer, off the hob and pour it over chunks of chocolate in the two mugs on the counter. Mine is a plain blue mug, but I've given Kaia Amalie's favorite mug in the world—a faded yellow Disney Goofy mug with several chips along the rim. As I stir the hot drink I wait for the onslaught of pain that is sure to come by giving this mug to another little girl, but it doesn't happen; it feels okay and so I place it on the table in front of Kaia. She stares at it for several moments, turning it around and taking in Goofy, running a finger around his outline. Her eyebrows scrunch together in a frown and she rests her little index finger in the white hollow of a chip, and glances up at me. Will she complain that I gave her this battered old mug?

"Thank you," says Kaia. "I love this mug."

"Do you?" I whisper, looking away for a moment into my own drink, where swirls of chocolate pattern the surface.

"Yeah. I think I have one like it. Or a bit the same. I think Noa gave it to me."

"Noa?"

"Yeah, she's my aunt. She helps Mamma with me sometimes

because they're sisters and best friends and Noa loves me almost as much as Mamma does."

"Ah, that's nice," I say.

"Yeah. Noa lives in Paris and I've never been there. They speak French."

"Yes, they do."

"Have you been there?"

"I have. Many times. It's a long time ago now, though."

"I can't go on a plane 'cause I'm sick. No, I *was* sick. Not anymore. Maybe I can go on a plane now. My mom lived in Paris, too, before I was born, and she says if I wasn't always sick and if I didn't always have to see the doctors, we could have lived there and it would have been so great because my mom loves it there and didn't want to leave. She only left it because of me."

"Oh. Wow, well . . . I'm sure your mom is so happy that she got you, even if it made living in Paris difficult." Kaia shrugs, and stares into her mug again. I am overwhelmed by a feeling of protectiveness toward her; something tells me she hasn't always had her mother's full attention. Iselin is so young, so nervous-looking; it can't have been easy for her. And yet, none of that is Kaia's fault. Kaia deserves the best; a mother who truly sees her and who doesn't feel like looking after her is some kind of sacrifice.

"Yeah, but she's sad because she has to do everything for me." Kaia takes a long sip of her hot chocolate and smiles up at me unguardedly; clearly this is the kind of thing she has been told over and over, and being seven, she doesn't understand that a mother shouldn't speak like that to her child. I'm struck still by a vicious contempt. I try to think whether I ever said such things to Amalie, and I'm sure I didn't. I had my daughter at thirty-eight, when I was financially, and emotionally, secure. Perhaps I shouldn't judge Iselin, yet I just can't help but feel furious at the thought of Kaia being made to feel unwanted.

being made to feel unwanted. Again, I am gripped by a visceral need to protect her and help her. If I was Kaia's mother, I would give her everything.

"What do you want to do now?" I ask.

"You could read me a story?"

"I would, but I'm not actually sure we have any storybooks here. It's a long time since the kids, uh . . . since Oliver was little." The books are in the attic, lots of them; old favorites and new ones we never got around to reading. *The Gruffalo*, *Peppa Pig*, Nancy Drew.

"You could tell me a story."

"Hmm, not sure I'd be any good, Kaia. I don't know that many stories."

"Yeah, I guess only mommies know stories." Her words hit me so hard, right in the gut, and like the burning, it tears at my insides. I swallow hard. It isn't her fault. She's so little, and clearly disadvantaged. I need to go back to earlier, on the ski slope, when I felt like my world had somehow righted itself. When it felt like I could love Kaia the way mothers love their children; forever, unconditionally, wildly. When it felt like Amalie was just below the surface, held inside Kaia, mine again.

"Actually, sweetheart, I do know a story. It's a pretty good one, I think." Kaia lights up then lifts the yellow mug to her mouth, obscuring her face as she empties it. I walk over to the sofa by the unlit fire and pat the empty space next to me. Kaia comes over and sits down close to me. I place my arm on the back of the sofa behind her and she looks up at me expectantly.

"Okay, so this is the story of the most beautiful horse in the whole world." Kaia smiles and claps her hands together. "Once upon a time there was an Arab horse called Fuego. He was jet black, so black that not a single hair on his body held even a touch of brown or gray. In spite of his name, which means fire, Fuego was very gentle. He belonged to a little girl called Mestifanie, who was a princess in a country called Baravaya. She lived in a palace bigger than any city in Norway—a palace so big it covered an entire valley, surrounded by snowcapped mountains."

Kaia is fully enraptured, staring at me as I speak, snuggling into the crook of my arm. I close my eyes for a moment.

Hey, baby bear.

I continue telling the story I used to tell my girl. When it's finished Kaia nods and leans her head on my shoulder. We sit like that for a long while, and I wonder whether I should keep talking, embellishing on the story like I sometimes used to, for Amalie. Kaia's head is heavy against my shoulder, and as if by instinct, I raise my hand and gently stroke her soft hair. Outside, the sky is bruising pink, and daylight won't last another hour. Kaia exhales deeply a couple of times, then her breathing drops into a steady purr. She's fallen asleep. I stay where I am, stroking her hair, looking out at long streaks of indigo on the sky. Tomorrow we return to real life, and I'll have to let her go. But how? I want more. So much more.

"Mills," I whisper. Kaia stirs slightly, her head rolling forward, chin touching her chest. I very gently lay her back onto the sofa seat and she draws her legs up. I place a woolen blanket over her and sit in the twilight, watching its rise and fall. Then I move a little closer. I peel the blanket back slightly from underneath her chin and place my hand very gently just below her collarbone on the left.

"Mills," I whisper again, Amalie's nickname as dangerous as a shard of glass in my mouth, and feel the strong, steady thud of my baby's heart underneath my fingertips.

41

ISELIN

After the sauna and the eucalyptus steam room, I have a long, slow swim in the countercurrent pool. I then return to the sauna, feeling exhaustion drip off my body along with all the sweat. I almost can't believe that I'm here, in a fancy mountain resort, whiling away the day at the spa. Equally hard to believe is that Kaia is off skiing. My baby, who couldn't walk across the room last year, skiing. I smile to myself—I'm here alone and I don't have to be anywhere at all. I focus on my breath, counting to fifteen as I inhale, and twenty as I exhale. It's as though restlessness has become a part of me because I've always had to rush around, tending to Kaia, and I feel the urge to get up and do something. Just holding my thoughts feels unsettling, but I make myself do another fifty breaths, and then I can feel the tension let go and it's the most incredible feeling as my

THE HEART KEEPER · 237

mind goes still. I think of hearts and birds and snow-covered mountains and wine and laughter, and how much everything is changing. It's as though my girl and I are on a whole new path and everything is shiny and exciting.

Afterward, I feel almost as dazed as I did after giving birth. I stand at the vast windows in the reception and look out on the mountains. They are smooth, rounded mountains here in Norefjell, very different from the black, towering ones in Nordland, where I lived as a child. The sun is burning low and amber on the sky, but in less than an hour, it will be getting dark. I could go back to the cabin now and change into my ski pants, and perhaps I'd make it over to the slopes in time to catch sight of Kaia skiing. Or I could sit in the bar for an hour, just relishing this unexpected time to myself.

I order a vodka martini and play around on my phone. I check Snapchat, but nothing fun comes up. I check Instagram for new likes or inquiries from people who might want to buy a drawing, but there's nothing. I scroll through random jokes and Mummy Needs Wine memes and old schoolfriends' winter-break photos on Facebook, when it occurs to me that Alison and I aren't connected on any social media. Alison is in many ways the kind of woman I resent. She has the big house, the million-kroner car, the mountain cabin, and yet there is something that doesn't fit. She's not like other people I've met, and I like her. For someone who has everything, she seems so jittery and unhappy. I admit I'm curious. I open the Facebook app on my phone; she's quite old, so probably more likely to use Facebook regularly. I type in *Alison Miller-Juul* and there is only one match. Her profile has strict privacy settings, so all I can see are the two profile pictures she's made public.

In the first one, posted in June 2011, she is wearing a white tank top and cutoff denim shorts and is sitting atop a large boulder somewhere hot and dusty. The photo has had 125 likes but no comments.

I click on the likes but am redirected to her timeline, which is empty; her friend list is also set to private. The second profile picture is a professional head shot, taken against a black backdrop. I stare at the picture—I almost can't believe it's the same woman. She looks polished and kind of golden—the kind of woman who can go to the hairdresser when she wants to, who can get her teeth discreetly bleached, her clothes altered to fit perfectly. She's not exactly beautiful, but she has a face that you want to keep looking at, maybe because her eyes are really arresting. Deep brown, flecked with light, almost yellow, patches, slightly slanted. She looks like she could be part Asian or something, except for the glossy American hair.

Alison doesn't look anything like this now—nothing. Her hair is wild and graying, and I've only ever seen it scraped off her face in a tight bun. She wears loose, plain clothes that look like she's borrowed them from her stepson, and maybe she has. The picture was posted in May 2017 and has had 281 likes and forty-two comments. I still can't see the likes, but the comments are public, so I scroll through them and the first one says *Gorgeous Ali.* There's one saying *You are absolutely stunning!* Another says *My favorite globetrotter in the entire world.* The rest of the comments read much the same, and I'm not surprised—she really does look radiant. Then I get to the last two.

My thoughts and prayers are with you, darling Ali, posted on July 11 last year. And underneath it, one last comment, this one posted on July 24: *Ali, my heart breaks for you. We love you so much and are here for you when you are ready.* I stare at the picture for a while longer before returning to the timeline to double-check that she hasn't posted anything else public, but there's nothing. I finish the vodka martini and order another.

I close Facebook and catch up on news and gossip on kk.no instead, but again and again my thoughts return to the beautiful, groomed Alison in her profile picture, and those final comments underneath it. I feel bad for snooping, but everyone looks up the people they meet on social media, that's just how it is. Maybe one of her parents died; I guess she's at the age when that is fairly likely to happen. Yesterday she mentioned that her father had died, and I had the impression it was kind of recent. That must be it. She was probably really close to her father and is still overwhelmed by his death. Poor Alison.

I finish the second drink and stand up, slightly woozy from the effect of the alcohol. Suddenly I remember that Alison was one of the customers who first contacted me via Instagram. I sit back down, open the app, and search for her, and there she is; Alison Miller-Juul. Her profile is private, so I can't see anything at all. I send a follow request anyway, and gather my stuff together; I want to be back at the cabin with Alison and Kaia, maybe playing a board game, watching fresh snow scatter, drinking some wine and talking after Kaia falls asleep.

42

ALISON

I don't want Iselin to come back. I stand in the kitchen, stirring a pan of pasta sauce that Kaia and I have made together, chopping onions, garlic, and tomatoes side by side. I loved the feel of the busy little person next to me, and kept my eyes on her tiny fingers carefully holding the chopping knife, avoiding looking at her face and breaking the spell. Now I occasionally look up and smile at the little girl muttering to herself in a cacophony of different voices as she plays with the Barbie and a scraggly soft toy she's brought.

"Hey," says a bright voice, and it's Iselin standing in the kitchen doorway holding out a bottle of cava. "I meant to give this to you yesterday, but I forgot. Well, I got drunk on red wine, rather." We both laugh and I take the bottle from her and place it in the fridge.

"Thank you, sweetie, you didn't have to do that."

"I wanted to. Oh, Alison, I've just had the most wonderful day. In fact, I don't think I've had many days as nice as today. It just feels so lovely to be here. Thank you." Kaia looks up from where she's playing, and smiles at us. Iselin is right, it does feel lovely to be here together, the three of us. But it felt even better when it was just me and Kaia. Cooking together side by side. Nestled together in front of the fireplace, telling her a story. Sitting closely together on the ski lift, looking out at the white, barren mountains, laughing out loud into cold air.

Kaia has been asleep for a couple of hours and a screeching wind has started up outside, chasing scuds of loose snow against the rattling windowpanes. I top up Iselin's glass with the last of the cava. I've just told her some stories from when I lived in Istanbul, and when I traveled in Thailand, and she hung on to my every word, wide-eyed, like Kaia earlier when I told her the fairy tale.

"You're just so brave," says Iselin. "I mean, I'd just never . . . I can't even imagine . . ."

"Not brave," I say. "Stupid. Crazy, probably." We laugh a little. "So. Tell me about Paris."

"Paris?"

"Yeah. Kaia was telling me you used to live there."

"Yes. Yeah, my sister and I moved there after high school to study. Well, I say study—my sister dropped out of school to write music. Then she became a DJ. Worked out for her, though."

"Noa, right?"

"Yeah. It was Nora, but she changed it for her music career." She giggles at this.

I smile, too. "I see. Kaia tells me you're very close."

"Oh, yes. She's almost like a second mother for Kaia . . ." At this, I feel a surge of jealousy. "Where we grew up was so remote it would have taken me an hour to walk to the nearest neighbor, so as kids it was just us sisters, really. It wasn't until I started school that I played much with anyone other than Noa."

"Wow. I can't even imagine."

"She and I have always had a really special bond."

"What's she like?"

Iselin thinks about this for a while, and when she still hasn't said anything, I grab a new bottle of wine from the wine rack and uncork it. Her eyes light up as she begins to speak.

"She's . . . She's different. Incredibly talented. Like, she cowrote a song that went to number one in the U.S. And she's worked with a lot of very famous artists. She's a risk taker, never had a plan B, never let anything or anyone stand in her way."

"That's impressive."

"Yeah. It's incredible. And strange . . ."

"Strange?"

"Well . . . I think at one point it felt like I'd left her behind, especially when I had Kaia. She seemed like a kid by comparison, and I guess she was. But now, watching her becoming so successful, it's clear that, really, it's Noa leaving me behind." Iselin looks suddenly deeply dejected, and she hesitates, clearly wanting to say something else, but trying to decide whether she can trust me. I settle back on the sofa and focus on maintaining my most calm and inviting expression. "I guess it feels like she has everything, and I have nothing."

"But . . . You have Kaia," I say, fury rushing through me.

"Yeah," she says, and smiles a little, but she doesn't look convinced. "I adore her. Every little thing about her is magical and I am so grateful for her. It's just been so hard at times."

"It doesn't sound like you've had much help," I say, trying to find some empathy for her. Maybe I shouldn't judge her so harshly—any mother knows how hard raising children is, for all of us. Iselin shakes her head and is clearly struggling to hold back tears.

"No," she says.

"Do you . . . Are you in contact with Kaia's father?"

"No. We didn't know each other well." I nod and make a point of not meeting her eye; I want her to continue without feeling pressed. She doesn't. I close my eyes and listen to the sound of the flames spluttering in the hearth, and the wind roaring down the chimney. "His name was Yoann," Iselin says after such a long time I'd almost forgotten she was here. "He was a sweet boy, from the south somewhere. Kaia has his blue eyes. We met in a bar, and though we dated on and off for a while, it wasn't very serious. He was one of a couple of guys I'd been seeing since I'd arrived in Paris. I liked him, though. A lot. We laughed at all the same things. I used to draw him, sleeping. When I got pregnant, everything changed. We both agreed I needed to have an abortion. I was going to. Until the last possible moment. But I just couldn't do it." At this new information, I bring my eyes back to Iselin. How can I judge a girl only just out of her teens for terminating an unwanted pregnancy with a man she barely knew? How can I feel such sudden, ugly hatred for this anguished, tired girl? But I do.

"What made you change your mind?" I ask, keeping my voice level.

"I was at the clinic. All signed in. A nurse showed me into a room at the end of a long white corridor. It was just a simple room painted a light yellow, but I still remember it so clearly. I was alone. I watched minutes drag by, one after another, until twenty minutes had passed, and I wondered if it was intentional, to leave girls like me waiting in there for so long they gave up and walked out. I looked down at my hands and realized they were clasped together so hard the knuckles were white, and I shouldn't have looked because my mind went to the baby's hands; its pink, tiny, see-through hands digging into the walls of my womb.

"I tried to just remain calm, to think of it as something that just *had* to be done. I looked around the room in search of something to focus on, but still, all I could see was the baby's hands, and I could feel them, too, clawing at my insides. I began to cry, and I hardly even noticed. I wished Noa was there with me, but that was impossible; for the first time I had kept something from her. I kept wondering what Noa would have said if she had known what I was about to do. But she'd never know. I would just do it, and everything would stay the same. I wanted everything to stay the same—so badly.

"But maybe it was thinking about Noa that made me stand up, that made me push the door open and run past the doctor who was just arriving. My sister always says *Listen to your heart.* I'd never thought it was good advice; my heart had never made enough sound for me to hear it. But it did, then."

I'm staring at her now, and Iselin notices and looks briefly alarmed. "Anyway," she says, lightening her tone. "Life's funny, isn't it? We don't have the answers. We just have to do what we believe is right. I still wonder, sometimes, about what could have been, what I've missed out on. Yoann never spoke to me again. Noa was so disappointed. If my parents had known, they would probably have been pleased I'd fucked up. Though it's not like I let them know I'd dropped out of school to become a teenage mother."

I reach across and touch my hand against Iselin's. I try to imagine her in the abortion clinic waiting room, how miserable and afraid she must have been, but instead I see Kaia the way Iselin did; desperately trying to hold on to life with her tiny hands. I want to go into the room where she is asleep and press my head to her chest and hold those tiny hands in my own. Instead I focus on keeping my face calm and sympathetic.

"Haven't your parents offered you any support?"

"No." Iselin purses her mouth and breathes a little ripple onto the surface of her wine. I nod and wait for her to continue, and I must admit, I'm curious now. Wouldn't it have been nice for Kaia to have grandparents? It was such a source of sadness for me, that my parents were halfway across the world and already old when I finally had a baby. They did meet Amalie many times, but they never had that easy closeness of family living down the road from each other. I'm glad my father died before Amalie did, that he never knew. He left the world thinking that his child and grandchild would be okay, and there must be a certain peace in that. I feel a pang in my stomach at the thought of my parents, and how my whole early life as their cherished only child is now long over. I also feel sad for Iselin's parents and everything they are missing out on.

"My father's an old drunk, and my mother waits on him."

My parents made me feel like anything was possible. I can't even imagine what it must be like to grow up in a home where sadness clings to the walls. "I'm sorry. That must be very difficult. They must miss you, and Kaia," I say gently.

"They've never met her," she says, and there is something cool and dismissive in her tone of voice, "and they never will."

"I see," I say, and I don't push her now, because I sense that there are stories here that perhaps should not be told. I get up and bring the bottle over to refill our glasses. Iselin glances at the bottle, and I can tell she is trying to calm herself down.

"There's something I've been meaning to ask you," I say. "What inspires your drawings, would you say?" I want to deflect from thoughts of her family—I'm worried this has all been too much and Iselin might burst into tears, excuse herself, and go off to bed, when what I need is for us to get closer. She looks grateful for the respite and takes another sip of her wine.

"Um. I used to draw mostly people. I think I got tired of that because so much of the time, people only show you what they want to, and I wanted to draw something that was . . . wild."

"Wild?"

"Mmm. Uncontrollable." She laughs nervously, sips at her wine, rubs at a spot below her left ear. "So then I started drawing birds."

"Why birds?"

"Well, I love their freedom. I guess I've felt so trapped and stuck at times and maybe I was drawn to birds for their amazing freedom."

"I can relate to that," I say, and this is certainly true. I think of Karen Fritz's birds, and how every detail of that image is imprinted in my mind.

"When did you start drawing the hearts?"

"Last autumn. I just couldn't stop thinking about the surgery Kaia had undergone. It was like I couldn't move on. And then I realized that birds and hearts have a whole lot in common. Both are wild. Uncontrollable."

"Indeed."

"The heart wants what it wants," she continues, and looks at me intently, as if to figure out what it is *I* want. I finish my wine and stand up; now I want to wrap up here before the conversation gets too intense—the conversation has brought me close to tears. I rinse out the wineglasses in the sink and close my eyes for a moment, summoning Karen Fritz's birds to mind; up high, held by nothing but the salty breeze, little walnut hearts galloping inside feathered chests, the hazy curve of the horizon ahead, tiny specks of people below, locked inside their houses, chained to the earth.

Iselin has come over to the kitchen area and is standing close to me.

"How is your hand now?" she asks, and when I turn to look at her, a powerful moment passes between us, as though she senses something in me I might not have chosen to share. I open my palm and glance down at it. I no longer need a bandage, but the scar is vivid and ugly, curved in a jagged C, distorting my lifeline and covering most of my palm. Iselin gently takes my hand and tilts it slightly so it catches the light.

"Would you let me do something?" she asks. Her lips are stained a dark red from the wine and her eyes are searching mine. I feel like the power balance between us has suddenly turned, that Iselin is now in control, but there is something soothing about letting her hold my hand, looking at my wound unflinchingly. I nod. She walks quickly down the hallway and into the guest bedroom before returning with a soft, black leather pouch. She leads me back over to the sofa and unfolds the pouch, revealing a row of pens, meticulously arranged by the size of the tips. Iselin selects a blunt-tipped one and smiles mischievously. I feel strangely excited, like a teenager led astray by one of the popular girls, and in this moment I can't decide whether I like this woman or not. She takes my hand again and uncurls my fist. Then she presses the pen to my skin. It hurts a little and I close my eyes; the moment is so strange, and I am woozy with the alcohol. When I open them again, I am taken aback at the sheer skill of Iselin's pen. She has drawn the outline of a wing around the scar, working the raised, pink skin into it to illustrate realistic musculature. When my hand is relaxed, the wing appears broken, but when I stretch it out, it becomes elegant and whole, ready for flight, its feathery tips reaching the base of my little finger.

I curl and uncurl my hand a couple of times and we both just sit watching the wing. Then Iselin stands up and smiles at me, but there is sadness in her smile, and again, I feel like she has the ability to look straight into me. For a crazy moment I consider telling her everything: that my daughter's heart beats in her daughter's body, that I mean no harm, that following your heart can sometimes lead you to dangerous places.

"Thank you," I whisper. I raise my hand again, in a wave, a high five, a slap, a surrender.

"Good night," says Iselin, then disappears back down the hallway.

It's 2:00 A.M. but I can't sleep. Iselin and I both went unsteadily to bed, but the alcohol has worn off now and my mind feels tired but clear. I get up from the bed, a chill from the floorboards creeping up my ankles, and stand at the window, but there is nothing to look at on this side of the cabin, only mounds of snow shimmering in the moonlight. I stare at my reflection in the windowpane: my face is drawn and sunken, and my hair, which I always took great pride in, is scraggly and unkempt. Could I become me again, or will I remain this person for the rest of my life?

I lie back down on the bed and play a mind game I used to play when I was much younger—imagine yourself in five years. I will be forty-nine in five years. If I had another child, which would most likely not be possible, that child would be four years old. Amalie would have been ten years old. Ten is so very young and yet twice as old as my child will ever be. In five years, Kaia will be twelve. She will have grown into her slightly awkward looks by then, and will be a young woman with a healthy porcelain complexion and arresting, blue eyes older than her years might suggest. She'll still be wearing her hair braided, but in a cool teen style, down one side of her scalp. I see her sitting at the breakfast bar at my house, drawing, humming under her breath, smiling up at me occasionally. In this vision, I am chopping some vegetables; the quiet and inevitable tasks of a doting mother. I try to envision

Sindre and then Iselin, but no matter how hard I try, I can't summon them to mind.

In the morning, I wake with a bad headache. I take a couple of Advil and spend a long time in the bathroom, splashing cold water on my face. I'm dreading today: the drive back to Oslo, having to say goodbye to Kaia, not knowing when I will see her again, *if* I will see her at all. The thought of coming home to Sindre and Oliver, resuming the draining routine of our lives, feels impossible.

I stare at myself in the mirror, and the woman staring back is even worse-looking than the hazy reflection I studied in the window glass last night. I always thought I had nice eyes; they are almond shaped and green, and in pictures they seemed to carry a playful glow that is now entirely gone. The color looks different, too; they look dull, slick, like mud. My lips, which were never full, but even and rosy, are wrinkled and pale. Is this what a bad person looks like? I wonder. Do bad thoughts make you ugly? The thoughts I had last night were those of a bad person.

I look down at my hand and Iselin's drawing is still intact. I open and half close my hand over and over, watching the broken ligaments miraculously straighten themselves, then crumble again.

For most of the night I was lying wide-awake, trying to rid myself of the images of Kaia and me in the future, together like Amalie and I should have been. It wasn't the possibility of a continued closeness to Kaia that was so unnerving, it was the realization that I want her to myself. I'm no more capable of keeping up this charade with Iselin than I am capable of letting go of Amalie and her heart keeper. I don't think the game of "where do you see yourself in five years" was ever a game for anyone that played it—it was always a plan. Because who would say, "Oh, in five years, I might be dead from cancer." Or "In five years, my husband will have left me for a younger, better-looking woman." Or "In five years, I'll be unemployed and unsatisfied, drinking too much."

The heart wants what it wants, and we say what we want for ourselves.

And I want Kaia.

PART III

43

ISELIN

I guess coming home is always hard when you've seen for yourself what "home" means for some people. Kaia, too, seems to deflate like a balloon as we fling our duffel bags to the floor in the cramped hallway. The pretty, pure snow that fell in Norefjell became slushy ice as we reached the motorway at the bottom of the mountain, and dense rain as we neared Oslo. And now everything is as before. In the kitchen, the clean washing-up is where I left it by the side of the sink. In the bedroom, the covers are thrown back, the vague imprint of Kaia's head still on the pillow. In the living room, the sofa bed I sleep on is folded away but a piece of the bedsheet is poking out from underneath. Kaia's toys are scattered around, a couple of unfinished drawings are spread out on the floor next to the sofa,

254 · ALEX DAHL

balls of dust have gathered in corners. It feels like I'm seeing this cramped, messy apartment for the first time.

I settle Kaia in front of a cartoon and put on some macaroni with peas and ketchup for a late lunch. Waiting for the water to boil, I switch my phone back on—it's been switched off since last night when I ran out of battery and realized I hadn't brought my charger.

Besides the water bubbling in a kettle and the tinny voices from Kaia's cartoon, the apartment is entirely quiet. I wish Noa was here, or Alison. It felt so good to open up to her last night. I haven't really spoken to anyone about those things before. I think about the bird in Alison's hand. It was the strangest thing—when she showed me the scar I just knew exactly how I'd cover it to make it beautiful. There is something nurturing about Alison, like she wants someone to take care of. And at the same time, she seems totally skinless, like she could disintegrate at the touch of a hand.

One thing this weekend has shown me, is how lonely I am. Perhaps I should get back on Sukker or Tinder and try to meet someone Kaia and I might have a real future with, but I just can't face the game of dating: the scrolling through face after face, reading "original" personal descriptions that all sound exactly the same, trying to sell myself as a person of interest who someone might want to make a life with. It's as if no one meets organically anymore, as if the Internet is the only place people can come together.

I reluctantly turn my phone over, and there are no new messages or missed calls. I check WhatsApp, Messenger, and SMS individually, but still, nothing. I have a few new likes on Instagram, but that's it. I feel worried about money again; after the orders I had in December and January, things have slowed down again, even though my Instagram followers keep increasing—almost three thousand now. I really need to find a dependable source of income on top of the drawing, or we'll get evicted.

I check my e-mail and two new messages come through. One is a newsletter from Norwegian Airlines, the other is an e-mail from a man whose name I don't recognize with the subject title *Your Illustrations.* I open it and my heart actually flips in my chest.

FROM: **Frans Høybraathen** <frans@speilet.no>
TO: **Iselin Berge** <isberg@online.no>
DATE: Fri, March 1st, 2019 at 10:12 A.M.
SUBJECT: Your Illustrations

Dear Iselin,

I hope this finds you well. I was sent a series of your illustrations by an old friend and colleague, Alison Miller-Juul, explaining that she'd bought some art from you and that you may be interested in more work. I haven't had a chance to take a look before now, but I wanted to drop you a line to say I was incredibly impressed by them. We'd love to work with you. In fact, some changes are happening here at *Speilet*—toward the end of 2019 we will no longer "only" be a newspaper, but we will be launching a weekend lifestyle magazine that will be distributed across Norway with our Saturday issue. Would you be interested in coming in for a chat about possibly coming on board as our in-house illustrator? I believe your style would be a perfect match for *Speilet Saturday.*

Let me know when might suit you—we have our offices at Tjuvholmen.

Very best regards,
Frans Even Høybraathen,
Editor

"Kaia!" I say, popping my head around to the living room, grinning like a goon. "Mamma might get a job! A really exciting job, drawing for a national magazine." Kaia turns to look at me and nods slightly before returning her gaze to the screen, where JoJo Siwa is bouncing about and screeching into a microphone.

"Okay," she says.

"Oh, Kaia, this is a really big deal. Give me a hug?"

"Okay."

I press my face into the hollow of her neck, running my hand down the length of one of her braids, her thin arms closing gently around me. After a while, Kaia tries to push me away lightly, but I draw her closer—I need to feel that sacrificing everything I wanted to do for her, for so long, was worth it. I've spent almost seven years in this apartment, mostly alone, shelving every ambition I ever had, losing confidence every day. But this could change everything. I try to imagine what it would be like, to have a job with offices in Tjuvholmen and coffee machines with free coffee and views over the harbor and actual colleagues who listen seriously to my ideas. And a salary. I could stop worrying about having to go back to NAV and rolling over for that bitch. Just the thought of the endless system of logging in and checking off everything Kaia and I ever do to receive a measly monthly government handout makes my skin crawl.

In the kitchen, I call Noa. It rings and rings, then goes to voice mail. *Hey, this is Noa. If I don't pick up, it's probably because I don't want to speak to you* . . . I hang up, and try again, and this time she picks up on the second ring.

"Hey," she says, her voice hoarse. It's just after 3:00 P.M. on a Sunday—she's probably been working and partying all night two days in a row. "I've been trying to call you."

"Hey," I say. "Everything okay?"

"Yeah, just busy. I'm going to Barcelona tomorrow."

"Oh. Cool."

"Where were you this weekend? I tried calling you, like, four times."

"Kaia and I went to Norefjell. She skied for the first time; it was amazing. She was actually really good at it, a total natural. Alison said she—"

"Wait, who's Alison?"

"She's my friend. I told you about her."

"What, the American? In Holmenkollen?"

"Yeah."

"Have you been hanging out with her?"

"Uh, on a couple of occasions, yeah."

"Isn't that kind of weird?"

"Why would it be weird? I can have friends, can't I?" Noa has this twisted idea that she reads people better than I do—it makes me so angry.

"You said yourself she seemed a bit strange, Is. What do you two have in common?"

"More than you might think, actually. Why are you acting all patronizing? Can't I have something in common with someone who is older or seems different on the surface? She's really sweet, and she and Kaia have really taken to each other. The cabin was so lovely. It was good for Kaia to get away for a couple of days and just do stuff that other kids do."

"Okay."

I make myself breathe deeply in through my nose and count as I exhale. I am not going to let a petty disagreement take away from the excitement I'm feeling about *Speilet*. "Anyway, the reason I'm calling is, I have something really exciting to tell you!" Noa is silent on the other end and she suddenly feels so far away. I imagine her dragging on a cigarette or weaving wax through her hair or playing around with a new tune in her mind. "I have a job interview! You know *Speilet*? They're starting a new weekend magazine and they want me to come and talk to them about the role as in-house illustrator!"

"Oh, wow! Sis, that's great news!" Noa sounds genuinely happy for me and I soften a little. I wish she was here tonight to celebrate. "Did they find you through your website? Or social media? Your Instagram is looking awesome, by the way."

"No . . . No, it was through, uh, Alison, actually."

"Right." There is something hard in Noa's tone again, something judgmental.

"She . . . She used to be features editor at *Speilet*. Still is, actually, but she's taking time out to write a book. Amazing, huh?"

"I just think you need to be a little careful who you let in, that's all."

"Seriously, what are you talking about?"

"Is, you said yourself she was a little strange."

"No, I didn't actually. She has been incredibly kind toward us."

"Fine," says Noa, but her voice is cool. I hang up without saying goodbye.

Where I come from, there was nothing to do but dream. So that's what we did, Noa and I. From our early teens we'd drink beer out of a plastic bag on the frozen beach, day after boring day, looking out at the fjord and the pink, low winter sky, the mountains in the distance, all that nothingness. Every day after school, we'd avoid going home for as long as possible, letting the school bus go without us, even though it was the only way to get back to the remote, drooping cottage clinging to a steep hillside that our parents call home.

Eventually we'd hitchhike home in the dark. I remember those rides home so clearly, Noa and me sitting perched up high together on some truck seat, the bearded face of a stranger barely visible in the darkness of the cabin. Then the long walk home from the district road, through the forest, up and up, until we'd finally reach the house, where our father was sure to be drunk, waiting.

Our early lives made Noa tough. Impenetrable. But I won't let her ruin this, I just won't.

I don't want to be someone who festers in her own misery—I want to make changes and move forward, I want to give Kaia a good life, and right now I'm thanking my lucky stars for having met Alison, who seems to have set into motion many of the things that may just make those changes possible.

"Hey, Kaia," I say, trying to clear my mind—I've come too far to linger any longer on my early life. I made it out, and really, that's all that matters. "Shall we order sushi?" I say it even though I'm not exactly rolling in money, but everyone deserves a treat sometimes. I take the macaroni off the hob and dial the number for Østerås Sushi.

After dinner, Kaia goes to bed easily, sweet face pale with exhaustion after her mountain adventure. Alison said she did really well on the slopes yesterday and it was impossible for me to imagine my Kaia skiing carelessly like other children, but she's a different Kaia now. I pour a large glass of red wine and sit down to draw, feeling encouraged by the e-mail from Frans Høybraathen. The darkness and cold of this seemingly endless winter all seem to disappear as my pencil sweeps across the paper as if by itself. A chest opened wide, surgical clamps holding ribs and yellow layers of fatty tissue back. And inside the empty cavity where the heart should have been, a bloody feather. When I finish, I stare at the drawing for a moment, before putting it to the side and starting another. I draw for a couple of hours, the evening deepening and my mind growing calm. I have three promising new illustrations by the time I put my pencil down.

I decide to call Alison and tell her about the e-mail from Frans Høybraathen, and dialing her number, I feel strangely exhilarated.

"Hey there," says Alison in her funny rounded American accent, picking up almost immediately. "You guys okay?"

"Yeah," I say, and only then does it occur to me that it's really quite late to call. "I'm sorry it's so late. I wanted to thank you again so much for the break in Norefjell. I didn't realize how much we needed to get away."

"No worries. Anytime. Seriously. Loved having you both."

"So, I have to tell you something," I say. "I got an e-mail. From that guy you mentioned. Frans Høybraathen. He says he wants me to come in for a chat about possibly working for *Speilet* as an illustrator!"

"Oh, Iselin, that's just wonderful! Yes!"

"I can't thank you enough for recommending me to him."

"You know I really like your work, and I'm just happy to help. When will you be meeting with them?"

"Not sure yet. Hopefully sometime next week."

"Well, listen, if you need any help with Kaia or anything, ask me. I'm wide open all week. I'd be happy to pick her up from school and fix her dinner or something. I'm sure you want to put your portfolio in order and maybe even start on some new stuff that would fit their profile . . ."

"Oh . . . Well, yes. That's probably a really good idea, huh," I say, looking down at the new drawings. They're good, and different, and I'm sure Alison is right in saying I should consider my portfolio as a whole before meeting with *Speilet*.

"Listen, I'd love to babysit. I'm trying to write an article on . . . wine making in the Caucasus—you know, trying to get back into it after quite a long sabbatical, and it's so hard! Would love the excuse to hang out with Kaia for a few hours. We could go for a hike or something."

"Gosh, she'd love that. If you're sure?"

"Of course I'm sure. I really want to help. I can only imagine how tough it must be, trying to do it all on your own. You really deserve some time to focus on yourself, Iselin."

I sit with Kaia as she sleeps and lay my hand to her chest, listening to the sweet sound of a strong, steady heart. Tears begin to drop from my eyes and I have to breathe slowly and deeply to keep myself from releasing a sob and waking her. I don't know why I'm crying. I'm not unhappy, at least not in this moment, but feeling the skittish beat of my own heart, I realize that I'm anxious. Everything and everyone is changing: Kaia, Noa, Alison, my whole life as I know it is turning to dust before my eyes.

44

ALISON

When I arrive home, I sit for a while in the car, just breathing. All the lights are on in the house and I need to go inside. Sindre will have heard the car pulling up, the engine being cut. The backseat fills me with dread. I turn around, forcing myself to look at the empty seats—Kaia really is gone. She will be at home, perhaps watching a cartoon, or maybe sitting with her mother at that cramped kitchen table, drawing. I switch on the light and pull my phone from my pocket. I take pictures of the inky wing in my hand, from every angle.

Outside, the air is clear and stars wash across the entire night sky. I consider turning back to the car, driving to Iselin and Kaia's little apartment . . . and then what? My life, or what remains of it, is here. I slip my key in the lock, but the door is open. Inside, it's hot and I can hear voices from upstairs, someone laughing. I shut myself into the guest bathroom underneath the stairs and run hot water around my hands, as hot as I can bear. The ink doesn't come off easily; I have to rub painfully across the new upturned skin with an old toothbrush to get it all off, and when I open the door after I'm done, Sindre is standing outside.

"Hey," I say.

"Hey." He moves toward me and pulls me close in an awkward hug. "What's going on, Ali?" he says. There is something hard in his voice, like in Mexico when I asked to see his phone and he refused.

"What are you talking about?"

"I'm asking you what's going on."

"And I'm asking you what you are talking about." Sindre laughs incredulously, and we both know he is going to say what he is going to say, no matter what I do. I listen for sounds from upstairs; I feel afraid to be here alone with Sindre, but now it's quiet, and it could be that the sounds I heard hadn't come from upstairs at all. "Where's Oliver?"

"Ali. I'm asking you, what's going on?" I pick up my holdall from the floor by the bathroom and wait for my husband to step aside so I can take my things upstairs to unpack. He doesn't. I turn quickly around and make for the kitchen instead, and as I do, I catch a glimpse of the wall where I'd hung Iselin's drawings, empty now.

"What—?"

"Ah, *now* she knows what I'm talking about."

I push past him and this time he lets me go. I go over to the empty wall, where the metal bolts that secured the drawings to the wall are still sticking out, and turn back around to my husband. His face is blank and unreadable. What does he know?

"Where are the pictures, Sindre?" I ask.

"I took them down."

"Why?" I don't want him to see me cry, but I can't help it.

"I can't imagine it can be that difficult to understand why. What, you don't understand how unbelievably inappropriate they were? Hey, look at me. Look at me, Ali."

"No," I say, and move toward the stairs, and he grabs hold of my shoulders, pulling me upward, forcing me to look at him.

"I thought you said things were getting . . . better. This! This is madness!" Could he know about Iselin and Kaia? No. It isn't possible. I need to distract him. I open my mouth to explain to him that I think the drawings are beautiful and raw and that they challenge everything I thought I knew about hearts—hell, about life and love and freedom, even—but it's like the words won't come, so I just wrench myself free and walk out, taking the stairs two at a time.

In the bathtub I stare at billowing steam clouds, feeling the tension and fear and anger seeping from me and into the scalding water. *Unbelievably inappropriate*, he said. I almost laugh at how he has no idea, none at all. How far I have removed myself from my husband and what was once our life together. When I leave the bathroom, I listen for a while on the upstairs landing for sounds of him. It is entirely quiet, but I can't relax until I've checked every room in the house. His car is gone, so he's probably not just out running. I send him a message on WhatsApp.

Where are the drawings? The two blue ticks appear almost instantly; he's read my message, but he doesn't respond. I sit at the kitchen table, letting my eyes move slowly across every surface. I stand up and look in the fireplace—could he have burned them? The hearth is cool and a draft from the chimney pulls at my hand.

I walk over to where the drawings hung and lightly run my hand over one of the metal bolts. I realize that the sofa has been pulled out a little and lean forward to look behind it, and there they are, placed against the wall. I hang them carefully back up and stand admiring them, relief washing over me. They really are incredible. Would I have loved Iselin's hearts as much as I do if I didn't know what I know, if I wasn't who I am? Maybe not, but I don't see what Sindre finds so disturbing about them.

I like the way the drawings suggest that a heart, and what fills it, is something altogether other than what you might think at first glance. I also like that the size of the heart in the little girl drawing is enormous compared to the body that carries it, which is portrayed as a mere shell in comparison to the vivid richness of the heart. It supports the theory that I have come to believe; that who we are— our very core essence—is carried within the cells of the heart. Our thoughts and beliefs may well reside in the brain, but it is the heart that holds the soul. My belief was reinforced when I placed my hand to Kaia's chest and felt the beat of Amalie's heart; it was as though it surged a little upon my touch, as if it knew me like I know it.

I turn away from the drawings, now back in their place, and go upstairs. I stand by Amalie's closed bedroom door for a moment, trying to gauge whether I am actually strong enough to open it. I am. In the last few weeks, since I have been spending time with Kaia, I have begun to feel some small, but unmistakable, changes. I sometimes think about the future. I am eating. I am not taking as many tranquilizers, and mostly drinking only at night. I'm not counting as much, and before we went to the mountains, I began to read a book. The unbearable pain of losing Amalie is softened, only a little, but still, by the presence of Kaia Berge. And tomorrow, I will have her all to myself.

45

ALISON

I very carefully unpeel the name label from the back of the iPad. I'd forgotten it was there, and thank God I removed the cover on a hunch, to double-check. *Amalie M-J*, it reads, with my phone number underneath. When it has come off, I hold the iPad up to the light and tilt it slightly. The dark screen is covered with fingerprints—Amalie's fingerprints. I take a deep, shaky breath and bring a moist cloth to its surface, press down, and wipe it clean. Then I put the iPad on charge. When it's full I will restore it to factory settings, deleting my daughter's apps and games, and then I will give it to Kaia.

My coffee is still too hot to sip, so I stand at the counter by the charging iPad and stare out into the garden. Today is a beautiful day, almost spring-like, with sunlight streaming onto the lawn, searing hollows in the snow. It's only 10:00 A.M.; how am I going to fill all the hours until I can pick up Kaia from school? I run a damp cloth over the breakfast bar, then the stove, finding satisfying overlooked blobs of oil around the gas rings. When I'm finished I take a few more sips of my coffee, considering whether or not to add a couple of vodka shots to it, but decide against it, as I have to drive Kaia later and I can't risk anything bad happening to her.

Is today the day I begin to think about Amalie's room; maybe at least clearing away some of the toys that lie scattered on the floor, taking off the bedsheets, letting in some fresh air, folding some clothes into boxes? I let my mind linger on each of these potential actions, and find that I am able to bear thinking about them. I pour out the rest of the coffee; it has gone from a touch too hot to a touch too cold and it disappears down the drain in a muddy swirl.

I go and stand by the window, looking out at the city held beneath a wispy mist. *I'm coming to get you, Mills*, I whisper, drawing two *A*s close together in the steam from my breath on the window.

"Hey, Kaia," I shout, and she turns around from where she is sitting high up on the red climbing frame with another little girl.

"Alison!" she shouts, her face lighting up. She shimmies down the gym's central pole and drops to the icy ground before running toward me and hugging me hard.

"So excited to be hanging out with you this afternoon!"

"Me too," Kaia says, waving goodbye to her friend. She picks up her backpack, then places her gloved fist in my hand.

"I thought we might go for a hike or something. The weather's pretty nice. Then we could go to my house and I'll cook something for us while you get a start on your homework. Sound okay?"

"Yeah." I pull out of the crowded parking lot and head left, toward

Røa. Traffic is slow because of the school run, and I glance at Kaia in the rearview mirror; she looks content but lost in thought, staring out at the murky snow pushed up high along the sidewalks by the snowplows, and the people walking home, faster than we are driving. After Røa, traffic loosens up, and instead of continuing straight ahead toward Holmenkollen and home, I turn left toward Bogstadvannet Lake. I park behind the gas station and turn to Kaia.

"We're here," I say.

"Where?" She looks outside the window, but can only see the road and the gas station's parking lot from where she is sitting.

"Bogstadvannet." Kaia nods. "Have you been here before?" I ask, focusing on maintaining a smooth, neutral voice. Kaia nods again. "I thought we could walk around it. It's nice, not too far."

"Okay."

We walk slowly around the south shore, occasionally picking up flat, gray stones and flicking them onto the ice covering the surface in patches, where they bounce around, faint echoes rising against the dense trees surrounding this part of the lake. Kaia remains silent beside me, walking dutifully in the controlled, calm manner of an adult. Amalie would have lurched, skipped, run, fallen down, stopping constantly to pick stuff up off the ground. A twisted paper clip, a funny stone, a frozen conker, a Coca-Cola bottle cap. I stop myself from looking at Kaia again, and keep my eyes on the lake. It's almost five o'clock and the sun is receding, slipping behind the tallest trees on the opposite shore.

I turn toward Kaia and realize she's fallen behind. She's thirty or so yards behind me on the path, looking out at the lake, entirely unmoving as though she's been frozen. I take in the overall shabbiness of her—the purple down jacket, the clashing green knitted hat, the bare, red hands held close to her sides, the stringy dark hair messily framing her face, the scuffed brown shoes. I smile at her, and she starts toward me, but I have to look away, because it hurts, how much I have come to love her.

"I have bad dreams," she says, stopping beside me and staring out at the partially frozen water.

"Me too," I say.

"I'm afraid to sleep because scary things happen to me in my dreams."

"What . . . What kind of scary things happen?" I ask, though I already know what she is going to say.

"I can't breathe. My heart begins to hurt. It feels bad again. Like before, when I was sick."

"How did it feel when you were sick?"

"Like I couldn't breathe. Like my heart sometimes was fast and sometimes too slow, and it burned."

"Burned?"

"Yeah, my heart felt like it burned."

"Mine feels like that, too."

"Are you sick?"

I look away; I don't want her to see the tears that blur my vision. "Not sick," I say, eventually, starting to walk again. "Sad, I guess."

"But . . . But why are you sad?"

"I wish I had a little girl of my own. A girl . . . like you."

"Oh," says Kaia, frowning. Then she places her fist back in my hand and I hold on to it tight as we start onto the forest path, back toward the car.

At home, I make a hot chocolate for Kaia and a coffee with milk and vodka for me. I'll have to drink a glass of water or two before I drive her home, but I feel so disoriented and confused after our walk that I just need something to soothe my nerves.

"I almost forgot," I say, "I got you something."

"A present?"

"Yes." Kaia claps her hands together and bounces up and down on the stool at the breakfast bar, where she's drawing. I unplug the iPad and hand it to her. She looks from the iPad to me and back several times, disbelieving.

"Can I borrow it?"

"No, you can have it, sweetheart. It's yours." I help her to turn it on and the apple appears on the screen.

"I've wanted one for so long! It's not even my birthday!"

"Glad you like it."

"I love it! My mamma is going to be so jealous. She wants one, too, but she can't have it yet because it's expensive."

"Well, make sure you share it with her."

Kaia nods solemnly. "But . . . But why don't you want it?"

"I bought a new one and I don't need two."

"Doesn't your boy want it?"

"Well, he already has one."

"Oh."

I smile at her and Kaia smiles back, but it's the sad smile of a child who suddenly understands that there are differences in the world, that some people have a lot and some people don't.

"Where is he?"

"He's gone to his mother's after school today. He lives here one week with me, and then he lives one week with his mom."

"Oh. Where's his dad?"

"He's . . . He's working." The truth is, I don't know where Sindre is. He didn't return home last night. He never answered my message about what he'd done with Iselin's drawings, though they are thankfully back in their place. I've tried to call him but his phone goes straight to voice mail. Then, just before I picked Kaia up from school, he sent me a message.

I have a late conference call with Houston, then running with
Espen in Maridalen. Home late.

I obviously wouldn't have brought Kaia back here to the house
had Sindre been home.

After dinner I drive Kaia home. She's stabbing away at the iPad,
pale face ghoulishly lit by the green light from the screen. I drive
slowly, mindful of the two shots of vodka I poured into my coffee
earlier. We're stopped at a red light at a deserted junction in Grini
when Kaia speaks.

"Why did you come to my school?"

"To pick you up, sweetheart," I say.

"No, I mean before."

"Before . . . when?"

"You came to my school once, before."

"No, sweetheart, that must have been someone else. Someone
who looks a bit like me, maybe?"

"But I saw you. And it was the same car." I pull away from the
junction too hastily, tires spinning on the icy ground, clutching
hard at the wheel. She didn't see me that day—she can't have. I
watched her the entire time, and never once did our eyes meet.

"Sweetheart, it wasn't me." I smile reassuringly at her, but she's
upset; her eyebrows are tightening in a frown and she's placed the
iPad facedown in her lap.

"But I saw you!"

"Okay, Kaia, that's enough. Lots of people look alike, okay? I can
think of so many times I thought I spotted an old friend in a crowd and
it turned out to be somebody else. Happens all the time, I'm afraid."

"Remember the first time you came to Mamma's studio and I was
there and I said I knew you? It was because I saw you at my school."

"Here we are," I say, too loudly in the sudden absence of the fan as I switch off the engine. "Don't forget your iPad, sweetheart."

Kaia looks at me, first defiantly, then seems to remember the iPad and the nice day we've had, and her expression softens. "You know, you shouldn't be sad. I can be your girl, too."

"What . . . What do you mean, Kaia?"

"You said you were sad. And that you wish you had a little girl of your own."

"Yes . . . Listen, I know I said that, but what I meant was that I was sad in that moment. Not all the time. I'm okay, I promise."

"Okay. If you're sad you can visit me."

"That's sweet of you to say, Kaia." I glance at the house, but Iselin most likely hasn't heard the car pulling up. "I think it's best that we don't tell Mamma I was a bit sad today, okay?"

"Okay," says Kaia, gathering her things. "Mamma is sad sometimes, too." I nod and then we walk the few steps to the door of the basement unit, Kaia smiling sweetly at me, clutching her new iPad.

At home, I call Sindre's name even though I know he's out late. I head straight to Amalie's room and shut the door behind me. I begin to remove the sheets from her bed, throwing them into a pile by the door. When I finish, I open the curtains wide, then the windows, letting the freezing night into the room. I pick up the discarded piles of toys from the floor and put them in the toy boxes. I take the folded clothes that have sat on her dresser since that July morning that started off much the same as other summer holiday mornings. I place them in Amalie's clothes closet, resisting the urge to press my face to the little T-shirts and cardigans for a trace of her scent. I close the window again and walk backward out of the room. It no longer looks like Amalie just left her room and may come back at any time. For the first time since July, I leave the door wide open.

It's past midnight when the phone rings. I was dozing, but the repetitive vibration of the phone against the wooden floor jerks me awake. It's Monica, Sindre's ex-wife. I sit up, fast, and my finger slips on the screen and I miss the call. My fingers tremble as I fumble to unlock the phone and call back.

"Alison," says Monica, "I need you to come here."

46

ALISON

Monica's face is scrubbed clean and weary-looking when she opens the door. She shows me through to the kitchen, where Sindre is sitting on a bench by the window, scrolling on his phone.

"What's going on?" I ask, looking from Monica to my husband, but neither of them will meet my eye.

"I thought Sindre needed a ride home," says Monica.

"What are you doing here?" I ask.

"I was out running and my mind got muddled, that's all."

"Sindre tried to unlock my door with the key to your house and it seems like maybe it's all been a little much."

"I'm fine," says Sindre.

"I didn't think he should drive back home," says Monica, the harsh light above the sink turning the papery skin underneath her eyes a deep blue.

"No," I say softly. "Thank you for calling me."

"Also . . . I feel concerned. For both of you. Because I care. Of course, you know how much I feel for you both. But . . . But my son spends half his life with you, and I'm wondering whether it would be a good idea for us to rethink that for a while. Until things get easier."

"No," says Sindre. "Monica, please. Look. I know things have been unstable. But please let him stay with us."

"Yes, please," I say, and as I catch Sindre's eye, a feeling of complicity and solidarity passes between us, the first in a very long time. "Oliver is grieving, too. What Sindre and I are going through is part of Oliver's history, too. I don't think it's the right thing to remove him, even if it's difficult now." Monica looks from Sindre to me and back. She nods, then stands up.

In the car, Sindre stares out the window, and there is something dejected and humble about the way he holds himself.

"Did you say you were going away again this week? You can't, Sindre. Not like this. You're not in a position to travel."

"Reykjavik. And yes, I have to." I don't answer—I learned a long time ago that there is little point in telling my husband what he can and cannot do.

"Where were you last night?" I ask as I pull into the driveway.

"Does it matter?"

"Doesn't it?"

"I . . . I'm not well, Ali. It's like my skin is on fire, like I'd do anything to get away from home and from myself."

"I know the feeling."

"I slept in the apartment in Skovveien, okay?" Sindre bought the apartment in his twenties, before he'd married Monica, and we use it occasionally for Airbnb.

"Alone?" Sindre stares at me, then opens the car door. I follow him into the house, my heart beating so hard he must be able to hear it. The moment of empathy I thought passed between us at Monica's is entirely gone. He goes straight into the living room and sees Iselin's drawings, rehung.

"Are you completely fucking insane?" he shouts right in my face. I make myself calm, looking him straight in the eye.

"I want you to tell me what the hell is going on," I say.

"*You* want *me* to tell you what's going on? How about this—how about you tell me what the hell is going on, Alison!"

"Where were you last night?"

"I've seen your search history. What the fuck are you playing at?" Sindre whispers, and this is more frightening than a moment ago when he was bellowing in my face. He begins to pace around the living room, rushing from one side of the room to the other, bumping into furniture, knocking books off the shelves, and comes to a stop in front of Iselin's drawings.

"Oh God," he says, his voice hollering again. "Did that woman draw these? Answer me! Answer me, goddammit!"

"How . . . How do you know?"

"I said answer me!"

"Yes."

"Jesus Christ." Sindre raises his hand and slams it into the wall next to one of the drawings. "What the fuck, Ali?"

"How did you know?" I need to know what he knows exactly.

"I found the article. About the girl. I Googled the mother and these same drawings came up. This is completely crazy. Have you been in contact with her? Answer me, Ali!"

"Only to buy the drawings, obviously," I say, softly.

"But why?"

"I liked them."

"You liked them. Can you even understand how fucked up this is?"

I nod miserably as Sindre slides to the floor and sits slumped over, holding his head in his hands. When he speaks again, the fury has gone from his voice and it comes out as a meek whisper.

"I've tried, Ali. I've really tried. I'm trying every day to forgive, or at least to understand, but the truth is, I'm not sure I can. I . . . I just can't believe she isn't coming back." I walk over to him and sit down on the armrest of the sofa next to where he is on the floor.

"I'm sorry," I say. And then my husband says the words that will echo inside my head for the rest of my life.

"Sorry isn't enough, Alison. I've tried so hard not to blame you, but the truth is, I do. She was five years old! Five! What the hell were you thinking? Tell me what you were thinking! Fuck! Alison, goddammit, how could you . . ." He begins to sob and pummels the floor with his fists. When I approach him and place my hands on his shoulders he leaps up as if he's been touched by a ghost, and then he spins around and stares at Iselin's drawings with uncensored hatred. He unhooks one and flings it across the room, where the glass shatters against the piano. I lunge toward him to stop him from doing the same with the second, but Sindre shakes me off twice, and the second time I fall and strike my face against the side of the coffee table. Sindre stands above me holding the framed drawing high above his head, his arms trembling, its chrome frame glinting in the low light. Then he brings it down onto me, smashing the frame to splinters against my arms, the glass slicing into me as I try to protect my face.

Then he leaves.

47

ALISON

I wake on the sofa, and it's already morning, the blazing sun framed in the floor-to-ceiling window and sending shimmering shards of light onto the parquet. It picks up the broken glass scattered across the floor, and then I remember last night. I clutch at my head; it's hurting terribly, like my brain has swelled up overnight, pressing against my skull. It's Friday, 10:25 A.M. I have nothing left and nothing to lose. Sindre is gone and there is no one to stop me or all the crazy thoughts rushing through my head. I don't even have Karen anymore.

If I turned up, would Karen Fritz still see me? I could tell her everything and then, surely, I'd be protected from myself and what I have become. She'd make some calls, and I'd have to go somewhere—a hospital where calm strangers know how to deal with someone like me. Or maybe she will say something that will give me some clarity; after all, that is what therapists are supposed to do. I'm still wearing the jeans and mohair sweater I had on last night and decide not to change, but in the bathroom I wipe the smudges of blood off my face and hands and apply some concealer to the dark bruise on my jaw.

I drive down past the ski jump glittering in the sunshine, past Slemdal, past Majorstuen Station, where my eyes linger on the bakery where I sat that day all those weeks ago, warming my hands on a cappuccino before walking over to Trudvangveien, where I came face-to-face with Kaia Berge for the very first time. I try to keep my thoughts on that moment and away from last night and how chaotic everything is now. Kaia, little beautiful precious Kaia, a vessel for the purest heart I've ever known. I'm doing this for her.

The look on Karen's face when she opens the door to find me standing there belongs in a horror film.

"Oh, Alison," she says, her face half-obscured by the doorframe.

"Can we talk?"

"Of course we can talk. Have you been receiving my calls? Will you take a seat? I can be with you in half an hour or so."

"But my session is at eleven." I'm aware that my voice is louder than it needs to be, and Karen glances discreetly back in the direction of whoever is in the room.

"You've been absent for a long time, Alison. But I will find you a new session, okay? Just sit down over there and I'll be with you in no time." I stare at her, then nod, but as soon as she closes the door I turn and walk back down the corridor, then outside.

I leave the car where it is and walk up to Uranienborg church and around the little park—it is such a beautiful day. I walk aimlessly back toward Solli Plass, then sit on a bench outside Kaffebrenneriet at the bottom of Skovveien in the cold sunlight, watching the blue trams hurtle past. What will Karen do when she opens the door and finds me gone? Why did I even go back there? She couldn't help me before, and she can't help me now—she just wouldn't understand what is happening with Kaia. How could I expect her to understand that it is a miracle—the universe's way of returning Amalie to me.

Two hundred and forty-five days without her. How many breaths have I taken since the moment she took her last breath? There is a number for it, and I'll never know it. How many times has my heart beaten? I think about all the tiny, minute things I still do— the things that we just keep doing, even after the entire world has ground to a halt: going to the bathroom, dressing, undressing, drinking coffee, changing lightbulbs, going to the bathroom, dressing, checking my phone, driving, going to the bathroom . . . Every single thing I do without her is another little betrayal. The fresh green buds shooting out on the branches of the tree next to where I'm sitting are a betrayal. The sun, shining—a betrayal.

It's too cold to sit still for long, so I begin to walk up Skovveien, and as I pass number fifty-one, I stare up at the windows of the fourth-floor apartment. It's where my husband says he spent the night. *I blame you*, he said. *What the hell were you thinking? She was five! Five* . . .

My husband is right, of course. He didn't say a single word I didn't already know.

I keep looking up at the redbrick facade, imagining Sindre moving around behind the gray gauze curtains. Maybe *she* is there with him, because why wouldn't she be? I have turned it over and over in my head. At first I felt nothing, except relief that Sindre has had something that has kept his attention away from me. But now I feel angry, too. He's probably been screwing her in Geneva and wherever the hell else he's gone since he went back to work. Not that it matters much—it means I could spend all that time with Kaia.

I pull my phone out.

Where are you? I write, but as I press send I remember he's traveling.

My phone bleeps almost immediately.

Hey you. I'm in Reykjavik until Tuesday, but we need to talk . . . Where are you? I'm so sorry. S x

Fuck you, I write back, my hand trembling. My head aches.

Of course he isn't here. I ring the doorbell several times in case his girlfriend is there, but no one answers. It occurs to me that of course she's gone to Reykjavik with Sindre. I'll go up for a moment, collect my thoughts. I could just turn around, get the car, and go somewhere. Anywhere. I could drive up to Blåkroken. I could take the ferry to Denmark and then just drive and drive, heading south, to France or maybe Spain. I could build a little life there, renting a studio apartment and writing features and walking on the beach— I've lived that life before. But I can't go anywhere without Amalie.

I close the door behind me and stand a moment in the hushed hallway. I could trash this apartment if I wanted to. I could hurl the furniture around and smash the bed and break all the windows. I could dismantle this little love nest my husband has enjoyed while I have mourned our daughter. I walk into the living room. It is just a normal, sparsely furnished room, and as I look around, all I can feel is sadness that Sindre has come here, in secret, with someone else while I was across town, alone, wild with grief.

In the kitchen, there's an empty wineglass in the sink. I open the fridge and notice a couple of beers and an open bottle of prosecco, a spoon emerging from its neck. He's been drinking here, with his whore. I take the prosecco from the fridge and sit down at the kitchen table and drink it straight from the bottle. Is it hers? It must be. I imagine them together, my husband's broad, strong body enveloping her in bed, her thin, pale hands clutching at his neck.

She's the one who's made him laugh late at night on the phone behind the closed door to his office. She's the one he asked *So, what are you doing today?* Every time I've asked who he was laughing to he just muttered "work," as if running a home security company could possibly be that fucking hilarious. Just thinking about my husband makes my mind recoil. I don't know what "Sindre" means anymore, or who my husband has become. He's a broken man. Dangerous, even. He hurt me, and I never thought he would. But anyone can be dangerous, every one of us can be driven to madness, I know that now, too. The realm of possibility has been extended for both of us, and I don't yet know where the limits to our potential for destruction lie. I wonder if he has that woman with him now, some stupid bitch who thinks she can piece my husband back together, and realize I don't give a fuck whether he does.

The prosecco is flat, but it doesn't matter to me. I get up and stand by the window, looking at normal, uneventful life playing out down there: a black car inching into a tight spot outside the grocer's, a couple of teenage girls walking from school and laughing together at something on a phone, a sparrow pecking at crumbs in the last of the patchy brown ice outside Baker Hansen. I sit back down and drink some more, closing my eyes against images of my husband standing over me, screaming in my face. I see him in the garage, with his gun. I see him standing over me, holding the framed drawing, then bringing it down onto me as I raised my arms to stop him. Afterward, he stared at his own hands as though they were capable of anything at all.

This must be it, the end of us, because where could we go from here? My phone vibrates in my pocket.

"Ali? Hey, it's me. Issy." Iselin's cheerful voice fills my ear.

"Hey," I whisper.

"Are you okay?"

"Yes. Just a little out of breath. I've been out. Running."

"Great. Such a beautiful day. It actually feels like spring! So, I'm going in to speak with them at *Speilet* on Monday."

"Oh. Okay. Yeah, that's great."

"And I was wondering, I mean, I know it's probably a big ask, and you might not have anything that would work anyway, or of course you might think it's really weird that I even asked, but—"

"Iselin, slow down. What do you need?"

"I was wondering if I could borrow a dress?"

I lie down on the bed. I'm so confused. Every time I close my eyes I see bad things. For all of these months, I've been speaking to Amalie, but her silence clutches at my heart with the most crushing force. I've been looking for her—in the lake, and in her room, in places she's never been, and yet all this time I was looking in the wrong places. In these last couple of months, she has returned to me, little by little, and it has become clear to me that she is still here, in every single beat of her heart. I need her, *you*, I need you, baby bear, and I think I know, now, how to bring you back. You, the very essence of you, is held not just within your heart. Every cell in a body is nourished by the heart. As blood passes through your heart and then around her body, you manifest yourself in all of Kaia. Your atoms run through her, spreading into every last cell. You and her, you're one and the same. I can't believe I didn't realize this before, that all of this time, you were right there. I have nothing left, nothing but you. I'm coming to get you and we are going to be together, baby bear, me and you.

48

Alison opens the door before we have a chance to ring the bell, and I almost don't recognize her. Kaia's mouth pops open, and she doesn't stop staring at her as we take our coats off in the hallway. Alison is wearing a beautiful high-neck emerald-green silk blouse, tucked into a pair of wide-leg dark jeans. Her hair, which I've only ever seen up in a scruffy ponytail or a bun, and which was streaked through with gray, has been dyed a warm brown, with subtle blond highlights. It gathers in soft curls around her shoulders, perfectly blown out. Her face is carefully made up, but underneath one eye, I can see she's attempted to cover up a long, raised bruise, and when she turns her head, I see another shadow underneath a thick layer of concealer on her jawline. She reaches up to hang our coats from the hooks running along one side of the hallway, and her sleeve rides up a little, exposing a series of black, ugly bruises on both of her arms.

"Have you seen *Annie?*" she asks Kaia. Kaia shakes her head. Alison starts the movie and Kaia slithers down onto a large bearskin on the floor in front of the television, taking the plate of cookies Alison hands her. I glance around for my drawings, but perhaps she hasn't had time to hang them yet. Or maybe she decided to hang them upstairs; it's a big house, after all.

We go upstairs, where I sit on a huge leather pouf in her bedroom while Alison brings out dress after beautiful dress.

"Where's your husband?" I ask, looking around the sleek, sparse bedroom as if for a sign of him. What I really want to ask her is *What has happened to you, and did your husband do this?*

"He's had to travel for work again."

"Oh." I pull on a thin gray merino wool sweater dress from Paule Ka and look in the floor-to-ceiling mirror.

"Yeah, uh, Copenhagen."

"Does it bother you, that he travels so much?" I feel like I can ask Alison things like that now—since we spent all that time together in Norefjell, it's like we've known each other forever. Like sisters. But how can I get her to tell me what's happened?

"No," she says, holding a silky dress up to the light, then handing it to me, though I've got my heart set on the Paule Ka. "It's actually quite nice, to get so much time to myself." I nod and take the dress she's holding out to me. Her gaze is sharp on me, as though she is willing me not to ask any more questions. But I'm her friend, and friends are there for each other. I open my mouth to ask *Has he hurt you?* In the end, no words will come, and I say nothing.

Alison is still on my mind on Monday morning as I walk across the bridge from the harbor front at Aker Brygge to Tjuvholmen, holding a latte from Kaffebrenneriet and wearing the dress from Paule Ka. Everything is new here on this little man-made island: the modern office buildings, the sleek cafés, the trendy hotel, the several overpriced galleries showcasing eccentric works of art, the incredible museum at the water's edge, signed Renzo Piano. Finally, I am here, in the middle of all of this. I wish teenage Iselin could see me now—a professional woman in her midtwenties, carrying a coffee through Oslo's finest district, on my way to speak with the editor of *Speilet*. And all thanks to Alison. If I hadn't met Alison, I don't know what I would have done. I'd be at home in my sweatpants, dreaming of being exactly as I am in this moment: going somewhere. She has helped me so much, and now I need to figure out a way to help her, too. But how?

I draw Alison's smart coat tighter around her dress; though we are in the second week of March, the temperature has dropped once again. The thawing cracks that had started to appear across the plates of pale blue ice in the inner harbor have congealed like scars. I lower my head against the bitter wind coming in from the sound, hurtling through the gaps in between the buildings.

I've arrived in front of *Speilet*'s offices, and the building is even more impressive than I anticipated. It directly faces the fjord, whose dark water and patches of white ice are reflected in the building's mirrored facade. Though I'm ten minutes early, I'm about to step through the revolving doors to wait in the warm reception, when I feel my phone vibrating in my handbag. I ignore it and it stops for a moment. I take a deep breath and step forward, but then it starts up again and I stop to fish it out. It must be Noa; she'll be back from Barcelona and eager to catch up. I don't want to speak with her right now; I haven't entirely forgiven her for giving me the third degree the other day about Alison, and I'm about to press reject when I realize it isn't Noa's number flashing on the screen, but the school's.

"Hi there, Iselin. It's Anne calling from school. I'm afraid Kaia isn't feeling too well this morning." My heart begins to race and my face immediately burns red.

"Oh, no. Oh gosh, is she okay? Where is she?"

"Now, I don't want you to worry. She's just here in the office with me. A headache, she says. Can you come for her?" I hesitate, and look up at the mirrored building, imagining myself inside it, working in an office of my own, looking out at the gently rippling water.

"Yes. Yes, of course. It will take me at least an hour to get there, I'm afraid. I'm in central Oslo, so . . . But . . . I could ask a friend."

"Sure. What shall I tell Kaia?"

"Tell her that I'll head home as soon as I can, and that Alison may come for her first."

"Also, I wanted to check with you—would it be okay for us to administer a paracetamol?"

"No. No, actually, don't give her anything. She's on immunosuppression medication; it could interfere with painkillers. I'll be there soon." I imagine my little daughter, lying flat out on the school secretary's sofa, clutching her head, face twisted in pain. I just want to be with her to make it better. I hang up and dial Alison's number. It rings for a very long time, but then she picks up, voice hoarse.

"Um, hello?" she says.

"Oh, hey, Alison, it's Iselin."

"Hi, Iselin!" Alison's voice noticeably brightens at the sound of my voice. "Finished already? How did it go? I bet you blew them away!"

"No, I . . . Shit, they just called from the school and Kaia's not feeling well and I'm about to go into *Speilet* and—"

"Calm down, sweetie. I'll go get her."

"I . . . I . . . Thank you."

"It's just down the road; don't worry about it. You know I'm happy to help."

"Could you bring her back to ours? The key's inside one of the rain boots to the left of the door. I should be back in a couple of hours. She needs her meds at three. Kaia knows how much, and where everything is."

"Of course. Hey, good luck today. Knock 'em dead."

"Thank you," I say, and hang up. I turn the phone on silent before putting it back in my bag. I smooth the soft wool fabric of the dress down and take a final, deep breath before going inside *Speilet*'s building, thanking God again for Alison Miller-Juul.

49

ALISON

"Can we play doctor and patient now?" says Kaia. I nod, taking her in: pale face, feverish eyes, little pursed mouth. Once again, I have the sensation that Kaia is a mere mirage; that the real child is Amalie, beneath the surface. Kaia gets up and disappears into the bedroom, before returning with a real stethoscope hung from her neck and a wry smile. What an odd object to own, but I figure it isn't so strange when you've been a heart patient your entire short life.

"I'm the doctor," she says.

"Uh-huh," I say. She reaches across and yanks my V-neck sweater down, placing the resonator in exactly the right place below my collarbone on the left.

"Oh, no!" she exclaims. "You're sick."

"I am?"

"Yeah. Your heart doesn't work."

"Oh . . ." I close my eyes, pretending to look extra ill, but really, I feel overwhelmed and close to tears, being so close to Kaia, feeling her hot, quick breath on my cheek. "Can you fix me, do you think?"

"Yeah. Maybe." She removes the stethoscope and places a little hand above my heart, fixing me with her cool blue gaze. "Does that feel better?"

"Mmm-hmm."

"Did you know you can die from a sick heart?"

"Yes. Yes, I did know that."

"You need medicines. Here, open your mouth." Kaia shoves a pretend spoonful of medicines into my mouth and I smile, pretending to swallow.

"So, do you know what's wrong with me?"

"Yeah. I told you. You have a sick heart. You're gonna need a new one."

"Do you know how it got sick?"

She ponders this before answering. "Bacterias probably."

"You think?"

"Yeah." I nod, resisting the urge to pull her close, to breathe her in like oxygen, feeling for the thud of Amalie's heart against my chest.

"Okay, my turn to be the doctor," I say.

"Nah," says Kaia and gets up from where she's been sitting perched on the armrest. She picks up the stethoscope and is about to walk away with it, but I hold her back by the wrist.

"Please," I say.

"No."

"Kaia, come on."

"I always have to be the patient!"

"Just one time, please."

She stares at me defiantly, crossing her arms across her chest. Then a thought seems to occur to her, softening her expression. "Will you give me a Hobby if I say yes?"

"A Hobby?"

"It's a chocolate! With raspberry jelly and banana marshmallow."

"Oh. Um, yes. Of course."

"Promise?"

"I promise."

The reality of what is about to happen strikes me so hard I can't bear to look at her, so I fix my gaze on my hands. Kaia sits down on the armrest again, leaning slightly toward me so that her chest is level with my face. She unbuttons the top few buttons on her blouse, unselfconsciously revealing the jagged, fleshy scar, then she expertly places the resonator on her chest, handing me the earpieces. I hold them for a moment before placing them in my ears, my eyes trans-fixed by Kaia's calm, deep gaze. I've wanted this for so long, since the moment I first saw Kaia, when she fell off the sleigh and I imag-ined the frightened scramble of her heart. Amalie's heart.

Heartbeats boom in my ear. The sound doesn't fill me with dread or exacerbate the black overwhelming panic I've lived in for the past eight months, like I'd feared. Each precise, perfect beat of Amalie's heart resonates at the very core of me, and like a miracle, it's as though they begin to draw the broken pieces inside me back together. I listen to it for a very long time, looking out at a violet afternoon sky, the way you'd listen to a concerto demanding your full attention, and still, Kaia does not appear to grow restless. Fi-nally, I pluck the earpieces out and look around, as if emerging from a dream. Kaia doesn't seem perturbed by the tears streaming down my face.

"It's okay. I know why you're sad," she says, handing me a nap-kin from a holder on the kitchen table that reads *Merry Christmas*. "It's 'cause it's sad that it was someone else's heart."

"Yes," I say, unable to move even an inch.

"They're dead now."

"Yes."

"Poor them."

"Yes."

"But not totally dead," she adds breezily, and goes back into the bedroom to put away her stethoscope. I don't dare speak again for fear of interrupting what she may say next, but she says nothing. She comes back out, and I notice that her eyes are red-rimmed and drooping. She settles into the crook of my arm and I close my eyes, too, feeling the soft rise and fall of her chest against my own. *We're going to go away together, you and I*, I think to myself, and I have to stop myself from saying the words out loud—Kaia can't know just yet. But in these moments, what had been a vague idea in my mind begins to take on the solid contours of a plan.

50

ISELIN

I open the door to the sound of Kaia's bubbly laughter coming from the living room. I place my handbag down in the hallway and stand a moment in front of the mirror. Iselin Berge, *Speilet*'s new in-house illustrator. I feel numb, and almost teary just at the thought. The amount of money they offered me is so much more than I could have imagined. Over three times what I'd been receiving in benefits. More than all of my commissions. I wipe away a tear and give myself a small smile. *You did it.*

"Mamma!" shouts Kaia as I walk into the room. She's lying on the sofa, and though she looks cheerful, her face is noticeably pale. I feel her forehead and she seems to have a slight fever. *Call us at the smallest indication of illness*, Dr. Harari said at our last checkup. The list of things that can go wrong for Kaia, especially in the first year after the operation, is long. I've made a decision to not spend all my mental energy obsessing over what could go wrong, and so far, she has surpassed all of my expectations health-wise. "Mamma, Alison and I played tea party! And then we played doctor and patient!"

"Fun," I say, and kiss her forehead. Alison is sitting in the old armchair by the window, looking more like her usual self than the glamorous version we saw last night. Her hair is swept back in a high, tight ponytail and her makeup is more natural, though she has clearly attempted to cover her bruises.

"You okay?" I say, and she smiles in Kaia's direction and nods.

"Yeah. Gosh, these little ones are energetic, even when they're feeling peaky. This little madam has bossed me around from her sickbed all afternoon." We laugh a little and Kaia pulls a goofy face. "So . . . when do you think you'll hear about the job?"

"Well . . ." I begin, enjoying the drawn-out moment and the anticipating look on Alison's face. "I got it, actually."

"What!"

"Yes!"

"Oh, my God! Iselin, this is huge! They offered it to you there and then?"

"Yes!" I didn't think they would—I thought they would run a long series of interviews, gradually narrowing it down. I didn't dare hope for more than a possible callback. I liked it there, in the airy, open-plan office on the third floor, the views every bit as spectacular as I imagined. The people were lovely, too, and the hour I spent with Halvor, the editor, and his colleague, Mina, felt more like a chat between old friends than a job interview. I felt that they liked me, but still I couldn't have anticipated what they said at the end of our talk. "We want you," they said.

Alison jumps up off the chair and hugs me tight. For a brief but sharp moment, I miss Noa so much—I can't believe it isn't her that's here with me and Kaia now. Kaia reaches her arms out for me, and when I hold her close, pressing my face into the little space between her shoulder and neck, I feel how hot she really is. I pull back, alarmed.

"I'm just going to give her consultant a quick call," I say. "They say to call immediately if she gets sick, even if it's just a cold or whatever." Alison nods, and her face is etched with worry. There's something else, too, in her expression: a deep sadness I've noticed before. Sometimes Alison's face goes from calm to anguished for a brief moment, before it returns to normal, as if she mentally has to force herself to keep a neutral expression.

"Are you okay?" I ask, again.

"Yes," she says, smiling, but this time, her smile doesn't reach her eyes, and she seems to realize it because she drops her gaze and stares out the window, her hand absentmindedly stroking her arm.

Alison drives us to the hospital. Fast, down a series of residential back roads, trying to avoid the heavy traffic that has built up around Røa. Dr. Harari and her team of angels are waiting for us when we arrive, and Kaia and I go up to the pediatric ward while Alison parks the car. She waits outside the room while Dr. Harari runs a series of tests on Kaia, listening to her heart, taking her blood pressure, shining a light into her eyes, taking her temperature with a laser thermometer that makes Kaia laugh, checking for a rash, drawing a blood sample to make sure her white blood cells are at the right level. Kaia doesn't complain or resist at any point, she just sits there in her pink Minnie Mouse underpants, her narrow shoulders trembling slightly, though the air is nice and warm.

"It's just a mild cold," says Dr. Harari, handing the stethoscope to Michelle, an older nurse who has also known Kaia since she was a baby. "Nothing to suggest cell imbalance or rejection. Keep her home from school for a full week, keep an eye on the temperature, and call me straightaway if it goes above thirty-nine. Kaia, you need to listen to Mamma, okay? No mountain climbing or scuba diving or para-chuting this week, do you hear me?" Kaia smiles tiredly and nods.

Back in the car, Kaia falls asleep, slumped over on the backseat. Alison drives slowly now, worry still stamped on her face.

"I don't know how I'll manage a job, and her . . ." I say, close to tears.

"You will," says Alison. "And I will help you."

"But . . . But, Alison, why do you help me so much?" Alison takes her eyes off the road for a moment and looks in the rearview mirror at Kaia sleeping, then at me.

"Look. I'm your friend. This is what friends do."

"I . . . Thank you." I feel tears stinging in my eyes and have to look away. I'm overwhelmed by gratitude for everything Alison is doing for me and Kaia. I am also feeling something else, something unsettling, and then I realize what it reminds me of: the atmo-sphere at home in Svartberget, when my father hadn't been drink-ing and was in a good mood; I knew, deep down, that it wasn't real, that it wouldn't last, that it could even be dangerous.

"What happened to your face?" I whisper, watching Alison care-fully. Her expression doesn't change; her face is open and calm.

"Oh, that," she says, turning right onto our street. "I was getting in the car the other day and managed to literally slam the door in my own face. So ridiculous."

"And your wrists?" Alison is silent as she pulls up in front of our house, and Kaia makes a soft mewling noise in the back, but doesn't wake up. She switches the ignition off and looks me in the eyes, but her expression is different, her eyes harder. Like my father's, when he was struggling to maintain his pleasant demeanor. I want to get out of the car, but immediately feel silly. Alison is the kindest per-son I have ever met.

"My stepson was very angry with me the other day. I took his phone away as he had broken the rules, again. He . . . He lunged at me trying to get it back. Completely unacceptable, of course. My husband was furious. It looks worse than it is, though. I bruise easily. Always have."

"I'm sorry," I say. "It's none of my business. I . . . I just worried about you."

"Don't apologize, sweetie. You can ask me anything you want." I feel stupid for trying to second-guess Alison after everything she has done for us. I'm just exhausted, mentally and physically. I gently, touch her hand, which is resting on the automatic gear lever, and give her my best, reassuring smile. "Want me to help you get her inside?"

"No, it's okay. I'm used to hauling this little munchkin around."

We exchange another smile as I step out of the car and pick Kaia carefully up off the backseat. She slumps against me, nestling her face in my neck, murmuring. Inside, I place her gently down on the bed, and pour myself a glass of red wine before I even take my jacket off. I got a job. An actual, well-paid job. Combined with the income from the drawings, Kaia and I could possibly move. We might go on holiday, for the first time. We could order sushi on any old Tuesday, without having to check the bank balance first. I wipe at a couple of tears running down the sides of my face, when my phone bleeps in my pocket.

Congratulations again, sweet Iselin, it reads. **It won't be easy, but it will be wonderful. A little celebration gift. Ali xx** And underneath: **YXB88N**

Thank you, Alison. And thank you for your help today. Not sure I understand the last part of your message?

It's a reference number. For a flight to Paris, use it whenever you want. You deserve a treat. Happy to watch Kaia.

51

ALISON

A week later

When I wake, it's still dark outside, and according to the alarm clock, it is 5:22 A.M. The room shimmers in the light of the moon and I contemplate getting up, perhaps even sitting outside at the edge of the forest with a mug of coffee; I know I won't be able to sleep anymore. It's strange I slept at all—a murky, empty sleep void of any lingering trace of dreams or memories; but perhaps not so strange considering I took a double dose of temazepam last night.

I've been waiting for this day all week, and when I think about what's going to happen, my stomach clenches. I very carefully get up from the bed, as though I wasn't here alone. Downstairs in the kitchen, at the back of the cutlery drawer, wrapped in soft, pink polka-dot tissue paper, I find the candle I bought especially. I slip it into the pocket of my bathrobe alongside a lighter and go back upstairs, avoiding my gaze in the mirror. I take extra care as I pass Oliver's room—he's always been a light sleeper, but then I remember that, of course, he isn't here. None of them are. I imagine him in his room at Monica's, tossing and turning, whiling out long hours scrolling aimlessly on his phone, writing on his grief forums, sitting awhile on his windowsill.

In Amalie's room, a flame flickers to life. Most days I find it hard to get out of bed, but she told me exactly what she wanted us to do on this day, and so we're going to do it. This week has been hard, but today won't be. It won't be bleak, even. It's her day, and we are going to celebrate.

Happy birthday, baby girl.

When Kaia spots me, she half runs across the playground, waving a gloved hand. It's only just after four o'clock but the sky is the pasty purple of wilting violets; daylight never stood a chance against the Norwegian winter.

"Alison," she says, and crumples into my arms, lifting her feet, just like she did with Iselin weeks ago when we came here together that first time. I smile down at her, taking in her healthy, rosy cheeks, the scatter of freckles across her nose, the water-colored eyes.

"So, I was thinking we'd do something really special today."

"Are we going to see the horse?"

"Not yet. Your mom says we need to be careful about animals for another few weeks."

"Because why?"

"You know why, sweets. Infection risk."

"So where are we going?"

Sandvika Storsenter is one of Norway's biggest malls. It spreads out alongside the E18 motorway by the Oslofjord on the western fringes of the city, and I glance at Kaia in the rearview mirror as I take the exit toward it, but she stares at the enormous building, showing no signs of recognition.

"Have you been here before, Kaia?" I ask, pulling into a parking space.

"What is this place?"

"It's a shopping center. A mall."

"Oh."

"You know, where I come from, malls are a big thing. On weekends, that's what kids do, hang out at the mall."

"What's it like?"

"They have any kind of shop and restaurant you can imagine, and a cinema and maybe stuff like bowling, too."

"No, I mean, what's it like where you come from?"

"Oh. Well . . . It's not too far from San Francisco. You probably haven't heard of it, but it's a big city. And beautiful, too. I grew up an hour or so north, in the hills, near the beach."

"What happened?" asks Kaia, her face serious as we step side by side onto the escalator, as though she anticipates some tragedy.

"What do you mean, what happened?"

"Why don't you live there anymore?"

"I . . . I guess I wanted to see the world and do other stuff, you know?"

"What about your mom?" Interestingly, it doesn't seem to occur to Kaia that many people have a mom *and* a dad.

"My mom is still there. Or . . . well, she's not at the house any-more because she got sick, so now she lives nearby in a home where she can get some help." I smile gently at her, and she nods seriously before absentmindedly handing me her hat, letting her eyes roam across the gallery stretching out in front of us.

"I was thinking we could get our nails done together."

Blank stare. "Get our nails done?"

"You know. A manicure." Kaia's face is still blank, and I wonder whether it was a mistake to bring her here. Perhaps she doesn't like the same things Amalie liked at all. "Nail polish, glitter, little animals stuck on your nails. Whatever you want." At this, she lights up and it occurs to me that Kaia just didn't know what a manicure is.

"Really? Can we?"

In the nail parlor, I watch Kaia choose from the tray on the nail technician's desk. Amalie always chose the same pink base, then added animal stickers and hearts over the top.

"This one," says Kaia, pointing to a ladybird, "for my pinkies." One of Amalie's favorites.

"Good choice," says the lady.

"And the bears for my thumbs and the hearts for the rest." *Good girl.* We smile at each other as we sit down side by side, and the girls start buffing and filing our nails. I notice the gaze of my manicurist as she takes in my chewed nails, the cracked cuticles, the raw skin where I obsessively scrub at them. I chose a French manicure, same as I always have, though it's been almost a year since I last got my nails done. As I watch Kaia's enraptured expression at this new, strange experience, it occurs to me that I was more like Kaia as a child than my own daughter. Growing up, I wasn't one of the kids who'd hang out at the mall, crisp dollars stuffed into their cute handbags. I was the loner, the dreamer and the tomboy, happier in the surf or playing war in the scraggly heather on the cliffs with the boys.

Amalie had the kind of life where money was never an object when it came to experiences. She had her own pony, she skied most weekends, she traveled from South Africa to Honolulu to Singapore to Cannes, and lived in a room with bespoke furniture, full of expensive toys and gadgets. I'd sometimes worry that we were spoiling her, but now I'm glad if we did. We could give her that life, so why wouldn't we?

I think about how unfair it is that Kaia has to live in that cramped, damp apartment. She doesn't even have her own bedroom, and God knows if the health and safety conditions in that place might hinder her continued recovery. If she stayed with me more, she'd at least have a respite from that depressing home.

"Ice cream?" I ask after we've paid, and are walking out of the nail parlor. Kaia nods, still staring at her little nails. Ice cream is followed by dress shopping and Kaia chooses three beautiful ones from Enfant Terrible. I worry that the shopgirl might recognize me; I used to come in frequently with Amalie, but I needn't have worried, she barely glances at me. She focuses on Kaia, loudly exclaiming every time she comes out of the dressing room, giving a timid little twirl.

"*Fantastique!*" the lady says, and I take a picture of Kaia in a navy-blue silk dress, the way any mother might. "Is it perhaps your birthday, darling?" *Yes. Yes, it is.*

"No," says Kaia.

"Oh, well, you are a very lucky little mademoiselle," she says, ringing up the sale. "Your mother treats you like *une petite princesse!*" I look at Kaia and wait for her to correct the lady, but she doesn't. She smiles wryly up at me and slips her warm hand into mine.

* * *

At the toy store, Kaia sits down at a little table with drawing pads and crayons and begins to draw.

"Kaia, have a look around. I said you could choose a toy." She looks a little uncomfortable, but dutifully scans the tall shelves behind her, stacked high with dolls that eat, dolls that sing, dolls that clap their hands.

"I don't need anything else today," she says.

"I know you don't need anything else, sweetie. I just want to treat you. Have a look around, choose whatever you want." She gets up slowly and walks around for a while, aimlessly taking in the vast selection of pastel plastic offerings. Finally she comes back over to me holding a small plastic pocket of crayons marked *50% off!* in big red letters.

"Can I please have this?"

I kneel down in front of Kaia and take both of her hands in my hands, but she gently withdraws them. "Listen, Kaia. You can have anything you want. Anything at all. Maybe you'd like a really big teddy bear? Or a Baby Born Doll? Or how about a Sylvanians house with a whole family inside?" At this, she brings her gaze back to meet mine, and it dawns on me that she has simply never been in this situation before and doesn't know what to do. "Come," I say, and take her hand, and together we go over to the Sylvanians village.

In the car, Kaia's quiet, and I just enjoy the moment, driving through the cold early evening with a tired and happy little girl in the backseat. The ice is breaking into large sheets on the fjord, as though someone has cut into it and wrenched it apart. It's almost seven o'clock and it's been dark for a little while already.

"I have one more thing for you, Kaia," I say, and she turns from the window toward me. Her little face is serene, sweet, partially cast in shadows from outside, and if I squint my eyes just a little bit, she could almost pass for Amalie in this light.

"One more thing?"

"Yeah."

"Where is it?"

"It's at my house." Kaia doesn't answer straightaway, but drops her gaze to her hands, resting on her lap. She twirls her thumbs around and around.

"I want to go home now," she whispers. I grab the steering wheel harder, feeling a rush of anger spreading through me from my fingertips to my toes.

"Soon," I say, keeping my voice light and neutral.

"No, now."

"Kaia."

"I miss my mamma."

"Honey, you'll see her in just a little while."

"I want to go home!"

"She's working."

"No, it's the evening now. It's bedtime soon!"

I messaged Iselin earlier this afternoon to say we'd head to Sandvika to catch a movie and something to eat and that we'd get back around eight, but then I switched my phone off. Partly in case she said no, and partly because I don't want my husband to call me.

"We won't be long, Kaia. I just want to show you something." She doesn't answer, and when I look in the mirror again, I see that her eyes are wide and wet with tears. A fierce empathy for her tears at me—I don't want to see Kaia upset at any cost; I can't bear the thought of her heart hurting. I pull off Vækerøveien into a bus lay-by, switch the overhead light on, and turn around to face her. She's dropped her head to her chest and won't look up; she'll be embarrassed to show me that she's crying.

"Hey," I say, and place a hand on top of hers, and she doesn't move away. "How cute are your little fingernails, huh?" Kaia nods slowly, miserably. "Hey. I just want to make you happy, okay? We'll go home real soon."

We leave Kaia's Sylvanians tree house and school bus and hospital in the car alongside her huge fuchsia Enfant Terrible bag full of dresses, and Kaia looks carefully around, as though she is here for the first time. She has calmed down and her eyes are shining again. There is something about her tonight that I can't quite put my finger on, something familiar. As she rushes ahead of me into the kitchen, I realize what it is. She's shuffling her feet in a strange little dance exactly the way Amalie used to. My heart picks up its pace and I'm swallowing hard at the lump in my throat. It's a very specific gait that Amalie used to do jokingly when excited; I think she started doing it after watching the salsa dancers on the street in Trinidad when we went two years ago, and I've never seen Kaia do it before. *Stay calm, Ali,* I say to myself. *Stay calm. She will come back to you.*

"Sit here and close your eyes," I say, and Kaia climbs onto the barstool and obediently clamps her eyes shut, giggling a little. I open the fridge and lift the cake carefully out. *Red velvet with pink glitter, your favorite.*

"Can I open my eyes now?"

"Not yet," I say, and take the candle back out from its polka-dot tissue paper in the drawer.

"Now?"

"Two seconds." I place the candle in the middle of the cake and light it.

"You can open them now," I say, and she does, her whole face lighting up at the sight of the beautiful cake, but then she takes in the candle, its shape like the number six, and her smile fades and she is confused. I close my eyes for a moment, and inside I say, *Happy birthday, my love, my angel, my baby bear, my sweet everything*, but then a strange voice cuts the air. I open my eyes and in the doorway between the kitchen and the living room stands Oliver, his face frozen in shock and horror.

52

ISELIN

"Mamma, Mamma, look!" shouts Kaia as I open the door. Alison has waited on the curb, engine on, but now she pulls away, waving as she goes. Usually, she'd come in for a tea and a quick chat, but she appears to be in a rush. I help Kaia inside—she's laden down with bags.

"What's all this?"

"Alison took me to the big mall! She bought everything I wanted! Everything! And look!" Kaia wrenches her gloves off and holds her hands out, tiny fingernails professionally decorated with ladybirds, hearts, and glitter.

"Wow," I say. "Wow. That is so pretty. Um, did Alison say why she was buying you all this stuff?"

"She said I deserved a treat. For being so good."

"But, Kaia, this isn't like a little treat. This is like Christmas and birthday at once . . ." I feel uneasy, the way you might as a child when adults are talking about something you don't understand over your head; you know there's something you're not getting, but you don't know what. Kaia seems unperturbed and empties the contents of two huge bags from Brio toy shop onto the floor. There are Sylvanians for thousands of kroner, three Barbies, and a pack of thirty fancy glitter pens, the kind I always say no to. "Wait, don't open that," I say, taking the Sylvanians school bus from her. "We are going to have to return this stuff, honey."

"No!"

"Yes, Kaia. I'm sorry."

"Why?" Kaia's voice is high-pitched and trembling.

"Because . . . Oh, honey, it's kind of complicated. The thing is . . . I know that Alison is really kind and just wanted to treat you. But . . . the problem with accepting gifts like this is that it places us in a weird position with people. Do you understand?" Kaia glares at me, shiny fingernails poised and ready underneath the sealed cardboard flap of the school bus. She shakes her head defiantly, eyes not leaving mine.

"I'm not giving it back!"

"Yes, honey. Yes, you are. Maybe when Mamma has been working at *Speilet* for a while, we can go and get a couple of new toys. Maybe then, okay?"

"No!"

"Kaia, put the box down. I've asked you to do something and you need to listen to me. Right now, please."

"No!" She flips the seal and rips the box's lid open. Before I reach her, she grabs one of the other boxes and does the same.

"Kaia!"

"You are so mean! Why are you always so mean to me?" I feel tears stinging my eyes. I'm tired, and I just don't feel like dealing with a tantrum.

"Just be quiet. Put all this stuff back in the bags, right now! Come on!"

"No," screams Kaia, face red and twisted. "Why are you so mean to me! You never give me nice things! I hate you! I wish . . . I wish Alison was my mother! She loves me much more than you do!"

"Shut up, Kaia," I say, through gritted teeth, turning away from her so she won't see the tears in my eyes.

"It's true," she continues, still shouting, and I think of Hanne Vikdal upstairs, pressing her ear to the floor to make out Kaia's words, nodding her head at her husband, listening, judging. I allow myself the thought I have had so many times over the years, but never let myself linger on. I want to walk away from this ugly apartment, from my child, even. I want to be free. I've done it once before. I think of Svartberget, how I got away; I proved to myself that it was possible to get out of a shit life and build another one. I was free, really free, for a short while, and then I went and fucked it all up. "You just want me to be sad! I hate you! I want another mother! We're not even a real family!"

"Fine," I whisper. "Fine. Just shut up. Please, please shut up. Keep the stuff, do whatever you want. And you're right, Kaia. We're not even a real family." Our words hang nasty and cold in the air between us, and we both look away, to the floor covered in chunks of cardboard and torn plastic shards. I leave Kaia in the living room and slam the door shut behind me—to hell with Hanne Vikdal and her twitching curtain and her fucking neighborly concern.

Only when the soothing warm water washes over me in the shower do I let all the tears loose.

* * *

My heart is pounding hard, and though Kaia is sleeping peacefully, nothing remaining of the furious red-faced monster she was earlier, I can't sleep. A new job at *Speilet*. The new friendship with Alison, all the help she has offered. And now this. My first thought was that we couldn't possibly accept all those gifts from Alison. It wouldn't be right. But then, thinking about it, and the consistent kindness and generosity she has shown me and Kaia, I wonder whether I am overreacting. Does it have to be so hard, to just accept someone's kindness toward us? I let myself imagine for one delicious moment what it would be like to leave Kaia with Alison, just for a couple of days, and return to Paris. What might it be like, to just walk down those streets again, feeling the warm spring sun on my face, being totally free, if only for a weekend? Considering the disastrous evening we have just had, it might do us good to have a couple of days apart.

A flight to Paris, use it whenever you want. Happy to watch Kaia. I message Alison.

53

ALISON

I pull away from Iselin and Kaia's house, and glance at Oliver, who is staring at the house, as though Kaia might reappear. He's calmed down now, but when I reach out to him, he moves away and glares at me. My mind is exhausted after the day I've just had. Oliver's face . . . I keep seeing Oliver's face when he walked in and saw Kaia. It went from shock, to horror, to disbelief and disappointment. How can I fix this?

"What happened to your face? And your hands?"

"I fell."

"You fell?"

"Yes. Right. Let's get you home," I say, heading toward the ring road.

"How could you do this to us?" he says, his lip trembling. "You should have told me." I drive fast; I just want him out of the car, away from me. Thanks to Oliver, the magic of celebrating Amalie's birthday has entirely faded. I am so angry I can barely see straight.

"And you should have told me you were coming home. It's Monica's week."

"But . . . But I live there."

"Half the time, yeah." Oliver goes quiet, and when I stop at a red light, I glance at him again, and his face is awash with tears. They drop onto his dove-gray sweater and I feel the stirrings of empathy for him, but only for a brief moment.

"You can't tell Sindre," I say.

"Is that all you care about? Being found out? Don't you understand how serious this is? You could . . . You could go to prison! You don't care about us!"

"Please don't tell Sindre. Please. I know you've told him about the article and that I'd go look for the family. And I know you told him about the drawings." He is weighing up his options, I can tell. Do the right thing, as he doubtlessly sees it—Oliver has a strong moral compass—and tell his father, or live with this big, ugly secret? Oliver doesn't know about Sindre's woman, or the fact that he and I are falling apart. Oliver will worry that Sindre will leave me if he found out that I had gone behind everyone's backs to establish contact with the recipient of Amalie's heart. For Oliver, that would mean spending every other week with Sindre on his own, no doubt eating instant noodles out of plastic cups, silently whiling away night after night in front of NRK's boring documentaries. It would mean losing me. Or . . . Or he can keep quiet . . .

"I want to meet her properly," he says after a long while. "Kaia. So I can decide."

"Oliver. Look. It . . . It's complicated. I'm going to have to cut off contact with her. As you said yourself, it absolutely isn't appropriate, and it's probably illegal."

"Why?" he says. "Why didn't you tell me? I found her first. You should have told me."

"Oliver . . . I . . . I never planned for this to happen. I just wanted to see her one time. Just once. You know? To know that she's real."

"You should have told me."

"I'm sorry." He stares at me coolly for a long moment, then refuses to speak for the rest of the car ride to Vinderen. I pull up outside Monica's house.

"Why did you come up to the house?" I ask, softly.

"Because . . . Because it is my sister's birthday. I brought her something."

"What did you bring her?"

"A present."

"What is it?"

"It's on her bed."

"Have . . . Have you spoken with Pappa?"

"Yes."

"Today?"

"No . . . Yesterday."

"You know he's in Reykjavik, right? Thing is, when he comes back, he's going to stay in the apartment in Skovveien for a couple of days. Nothing to worry about, okay. Just . . . Just we're . . . Things are a little . . . We just need a few days to ourselves. But if you come here as usual on Friday, Kaia will be at the house. She's going to be staying for a little while."

"Staying? Why? I don't understand . . ."

"Her mother is going away, that's all. Listen, Oliver. You cannot tell Pappa, no matter what. Okay? I need to know that you won't. I trust you now." Slight nod. "If you're smart about this, you can come and meet her, and you will realize what I've come to understand. You were right, all along. About cell memory."

"What?"

"Amalie's still with us, Oli. She's there. In Kaia . . . It's incredible. It really is."

Oliver looks afraid, and when I have to stop for a moment to wipe at my tears, he looks toward the house, as if hoping his mother will spot the car in the driveway and come for him.

"But . . . What do you mean?"

"She's there, in Kaia. She's not gone, sweetie. Not anymore. We can have her back."

Oliver looks at me, and then opens the door. "I'll, uh, see you on Friday."

At home, I go into the kitchen and put the untouched red velvet cake into a plastic bag, tie it shut, and place it in the bin. I pour myself a tequila and top it up with just a dash of gin, then orange juice. Oliver's face . . . I see it in my mind. Can I trust him to keep his mouth shut? I know my stepson and he has a solid head on his shoulders. When he gets to properly meet Kaia, he will know what I know. He will love her like I love her, I know it. And so what happened tonight is a good thing; when Oliver fully understands what has been going on, he will also understand why I have to do what I am about to do, that it's the only way to bring Amalie back. Maybe one day he will be able to convince Sindre, too, and then it can all go back to the way it was before. We'll live here together again, all of us; Sindre, me, Oliver, and Amalie.

Though it's all crystal clear to me in this moment, I realize that it could all be seen differently. Someone else could think that I'm delusional, crazy, desperate, clutching at straws, playing a dangerous game where there can be no winners. I stand by the window, watching a full, blue moon, its face bruised by dark shadows like mine, feeling more alone than I have in all my life. I look toward Østerås; Kaia is down there sleeping the sweet sleep of a child who has just celebrated her birthday, little newly painted nails glinting in the moonlight, face calm, dreaming happy dreams this time. Amalie's heart sluicing her unique DNA throughout her host's body. What mother wouldn't believe what I have come to believe?

54

ALISON

It's late when she calls, after ten.

"Hi, Ali," Iselin says.

"Oh, hi there, Iselin. Everything okay? I hope Kaia was pleased about this afternoon?"

Iselin pauses. "She was ecstatic."

"Good." I laugh a little and refill my gin-and-tequila concoction. "And I'm so pleased you've decided to go to Paris. You deserve to be spoiled. And so does Kaia."

"Yes. I am so excited. And thankful, I hope you know that." She pauses for a long moment and draws a shaky breath before continuing. "So, I was wondering if we could talk a little about, you know, today. The gifts and stuff. I am kind of worried you're going to think I'm being really ungrateful saying this, and I don't mean that at all, it's just, I'm not used to . . . to having things given to me, and Kaia isn't, either. I guess I worry that by accepting them, I'm, you know, putting myself in a position of . . ."

"Of what? Being beholden to me somehow?" I keep my voice calm and level, but inside, my heart is lurching. Have I gone too far? Is Iselin pulling back from me, taking Kaia with her? I won't let her. "Iselin, sweetheart. I'm glad you feel able to talk to me about this, because I would never want you to feel like that." She's quiet, thinking, and I picture her in this moment, sitting at her kitchen table, Kaia snoring softly in the next room.

"I know," she says. "It's just—"

"Look, Issy," I begin, making my voice falter slightly. "I've been lonely. So lonely. Some really bad things have been going on at home. And having you and Kaia in my life has just been such an incredible breath of fresh air. I am so sorry if it felt too intense. I just wanted to show you how important you both have become to me."

"What kind of bad things?" asks Iselin, her voice softer now.

I picture Amalie sleeping softly, holding Dinky Bear, and unleash an anguished sob.

"Alison? Oh my gosh, are you okay? I'm sorry, I didn't mean to upset you . . ."

"It's okay," I whisper, then let myself cry again.

"Oh, Ali, I'm sorry. I wish I knew what you are going through. I'm here for you like you have been here for us."

"I'm ready to tell you everything, Issy. I"—sob, heavy breathing, croaky voice—"I'll tell you when we next meet. I just can't do this over the phone."

"Well . . . Do you want to come over? I can't leave the house. Kaia's sleeping—"

"Now?"

"Yeah."

"Would that be okay?"

My tears were real, and they keep falling as I drive down the hill toward Østerås. The thought of losing Kaia as well rips at my heart, especially now when we are so close—I just can't afford Iselin pulling back from me.

She opens the door, a worried expression on her face. She holds her arms out to me, and it feels good to be held by her, in spite of everything.

"Do you want a cup of tea? Or maybe something stronger?" The look on my face must tell her everything because Iselin pours me a large glass of red wine, and a smaller one for herself. I sit at the kitchen table, leaning my head against the cool glass of the window. In the next room I can make out a pile of torn cardboard boxes, shredded scraps of Sylvanian faces staring at me, from the toys I bought Kaia. I make myself cry again.

"Talk to me," says Iselin.

"I'm sorry to come here like this."

"Please, please don't apologize, Ali. I'm here for you. That's what friends are for. Friends." She strokes my hand as lightly as if with a feather and looks at me with such warmth that for a moment, I feel bad. For who I am and for what I have to do.

"My husband has left me. For another woman." Iselin's mouth draws tight in a little O and she covers it with her hand.

"Oh. Oh my God. I am so sorry. When did this happen?"

"It's been bad for a while. He's . . ." I take a deep breath here, keep my mind dark, and cry fresh tears. "Sindre has been abusive toward me."

"Oh, Alison." She strokes my hand gently again, and I pull my sleeves up, revealing the green-and-purple splotchy bruises. "I was afraid that was the case. The other day. When Kaia and I came to your house."

"It happened because I found out about the other woman. He went completely crazy."

"Where is he now?"

"He's staying at an apartment we use for rentals in Skovveien. I've changed the locks at the house."

"Has this happened before?"

"Not exactly. Sindre's not a bad man. But he suffers with trauma. He was in the army; he's seen bad stuff. Really, really bad stuff. And sometimes, his mind turns dark. He's always been gentle with me and Oliver; I just can't believe this is happening to me. I honestly thought we were happy, you know?"

"I'm so sorry you're going through this. I wish there was something I could do."

"You are doing something, though. Listening, being here. Thank you."

"You don't have to thank me."

"I just feel so alone."

"You're not alone. You have us now."

You have us now. But I only want Kaia. I can give her everything, and she can give me everything in return; the whole world and all its joys, held within one little girl.

We remain at the table for a while longer, discussing the logistics of the weekend, me absolutely insisting that it would, in fact, make me feel better to have Kaia around.

"She makes me feel less alone," I say. Iselin nods sympathetically, like I hoped she would.

"Crash here, on the sofa. Not like you can drive home after that," says Iselin, indicating the huge, empty wineglass. *Not like I*

320 · ALEX DAHL

don't routinely drive with significantly higher alcohol levels, but I don't say that, I just nod miserably. It's past 1:00 A.M. and Iselin is rubbing her eyes. She gets up and comes back with a towel and a spare toothbrush, still in its plastic packaging.

"Thank you," I say, and give Iselin a light hug. I find it hard to meet her eye. I slip into the sofa bed which Iselin has unfolded for me and close my eyes. It's strange, to be here, in this cramped apartment, on an uncomfortable sofa bed, the metal springs underneath the mattress digging into my back. I wish I was Iselin in this moment, sleeping closely curled around Kaia on the alcove bed.

I lie awake a long while, my thoughts drifting, and I'm finally growing tired when I notice something strange. A shaft of light falls from the streetlight outside onto the kitchen wall. At first, I think I'm imagining it, but as my eyes fully adjust to the darkness, a long line of bears—Amalie's bears—becomes clear, penciled along the baseboard. I get up and creep back into the kitchen. I squat down next to the drawings and they really are hers—I would know them anywhere. I run my finger along each darling little bear: another sign. Any sliver of bad conscience I may have had evaporates—Kaia doesn't belong to Iselin. Not anymore.

55

ALISON

Two days later

I wait in the parking lot at the KIWI store until I see Iselin and Kaia leave the house and watch as they walk up the long, gentle hill toward the school. When they have gone, I wait another ten minutes before switching the engine on. It isn't hard to pass the time; I feel like I'm drifting through a dream, as though what is happening couldn't possibly be real. But it is. I put the car into drive and it takes me less than two minutes to pull up opposite Iselin and Kaia's house. I wait a moment in the car, steeling myself, staring at the basement flat where Iselin and precious Kaia live their lives. No child should have to live in a cramped, damp flat with a mother who seems more than a little resentful about taking care of her own kid. I just can't bear the thought of Kaia waking up, day after day, in that windowless space they call a bedroom. Does Amalie's sweet, pure heart ache at the thought of a comfortable home and a stable family?

Kaia will be at school until two o'clock and Iselin is heading into *Speilet* today, to sign her contract. Tomorrow, she will fly to Paris for her well-deserved rest, and Kaia will stay with me. Everything is nearly ready for her at home; I just can't wait to see the look on her face when she takes it all in. I leave the car and cross the street quickly, drawing my coat closer around my chest against the wind. Instead of continuing straight ahead to Iselin and Kaia's door, I walk around the front of the house and take the steps up to the upper level. The section occupied by the homeowners looks significantly better taken care of than the lower level they rent out to Iselin. It's recently been painted a chalky white, with dark red windowsills. I knock on the solid oak door and it opens almost immediately. The woman standing there is around my age, with fine white-blond hair swept into a severe-looking bun on the top of her head and a rather angular face. Her lower jaw juts out, but she is clearly aware of it and inclines her head downward.

"Hanne Vikdal?" I ask, and she nods curtly, taking me in. I've applied a full face of makeup and put clean, ironed clothes on for this visit, and though I may appear a little tired and haggard, I think I pass for a normal person. "I'm sorry to turn up like this . . . I just wondered whether you had a moment to discuss a rather sensitive matter. It's about your tenant, Iselin, and her daughter, Kaia. The thing is . . . Well, frankly I'm concerned for the child's well-being." The woman's eyes bulge and become instantly animated. There is something repulsive about her obvious glee. I could turn back around—it's still not too late; she'd never know what I was going to say, or where what I'm doing here might take us.

"Come in," she says, reaching out and pulling dramatically at my sleeve, as though we might be watched outside. I step into her meticulously tidy hallway, the walls hung with large black-and-white photographs of three unremarkable-looking young boys posing dutifully for the camera. Hanne Vikdal follows my gaze and smiles proudly.

"Magnus, Georg, and Philip, my sons. Wonderful boys," she says. She shows me into a kitchen and quickly fixes us each a cup of milky tea. When she sits down opposite me by the window looking down over Iselin and Kaia's porch, she raises an eyebrow as if to say *So, what have you got?* For a moment, I feel bad. I glance out the window, at the exact space Iselin probably stands every day, fumbling around in her bag for her keys, stroking Kaia's hair absentmindedly as they enter their little flat. Can I take it all away from her? But the heart wants what it wants, and I am acting in the best interest of a child.

"Iselin and I got to know each other kind of randomly," I begin, paying attention to my tone of voice, trying to appear soft-spoken and concerned. To get this woman on my side is crucial. "We . . . uh, have socialized on quite a few occasions now, and I have helped her out with Kaia quite frequently. You might have seen me around, actually." Hanne Vikdal nods vigorously, she has indeed seen me around, has indeed been watching. "That's my car over there." I point to the gleaming XC90 and a glimmer of appreciation crosses Hanne's face.

"I've been happy to help Iselin out with Kaia. You know, she's very young, and with Kaia's medical issues, it can't have been easy. Just . . . And I have really debated whether I should talk to anyone about this . . . I do believe we all have a duty to speak up in the interest of a vulnerable child. I don't think everything is quite right at home, and I wanted to check in with you, to see whether you'd noticed anything unusual. I will be honest with you—I am intending to file a report of concern with child services."

Another vigorous nod. "Yes," says Hanne, bland eyes narrowed. "Yes, unfortunately I have been thinking along the same lines myself. Something's just not right. Every night, that poor child screams like a banshee. I think she must hurt her, I really do."

"Really? I suppose with her medical situation, she could be in some kind of pain, or it could be a side effect of the drugs she has to take . . ."

"You haven't heard it. It's bad."

"My goodness," I say, face serious and sad.

"I have never seen the father around. God knows where he is. And the mother shouts a lot. They both do. The other day they screamed for a long while, then I heard a loud bang and then it went quiet."

"Oh," I say. I'm glad, now, that I went to the lengths of coming here—it just goes to prove that my gut instinct wasn't off. It's just too much for Iselin. She needs help. And my baby bear needs to come home.

"I . . . I've noticed some things that I really believe are cause for concern, too. I think Iselin drinks," I say. Hanne Vikdal's mouth drops open. "Yes. She came with me to my mountain cabin a while back and I noticed that she seemed to be drinking during the day. You know, liquor. She has also asked me to babysit so she can travel abroad. To a party or something. I mean, I'm happy to babysit Kaia; she's a sweet kid. But she has just had major surgery less than a year ago and is still on a long list of medicines. I suppose I feel that it's a little irresponsible of Iselin to even contemplate leaving her in the care of someone who is practically a stranger. We've known each other less than two months, you know? I just find it a little disconcerting that a mother would feel the need to travel far away from her sick child . . ."

"Goodness me," says Hanne. "That's just absolutely unacceptable."

"Well, I think so. What I suppose I wanted to know is whether you'd be willing to back up my report to Barnevernet concerning whether Iselin is in a position to take care of Kaia."

"Oh yes. Yes absolutely," says Hanne, eyebrows scrunched tight together in light of this new and delicious information about her tenants.

"Well, I must say that it's lucky for Kaia that she has a vigilant neighbor such as yourself on her side. It is of the utmost importance to make sure the poor child is taken care of in the best possible way."

Back in the car, I drive fast toward home, then a thought occurs to me and I take a left at Røa, toward the lake.

I don't go the usual way. Instead I head north, to a quiet stretch of the lake that isn't as easily accessible for walkers. I have to push through some shrubbery and some young trees that have blown over during the winter, and then I reach a thin sliver of pebbled beach, impossible to see from the graveled pathway that encircles the lake. This is where I will bring her—it's perfect. I sit down on a flat rock and close my eyes, running through the plan.

The thing is, baby bear, I needed to learn to listen. All those months I spoke to you, I was so, so sad because I couldn't hear you—I didn't understand then, how you would come to speak as clearly as before, only differently. I just needed to listen. When our girl looks at me, I see you in her eyes. I feel you in everything she does. The beat of your heart is clearer than the sound of your voice. I can't live without you, and because of the girl, I won't have to.

56

ISELIN

The club is a pop-up in a huge basement near Bastille, down an alleyway from Rue Philistène, which used to be seedy, but is now the height of cool. I'm in the VIP section with Enzo and his handsome friend Matthieu, who Noa is trying to set me up with. We're not far from the booth, where DJ Noa and DJ Tantalyze are playing. My sister's hair is sprayed a silvery violet and slicked back into a futuristic, chic bob. She's wearing sequined Chanel hot pants, a leather halterneck top, and studded Valentino shoes. My sister, Nora Berge, from the dilapidated cottage on the far side of Svartberget, is regularly mentioned in the same breath as the likes of Harley Viera-Newton and Leigh Lezark. I feel a tremor of pride, watching her, and also something else—I feel freed from envy. She was born to be up there—this is her world, and it feels okay, in this moment, that it isn't mine.

"Issy," says Enzo, Noa's handsome but somewhat intense boyfriend. I lean toward him but can't hear what he's saying over the music. I laugh as though I did, and that was clearly the right response. I check my phone—nothing. Kaia will have been in bed a long while now. I wonder if Alison remembered to give her the azathioprine at seven. I have to stop worrying—I know Kaia would remind her even if Alison forgot. I can just *be* here in this moment, young and free again. Matthieu presses another beer into my hand and I drink fast; it's so hot and sweaty in here. He says something to me, and again, I just laugh. I excuse myself and go to the bathroom. Even inside the cubicle, the air is clammy and the music thumping uncomfortably loud. How does Noa bear it, night after night? And what will she do if she and Enzo have kids or she wants to leave this party world behind?

In this moment, Kaia will be asleep, her little face bare and resting. What will she do if she wakes in the night, needing me? Does being here make me a bad mother? And why did I say such awful things the other day—did I really think that being drunk in a warehouse full of strangers, listening to this weird electropop music, would be so much better than being at home? *I'm having fun*, I tell myself. *Stop sabotaging yourself.* Matthieu is cute. He's the kind of guy I should be looking for—he's an architect, so we'd have something in common, he's handsome and a bit shy, his eyes are mellow and kind. I look at myself while I wash my hands. I haven't had sex in four years. I've never had sex with the same person more than a handful of times. I could make it clear that I'd be interested in something with Matthieu. I try to reconnect with that girl I used to be, the one who'd bring guys home from Stella's bar in Saint-Germain, the one who'd laugh easily at their jokes, the girl who would shed her clothes without a shred of shyness, but who never did let anyone in. But that girl is gone, I know that now.

I hover a moment in the vestibule area and check my phone again. I don't want to seem hysterical, but worry is niggling at me and I feel both slow and emotional with all the alcohol, so I text Alison even though it is well past midnight.

Hey, just wanted to check that bedtime went okay, I write.
Give K a big hug from me! Issy X

I buy another beer and drink it down quickly while scrolling through Instagram, trying to recapture the feeling of giddiness and uncomplicated excitement I felt on the way here, sitting beside Noa in the Uber. I took a picture of us sipping with straws from a magnum of Moët and it's already had 195 likes. I'm about to go back in when a message ticks in from Alison.

The sweet little nugget is fast asleep after board games, banana bread baking, and bath. Will have her call you in the morning. Xo Ali

The phone vibrates again and in comes a photo of my girl sleeping, hair unbraided and wild. In her thin white arms lies a purple bear, snug. She's wearing boyish Rupert the Bear pajamas I've never seen before, probably a castoff from Alison's stepson. She's safe and well taken care of, and my heart feels so full looking at her. It's good to know that I would choose my life over this one—maybe we all need a reminder sometimes. I put the phone away and push my way back through the crowds, smiling to myself, feeling young and happy again.

It's almost 5:00 A.M., and back at the apartment, the four of us float around aimlessly, fixing drinks and slipping out of uncomfortable clothes, before collapsing on the huge black velvet sofas underneath the skylights. I'm in my yoga pants, holding a Bloody Mary, pleasantly drunk and still buzzing. Enzo cuts the lines of coke as casually as if he were slicing cheese, and I'm about to say *Thanks but no thanks, I don't do drugs*, but then I think to myself, why not? Why the fuck not? Noa watches me as I draw the lines, first one, then another, and I can tell she's surprised—she probably thinks of me as a party pooper. I wonder how she speaks of me to Enzo and their friends. Am I the poor, unfulfilled older sister who got stuck in an awful life? Or am I the tired but fun, hopeful person I perceive myself to be?

We still share the same bond that we always have, but we're very different people. I can't believe that my little sister has been in a relationship with Enzo for five years, that they own a beautiful, if small, apartment in central Paris together, that Noa somehow went from knowing three words when we moved here (*bonjour, baguette,* and *merci*) to being totally fluent in French without me noticing, that in spite of the crazy hair and the parties, she is a real adult now.

"Come here, big sis," says Noa, pulling me close in a sideways hug. "Matthieu," she says, "don't you think Iselin should move to Paris?" Noa pronounces my name with a French accent, stressing the last syllable instead of the first one. Is–Céline. I like it, but could I be her? Matthieu nods and laughs, rolling a spliff between his fingers, his eyes glassy and distant. I close my eyes and immediately feel myself drifting away on a strong current, the smell of pot and cigarette smoke in my nostrils, the bitter taste of cocaine at the back of my throat like a burn.

57

ALISON

"I have a surprise for you," I say. I just can't wait to see Kaia's face when she sees what I've done. It wasn't as hard in the end as I had feared it might be. It would have been different, had I done it for any other reason than to make a beautiful space for Kaia. She takes my hand as we climb the stairs, and Oliver trails behind. He has barely spoken a word to me since he got here last night, but is watching Kaia intently. When she smiled shyly at him, he looked away, and I could tell that her presence moved and unsettled him. I pause for effect outside what was my daughter's bedroom. Then I open it.

"Your room," I say, and the stunned look on Kaia's face grabs me by the heart. It's quite a big bedroom, with pink-and-green flowery curtains. It has a deep wooden sleigh bed that was Sindre's childhood bed, then Amalie's. The headboard has intricate wooden carvings, and if you were to look closely, you could see where Amalie once traced over them with a purple crayon. There's a desk, neatly stacked with drawing paper, freshly sharpened pencils, and a box containing scissors, Scotch tape, and little pots of glue and loose glitter. In the corner stands a large antique French wardrobe, its doors open, showing neat rows of clean, folded clothes.

"Who . . . who lives here?" asks Kaia, and a raw, stricken look crosses Oliver's face before he regains his composure.

"No one, darling," I say. "I've made this room for you."

"But . . . But, who do the toys belong to? And the clothes?"

"You, Kaia. Everything in this room is yours."

"But . . . I'm only here for two days. Mamma said." I feel Oliver's eyes on me; he, too, believes that Kaia is only here for the weekend. He doesn't yet understand that she belongs here with us.

"Don't you like it?" I want her to be grateful. She needs to realize that the person who can give her everything—from full maternal attention to a beautiful, comfortable home and a real family—is me.

"I love it," Kaia says quietly, smiling shyly up at me. She's just overwhelmed; the poor child is used to living in that dreadful, cluttered space. "Can I draw?"

"Of course you can, sweetie," I say.

"Uh," says Oliver. "I got you a, uh, present. It's on Am—uh, your bed . . ."

Kaia lights up and walks over to the bed. She picks up the clumsily wrapped present and looks nervously from Oliver to me and back. I smile at Oliver—I've never been prouder of my stepson. I just knew that he would see what I see.

"Open it," I say. Kaia tears the paper and inside is a fluffy purple bear wearing a Queen Elsa T-shirt. Amalie had wanted this bear, and as I watch Kaia hold it solemnly to her chest, my heart feels like

332 · ALEX DAHL

the anatomical heart in Iselin's cross-section drawing: cracked open, its intricate, gory innards bared to the world. I look at Oliver, and judging by the look on his face, he feels the way I do.

"How did you know I wanted this bear so much?" asks Kaia, and unselfconsciously launches herself into Oliver's arms, clearly unaware of the tension in the room. "I've never seen this bear before! But it was exactly what I wanted!" Kaia whoops and claps her hands together before twirling around on the floor, laughing loudly. A little girl, holding a bear, laughing in this room. Could life become livable again?

Oliver and Kaia played Snap. They baked banana bread, Kaia standing on a chair next to Oliver, wearing Amalie's old baker's hat. They collected sticks in the forest just beyond our garden, the way they used to. They threw the sticks into the hearth and sat on the floor sipping hot chocolate with marshmallow hearts, listening to the spit and crackle of the flames. Oliver even sat next to Kaia at the little desk, drawing for her. When it was time for bed, Oliver read *Rupert the Bear* to Kaia, which she had never heard before, and when he finished, she fell asleep holding the book in one hand and the purple bear in the other.

It's past midnight now, but I feel wide-awake, roused as if from a blank, deep sleep by Kaia's presence in this house. I am sitting at the edge of her bed, watching her sleep. She seems much less restless than she did a few weeks ago in Norefjell. I believe that my presence in her life has had a calming and positive effect on her. *Kaia is entirely at the mercy of a volatile, irresponsible mother who expresses feelings of bitterness toward the child*, I wrote in the statement to child services. *She is timid and understimulated. She deserves a more stable home—just more of everything.* It wasn't an easy step to take, and I have had moments of guilt and doubt, but the main concern here is

Kaia. I love her in a way I don't think even Iselin could. When you have regained something you had lost, you hold it dearer.

I stroke Kaia's hair and she stirs in her sleep. I gently insert my hand underneath her pajama top and let it rest above her heart. I stay like that for a long while, just drinking the faint thuds in, like oxygen. My phone vibrates, and it's Iselin. I can't even picture her in this moment, it's as though she has been conveniently erased from the situation. And soon enough, she will be. I write back to her and include a sweet picture of Kaia. Then I put the phone away and snuggle up next to Kaia.

"Welcome home, Mills," I whisper, nestling my face in her hair.

58

ISELIN

"Let's do the old haunts," says Noa, remarkably bubbly at 10:00 A.M. for someone who went to bed just a few hours before, high as a kite. Enzo is still asleep in their bedroom, and Matthieu is sleeping on the sofa and grunts loudly when Noa opens the shutters.

"Okay," I say, a little reluctantly, just because being back here in the city I have pined for has been surprisingly uncomplicated so far, and I worry that my old neighborhood would make me sick with longing. I love this city as much as I always have, but my home is with my child and I crave her in a way that feels physical. Like a part of me is missing.

We meander up rue Mouffetard, admiring the Pont-l'Évêque and Livarot from the cheese stands, running our fingers across plump, fuzzy basil leaves, and eating fresh croissants straight from grease-

stained paper bags. We have a glass of wine before lunch at the Place
de la Contrescarpe and smoke thin French cigarettes sitting underneath a monochrome awning as the sky unleashes sudden torrential
rain. We walk down the rue des Écoles, giggling and reminiscing
about all those nights walking home the same way from Stella, a
dive bar on the lower slopes of Montmartre where we worked part-
time when we first arrived. We have avocado and fried eggs on sour-
dough bread with Bloody Marys at Coffee Parisien on the rue
Princesse, and for a moment it is as though I've entered a time lapse
and I am right back there. I sat in this exact same spot on the day I
told Noa I was pregnant. She'd rolled her eyes and shrugged, not
thinking for one second that *staying* pregnant was even an option.

"Oh, fuck," she'd said. "How soon can you, you know, get it out?"

We've asked for the check and are down to our last couple of sips of
Bloody Mary number two when Noa interrupts something I'd been
saying about the contract I've just signed with *Speilet*. Judging by
the serious tone of her voice, she has been waiting for the right
moment to broach this subject with me.

"So, Is. Let me just get this totally straight. Alison recommended
you to this Frans guy, who then interviewed you and offered you
the job?"

"Yeah. He's the editor in chief."

"Okay. And Alison recommended you to her own actual work-
place based on the couple of illustrations you've done for her?"

"Yeah. Well, I mean she's seen most of my stuff, I think. She first
found me on Instagram, and pretty much everything is on there."

"Let me see her."

"What do you mean?"

"Let's see her Instagram profile."

"Oh. Yeah, okay." I sent Alison a follow request when we were in Norefjell but it occurs to me now that I can't remember seeing a notification that she'd accepted. I scroll through the people I follow and see that my follow request to @millerjuulfam is still pending. Noa motions for me to hand her the phone.

"She doesn't really use Instagram," I say.

"You just said she found you there first?"

"Yeah, but she doesn't, like, use it generally."

"She's posted four hundred and eighty-eight times and has two hundred and sixty-four followers, though."

"Yeah. Okay, well, I don't get the impression she checks it often."

"Facebook?"

"I looked her up on Facebook but she's kind of just a bit old for the social media stuff. You know what people over forty are like," I say. "They just don't get it."

"Hmm," says Noa.

"Anyway." I'm finding it increasingly annoying that Noa seems to constantly want to catch Alison out at some weirdness. She must be jealous, after all—I've never really been that close to anyone but Noa.

"So, what's her husband like?"

I pause. I really don't want to get into Alison's personal life with Noa. "Sindre? Oh. Solid. Maybe kind of typical Norwegian, you know, more comfortable in the woods than he is in a restaurant." I chuckle a little, trying to lighten the mood, but Noa's eyes are narrowed.

"What's he like with Kaia?"

"Um. I don't . . . She hasn't met him, actually."

"What?"

"Yeah, you see, he travels a lot. He was in Geneva, and then Reykjavik and, like, Frankfurt or something, all in a few weeks. And Copenhagen. He runs his own company, doing some kind of home security systems."

"Wait. Issy, hold on. Are you saying Kaia's staying at these people's house and she's never even met the guy?"

"He's not there this weekend. He's—"

"Traveling."

"Uh, yeah."

"At the weekend? For work? Seems odd, no?"

"Okay, maybe it wasn't for work. Alison told me where he was going. Could be hunting or something." I'm not going to tell Noa that he has left Alison for another woman, but for the first time, I feel uneasy about how completely Alison's home life has unraveled in the last few weeks and that I've placed Kaia right in the middle of it. What if the husband comes back to the house, furious, and threatens Alison? I already know he can be violent. Kaia could get caught up in something dangerous.

"Right. But, when you met him, you thought he seemed, you know, nice and normal?" Fear, sharp and unexpected, simmers in my stomach with the Bloody Mary. I stare at the chunky rings on my left hand, turning one round and round, exposing a band of green, stained flesh underneath. Do I tell my sister the truth, or do I chance a soft lie?

"I . . . I haven't actually met him, either."

"What? Are you serious?" I nod. "Issy, you realize that is super fucking weird, right?"

"Noa, listen. I've spent a lot of time with Alison. She's absolutely lovely, and—"

"You've told me before that she's weird."

"No, not weird."

"You did. When you went round to her house and she sliced herself with a glass or whatever? You said there was something strange and sad about her."

"Yes, okay. She is a little . . . mysterious. I think she's lonely.

She's taking time out from her job and I don't think she has a lot of friends in Norway. It's not easy to make friends especially if you don't have kids. I mean, where would you even meet people—"

"Why is she taking time out?"

"She's writing. A book."

"Right."

"Seriously, Noa, what is up with you? You can meet her next time you're in Norway and you'll see for yourself that she's really lovely. Totally normal. It's not like I would let her babysit Kaia if she wasn't."

"My point is, Iselin, why do you think that this woman, who is—what?—twenty years your senior and has had this extremely successful international career, but is now suddenly and strangely unemployed, is interested in hanging out with a young, exhausted single mother whose drawings she bought? It's weird! She wants something from you."

"Why is it always the same with you?" I can't help but raise my voice at Noa, making the foursome at the table close to us fall momentarily silent. "It's like you just can't accept that I, too, have a life! It's not all 'Poor Iselin this, poor Iselin that'! I'm my own person and I make my own decisions, and trust me, I am capable of making friends who are there for me without some secret fucking agenda!"

"What's her husband's name?" Noa is punching something into my phone, then scrolling down, fast. I breathe exaggeratedly; Noa has typically gone off on one of her unstoppable quests.

"Sindre Juul, I think." Noa taps again and again, and then her finger hovers over something I can't see from here. It's as though she's about to throw up, and I guess this could be the case because we have been drinking nonstop for two days, not to mention the coke, but her face is crumpling into a strange grimace of horror and shock and she hands me the phone in silence. I stare at Noa, not at the screen; I know already that I won't want to see what she has found.

"Jesus Christ," she whispers as I force my eyes to the little blue square and begin to read.

I've seen photographs of Sindre before—Alison showed me a couple on her phone in Norefjell. *Veteran Skarve-enthusiast* reads the caption, and in this one I see that he is a very handsome man, with soft, brown eyes and messy blond hair. In the other photos, his head is clean-shaven, giving him a much harder look. I scroll again, to the next picture of Sindre, and it's this one that makes my heart drop in my chest.

59

ALISON

For breakfast, I make Amalie's favorite; thick American buttermilk pancakes with maple syrup and fresh strawberries. Oliver and I watch Kaia, transfixed, and at one point she realizes and blushes self-consciously, perhaps thinking we were being critical of her. She pulls at my heartstrings with her trusting, big eyes and I have to look away.

"Hey, Kaia," I say when she's finished. "I have another surprise for you."

"What!" she shouts, and claps her hands—she's getting used to one nice surprise after another around here.

"We're going to go see the little horse now. Misty."

"Yes! Misty! Misty!" Tiny hands clapping, little face glowing. Oliver looks from his phone to me. He is different from last night—these adolescents have the most bizarre mood swings. He's been terse and shifty all morning, hardly glancing up from his phone.

"Do you want to come with us, Oliver?"

"Nuh," he grunts. "I might, uh, see Celine later. She wants to go to the mall."

"Alison?" says Kaia, face suddenly serious. I smile at her, stroking her hair off her face.

"Mamma won't let me go to the horse," she says. "She says it's because of one of my medicines . . ."

"Your mom won't find out," I say, smiling, and Kaia considers this for a brief moment, before excitedly nodding, naughtiness sparking in her eyes.

"We won't tell her!"

"No. We won't."

"Go put some warm clothes on and we'll go. I've put some out for you on the bed." Kaia runs off to get dressed. I rinse my coffee mug in the sink, and when I turn back around, Oliver is glaring at me.

"What is it?" I ask.

He forces a little smile, shakes his head slightly, and gets up. He slips his phone into his pocket and hovers a moment.

"Nothing," he says in the end, and walks away.

Misty knows it's you straightaway, I can tell. All these months, when I've come here, she's just stood there, scratching at the ground, looking past me, looking for you, but now she twitches her ears merrily and pushes her muzzle into your open hands. You look up at me and your eyes are full of love and wonder. You understand, now, like I knew that you would. Misty is yours and you are mine.

Misty snorts several times and rubs her forehead with its round white patch against your chest, where your heart sits. She knows it, and she knows you, and this was what I needed—to be sure. It's time, baby bear.

60

ISELIN

He's standing with his skis still on, having clearly just passed the finish line, a gently rounded, snow-covered mountain behind him. A young boy stands behind him, laughing, squinting in the sun, a patch of angry acne on his cheeks. And to his right stands Alison, beaming, wearing a pink ski jacket and silver Moon Boots. On her arm perches a small child, perhaps around four years old—a girl, judging from her pink hat and Queen Elsa snowsuit. There's something about the confident, relaxed way that Alison holds the child that leaves me in no doubt that she's her mother.

"Oh my God," I say. My heart's racing and I can feel a rash burning up the side of my neck.

"Yeah," says Noa, looking around again for the waiter. "We need to go."

"Okay . . . Wait. We don't know anything! This could all be completely innocent!"

"Why would Alison lie about having a kid?"

"Just wait a second." My thoughts dash back to yesterday morning as I got in the taxi, to Alison's relaxed, possessive hand on Kaia's shoulder as they waved me off in the window. What could this mean? I need to know what it means. Perhaps it means nothing at all, maybe the little girl is Alison's niece or something.

Quickly, my fingers trembling and stumbling over the search pad, I Google *Alison Miller-Juul*. Google asks *Did you mean Alison Miller-Hughes?* There are links to articles in publications from *The New Yorker*, to *Dagbladet*, to *Paris Weekly* and the *Guardian*. Her impressive career is certainly no lie. I type in *Alison Miller-Juul mother* and toward the top of the search results is an article in *KK* magazine from 2014. *What Motherhood in Norway Taught Me about American Values*, reads the title. I click on it.

> *When my daughter Amalie was born in 2013, I realized that American women are shortchanged when it comes to motherhood. We are taught that it is natural to work up until the day we give birth, and again pretty much straight after, leaving our baby in the care of strangers. In Norway . . .*

My heart is beating so fast I actually place my hand above my left breast, trying to restore its usual rhythm. Fifteen in, twenty out. *Come on, Iselin, use your brain.* I try to employ my old technique of isolating one aspect of a problem and analyzing it before moving on to the next. Alison has lied to me about having had a child. This doesn't necessarily mean anything. She doesn't owe me full disclosure about her past or her family life. Something must have happened to her daughter, something terrible—it would explain the sensation I've sometimes had, of something painful lingering beneath Alison's surface.

"Read this," I say, handing Noa the phone.

We swap phones and I type *Amalie Juul* into Google on Noa's phone, but it asks *Did you mean Amalie Iuel, the world championship hurdler*, and all the images that appear are of the athlete. I try *Amalie Miller-Juul* and there are several hundred hits. *Dagbladet, VG, Bergens Tidene, Drammensposten, Morgenbladet, Aftenposten*: all of Norway's mainstream press. I breathe deeply and click randomly on the third article, from *Aftenposten* on July 20, last year.

No formal inquiry will be launched into the death of five-year-old Amalie Miller-Juul, who drowned in Bogstadvannet on July 6, confirms Egil Minnevold of Majorstuen police station.

I click on the first one, this one from *VG* on July 9.

The little girl who tragically drowned in front of hundreds of families on the hottest day of the year earlier this week has been formally identified as Amalie Miller-Juul (5), of Frognerseteren.

There is a photograph of Amalie; a typical nursery school head shot of a smiling child. She has a sweet, slightly narrow face, with dark almond-shaped eyes like Alison's, and thick, dark blond hair fastened back from her face with red bows. I can't think straight. I stand up. I touch my heart again, and it's scrambling like a trapped bird in my chest. Noa says something, but I'm already running, and on the street, heaving with the cool Parisians of Saint-Sulpice, I can't help but unleash a wild cry. Noa puts her arm around me and we begin to run, toward the rue du Four, where Noa flags down a taxi. "Orly," she says.

In the quiet car, maneuvering through the streets of the sixth slowly, my sister and I stare at each other.

"It's her, isn't it?"

"What do you mean?" whispers Noa, eyes wide and afraid, her face soft and sweet without all the makeup.

"Alison is the mother of Kaia's donor."

"What?"

"I just know it. July sixth, Noa."

"Oh my God," whispers my sister. "Try her again, Is." I do, but Alison's phone goes straight to voice mail. I look at my WhatsApp, and it says Alison was last online at 01:34 this morning. Was she tending to Kaia? Has something happened? I know that Alison would never hurt Kaia. She wouldn't hurt her. She couldn't. But what does she want? I think about when she crushed the wineglass in her hand, how anguished and wild her expression was, as if the pain she must have felt was a release. She wouldn't hurt Kaia. Would she?

"I'm trying to find Sindre's phone number," says Noa. "And am going to call Norwegian Air. There is a flight at four; I think we'll make it. Issy, I think you should call the police!"

"The police?"

"Yes! Yes, of course. Call them now."

But just then, my phone rings.

"Hello?"

"Is this Iselin Berge?" A stranger's voice, calm and unhurried.

"Yes! Who is this?"

"This is Silje Mathisen from Bærum Barnevernstjeneste, children's services."

61

ALISON

As I drive away from the stables, my phone begins to ring, but it's in my bag in the trunk, so I can't reach it. It stops, but then immediately starts up again. And again. I look in the rearview and Kaia is holding the purple bear, mumbling sweetly to herself. Her eyes are still glowing with the excitement of meeting Misty. She notices me staring at her and looks up at me. Perhaps my gaze is too intense because she looks taken aback. She hesitates before she speaks, as though she has learned to be afraid. That mother must have taught her that, poor baby.

"When is Mamma coming?" I don't answer her—I'm distracted by the phone ringing, again and again. As soon as it goes to voice mail, it starts up again. Kaia is noticing, too, craning her head around to locate the sound. "Is that Mamma calling?"

I ignore her. "Hey, Kaia, do you know what I was thinking?" Slow headshake. "Tell me, how much did you love Misty?" She considers this, eyes lighting up.

"A lot."

"What if . . . What if Misty was your horse?"

"I wish she was my horse," says Kaia, eyebrows drawing together in a frown, "but . . ."

"But what?"

"Mamma would never let me."

"That seems a bit mean, don't you think? Surely she'd let you have a sweet little pony?"

"No, I don't think so."

"I'll speak to her about it if you want. I'd like to give Misty to you. You deserve a beautiful pony of your own, Kaia."

"But . . . But, Misty is Oliver's pony."

"Yes, that's right. But he's getting too big for her now. You saw how tall he is, he's a big boy, and Misty is a very little horse. She's perfect for you. Anyway, it was Oliver's idea."

"It was?"

"Yeah. You know, Oliver likes you so much. He wishes he had a little sister just like you."

"Oh."

"Do you ever dream about living in a big house and having your own horse and that kind of thing?"

Kaia says nothing, but seems to consider this, looking at Oslo spreading out below as we drive up Holmenkollveien, past the ski jump. "I want my mamma," she says, making my gut clench in anger. I grip the wheel so hard my knuckles turn a white-blue, like ice. We are approaching the bottom of the hill that leads to the house, and still, the phone hasn't stopped ringing. I am getting stressed about it—who could be wanting to call me over and over? Sindre? I try to picture my husband and find that I can't—he's become hazy and shadowed in my mind. Why would Sindre call me repeatedly? On impulse, I pull over by a bus stop and, leaving the engine running, get my handbag out of the trunk. Still the phone is vibrating and chiming as I wrench it free from a side pocket.

I have nine unanswered calls from Iselin, twelve unanswered calls from Sindre, and three from a private number. My heart begins to rush in my chest, painful and loud. They know. A message comes in, from Sindre.

Hey. I'm back early from Reykjavik. I'd really like to speak with you as soon as possible. Can you call me? I'm sorry about everything. So sorry. I love you.

He definitely knows. Oliver told him. He must have gotten cold feet; he acted weird all morning, stabbing at his phone, refusing to engage with Kaia like he did last night. And the way he looked at me . . . How could he do this to me? I am not going to let a fourteen-year-old, acne-ridden, limp little Goody Two-shoes ruin this for me. I'd rather kill him.

I get back in the driver's seat and push the pedal down, making the Volvo spin on the salt grit left on the road from winter.

62

ISELIN

The plane shudders through the clouds. Noa's hand is clammy in my own. Afternoon is blushing on the horizon and I begin to pray inside my head, the same kind of prayer I used to turn to whenever it was touch and go with Kaia. My baby. *Please, please, please*, I whisper.

When I was little, trying to just get through the days up there in Svartberget, I taught myself a technique for managing my feelings. I sensed that you can't fix everything all at once, sometimes you just have to focus on getting your breathing steady, and then you can begin to bring the problems you have out into the air, one by one. I used it when my father would scream at my mother, his voice reverberating around the flimsy walls, until she burst into tears. Noa and I would sit in our hiding place in the attic, drawing

THE HEART KEEPER · 351

doodles in Biro on our wrists. I'd keep all my focus on my breathing, counting to fifteen while inhaling and twenty while exhaling,
until I could be sure he'd passed out drunk. I used it when Kaia was
fighting for her life. I'd stroke her hand through the hole in the
incubator lid, inhale and exhale, always fifteen in, twenty out, and
allow myself to focus only on that and the image of her baby face
etched on my mind. Breathe and pray. Pray and breathe.

The plane is ushered north by a strong tailwind and the flight is
mercifully short. As soon as the doors are opened, Noa and I are
helped off by two men. A little indoor van is waiting by the gate
and they drive it fast through the terminal building. They know it's
an emergency, that a child is in danger, that the police are involved,
that I'm the mother of the little girl who has been taken. My phone
is bleeping nonstop with an onslaught of missed calls and messages.

   There's no trace of Alison, reads the most recent one. It's from
Sindre Juul.

63

ALISON

The house is empty. That little shit must have had the sense to call his mother. It's lucky for him, otherwise I would have broken every fucking bone in his body. I would have run him over with the car. His head would have smashed underneath the wheels—I picture it clearly in my head. I'm not going to have a lot of time, but I have to get the bag. You're in the car, strapped in and waiting. I see you from the window at the top of the stairs, sitting motionless and obedient in the backseat, tiny milky hands held still in your lap. I kick Oliver's door open, just in case he's cowering in there, the goddamned fucking traitor, but the room is empty. I grab the bag from your room and run back downstairs.

Again, I drive fast; much, much faster than is allowed, and I can

THE HEART KEEPER · 353

tell by the look in your eyes that you're afraid now. Very afraid. I want to tell you that everything is going to be okay.

Got your passport. Got Dinky Bear. Got everything but the girl. But we're fixing that. We're going to fix it, baby bear. Everything is going to go back to how it was supposed to be. It's going to be me and you—the heart keeper. I know now that you can hear me, and that you can see me, and feel me. I know what you need me to do and I will do it because then everything will be undone. Fixed.

"Are we going home now?" you ask in a thin voice.

"No, sweetie, not just yet."

"I . . . I want to go home."

"No," I say, and turn left at the junction, toward Bogstad.

"Where are we going?"

"We are going to play a game."

"What kind of game?" I don't answer you, because you don't need to know everything at once; children need to learn about patience. I look from the road to you and back to the road, and my heart is trembling in my chest, with my enormous love for you. I almost laugh out loud at the unbelievable turn of events, at what is about to happen, at how in spite of all this stress, miracles really do exist. I wasn't going to do it yet, but after what Oliver has gone and done, I've got no choice. Your face is drawn and afraid and I hate to see you upset because all I ever wanted was to take care of you and to love you and to keep you safe.

"Don't worry, Mills," I say, and give you my most loving, reassuring smile.

"Who is Mills?" you ask, and your words fill me with anger because we're past this now, we've come to a place where we no longer need to pretend or lie. We can just be together, open to this new life, and to miracles. I breathe deeply, and consciously let go of my anger, and of everything that has happened. It is a beautiful day; the sun is shining after a rainy morning, just like I hoped it would, and here we are, you and me, the Juul girls, on our way to the lake.

64

ISELIN

A police helicopter hovers low over the E6 eastbound and I force myself to keep my eyes on it. We pass it, and I try to decipher the crackle of the police radio.

"Is that helicopter for my daughter?" I ask, and the young, red-haired police officer driving the van hesitates, then nods.

"We're about to block the main roads out of the city," he says. Noa and I exchange another glance. Where, where would she take her? What does she want? I know what she wants. She wants Amalie's heart back. I see her in my mind, at Blåkroken, my trusting child sitting beside her, unaware that this woman could hurt her. A new message appears on my phone, the husband again.

Oliver knows where they might have gone! Hurry!

65

ALISON

"Farther out," I say, my voice dancing across the cold, dark water. You're so very afraid now, but that's because you don't understand. We always fear what we don't understand. I've learned this over and over in my life, and now you will learn it, too. It will all make sense soon. You shake your head and turn away from me, staring out at the lake. We've come to the north shore because it is quiet, far away from the road and the little beach on the opposite shore where people like to walk; no one will see or hear us here. I am standing in the exact same spot I chose just a few days ago and it really is perfect.

"Please can I come back now?" you say.

"No! Farther out! I told you what to do!" You've started to cry, and you are shaking both with sobs and with cold. Your body is so thin and pale it's a translucent blue; like the meek sky, like the water itself. The scar on your chest is so long it looks like someone tried to saw you in half, and it is dark and purple, now, in the unforgiving daylight. It wasn't there before, but it doesn't matter, we all change with time, and life scars us all. In the end, it's your scars that make you beautiful, and I hope you will come to know this. You take another couple of steps out into the lake, your arms held awkwardly to your sides, then you stop and turn back toward me. *I can't swim*, you whispered when I explained what was going to happen. *You won't need to*, I said.

I close my eyes. I'm back there. So are you.

"Now get under," I shout. You don't say anything, but you drop slowly to your knees in the water, and it rises above your waist. I close my eyes, ready. You begin to wail and the sound of your voice closes around my heart, but there is another sound booming across the lake and it sounds like a helicopter tearing at the air. It's working; we really are back there, even the sounds are the same.

"Now!" I shout. "Say it!"

"Mamma," you shout.

"No, Mommy!"

"Mommy," you say.

"Louder!"

"Mommy," you scream. "Mommy!"

All I wanted was to hear your sweet voice calling me, needing me, and I charge into the freezing water, screaming your name, feeling around for your flailing body, and manage to grab hold of your slippery, thin arm. I got you. I got you, baby bear, and I will never let you go again. We fixed it now, it's all different, it's all undone, and we can walk away from here together. We can go to California, or to the South of France or to Paris or anywhere else in the whole world. Together.

But the sound of the helicopter doesn't desist even though we don't need it anymore. *I got her*, I shout. *I got her, she's here, I found her, it's all fine now*, and I'm laughing and crying, spitting stale, earthy lake water, but it's so loud and I have to cover my ears. The helicopter is directly overhead, whipping the surface into frothy wavelets and I can't both cover my ears and hold on to you and you slip away from me, back into the dark water, or no, you're carried away, and I'm carried away, too, or dragged, rather, and placed on the ground, hard hands hurting me. There are voices shouting in my ears and over my head and people crying, but no matter what, I won't open my eyes.

Epilogue

ALISON

Gaustad Hospital
Four months later

There is a garden here and every day I sit in it for a few hours. It doesn't matter if it rains—nobody says anything, or tries to stop me. It's raining today, though it's July, and the raindrops that fall onto my skin are plump and warm, carrying particles of sand and earth from other places.

Soon, you can go home, Alison.

I don't know what that will mean.

The medicines they give me make my thoughts clear, like diamonds lifted from crumbling, black earth. They come to me one by one now, not all at once, and I can turn them over and around in my mind, before letting them go. I understand everything now. I understand that the truth, no matter how painful, is all we've got.

Oliver told his father the truth. It was the right thing to do. Now he comes here to sit in the garden with me, every Thursday after school. He's coming today, and we will sit a long while with our heads thrown back, letting the warm summer rain wash across our faces. Oliver will let me hold his hand and he will try to hide the fact that his eyes are still sad. Before he goes back out to where Monica waits in the parking lot, I will tell my boy that I love him.

Sindre fell apart, like me. He's at home again, and soon I will be there, too. I don't know if we can share a home again, Sindre and I. How could we? He comes sometimes, too, but we don't speak much, we just walk around the garden or stare at the walls in my room.

I imagine Kaia Berge is at home with her mother, wherever they are now. Iselin wrote to me, which was more than I could have hoped for. She's going back to art school and they will be moving far away. A fresh start, she called it. Iselin asked me to not write back or try to look for them, and I never will.

Amalie is gone. She isn't in the lake, or in her room, or in the heart beating in Kaia Berge's chest. She's gone, and she isn't coming back. Still, I sometimes feel her in the soft evening breeze, in the impossible beauty of the tight pink rosebuds in this garden, in the shimmering light of the uncountable stars strewn across the infinite darkness of the night sky—every last one of them another world.

THE
HEART
KEEPER

ALEX DAHL

BEHIND THE BOOK

As a person, and as a novelist, I am interested in the human mind and in the workings of the heart, especially when it has been broken into shards. I will forever be especially interested in motherhood as a theme in fiction, because for me, motherhood is a love only matched in its intensity by fear, a fear that is visceral and deep-rooted and sometimes difficult to manage. It is also universal, in the sense that whether we are mothers or not, we can relate to the bond between mothers and their children, and the deep fear evoked by any threat to this bond. Motherhood runs as a thread throughout my work; from highly strung, scheming Cecilia Wilborg in *The Boy at the Door* (2018), who is driven by something many women unfortunately can relate to—society's relentless pressure on women and the quest for perfection—to broken Alison Miller-Juul in *The Heart Keeper*, who speaks to her lost daughter and succumbs to dangerous impulses in a desperate attempt to bring her back.

The idea for *The Heart Keeper* came to me in the summer of 2017. I happened to have read a few interesting stories about people who purported to have "inherited" traits and memories from their donors after receiving lifesaving organs. Interesting enough in itself, I thought, but the idea really came into its own when a character very insistently came to me—Alison Miller-Juul, a desperate, grieving mother who has lost her only child and becomes dangerously obsessed with the child that received her daughter's heart. What caught my attention initially was the emotional plausibility of such a thing happening. In that situation, would you not do anything, believe anything, anything at all, to hold on to what you'd lost? It resonated with me, because though my own personal circumstances are very different from Alison's, I've been there—right there, in the most impossible of places—hoping against all the odds, begging, praying, for the life of my irreplaceable child.

When my son was six days old, he came very close to dying from meningitis. Half-an-hour-later-and-it-would-have-been-too-late, kind of close. For several weeks, he fought for his life on life support, enduring numerous blood transfusions, painful procedures, life-threatening sepsis, and a very close call with needing part of his hand amputated. He made it, but only just. We went home. But the trauma of that life-changing experience simmered and burned beneath the surface.

At the time, I didn't deal with coming that close to losing Oscar. I was anxious and nervous for years after, all the time. It is perhaps unsurprising that living on high-alert for such a prolonged time has a profound effect on both mind and heart. During Oscar's illness, I just prayed and prayed—show me the atheist in the neonatal intensive care unit. I made a deal with the devil and all the Gods and every spiritual creature imaginable—

if only I could keep him, if only he would live, I would be the best mother, the most grateful, considerate human being, the kindest, most mindful woman, who'd live a serene, peaceful life with my child. I would be perfect. And there began a quest for the unattainable, of feeling a failure every time I inevitably couldn't uphold my end of the deal—after all, Oscar lived. And after we came home was almost as difficult as our time in the hospital, but in a different way, a way I just couldn't talk about. I was supposed to just continue as though nothing had happened. As though my world hadn't just been suspended at the gates of hell for months. As though my frightened, tired heart didn't believe deep down that he could still die at any minute.

I hated myself for occasionally resenting motherhood, for feeling exhausted, for craving a career and a life of my own in addition to motherhood. I got the only thing I had ever wanted—Oscar survived against all the odds, and yet I failed at being perfect. My stress levels were off the chart—I could cry for an hour from the sound of a set of keys dropped to the floor, and sometimes I felt so anxious being around my beautiful, boisterous, unaware baby boy that it was almost unbearable.

I ran through the events of the night he almost died over and over. He was only alive thanks to sheer luck, a fluke, a split-second decision to just show up at the hospital when we'd been blown off four times on the phone, so who was to say he couldn't as easily be taken from me? In my head and heart, it was like I had lost him and then somehow got him back, but I was still reeling from having gone so very close to that place, the impossible place where mothers bury their children.

I'll never forget that place.

Time did heal, as time inevitably does, or masked the cracks, rather. Then, as I set out to write *The Heart Keeper*, the trauma of Oscar's early life began to rear its ugly head again. *I know your fears,* it would whisper, at night, or when I was writing, or simply in an everyday moment browsing the aisles at Whole Foods. *I know how deep your fear is and I'm going to bring you to your knees.* I couldn't breathe. My mind went blank. My whole body was tense and struck by an impenetrable haze of dread. It got personal, because as writers we go with our characters to the deepest, darkest places, of course we do; we have to. And then, *The Heart Keeper* became therapeutic in forcing me to finally face the fear we mothers live with, a fear I think every mother can relate to, and begin to deal with it.

It is a process and never a cure, but I am increasingly able to see that the deal I struck with the beast in my head those nights my child was hooked up to countless tubes and frantically bleeping machines wasn't real—there is no law stating he will be taken from me if I fail to be perfect. I am finally talking about what happened when Oscar was a baby, I am beginning to touch upon that darkness, so it doesn't manifest itself by taking my breath away, and learning to accept that love and fear are two sides of the same coin.

I'm proud of *The Heart Keeper*, and hopeful that it succeeds in describing the nuances and intensity of motherhood; the love and light, the fear and darkness, and the hope.

QUESTIONS FOR DISCUSSION

1. Who is your favorite character in *The Heart Keeper*, and why?

2. How do you feel about the notion of cell memory?

3. Why do you think Sindre and Alison are unable to support each other in their grieving processes?

4. What do you think of Kaia's similarities to Amalie after the heart transplant?

5. Which character(s) elicited the most and least sympathy from you, and why?

6. Can you understand why Alison does what she does with Kaia at the end of the book?

7. Did the story change or challenge your ideas about organ donation? If so, how?

8. How do you think the experience of growing close to Alison will change and affect Iselin and Kaia in the future?

9. What were your thoughts on Iselin's parenting style?

10. What did you believe Alison's intentions with Kaia were as the story neared its end?

11. What are your thoughts on how Sindre managed his feelings toward Alison after the loss of Amalie?

12. What purpose do you think Oliver serves in the story?

READING LIST

"If you want to be a writer, read," they say, and I think it's true—I know that certain books have been as formative as anything else in my life, both as a person and as a novelist. I like books that make you *feel* something, and writing that "twists the knife in every sentence." I don't appreciate writing that seems too calculated or controlled; for me, there has to be something emotional and a little wild beneath the surface. I like the rule-breakers and the game-changers and the books that make me cry—most of all, I like the sad stuff. Here are some favorites, past and present:

Away
by Amy Bloom
Away is everything that I love about Amy Bloom—heartbreaking, masterful, and raw. It's a wide-reaching story of motherhood and loss, with razor-sharp prose and a wondrously light touch on dark subjects.

Gilead
by Marilynne Robinson

Gilead is my favorite book, and I suspect it always will be. I picked it from my mother's bookshelf randomly, and it changed my life. I tell everyone to read it, friends, family, strangers on the street. But only if you like a heart-bashing.

I AM I AM I AM
by Maggie O'Farrell

I love pretty much everything by Maggie O'Farrell for all the reasons! This was brave, beautiful, moving, original. One of the books that made me want to be an author was *After You'd Gone*, also by Maggie O'Farrell—I was quite shocked that reading a work of fiction could have such a profound emotional effect on me.

Days Without End
by Sebastian Barry

Incredibly original and masterful, with the most exquisite prose—I had to stop every few sentences just to reread and savor, and this book made me bawl—just the way I like it.

Reservoir 13
by Jon McGregor

This is a new addition to the list, and easily the book I enjoyed the most last year. It was like a poet decided to write a thriller—loved it!

Cloud Atlas
by David Mitchell
An eternal favorite—rich, original, moving, exciting, funny, sad—all the feels with this one. If I had to take only one book to a desert island, it would be a tie between *Gilead* and *Cloud Atlas*.

Next up are *Red Snow* by Will Dean and *The Dead Ex* by Jane Corry. Though I write psychological thrillers, I don't tend to read that many of a similar genre, simply because I want to develop my own voice and avoid becoming influenced by other authors' styles and voices . . . I do love a page-turner, though, and I am looking forward to these two!

Ready to find
your next great read?

Let us help.

Visit prh.com/nextread

Penguin
Random
House